Spellbound

Book Three of The Gwen St. James Affair

Nicole McKeon

TOWER ROOM PUBLISHING

Contents

www.towerroompublishing.com

Content Notice

MAY CONTAIN MILD SPOILERS

This book was written for an adult audience and contains mature themes that may not be suitable for every reader. Content includes but may not be limited to:

- Profanity

- Violence and death

- Substance use

- Grief

- Assault

- Mental Health struggles

- Disability of a loved one

- Sexually explicit scene (Ch 21. To read a summary without the sexual content, go to Chapter 21.5 at the end of the book)

- Anxiety and PTSD

- Fire injury

- Anxiety attack

Pronunciation Guide

BOLDED SECTIONS INDICATE WHICH SYLLABLE IS EMPHASIZED

1. <u>Fleur:</u> Fl-uh-r

2. <u>Obyrron:</u> **Oh**-buh-rohn

3. <u>Manannán Mac Lir:</u> Man-an-**on** Mac Leer

4. <u>Graohw:</u> Gra-ow

5. <u>Harl:</u> Hah-rl

6. <u>Titania:</u> Ti-**tahn**-ya

7. <u>Gaelethsdaughter:</u> **Gay**-leths-**dott**-ir

8. <u>Geis:</u> **geh**-sh

9. <u>Aes Sidhe:</u> Ay-s Shee

10. <u>Grimoire:</u> Grim-**wahr**

11. <u>Mordegant</u>**:** **More**-duh-gant

Dedication

To my readers: this is for you. It has always been for you.

1

Familiar Shadows

TONY

Anthony Hardwicke was one of the toughest inspectors to walk the streets of New London; he had arrested murderers, stopped kidnappers, fought vampires, and battled supernatural spirits...and none of it scared him as much as Thursday dinner with his parents.

His mother's face lit with pleasure when she opened the door, but as she hugged him, she whispered, "Today is not a good day."

He was grateful for her warning. It gave him a chance to prepare himself.

"Anthony is here, dear!" his mother called a moment later as she led him into the small sitting room.

A couple of mildly tatty chairs, a chaise with a poorly repaired leg, a desk covered in little oil paintings featuring Tony and his brothers, and a table were the only pieces of furniture in the room. But it was warm, and his mother had added homey touches, like a vase full of flowers dried before the weather turned cold, and bits of embroidery in wooden frames. The bright little fabric birds stared back into the room with curious expressions in their button eyes.

His father sat by the hearth with a blanket draped over his legs and an unlit pipe in one bony hand, his white hair glowing in the firelight. The familiar surge of pain was like a knife in Tony's chest, but he ignored it. It would pass.

"Good evening, Father," he said, kneeling by the chair and pressing the old man's hand.

"Tony," his father said, smiling. "Did you know I ate three eggs today? Three. Your mother was very impressed."

"As she should be. That is a prodigious number of eggs."

"Quite so. I'm going to need my strength for when I reopen the business and there is nothing so good for regaining one's vitality."

"When is the business to open?" Tony asked, beginning the first steps of the dance they repeated every Thursday night.

"As soon as I secure investors, we'll be well on our way. And then your mother can stop selling those little bits of flimflam"—he waved his hand at the unfinished embroidery in the wicker basket next to her chair—"and I can fit her up in fine silks, again. No one looks as handsome in silk as your mother."

He gave her an adoring smile, took a puff from his pipe, realized it wasn't lit, and frowned at the bowl.

"Here, Father," Tony said, "I'll pack this for you."

"You always were a good boy."

He carried the pipe to the desk, opened a drawer, and pulled out a nearly empty packet of tobacco. His mother joined him, her expression defiant.

He tried to keep his tone casual as he packed the bowl. "You did not tell me you were selling crafts. And you didn't tell me father was out of tobacco, either. Why the secrets?"

"Parents are meant to care for their children, not the other way round. If I want to earn a few pounds a year to pay for your father's pleasures and small odds and ends, I have that right."

Tony clenched his jaw, took a deep breath, and let it out slowly. "I didn't mean to say you don't."

"Anthony." She touched his arm, forcing him to look at her. "You already do more than enough, more than any parent should expect from their child. This is the only dignity I have. Please do not make me feel guilty for it."

He fished a pinch of tobacco from the packet, which lay yellowing on the tablecloth, and swallowed hard. She had carefully repaired the cloth so many times there wasn't much left of the original design. It was a lovingly maintained illusion of gentility that would fall apart with the slightest stress, but his mother's neat stitches held the fraying edges together with relentless optimism.

"Of course, I won't," he said, meeting her gaze.

She had such beautiful eyes, light blue and clear as the sky. As a child, he was convinced her extraordinary eyes were a sign she was a secret fairy princess. Now they were surrounded by a mess of lines, resting on purple pillows that were evidence of the weight of her daily struggle to make their life joyful despite his father's injury. And for the most part, she succeeded.

But no amount of effort could return his father to the bluff, hardy man he had been before bandits waylaid him and left him on the street to die with empty pockets and a cracked skull. Neither his mother's clever stitchery nor his hopeful promises had been enough to keep his parents from walking the tightrope of poverty.

Bile burned the back of his throat as guilt flexed slimy fingers in his stomach. If his brothers would have seen fit to contribute more to their parents' maintenance, perhaps things would have been different, but...

His mother's grip tightened on his arm and her voice hardened as she said, "Don't do that to yourself. Don't you dare."

He schooled his expression, kissed her cheek—which always mollified her—and brought the pipe back to his father.

"Ah, Tony!" he said, looking up at his son with a smile. "Did I tell you I ate three eggs today?"

There was the pain, again, opening like an endless hole in the center of him. "You did, Father. That was well done."

"It certainly was. Oh, my pipe! I wondered where it had gone. Thank you, boy."

They ate a simple stew with brown bread and butter, opting to stay by the fire instead of adjourning to the small dining room. The place had no hearth, and in winter it was far too cold for Mr. Hardwicke to bear.

Tony told them of his impending promotion to detective, and his father regaled them with stories from his days as a merchant, fending off pirates and bribing foreign customs officers. The experience was exactly as painful as every Thursday dinner.

When it was finally time to say goodnight, he ensured his father had a freshly packed pipe, kissed his mother on the cheek, bundled up in his wool coat, scarf, and hat, and hurried out into the biting wind.

When he was promoted, their lives would be different. He would buy dwarven heaters to keep his father warm, even in their chilly dining room at night. And his mother wouldn't have to sell the work of her hands just to have spending money.

Until then, every visit would feel like an arrow to the heart. The freezing winter air was preferable to hours of having his failures as a son thrown repeatedly, though unconsciously, in his face.

He reminded himself to pick up a bag of salt for their stairs, which sported a fine coating of ice, pulled up his collar, and tucked his fists into his pockets. Despite the heavy layer of clouds, it did not snow, but his cheeks and nose burned with cold.

The one benefit of the frigid air was that the reek of horse manure, auto exhaust, or garbage warming in the sun had been dampened. The air smelled almost fresh. His parents lived too far from the Thames to suffer from the miasma that rolled off the river during the hot summer months, which was why he paid so much for their rent. His walk home was longer than it otherwise might have been, but knowing the fetid stink wouldn't make them sick was worth it.

The few people brave, or foolish enough, to be abroad so late kept their distance, only glancing at him from the corner of their eyes above scarves pulled up to protect their noses. He was tall and broad across the shoulders, which made his current scowl even more intimidating. They clearly thought he was not the kind of person to risk an encounter with at night. Good. He wasn't in the mood for even a passing conversation.

A cab rumbled past, the sound of horses' hooves echoing off the cobblestones as the driver gave him a pointed look, but Tony waved the man on. He'd rather walk and work out his emotions on the unforgiving pavement. Still, his eyes followed the retreating vehicle as it passed beneath the electric street lamps that buzzed and flickered.

A head of familiar tousled dark blonde hair caught the lamplight half a block away. He froze for a surprised heartbeat. Samuel? The teenager was the ward of his—what should he call her? Friend? Paramour?—Lady Gwenevere St. James.

The boy would soon be fourteen and had finally begun growing. Now that he ate well and regularly, he was filling out. In a few years, he'd be a strapping man, but the former pickpocket currently had the too-long limbs and awkward, coltish grace of someone unaccustomed to their changing body.

He should have been at the townhouse on Grosvenor Square, warm in his bed, not on the border of the east side at eleven o'clock at night. Tony altered his course, taking to the shadows of the row houses. He increased his speed but kept his gait casual.

Sam turned left, passing through a pool of light and then disappearing into the darkness between lamps. Tony took the long way round, sticking to the shadows, and followed the boy onto Church Street. The homes and businesses in this part of town were a few short steps above neglect. They bordered the neighborhood where Sam had grown up, and while the place was not impoverished, it wasn't far off.

Abandoned buildings punctuated every block. Stucco had been added to the brick in the days when the inhabitants were affluent enough to hope for a better future. But progress crouched in the shadows like a hungry wolf, waiting to eat up whoever got left, or pushed, behind. Exposed brick showed through crumbling holes, and boarded-up windows let in more cold air than they kept out. The once-fine houses now looked like aging actors trying to hide the passage of time beneath too many layers of makeup.

He gained on the boy a little at a time, but never fast enough to be noticed. Part of him was tempted to grab Sam by the back of the neck and drag him home to Gwen and his sister. The other part knew that if he asked Sam why he was creeping through town in the dark, he would respond with a plausible lie and never let Tony catch him again.

Helping the boy would be impossible if he did not know what was happening, so he kept his distance. They entered the south end of the neighborhood less than thirty seconds apart.

A crumbling gothic church dominated the landscape, looming over the houses like a vulture waiting for residents to crawl through its doors with their petitions in one hand and their coin in the other. Neither their coin nor their prayers had been enough to save the church from the erosion of time and progress, and only its bones remained to protect the graves of the parishioners buried there.

Sam stopped outside the boundary of the wrought-iron fence and turned his head to the side as if listening. Tony slipped farther into the shadows and froze. The boy had good instincts. Tony may have spent his entire career catching criminals, but Sam had spent his young life avoiding being caught. Satisfied no one was following, he hopped the fence in a single bound and wove through the tombstones toward the doors. Before he crossed the threshold, two men stepped out of the darkened doorway and barred the way.

Sam stopped, hands up, then slowly pulled his jacket open at the throat. The guards stepped aside to allow him through, and he disappeared into the dark maw of the church. Tony edged farther down the street, waited for the guards to retreat, then crept alongside the building to listen. The stone beneath the broken stained-glass windows was cold against his back, sucking warmth through his jacket like a starving babe.

He heard nothing but the distant rattle of wagons and the occasional echo of conversation or scuffing shoes as the guards inside shifted their weight. Wherever Sam had gone, he either wasn't in the church, or his business there required little conversation.

Tony circled the building once, then returned to the front, satisfied there was only one viable exit from the building. If no one had yet caught Sam sneaking out of the house, and he was certain Gwen would have mentioned something if they had, the boy must have a way to and from home that kept him out of sight. To stop such escapades in the future, Tony needed to see what it was, so he waited and considered the situation.

It would break Gwen's heart to know her youngest ward was creeping about the city at night, engaging in criminal activity. The children had no need of money since inheriting Claire Monmouth's estate, so what could force Samuel to return to a life of crime, knowing it would hurt both his benefactor and his sister?

Sally Dawes, Sam's older sister, was a clever, good-hearted girl of nearly seventeen, who loved her brother with the ferocity of a mother bear. She'd worked herself to exhaustion learning anything and everything that might give her a leg up in the world: history, geography, chemistry, and alchemy right alongside etiquette and comportment. The girl was determined to make a good life for herself and her brother, and it would devastate her to know he was putting himself in unnecessary danger.

And Tony had to be the one to tell them. Or to tell Gwen, at least, which was guaranteed to be an enjoyable conversation. The grim irony of that thought made his mouth twist into an unhappy line.

Didn't they have enough hurdles to deal with in their relationship without adding this to the list? Apparently not, because he couldn't see a way out of telling her. He'd rather kiss her into insensibility, or bury himself—well, there was no use thinking about impossibilities.

Gwen was convinced she'd break his heart if they entered into a committed relationship, and he hadn't been able to un-convince her, so instead of kissing the ironic smile off her face, he'd be explaining that the boy she loved was skulking about unsafe parts of the city at night. As he ruminated on that unpleasant thought, Sam crept out of the church and started down the street. Tony waited for the boy to gain a lead, then followed.

First, he'd find out how Sam had crept out of the house under the watchful eyes of Mrs. Chapman and Mr. Yates, then catch him and give him the opportunity to come clean. If he refused, Tony would have to do it himself.

He had always believed the boy honorable, even if he was a bit of a scamp. Perhaps there was a good reason for him to be here at night, alone. Perhaps his excuse would make sense. He hoped to hell that was the case because he couldn't stomach the other option. If Sam was breaking the law, he didn't think he could hurt Gwen by doing his job and hauling the boy to Scotland Yard.

He was so distracted by his own thoughts he didn't realize he was being stalked until a rasping voice said from behind, "You shouldn't be out so late, guv."

Tony turned, half disgusted with himself for missing the tail, half relieved that he might be able to vent his anger on someone who actually deserved it. Sam disappeared around the next corner.

"It's dangerous in these parts, after dark. You'll want to get home safely, eh? We can make that happen. For a price, a'course."

The man was a head shorter than Tony but just as wide, with the forearms of a blacksmith and a jaw like an anvil. He showed off scarred knuckles by flicking a thumb across the bottom of his nose. A bowler hat was pulled down low enough that Tony couldn't see the color of his eyes or the shape of his features. Clever.

What wasn't clever was trying to extort money from an officer with Tony's experience, an officer who was already aching for a fight. He said, with a hint of a warning in his voice, "I can find my way home just fine, thanks."

"'Fraid we can't allow that," the Bowler Hat said, raising his hands at his sides. "Wouldn't be neighborly to let you get hurt. Hard for a man to work with broken fingers. But don't fret, guv. It'll only cost you a few pounds. Pull out your wallet and you can be on your way."

"This isn't the fight you want to pick, friend, unless you enjoy breathing through a broken nose. But I'm feeling charitable. I'll overlook your attempted extortion if you turn around, call off whoever is waiting to ambush me, and walk away."

The man snorted, pushed up his sleeves, and flexed his fingers, making his knuckles pop ominously. "So much for being polite and businesslike. Let me make this clear, eh? You ain't the one making the rules. Be a good lad and pay up, or you'll suffer worse than a broken nose for our trouble."

Someone behind him and a little farther up the street chuckled: the accomplice who would make sure he either paid or regretted not paying.

"There you are," Tony said, turning far enough to keep both men in sight but staying close enough to finish the first man off before the other reached them. "Now the odds are fair. Maybe. Come on, then. I have places to be."

The men exchanged disbelieving glances, but Tony waited. He couldn't strike first, not if he wanted to arrest the man for attempted extortion and assault. Not if he wanted to use force. And he did.

Bowler Hat shrugged, reached into his pocket, and slipped on a pair of brass knuckles. "Your funeral, mate."

He lunged.

The fellow was a brawler, strong and tough, but unskilled. Tony had spent more than half of his life training as a pugilist—it was one of the few legal ways he could take out his frustration with the world—so when the fellow threw a looping hook, he ducked, stepped to the outside, twisted his hips, and struck the man in the diaphragm with a tight blow.

Bowler Hat crumpled with a gasp and flopped on the ground, trying to get his wind back. But it would be another ten seconds before he breathed again, and most fights didn't last that long.

"Disappointing." Tony turned to face the man's partner. "Can you do any better?"

Men who made their living on the streets weren't dumb. Harassing a random stranger for money involved little danger, especially working with a partner. Fighting one-on-one against a skilled opponent was another matter. Tony casually unbuttoned his jacket and flashed the badge pinned to his waistcoat. The second man glimpsed the metal, then turned and ran.

Tony sighed, replaced his badge, and stripped the brass knuckles from Bowler Hat's fingers. He removed the nippers from his coat pocket and slung the rope around the man's wrists with practiced ease. Once he pulled the t-shaped handle into place, the man was securely bound.

"Come on, my lad," Tony said, hauling the man to his feet. "Time to go for a walk. You ruined my night, so I wouldn't be averse to another sparring match if you're still feeling tough. Here's your hat, let's go."

He dragged Bowler Hat to the closest lockup, still fuming that he had lost the boy and been denied the release of a good fight. Tomorrow, he'd have to tell Gwen what he had seen and bear the look on her face when worry, disappointment, and fear replaced her usual humor and confidence.

That happened to his mother every time his brothers failed to write or call when they were home on leave; every time they promised visits or money and disappointed the woman who raised them. The idea of Gwen suffering such pain made him clench his jaw against a growl of frustration.

He hoped his boxing club was open late because he desperately needed to hit something.

2

A Perverse Bit of Nonsense

GWEN

No matter how frustrated, irate, or furious I became, I would never throw a book. Books were repositories of knowledge handed down through generations, providing an insight into the minds of people long gone.

Every book is sacred...every book except the Mordegant Grimoire. That book is a perverse piece of nonsense designed to test the will of even the most patient scholar and tempt them to sacrilege.

Rather than throwing the grimoire across the room, as I so desperately desired to do, I threw my empty glass of sherry. It struck the bust by the window and shattered into a thousand sparkling pieces, sending Aristotle, my raven, flapping angrily into the air. He landed on the bookcase and croaked at me in reproach.

With deliberate care, I slid the damned book to a safe corner of my desk, pushed my papers aside, and pounded my forehead on the unforgiving wood.

"Why—won't—this—work?" I demanded between thuds.

Mrs. Chapman appeared in the doorway with one hand on her chest, her hawkish features set in lines of concern. God's breath. Why was she still awake? As she took in the discarded piles of notes, the empty bottles on my desk, and the shattered glass on the carpet, her mouth thinned and her eyes narrowed. I tried to mollify her before she built up a full head of steam.

"Don't worry, Mrs. Chapman," I said, flicking my fingers at the mess. "I'll have all this cleaned up in no time. You can retire."

She snorted and put her hands on her bony hips. "As if it's the mess I'm worried about. Glory be." Then she stalked into the room and loomed over me, glaring down with resolute grey eyes. "You have not given yourself a break in months. You're too thin, you barely see anyone, and now you're destroying your father's study, rest his soul. Well, I'll not have it, my lady. Your mother, the duchess, would have my hide if she knew what I've allowed. But I've not said a word because you told me the book was important. And it may well be. But"—she reached over, shut the book with a loud *fwap*, and took me by the wrist—"that will be enough for tonight."

"Mrs. Chapman," I began, but she ignored my protest and hauled me to my feet. She was surprisingly strong for such a slender woman.

"I'll not hear another word," she said, dragging me behind her and out of the study. "What your mother would say, I shudder to think."

"You are rather saucy for a housekeeper."

"I was your nursemaid first, and that's not a job so easily forgotten. Staying up late and drinking too much. What was I thinking to allow it? When is the last time you've done anything but work? You haven't even seen Lady Ashcroft in months!"

"I have an appointment with her next week," I said. Which was true. Edith and I had become fast friends since Tony and I saved her and Lord Ashcroft from a vampire last summer, and we were scheduled to see the opera together. Of course, I had every intention of cancelling my plans, but Mrs. Chapman did not need to know that.

She made a clucking noise as she led me past the great clock in the hallway—was it two in the morning, already?—and pulled me up the stairs to the second floor, where the family bedrooms were located. Sam's door opened and a sleepy face topped by a head of tousled blonde hair popped out.

"Samuel Dawes," Mrs. Chapman's voice cracked like a whip, "if you don't get to sleep this instant, I swear—"

He disappeared like a startled anemone and slammed the door behind himself. I swallowed a chuckle, certain Mrs. Chapman wouldn't appreciate my levity, and allowed her to bustle me into my room.

"I am quite capable of—" I began, but she cut me off.

"Are you? Are you capable, my lady?" The anger in her voice shocked me. She scolded me my entire life, but rarely had she been truly angry. "Because your behavior over the past few months makes me question whether your mother is right to stay in the country and leave you here."

"I am nearing thirty years old, Abigail," I said gently.

Anger fought to remain in control of her face and voice, but lost the battle to concern. "I know how old you are to the day and maybe even the hour, Miss Gwen. And all things being equal, I trust you to care for yourself and those children. But something about that book..." Her whole body tightened. It was like watching a rubber band being pulled back before being flung across the room.

She controlled it, relaxing with a long sigh from deep in her chest. "Something about that book has got its hooks in you, and it worries me. If you don't find some balance and start taking better care of yourself, I will send a telegraph to your lady mother."

I opened my mouth, but she puffed up and said, "See if I don't! Now you'll sleep or I'll have an answer as to why. Breakfast will be saved for you, and I'll see to the children's tutor in the morning."

Expecting obedience, she closed and locked my door with a final *click*.

How long did I stand there, suspended between amusement, surprise, and sorrow? Mrs. Chapman was the least tender hen to ever adopt an abandoned egg, but I could not have loved her more. And I had apparently been worrying her for months. Now those sidelong glances and furrowed brows made sense.

Of course, she did not understand what was at stake, what kept me up late every night. She did not know that, for centuries, faeries had been sneaking through the wall that separated the Sunset

Lands from the mortal world. Or that they lived among humans, elves, and dwarves in secret, protected by the glamour that allowed them to appear in any form they chose.

She didn't know that creatures like strzyga, werewolves, and harpies—monsters that had become rare to the point of extinction thanks to dwarven industrial advances—were being sighted more frequently now than in the last hundred years combined. Ever since our fight with the vampire, Cyrus and Alix sent telegraph after telegraph reporting monster encounters.

And she didn't know that the potential answer to why these things were happening lay in that book; the book almost every advanced society had banned shortly after the Great War nearly wiped out both mortals and fae. All copies were publically burned whenever they were found. No one believed the original still existed. But it did.

I killed a vampire, destroyed creatures made of darkness, and rescued a faerie woman to get my hands on it. If the authorities knew it was real and in my possession, they would likely jail me for treason.

Perhaps more important than any of those things, however, was the fact that the book may hold the key to bringing my twin sister back from the Sunset Lands. She'd been imprisoned there since she was stolen from a faerie ring when we were sixteen. Ophelia had stepped into the circle of mushrooms and disappeared. Finding her was my life's mission.

After years of searching, the only hope I discovered for bringing her home was inked in the calfskin pages of the most dangerous book I'd ever heard of. But I couldn't make the spell work.

Risking Mrs. Chapman's wrath, I opened the lock with a hairpin, checked the hallway, and snuck back downstairs just in time to see her enter the kitchen with a dustpan full of glass shards. Guilt sunk its teeth into the back of my neck, but I hurried into the study anyway, lifted the heavy book off the desk, and secreted it upstairs.

I needed to see, one more time, if I could crack the spell. A little more than a year ago, a witch had tried to use it to save her sick daughter's life. She hadn't known the spell's primary purpose was opening a door large enough for a whole troop of faeries to invade our world.

That's when I had seen Ophelia, my sister, standing on the other side of a spectral gate, her arms open in benediction. My heart froze in my chest at the sight of her. I never wanted anything in my whole life as much as I wanted to open the door.

My soul called to my lost sister like a lighthouse calling to ships in a storm. But, Instead of opening the door, I'd broken the spell circle and closed the gate to save the children, dooming the witch and her daughter to death, and separating myself from my sister again.

I ran my hand over the engraved leather of the cover and flipped the book open to the familiar page I'd spent countless hours studying. Magical symbols in faded ink seemed to float across the vellum, moving but not moving, flowing like water but always in the same place. Or perhaps that was simply my tired eyes.

A knock at the door made me jump, and guiltily close the book. "I'm changing for bed, Mrs. Chapman," I said.

The knob turned, and Sally poked her head through the crack. "Lady Gwen? Are you alright? I heard Mrs. Chapman, and the light stayed on under your door."

I motioned her inside, and she pulled her shawl tighter across her shoulders as she passed. The girl was of a height with me, now. When had my foul-mouthed little street urchin become an adult? Sally possessed more brains and courage than most people twice her age, but standing next to her now, it was painfully clear her childhood years were nearly done.

Not that she had much of a childhood. Her mother died when she was only ten years old, and her father abandoned them shortly after. Sally had scratched out a living on the streets with nothing but cunning and determination before I stumbled upon her.

Since then, she had saved Samuel from being kidnapped, fought to rescue the children Lady Monmouth tried to use as sacrifices, and spent her days learning everything she could; when she wasn't trying to mother me, of course.

"I'm fine, darling girl. Just stayed up too late reading and worried our dear housekeeper, that's all."

She blushed. "I have done that myself, on occasion."

"I know you have."

"What were you reading? The grimoire, again? Have you made any discoveries?"

She was too clever by half. And because of her involvement in the kidnappings, she knew more about the state of things than she should.

"No," I said, opening the book once more and looking down at the spell laid out in completely indecipherable symbols. "Not since the last failed experiment with Delilah. I have cross-referenced this spell with every other in the book, but not all of the runes translate."

Sally padded over on stocking feet to stand next to me and stare down at the symbols. "The circle is to contain and control the magic," she said as if repeating lessons, tracing the point of one finger along the diagram. "And the symbols give the magic shape and direction. But where does the power come from?"

"That is part of the problem. A witch creates and channels it through herself or her coven, using the spell like a funnel to direct the force according to her will. But our bodies were not made to channel magic. That is why most witches appear to be broken, even when they are not old."

"It ruins their bodies," she said. "I saw it happen to Lady Monmouth. Her hands were twisted and covered in age spots. And other strange things, too, that didn't have anything to do with growing older."

"Correct. But she was also using your life force, yours and the other children's, as a kind of amplifier. This spell requires a great deal of power."

Sally tucked a stray hair behind her ear, considering the problem. Ever since taking the children as my wards, I had learned not to underestimate either of them. They were smart and capable...and stubborn.

There was no use in trying to hide things from them, as we had all agreed to do with Mrs. Chapman after the vampire affair. They would simply snoop until they were either caught or learned what they wanted to know. Growing up on the streets had left both of them with a rather questionable sense of propriety where the secrets of others were concerned.

She frowned down at the book and said, slowly, "We can't create and channel the magic, so we need another way to activate the spell. But we can't use the runes Delilah used to copy the kidnapping spell? That one powered itself with natural forces."

"That was a small working," I said. "It required little energy and had a limited range. That's why it didn't call every orphan in the city to come running."

"So...could we use the runes to start the spell and then find some way to strengthen them?"

"Find an amplifier of our own? I don't know of any strong enough to hold so much energy without exploding. And a damaged spell is incredibly dangerous. You remember what happened when I broke the circle?"

She swallowed and nodded. The resulting explosion had scorched the grass for a hundred feet and sent a pillar of light burning into the sky. Nearby farmers mistook it for a lightning strike. I had only survived because of the crystal necklace gifted to me by a coven of witches, the extraordinary skills of a dwarven artificer, and the engraved wire felted into the coat Percy made me.

Those items had acted like a Faraday cage, warping the energy so it traveled around instead of through me. But it had not worked perfectly. My legs were scarred from the burns.

I closed the book and rubbed my hands on my skirt. It was easy to forget how terrifying that night had been. All my focus was bent on finding a way to bring my sister home, and that did not leave room for much else.

"Would the witches—the Triumphant Sisterhood, I mean—would they know of such an amplifier?"

"They might. But chances are they would keep it for themselves if they did. And they are not my favorite people to deal with."

Sally straightened and nodded once, as if it were decided. "I'll go with you to meet them, and we'll see what we can learn," she said.

Before I answered, she kissed me on the cheek and escaped back to her room. I stood there, once again confounded by the women in my household. How did they manage to get the better of me twice in one day?

I clearly wasn't getting enough sleep.

After stripping down to my chemise and drawers, I climbed into my cold bed and snuggled beneath the covers, rubbing my feet to warm them. For a moment I regretted—as I often did—telling Tony a relationship between us would never work.

I regretted even more that he refused to allow himself to be tempted into my bed without some kind of commitment. If I dragged Tony to bed, he would want far more than I was willing to give. He was not selfish, but it was his nature to commit fully and to expect the same commitment from the people in his life.

And I would never marry.

I refused to spend my life wondering if the man who married me did so because he loved me, or because I would inherit my father's estate, title, and extravagant wealth...which he would share.

Worse, Tony was a genuinely good person with a whole heart, and mine had been broken for years. It would be a terribly unfair exchange. But laying alone in my cold bed, tired and unable to sleep, made any warm body sound worthwhile.

At the thought of warm bodies, an unwelcome memory wriggled to the front of my mind, like a worm in a corpse. No matter how much I tried to suppress it, it always came back when I was at my weakest.

My fingers strayed to the juncture of my neck and shoulder, where the skin was raised in an oval scar.

The vampire was dead—we had destroyed his body to be certain—but his bite would mark me, forever. In moments like this, I still felt the horrible, sickening pleasure of it trying to drag me under, to make me enjoy what he called his 'kiss.'

I shot out of bed and paced the floor, rubbing my arms against the goosebumps. My mind was too wrung out to get anything useful from the book, and there was no one to distract me from the welter of thoughts and emotions sloshing about inside my head. Something had to be done, and I was out of brandy.

A few moments later, a comforting little fire crackled in the hearth. I pulled the blanket off the bed, wrapped myself up, and curled into the chair, watching the flames and trying to let them burn away the memory.

A familiar tapping sounded at my door.

Aristotle stood on the carpet in the hall when I opened it, looking up at me sideways, the flames painting his black feathers in oily orange light.

"You can't sleep, either?" I asked.

He walked in, as stately as Poe had dreamed, and hopped onto the arm of the chair. When I sat down again, he snuggled into the hollow created by my bent legs, laid his head on my knee, and clicked his beak twice in command.

"You are a pushy fellow, Aristotle," I said, but ran my fingers obediently along the top of his head until his eyes closed. Not the warm body I was hoping for, but absurdly comforting, all the same.

Perhaps I needed to take a new lover, someone distracting to pull me out of my head when I got lost inside. Of course, I would have to hide them from Sam and Sally, which wasn't ideal. Neither was spending every night pouring over the damn grimoire until my vision blurred.

I needed help. Sally was right.

Tomorrow I would reach out to the one person in New London I did not want to speak to and find out if she had any insight into making the spell work. And I ought to take Sally with me. She was already involved in the affair, so it was safest to arm her with as much information as possible.

If I made her search it out on her own, she would find more than she bargained for.

Aristotle made a disgruntled little noise and waggled his tail. I resumed petting his soft feathers, running my fingers down his neck and back as he purred. That sound lulled me to sleep too many nights to count, and my eyelids grew heavy as a sense of peace stole over me.

I needed that peace because tomorrow I would be forced to ask a favor of a witch, and who knew what she would demand of me in return?

3

Asking Favors of Witches

GWEN

Sally and I climbed out of the carriage late the next morning and joined a gaggle of pedestrians on their way to Sevil Park. We needed a bit of privacy for this conversation, and there was no better place than the tree-lined paths, hedges, and intimate walkways of Sevil.

Well-known as a suitable place for young lovers to get better acquainted, it would provide the perfect cover: no one would eavesdrop on the three of us talking about magic, because no one wanted to get close enough to overhear gooey declarations of love.

Evergreen shrubs pressed against the wrought-iron fence and spilled over into the street, giving visitors secluded avenues for tête-à-tête. Pale blue winter pixies flitted amongst the branches, searching for ice and frozen dew drops.

They were exceedingly rare in cities where natural spaces had been destroyed in favor of streets and buildings. But gardens in the city were cultivated with pixies in mind and Sevil Park flourished year-round because of their gentle magic.

Madame Matilda stood in the sunlight near the entrance to the park, as beautiful in a walking dress as she was in formal evening gowns. Her dark curls were piled atop her head beneath a pale, fur-lined hat, her hands tucked inside a similarly styled muffler. The ivory gown made her olive skin and dark eyes glow.

As the head of the Triumphant Sisterhood, the only coven of witches in New London, she always met with me in the safety of the building they owned—her territory, so to speak. So meeting on neutral ground was a step of faith on her part, especially since witchcraft had been outlawed for more than a century and the Sisterhood operated in secret.

"I appreciate your joining us," I said when we reached her. And I meant it. My late night made two things clear: if I believed something significant was happening in the world, and I did, I required more allies. And, to build any kind of working relationship with the witches, I needed to extend trust and goodwill rather than constantly battling for the high ground.

"I hope it will be my pleasure," she said with an elegant nod.

Madame Matilda was one of those women, women like my mother, who must have been bathed by the gods in feminine elegance.

She was certain to draw attention wherever she went and equally certain to be the de facto leader of whatever group she happened to be a part of. She wasn't merely elegant, but fiercely intelligent.

And I hated admitting that because I still had not forgiven her for the Cassandra Monmouth affair...but I needed her in my corner. So I said, "I hope so, too."

"And who is this?" She asked, offering Sally a smile.

"This is my ward, Miss Sarah Dawes."

"Miss Dawes?" Matilda asked, tilting her head as a small line appeared between her perfectly arched brows.

"Sally," she corrected with a neat little curtsy I wasn't aware she'd been practicing. I would have to ask her about it later.

"It is a pleasure to meet you, Sally. Please call me Matilda."

We began walking, for all appearances a polite and respectable group of ladies. Except we were a group of outcasts: a witch, an orphan, and a social pariah. And here I was, strolling through a park with a witch as if it were a perfectly normal morning activity. My life had truly reached a new and unexpected level of strangeness.

"I was surprised to receive your invitation, given the tenor of our last meeting," Matilda said.

I had been preparing myself all morning to swallow my pride and ignore past insults, but it proved even harder than I expected.

I did manage to say, with at least some honesty, "I do regret that. As you can imagine, the events of the last year or so have been rather disturbing. It doesn't put one in a trusting or friendly frame of mind."

"Understandable. I shall assume your ward is aware of the situation?"

"She is."

"And she can be trusted to be discreet?"

That question tested the bounds of my desire to be cordial. I took a steadying breath and said, "Sally was one of the children involved in Cassandra's bid to save her daughter's life."

Matilda's gaze sharpened as she looked at the girl. "I see. I am sorry you were forced to suffer such a thing, Miss Dawes."

Sally's face paled, but she kept her chin up and gave Matilda a polite nod.

"With that out of the way," I said, once we were clear of the crowd and turned to the lee side of a large hedge, "I hoped you might help me with a problem. I am struggling with the translation of the spell Cassandra used to punch a hole through the wall."

One dark brow arched. "In what way?"

"It appears to require a great deal of power to activate and sustain."

"So it does."

"Is there a way to lessen the power requirements? I have seen it done with much smaller spells, but never one of this magnitude."

Matilda was quiet for a long time, looking down at her muff as we walked. When she finally spoke, her voice was thoughtful. "Am I to assume you plan to repeat the spell?"

"How could I? I am no witch."

She gave me a sidelong glance through her lashes, likely catching the hint of dishonesty beneath the truth. I was no witch. But Delilah and I had discovered how to power magic through artificery when we broke down the spells Cassandra used to kidnap the children, and that may let me replicate it if the power requirements became more manageable.

"No, you are not. You realize that magic would allow anyone on the other side a safe door to the mortal world?"

"Of course. And you realize," I said, changing the subject and taking my first leap of faith in this conversation, "faeries have been finding their own way through in greater numbers recently?"

"Of course."

"And that monster sightings and encounters have been increasing rapidly, as well."

"I assumed as much, given what happened with Lady Chatsworth's housekeeper."

"And," I said, introducing the last and most uncomfortable topic of all, "that some of them may be interfering in mortal affairs beyond simple predation."

She hesitated before taking her next step, though she recovered quickly. "Please explain."

This was an experience I did not particularly want to relive, but if I was to gain her confidence and convince her to share knowledge with me, she would require reciprocity.

"We killed a vampire in the forest on the Chatsworth Estate. I believed him to be involved in the disappearance of the housekeeper, but I was mistaken. He had enthralled a guest, a member of the House of Lords, and was using the man to gather and pass information."

"For what purpose?"

"The vampire was dead before we could ask him."

"That was an oversight."

You are polite, calm, and charming, I reminded myself. But I wasn't quite able to remove the pertness from my tone when I said,

"If the Sisterhood had seen fit to lend a hand, we may have been strong enough to capture him without killing him."

"You know very well why we could not."

I didn't bother responding. While the coven claimed to sponsor charities and good deeds, I had yet to see them myself.

"He did mention creating a world where the strong no longer hid from the weak," I added.

She took a moment to mull over everything I said and implied, putting information together in her clever brain. She would likely take the same logical path I had, weighing the chances that the vampire was working alone, an anomaly, against the possibility that everything happening was related.

But would she also assume my interest in the spell was only related to those events, and not to my desperate need to finally regain my sister? I pursed my lips and let her come to her own conclusions.

At last, she said, "If these incidents are related and we treat them as if they are not, then we are voluntarily putting ourselves and the kingdom in danger. I think, for our safety, we must assume they have a single point of origin."

"Sound logic," I said, breathing an internal sigh of relief.

"And you believe the origin lies on the other side of the wall."

"I have my suspicions."

We rejoined the main path that circled the central lawn, silent while other ears were so close. Sally walked with her head down, brows knitted. Her gloved hands were shoved into the pockets of the wool coat Percy—my favorite designer who also happened to be a fae selkie hiding on this side of the wall—finished for her last week.

Slowly, as if thinking her way through the problem, she said, "In the books I have read on medieval warfare, a besieged castle would purposely draw attention to weaknesses in their fortifications because it allowed them to predict and control where the enemy attacked. "

Matilda looked up, surprised. "That is an astute observation. And you are right. Outside of warfare, in any relationship between peoples, whoever controls the port has power. If we control the doors, we have an advantage in any future encounters."

Oh, my Sally. Her eyes flicked to me for only an instant, but I saw what she was doing: giving Matilda more reasons to assume that I needed to understand the spell from a tactical perspective. And nothing in my history would lead her to think otherwise, aside from my sister's disappearance.

But most of society believed Lia had either run away, been sent away for an indiscretion, or been killed. How many people, witches included, would believe she was kidnapped by faeries?

"As with any spell," Matilda began, "the ability to alter it depends upon the witch who created it. Sometimes safety measures are built into the spell, other times it is, for lack of a better analogy, a simple recipe that can be expanded upon without ruining the original. You must find out what kind of spell it is."

It was my turn to hesitate. "You don't know?"

"Despite what you may believe," she said, looking at me down the length of her nose, "I do not study magic to seek power for myself. The Mordegant Grimoire was outlawed for a reason, and

I do not think it came to Cassandra by accident. We are all safest if the grimoire remains in non-magical hands."

"You gave the book to me to protect your coven?"

She smiled. "That, and because I trust you not to blow England up with it."

"How do I go about discovering whether the spell has been rigged?" I ground out, irritated that she managed to get the better of me in three ways at once.

"You are an intelligent woman. Puzzle it out."

I thought I might choke on the words, but I managed to say them without also losing my breakfast all over the path. "Will you not help me?"

She stopped walking, tucked her hands deeper into the warmth of her muffler, and said, "I will help you protect the city. I will give you what advice I can. But it is safer for my coven if we use our own spells for our own purposes, and stay as far from the mind of the witches who wrote that grimoire as possible."

My jaw clenched hard enough to send a spike of pain shooting up to my ear. How was I supposed to get Lia back if I could not make the spell work? And how could I convince the woman to help me without giving away the one weakness she could most easily exploit if she chose?

I might be willing to recruit her to help protect the city from whatever was happening, but I certainly didn't trust her with my most vulnerable secret. She'd have to earn that.

"What about an amplifier?" Sally said. "Might a witch use one for a spell like that instead of drawing power from people?"

Matilda tapped her chin with one gloved finger. "It might, depending upon how stable the amplifier is. But artifacts like those are rare and valuable. And"—she raised one finger—"if they are not perfect, they may explode and release the stored energy."

She made a little expanding motion with her fingers and mouthed the word, boom.

"How would one know if an artifact was of the right kind?" Sally asked. Her eyes were focused, her body still, like a cat who sighted a bird.

Matilda noticed it, too. "Crystals and precious gems often serve as amplifiers because of the way they transmit and refract magical resonance. But they are also brittle. Better is an amplifier built for the purpose."

"Can you build one?"

"Yes."

"Will you?"

"No."

"Will you teach me to build one?"

"Certainly not."

"Why?"

"Because I have no intention of helping anyone open the wall to the Sunset Lands. Controlling the doors is one thing. Opening them for invading fae is another."

"Sharing knowledge is not opening the door."

Matilda's smile was full of knowing. "Oh yes, it is. Knowledge is a door. And the sooner you learn that, the closer you will be to wisdom. Knowledge, true knowledge, must be earned if it is to mean anything, Sarah." She dipped her fingers into the pocket of her coat and pulled out a small white card. "If you find you want to learn, let me know."

I stepped between the two of them and snatched the card before Sally touched it. "Do not proselytize my ward, if you please."

She held up both hands, winked at Sally, and turned to walk on, sashaying down the path, through a vine-covered arch, and out of the park. Apparently, our meeting was at an end.

"She gave that to me," Sally said. There was a note of steel in her voice I recognized immediately from my teenage years.

"Yes, she did," I said, dropping it into my pocket. "And we will discuss that before you take possession of it."

She crossed her arms. "You're the one who said we should learn as much as we can about dangerous things."

"I did. And why do you think I have never tried to do magic, even small magic, despite how much I know of it?"

"Because the gift of witchcraft must be in your blood to do magic," she said with the vocal equivalent of an eye roll.

"Because having a key to a door and opening a door are two very different things, Sally. Matilda was right about that. What she did not say is once you have opened the door, it can never be shut again. And when you have tasted the power of changing the natural world as you see fit, you might like the flavor of it too much to care who or what the open door lets through."

"People change the world all the time with money, or laws, or..." She threw her hands into the air. "What makes magic different?"

"Because the ways in which those people change things are not fundamental. If they cause a drought, it is because they used up all the water, not because they changed the water into gold. Or wine. Or sent the clouds off to another part of the planet."

Her eyes grew wide.

"Oh yes, all of that is possible. Magic can fundamentally alter things. It can also affect your mind and your body. Why do you think we wear the amber amulets?" I touched my neck where the necklace rested against my skin.

"Why don't witches do that, then? Why not just fix everything or...I don't know, win wars?"

"Do you remember the way the magic changed Lady Monmouth's body?" I asked, taking her arm in mine.

Sally shivered. "Yes."

The woman had gone from a lovely mature beauty to something barely recognizable as human in a matter of minutes as power twisted her body.

"Most witches are solitary, and their power eventually changes them so much they are forced to live reclusive lives. But the Sisterhood has discovered a way around such danger. They share the power and channel it together, so the strain weighs on them equally. And they don't try to work magic that is too strong, because it would harm them despite sharing the burden."

Sally remained quiet, thinking as we neared the exit. Finally, she said, "But you could still find an amplifier. And if you can activate the spell the way you do with the artifice Delilah makes"—she gestured to the umbrella hanging from my forearm—"then add an amplifier to it, you could open the door."

"So it would seem. I had hoped Matilda would be of more help but, I must admit, hearing her confirmation eases my mind. It means I have been on the right track."

James pulled alongside the walk and stopped the coach, then jumped down and opened the doors, handing us up one at a time. Sally got herself settled, flipped the switch on the little dwarven heater placed in the center of the coach, and held her hands out.

The device had been charged the night before in the kitchen hearth and began pumping out the stored heat with a happy humming sound. Before a minute passed, the space was warm enough to make me pull off my gloves.

"Can I at least search the library for mentions of amplifiers?" she asked a moment later.

I knew, perhaps better than anyone, that denying a determined mind is the surest way to force it to seek other options, so I said, "I was hoping you'd ask."

She smiled, but it was the smile of someone accepting a hug instead of a kiss. Sally would concede...for now. But only because she fully intended to fight for what she wanted later.

I was tempted to ask James to turn the coach around so I could say a few choice words to the witch.

Sally disappeared into the study as soon as we arrived home, stripping her winter clothing like a shedding bear. I followed, picking up gloves off the floor and smiling as I leaned against the doorframe. She searched titles on the shelves, shooing Aristotle as he tried to help by pecking at random spines. After choosing a few books, she set them on the table near her favorite chair for serious study.

Mr. Yates entered the hallway, his measured pace and steady tread warning me of his presence long before he said, "Inspector Hardwicke to see you, Ma'am."

Tony.

He liked the idea of my dabbling in witchcraft even less than Madame Matilda did, but he also knew how far I was willing to go to find my sister. I hoped he hadn't visited purely to fight me about it again.

Once we discovered the elusive Mr. Capstone was, in truth, a mirage created by the vampire, he'd been able to spend his time on the more mundane cases dropped on his desk at Scotland Yard. Which meant he also had more time to order me around.

Not that I minded his ordering...especially when it ended in frustrated kisses.

"Thank you, Mr. Yates," I said, handing him Sally's bundle of clothing. "He's in the drawing room?"

"Yes, ma'am. I have already taken the liberty of offering him a glass of his favorite whisky."

"Did he accept?"

"He has finished his second glass, my lady."

"Yates," I said, touching his cheek fondly. "You think of everything. What would I do without you?"

He didn't smile. He rarely smiled. But the corner of his eyes crinkled, and he dipped his head to the side in a very formal acceptance of my compliment.

If Tony drank two glasses of whisky, he was either nervous, under a great deal of stress, or both. It was Friday, so he'd visited his parents last night. I unbuttoned my jacket, handed that to Mr. Yates as well, and headed off toward the drawing room, prepared for the worst.

Tony stood near the window with a half-empty glass in one hand and a silver coin in the other. He didn't look at the coin, just fiddled with it, turning the smooth silver over and over, running his fingers across the faded surface with his blonde brows drawn low over his eyes.

He was nervous.

He also looked incredibly handsome in a wholesome, silent, square-jawed way. Nervous and handsome was not a good combination, because it activated whatever caretaking instincts I had. That would naturally remind me of how lonely I was and how much comfort I might find in the joining of bodies.

I cleared my throat and entered the room. "Tony! How good to see you. Are you—"

The words stopped in my throat at his expression. He fumbled the coin, tucked it into his waistcoat pocket, considered setting his glass on the table, then thought better of it and threw back the rest of the whisky.

Oh, no.

I recovered nicely with an, "Are you quite well?"

"Gwen," he said, his eyes darting over my shoulder, then back to my face. A moment of unadulterated longing flashed in his eyes, only to be smothered by apprehension. His hands curled into fists. "I...I must tell you something," he said at last, marshaling his courage and setting his shoulders. "Though I wish I was not the one to deliver the news."

Lovely. I rallied my intestinal fortitude and prepared for the blow.

4

Revelations and Grenades

GWEN

Sam strolled into the sitting room with the confidently lazy stride young men adopted when they finally recognized they were growing into their adult bodies. Taller, leaner, his face a bit more angular than it was this time last year, he had all the promise of being a rather handsome and well-made man.

If I didn't kill him first.

No, Sally would be angry with me if I did that. And it would distress Tony. He might even arrest me. I gestured to the chair across from where I sat, and he flopped into it, oblivious to the tension in the room.

Sam got into trouble regularly—small things, for the most part. But he had a good heart, and I was trying, unsuccessfully, to give him the benefit of the doubt. He'd proven to be honest and courageous more than once, even when he disobeyed.

I hoped, desperately, that he would prove himself again. And I was terrified he would not.

Tony stood behind my chair, to one side, his breathing calm and even.

"Sam," I said, then cleared my throat and tried again. "Samuel. You know how much I care for you."

He blushed and his eyes flicked to Tony as if he wished the older man hadn't seen such an intimate exchange. "Me, too," he mumbled. Then, more suspiciously, "What's all this, then?"

"Is there anything you'd like to tell me? Anything at all?"

He glanced between the two of us, first at Tony, then at me. "No. Why?"

Damn, the boy was going to make this hard. "Nothing? You wouldn't like to tell me why you snuck into an abandoned church last night when you should have been sleeping?"

Sam leaned back, his body stiffening as if he'd been sucker punched. I supposed he had. But surprise was often the most effective way to get the truth out of someone before they had a chance to school their features and prepare a story.

"What?" His voice was hoarse.

"I saw you, scamp," Tony said. "Followed you to the church, and waited outside. In fact, I was jumped by a couple of toughs, or I would have followed you home, too. That's not a safe part of town, Sam. Why were you there?"

Panic twisted Sam's face for a heartbeat, but he covered it with a laugh. "Just meeting with some of the boys, you know? From the old neighborhood. Haven't seen 'em in so long, I just—"

"Then you wouldn't mind if I did a bit of reconnaissance tonight."

"No! I mean, that's not a good idea, Tony. Not for a cop, they'd never allow you in. You've gotten good this year"—he was referring to the lessons in crime he'd been giving Tony since the inspector first learned he was protecting himself from pickpockets badly, as evidenced by the handful of goods Sam had nabbed from various pockets without Tony realizing it—"but not good enough to get in there."

"Suppose they would if I showed up with my badge and a dozen constables."

Sam's face went absolutely white. His eyes flashed across the room as if looking for an escape, and the leather armrests dented beneath his white-knuckled grip. My stomach twisted free of my body and dove into my toes.

Something was very wrong.

I left my chair and crouched before him, gripping his wrists. "Sam. What's happened? Whatever it is, we can fix it."

He slumped, his eyes misting with unshed tears. Samuel Dawes crying? "No, we can't. This can't be fixed, my lady."

"You have no idea what I am truly capable of, Sam. Do not force me to do something stupid to protect you because I will bloody well do it and damn the consequences. You will tell me what is happening. Right. Now."

It may have been the growl in my voice, or the strength with which I was gripping his wrists. Or, perhaps, it was the barely leashed insanity in my eyes that convinced the boy to speak. Either way, it worked.

"I just wanted to help," he said, lip trembling. He looked much more like the small twelve-year-old scamp than the nearly fifteen-year-old young man.

"How?"

"You were so worried about Mr. Capstone," he said, speaking as if the floodgates in this chest had opened. "And I thought maybe some of my boys had heard gossip. Street kids hear more than you'd think. So I snuck out and walked back to the old neighborhood. But they were waiting for me."

"They, who?" Tony asked. His voice was low and rough.

"The King's men."

There was a heartbeat of silence, the intake of someone's breath—Tony's or mine, I wasn't sure—and Tony said, "The Cutthroat King?"

Sam nodded miserably.

"I thought he was just a myth," I said.

"He is. Or a legend. Or a ghost," Tony said. "We've been after him for years, and never caught more than whispers."

"Because he's the King," Sam said as if we were both stupid. "He wanted me to do some spying for him since I was...well, since I was a fancy lad now, and I could get into fancy places."

"And you agreed," I said.

"He said"—Sam looked away, jaw clenched—"he said he would come after Sally to help him if I didn't."

Something clicked into place in my mind behind the sudden fury that made my chest feel like it was on fire. "Lord Ashcroft," I said.

Sam nodded.

I had been so distraught after that incident, and so grateful everyone I loved was still alive, that I had forgotten to push Sam for more information, neglected to ask why he'd suddenly appeared in the country when he was supposed to be safe at home.

"I went back afterward," he said, trying to justify, to make us understand. "I told him I was done, that I did what he wanted. But he won't let me go. He says I'm too useful. I'm sorry, Lady Gwen." He grabbed my hands, squeezing hard. "I never meant to dishonor you like that, but I didn't know what else to do, and if I told you..." His eyes strayed to Tony. He swallowed painfully, and said, "I suppose you'll have to arrest me, now. Maybe that's safest, anyway."

"You little idiot," I said, shaking my head.

"Gwen—" Tony began, but I spun and locked him in place with my eyes, feeling as if they would burn themselves right out of my head. He froze.

I turned back to the boy. "This is done, Sam."

"I wish you saying it would make it so, my lady."

"It is done because I say it is done. If he comes after you, he'll have me to deal with."

He gave me a sad, hopeless smile. "And what if he burns the townhouse in the middle of the night? Or kidnaps Sally when she goes shopping? You can't be with us all the time."

"Sam—"

"It's too late," he said, sitting forward, his eyes boring into mine. "Don't you understand? I can't go back now, I'm...I'm marked."

The fury burning a hole through my chest hiccuped and sputtered. "What do you mean?"

Cheeks red with shame, Sam fumbled with the buttons of his shirt. He pulled the collar aside to reveal a raised circular scar on the right side of his torso, just below the collarbone. It was a man's head with a cut throat. It had healed clean, but the message was clear: it was a brand of ownership.

I fought to control my voice as I asked, "Did you agree to this, Sam?"

"No!" he shouted, then licked his lips and began buttoning his shirt. "No. He held me down. Sat on me, actually."

I grabbed his face between both hands, staring into eyes I saw over the dinner table every night. How much would this boy have sacrificed? How many nights had he kept secret? How much fear had he endured? My fury cooled, hardened, solidified into ice, and flowed through my veins, freezing everything in its path.

"Do you want to be a servant of the Cutthroat King?" I asked, my voice low and cold.

"No."

I nodded, stood, said, "You will stay here until I tell you otherwise. Do not cross me in this, Samuel Dawes, or I will not be responsible for my actions," and left the room.

"Gwen," Tony's voice followed me, but I didn't stop. Sally stood in the hallway, tears running down her face. She hurried into the drawing room as I left. There was shouting, but I couldn't grasp the meaning of the words.

My focus had thinned to a razor's edge, cutting away everything that did not matter as I planned to make the Cutthroat King regret putting his hands on my boy.

"Gwen, stop."

Most of my gear was safely in the study, stored away after my adventures on the continent. It was time to reacquaint myself with my tools. I would need smoke grenades, actual grenades, my umbrella, a pistol...my jacket had been destroyed during the fight with the Reavers, but the replacement might be wearable. Would Percy have it at his shop? Did I have time to stop?

"Gwen!" Tony shouted, turning me about by the simple expedient of grabbing my upper arm.

Tony was a friend. I shouldn't attack him.

"You cannot go after the Cutthroat King," he said. "You'll never find him. He is the literal ruler of the underground. Those who wear the King's mark will serve him to the death because they are more scared of him than they are of constables or prison." He shook me once when I did not respond. "Do you understand me?"

"Tony," I said, in a very reasonable tone. "Either help me or release me and get the hell out of my way. I am going. I will protect Sam. If you try to stop me, I will kill you."

He stepped back, eyes wide. I turned to resume collecting supplies.

Sam said he had entered whatever existed of the King's domain through that church, which was guarded by at least two men and probably watched by several more. I opened a drawer of the bureau against the rear wall and pulled out a boiled leather corset that had several loops and straps attached.

I knew that church, and if the door to the King's domain was there, the rest of the lair was likely underground, because all the other buildings on that block were houses. Some were abandoned, so I'd need to be certain they were empty before I tried the front door.

Two silver knives slid silently into sheaths fastened to the back of the corset, followed by the green smoke grenades I had perfected late last year. The criminals would certainly have firearms, and the umbrella would help, but I'd need additional armor to reach the King. And where was my grappling hook?

"Dammit," Tony said, his voice weary and defeated.

You'd think the drive to Percy's shop would have given me time to come to my senses. It did not. Instead of buildings and traffic, I saw the angry scar on Sam's skin, the way his lips trembled, and how Sally's face twisted into lines of shocked grief.

The ice had frozen me from the inside, leaving no room for anything but cold determination.

Percy's shop was barely on the fashionable side of the invisible line that divided the West End from the center of town. Windows featuring his latest fashions lined the front, displaying abundant wealth and skill.

Once upon a time, he had been a milliner, specializing in the most gorgeous hats I had ever seen. But after outfitting me for the party at Lady Chatsworth's country estate, he was now the most sought-after designer of women's fashion in New London.

I paid him an exorbitant amount to be my personal designer, but he subcontracted at least four sewists to work under the name of his house, while he focused on more...elaborate designs for me; usually, ones that kept me from dying in the dangerous situations I seemed to find myself in, lately.

"Percy!" I shouted as I pushed open the front door.

The girl behind the desk jumped, recognized me, and opened the little gate that divided the front of the store from the back. She cringed away from me as I passed. He was in the back, yellow measuring tape flung over one shoulder, pins stuck in the fine white lawn of his shirt, a needle and thread hanging from his lips as he tacked a pleat in place.

"Have you finished the new jacket?" I asked without preamble.

He jumped, too, one hand over his heart as he turned to gape at me. Beneath the wide, elegantly upturned eyes and pointed ears of his elven glamour was an equally beautiful creature, still dark of skin, but fae and not elvish.

To anyone who had never seen him without his glamour, he was an elven man. But he was, in truth, a selkie who had crossed the wall hundreds of years ago. He'd never said why, and I didn't ask.

"Gwen!"

Several mannequins lined the walls wearing unfinished pieces of clothing, but I approached one in particular. It was a wool coat of dark, desaturated blue-grey that would cover me from wrists to ankles when it was fully buttoned. It was beautifully made, but that wasn't why it was special.

Sewn into the fabric with metallic thread were runes he and I had developed with Delilah, runes similar to the ones engraved in my umbrella that caught and redistributed energy. It was, for all purposes, a suit of armor; not strictly artificery, like the mechanisms Delilah made, but a hybrid child of sorts.

It blended faerie magic with dwarven artifice to form something unique. In essence, the two of them had been using me as an experiment to test what was possible with these new techniques, and what was safe to release to the public. I had many bruises to prove it.

"Is it done?" I asked again, turning the mannequin to check the finish.

"No. Well, yes, but Delilah and I aren't scheduled to test it until next week."

I removed my leather corset, pulled the jacket off the mannequin, and shrugged into it, testing the fit. "It will have to do."

"Wait, what on earth are you talking about? Gwen, we haven't tested it! If the runic sentences are wrong, it's just as likely to kill you as it is to protect you. It could explode or catch fire, or gods know what."

"I'll just have to take my chances," I said, pulling the corset harness on over the coat.

"What? Why? Gwen, what is going on? Stop!" He grabbed my shoulders. "What happened?"

For a moment I considered breaking his fingers, but Percy, too, was a friend. His kindness had protected my soul on more than one dark night, just as his magical garments protected my hide.

So I said, "The Cutthroat King forced Sam into his service. He *branded* him." The word stuck in my throat.

Percy's face went ashen, his mouth open in shock. "Why?"

"So he can use him," I said, resuming fastening buttons and buckles. "Why else?"

"And...you're going to stop him." It wasn't a question.

"I'm going to make him regret ever even thinking about touching my boy."

Percy's eyes softened as he watched me, and Tony's words from that summer floated through my mind. *You are a mother in every way that matters.* And what mattered now was putting Sam forever beyond the reach of the Cutthroat King.

By any means necessary.

Tony insisted on coming, and I hadn't the heart to talk him out of it. Whatever remained of my sane mind told me he was taking too great a risk, both for himself and for his family's sake. But I needed whatever help I could get.

He did not suggest bringing more constables, knowing as well as I did that more people would only scare our rabbit from his den. We had to take another approach. While it was more likely to get us through the door than showing up with twenty constables, my plan was also several times more dangerous.

And since I had no intention of dying tonight, I had to be thorough.

After canvassing the area during what remained of the afternoon, we squatted in separate abandoned buildings and watched night fall over the decaying neighborhood. For a moment, the last rays of sunlight lit up the withered remains of the old church, cutting through gaps in crumbling mortar and glowing in leftover shards of stained glass.

For a few moments, the ruins were as beautiful as a moss-covered skeleton in the woods. But then the light died, and it was only the remnants of a religion slowly fading into the past.

Stars peeked between breaks in the clouds. Mist began to settle in the low places and build up until it was a white sea that obscured every shape and softened every corner. Street lamps became islands of safety in the fog.

Still, we waited.

When even the most committed laborer was safe in their beds, I took two grenades with long fuses and positioned them by the windows. After lighting the fuses, I crept out of the building. My blue coat turned me into another shadow as I slid along walls and edged down the street.

During the long walk to this part of town, Tony told me that Scotland Yard had given up hunting the King. They'd been after him for years, but his lair moved regularly, his servants were zealots, and it was certain he had either bribed or blackmailed many well-placed officials.

It was more profitable for the department to focus on criminals they could catch. He seemed certain we'd find nothing beneath the church, provided we managed to get in. But I planned to make a lot of noise.

I had a few suspicions about the King's motivations, and we were about to find out whether I was right.

Once I reached the side of the church just behind the entrance on the right, I double-checked my preparations and waited. My nose and cheeks burned with cold, but I hardly noticed. There were more important things to consider...like whether I had given Tony enough time to reach his position on the other side before my distraction activated.

I was going in, whether he joined me or not. But I was much more likely to live if he did.

So, when the bottom floor windows blew out of the building in spectacular fashion, I rushed the front door.

5

Royal Introductions

GWEN

Broken glass, chunks of stone, and bits of boards peppered the sides of the nearby buildings as a gout of flame soared twenty feet in the air.

Both guards stood on the top stair facing the blast, their faces slack with surprise and bathed orange light. Tony and I took them from behind. I snaked my elbow around the throat of the man on the left and locked it in place with my other arm, then arched back and squeezed.

He thrashed for a moment but went limp as the blood stopped flowing to his brain. I fisted my hands in his jacket and dragged him off the porch and into the shadows, using a length of rope to secure his wrists and ankles, and ripping a strip from the hem of his shirt to stuff into his mouth.

Tony met me outside the doors seconds later, pistol drawn. I opened the umbrella, crouched so he could position the weapon above the canopy, and we entered the church in a kind of two-person phalanx.

I pulled out a smoke grenade, lit the fuse with one hand, and tossed it into the nave.

Yes, it was sacrilegious, but I had more important things to think about, like the coughing that followed the grenade as it bounced around the corner, spewing green smoke. A man ran out of the haze, one elbow bent over his nose. Tony stepped out from under the cover of my umbrella and punched him. The neat jab rocked the man's head back before he toppled to the ground, dazed. We tied his hands and feet and hid him behind piles of rubble where the pews had been.

We advanced in formation again, watching for more escapees, when I noticed something peculiar.

"There," I whispered. "Behind the pulpit."

A trail of green smoke was being sucked downward between two paving stones. Tony dug his fingers into the crack and grunted, lifting the stone to reveal narrow stairs leading down into the dark. He looked up at me, a question in his eyes.

"I'm not going back," I said, flatly.

He nodded, checked his pistol, and motioned for me to lead the way. I shut the umbrella, shoved it through the opening, and opened it again, holding it beneath me like a shield. Tony followed me down into the greater darkness where not even the light of the dying fire could reach.

A small dwarven torch hung from a strap on the front of my corset. I flicked it on and turned the dimmer down. Delilah had

called it a thieves' lamp, and it cast a dim, narrow beam at the
floor that would be almost invisible from a distance.

The passage ran in one direction, down. We followed it until
more voices echoed up toward us.

"...sound? It were too loud to be normal."

"...do you—it was?"

I switched off the lamp, and we crouched behind the umbrella. A bright light came around the corner at the end of the
corridor. Two dark figures climbed toward us with a torch of
their own pointed at the ground. When they saw us, things
would get loud.

"Brentus should have reported," one said in the kind of voice
only earned through years of cigars and whisky.

"What the bloody 'ell is that?"

"What?"

"There!"

Silence.

"Is that...an umbrella?"

Footsteps. "Who left an umbrella—what the 'ell?"

The passage erupted with gunfire and the umbrella glowed
with blue shockwaves where the bullets struck. I braced my
shoulder against the impact, gritting my teeth as the runes
along the shaft lit up and grew hot. Before they were too hot
to hold, I triggered the release.

A bolt of stored force shot from the tip of the umbrella, expanding as it flew, and knocked both men off their feet. Tony rushed
from cover, gun drawn, and fell upon them. By the time I joined
him, there wasn't much left to do but tie the wrists and ankles of

the dwarven man, who must have hit his head when he fell because he blinked numbly at the ceiling.

"So good so far," Tony muttered.

"You mean we haven't had to kill anyone yet?"

"And we aren't dead."

"Yet."

"You are so comforting, my lady."

I grinned, showing all my teeth, and opened the umbrella again.

We followed the passage until it bifurcated, splitting at a ninety-degree angle, and stopped to listen. The air moved past us in a semi-constant flow from right to left and carried with bits and pieces of muffled conversation and...music? I jerked my head to the right, and we continued creeping deeper into the caverns, following the sound of activity.

"This is going to be messy," I breathed. "Stay behind the umbrella and let me take the brunt of the attacks. My jacket will protect me."

Tony's jaw muscle flexed, but he nodded.

The passage widened, opening up to allow for a door to a larger room. Music, laughing, and the scent of cigars and roasting meat wafted toward us. I turned off the torch, raised my last smoke grenade, lit the fuse with a twist of my fingers, and tossed it through the door.

"One, two," I counted, and then the swearing started.

We rushed into the smoke amidst the coughing and shouting, holding our breaths. I spotted a door through to the other side and led Tony toward it, but the first shot split the air before we'd gotten halfway through. The impact lit up the canopy of the umbrella as

I turned to keep Tony behind me and braced the reinforced ribs against my shoulder.

Tony straightened, sighted, and returned fire as we traversed the space. I could protect us for a few moments, but not long enough to get through the door before someone flanked us and started shooting at our unprotected backs.

Two more shots hit the canopy, someone screamed, and several criminals rushed us. I let fly another blast of stored force that blew a channel through the rushing attackers, then spun so the canopy protected Tony from knee to shoulders. With a quick twist of my arm, I shoved him backward and away from danger.

He stumbled and swore, but he was too late to stop me. The first bullet that struck my jacket felt like a fist in the ribs, and a wave of warmth wrapped around me like a perverse hug to spread the impact. The smashed bullet made a little ping as it bounced across the stone floor.

I leaped forward, grabbed the closest combatant, pulled him against me, and pressed the barrel of my pistol—the silver one I'd taken from the vampire we killed—against his temple.

"Take me to see the King," I shouted, "or he dies!"

The room quieted for a moment. Could it be as simple as that?

Someone said, "Then he dies," and fired at me.

I felt the impact as the bullet slammed into my hostage, traveled through his chest, and struck just above my left breast. His body had absorbed most of the force, so it was less of a shock than the first bullet, but the resulting heat made sweat break out on my forehead.

Tony returned fire, and whoever shot the man crumpled to the floor. A spear of regret pinned my heart to my ribcage for a painful instant. Two men were likely dead because of me. But I did not have time to mourn them or feel guilt, not while Tony and Sam were still in danger.

"Take me to see the King or more of you will die," I said, trying to hide a wince as another bullet struck me, this one in the stomach. It felt like getting kicked by a mule.

"She don't fall," someone whispered.

"That's right," I said. "You can't kill me. But if you don't take me to see the King..." I pulled the final grenade, pinched the fuse between my fingers, and snapped, activating the gunpowder that lit the tip. It made a popping sound, and I held it up as the fuse sent a trail of smoke into the air. "I will kill all of you."

"Bloody hell," someone said, and the room emptied as people stampeded toward the opposite door.

A gasp from behind me made a shiver of dread slide down my spine. I twisted, bringing the barrel of my gun to bear on the handsome face of the man holding a knife to Tony's throat. A little trickle of blood trailed down his neck from the knife point.

"I understand you'd like to request an audience, Lady Gwen," the man said, his voice smooth and cold and vaguely amused.

My stomach twisted at the thought of anyone hurting Tony, but I tossed the grenade into the air, caught it, then raised an eyebrow at him. "I'm not asking."

"Surely you don't intend to kill the inspector?"

"To protect Sam? I would burn down the catacombs, the church, the neighborhood, and everyone in it. Starting"—I thumbed back the hammer—"with you."

He smiled. What I mean is that his mouth moved, curled in a facsimile of human emotion, but it never reached his eyes. If a snake could smile, it would look something like that. He released Tony and said, "Very well. Please, follow me."

Tony stumbled forward, one hand pressed to his neck. I picked up the umbrella and checked the wound, trying to maintain the cold that had sustained me since that afternoon, but finding it hard while seeing Tony's blood.

"It's a scratch," I said.

He nodded, his face furious as I pressed the umbrella back into his hands. He did not want to take it, but he had seen my jacket at work and he had common sense. I would not tell him the sweat on my forehead was a result of the heat energy trying to dissipate so I didn't burst into flame. Let him believe I was winded instead.

I would allow myself to feel the pain sometime later when I had more time.

We followed the King—for it could be no one else—through another antechamber and into a smaller room. He moved with the lazy grace of a lion amid his pride, unconcerned about his exposed back and the gun I kept trained on it. He knew, as I knew, that if I killed him, every thief, murderer, and felon in the place would come down on us at once.

We would not leave these catacombs alive without his permission, and I refused to leave until Sam was safe.

He sat in a wooden chair at the head of the room, lifted something off the floor, and placed it on his head. It was a crown, of sorts, made of silver spoons. It should have looked ridiculous, particularly accompanied by an outfit that looked like a holdover from the sixteenth century, but it did not.

Once he was settled, he held out both arms and said, "The King would be happy to grant you an audience. Lady Gwenevere St. James, future Duchess of Wainwright, and the honorable Inspector Anthony Hardwicke. It is our pleasure to meet you, at last. To be honest, lady, given your reputation, I expected you somewhat sooner."

"You are lucky I did not discover what you have done until it was well healed, or I would have bombed this church and watched it crumble."

"I cannot understand why you are so angry, lady. Sam is now safer than he has ever been. Isn't that what you wanted?"

"You branded him," I snarled. "As if he were cattle."

"And that brand is greater protection on the streets of New London than an armed guard. We want the same thing, you see. I just accomplished it in a different way."

"We do not want the same thing. I want to protect Sam, and you want to use him for your own benefit."

Hollow laughter echoed off the low ceiling, but the King's eyes were hard. "You don't want to use him? Of course, you do. You want to force him into the mold you think best for him, and not for his good, but for your comfort. Oh lady, if only you could see how much we are alike. How we are both willing to sacrifice even the innocent for what we want."

I pulled the trigger.

Pieces of wood splintered from the corner of the chair and tumbled through the air. The Cutthroat King didn't even flinch, and he ignored the traces of blood that trickled down his cheek from the flying splinters.

"Where are your manners, my lady?" he asked, his voice dangerous.

"I reserve my manners for those who deserve them," I said, hanging onto my anger so he would not see how close his jibe had come to the truth. "You and I are nothing alike. If you do not release Sam from your service, my next shot will do it for you."

He smiled and leaned back in his chair, settling into a comfortable sprawl. "You will not kill me, Gwenevere. Because if you do, the handsome inspector will die. And despite your protestations, you will not sacrifice him."

"She won't have to," Tony said, raising his pistol.

"What a team. Such heroes." He leaned forward and pointed at us. "You didn't even kill the guards on duty. You could have gunned down at least half of my subjects, yet you chose the path of least carnage. Do you truly think I would have allowed you this far if I didn't know you well enough to predict that much?" He leaned back again, relaxed. "Have a little respect for the King of the Underground. I am no fool."

"Since you know me so well, you know I will not leave you in peace, or alive, until Samuel is free of you. No, your majesty. You think you know me, but you have made a grave mistake." I began stalking toward him, gun barrel never wavering. "I have never had children to care for, and while I have no intention of ever being a mother, I find within myself a rage I did not know existed. Believe me when I tell you"—I pulled the crown off his head with my free hand—"that my life, and yours, mean less to me than slag compared to my need to protect that boy."

I squeezed. The crown of spoons bent with a metallic whine before I tossed it over my shoulder. "Let him go, and we leave without further trouble. Refuse, and I will kill you. Right now. And damn the rest."

"I liked that crown," he said after it clattered to a stop.

"How disappointing for you."

He studied me for a while, expressionless, unimpressed. Then he stood, bringing his face mere inches from mine. The hammer on Tony's pistol snapped backward with a click.

"I have another offer for you, my lady," the King countered. His hand moved so fast that I could not track the motion. He gripped my chin between his thumb and forefinger, tilted my face up, and squeezed. I refused to cry out, but breath of god, I wanted to.

"Take his place. Do me a favor, and I will let him go. You may leave with the inspector, and with my word that the boy, his sister, your harridan of a housekeeper, and the staid Mr. Yates will be safe from me and mine. I will extend the same offer to you, Inspector. Stay out of my way, ignore the lady's pursuits in my service, and your lovely mother and ailing father will be safe from me."

I could almost hear Tony's teeth grinding behind me.

"But kill me," he said, his voice wrapping around the words as if he wished I would, as if the idea were exciting, and squeezed harder, "and the men I have stationed outside your homes will set fire to them and bar the doors until everyone inside is nothing but charred flesh and ash."

Perhaps I stood there silent longer than I should have. My finger might have tightened on the trigger. But it was hard to maintain my icy fury knowing so many people were in danger. He may have been lying, but his actions told me he had not only anticipated this attack, he had desired it, planned for it. He may even have drawn Sam in purely because it was a pathway to me.

Sam would bear a scar for the rest of his life because the Cutthroat King wanted something from me.

"What proof do I have that you will keep your word when you have broken it once, already?" I hissed between teeth gritted in anger and pain.

He tilted his head to the side as he closed the distance, bringing his chest flush against mine before reaching around behind me to pull my dagger from its sheath. After a breathless second, he released me and pricked the pad at the base of his thumb. Dark blood welled up and ran in a shining rivulet down his wrist. He produced a small piece of parchment from his pocket and smeared his blood across it.

"If I do not, give this to your witches. They will know what to do with it."

He held the paper up between two fingers, not bothering to stop the flow of blood. I reached for it but he pulled it away, a smile teasing the corners of his mouth, forcing me to step closer. I wasn't slow, either. My hand shot out, fingers locking around his wrist, and I clamped down with all the strength I could muster. His wrist bones rubbed together under the force.

His eyes widened, then narrowed. "I thought so," he said.

I holstered the gun without asking what that meant, snatched the paper, and released him. The Cutthroat King picked up his crown, winked at Tony, and resumed his seat, still bleeding.

"Before I agree," I said, "I would know what this favor entails."

The King's men, a rag-tag combination of humans, elves, and dwarves, tumbled in through the door with random weapons drawn, shouting imprecations that would have made even Sally blush.

"It's a bit late for that," the King said, flicking his fingers at them in dismissal. They exchanged chagrined expressions, knowing that punishment awaited them, and slunk back the way they had come.

The King watched them go, then returned his attention to me. "Someone stole something from me, and I want it back."

"Oh, the irony."

"Indeed. I believe you are acquainted with a man by the name of Lord Rutledge. Samuel has confirmed he possesses a construct, a dog, in fact, that belongs to me. I want it back."

"What kind of construct?"

"The kind that does not belong to him," he said in a stern voice. "The man is a great collector of items he has no business possessing. Return it to me, and our bargain will be complete. Precious Samuel will be free. And if we have any future business after that, we will negotiate it in good faith. I doubt we will—"his dark eyes trailed down my body, then drifted to Tony with the same lazy insolence. "But I hope we do."

"Is there anything I should know about the construct?" I asked.

"Yes. It must be bonded to its owner, and to get it safely away from the perfidious lord, you must reset the construct with a key and in the proper order." He dug something else out of his pocket and held it up. A brass key engraved with runes and swirling symbols reminded me of the fae magic Cassandra had used in her kidnapping spell.

"There is a locking mechanism on the back of the construct's neck. When unlocked, a device will appear that requires a drop of your blood. Once you have done this, it will bond to you. Until you do it, your life will be in danger. But"—he waved a hand, flinging drops of still-flowing blood to spatter on the floor—"you are faster and stronger than you have any right to be. You should be fine."

"Where is the construct?"

"He keeps it with him, always. Or so our Samuel has told me."

My lip curled into a snarl. "He is not ours. He is mine. You will remember that if you want to live."

He held the key out and Tony took it, not trusting me to get close to the man again. Which was wise.

"If you need assistance," the King said magnanimously, "send word."

It took a moment to force myself to reply, and when I did my voice was dripping with disdain. "I will take nothing from you."

"Nothing except my blood, dear lady. And this." He flicked something into the air and it spun, flashing. I caught it. On my palm lay a silver coin embossed with the same symbol that had been burned into the skin of Sam's chest.

Fury boiled back to life, making my skin tingle and my muscles tense. He smiled at my reaction, the first real smile I had seen, and it lit his eyes on fire. Tony bustled me out of the room while the Cutthroat King's laughter echoed off the walls behind us.

6

The Birmingham Screwdriver

TONY

The King's men gave them a wide berth as he dragged Gwen out of the catacombs. Now that she was working for their master, they had no desire for confrontation, but he suspected she was too flustered to notice.

They walked a few blocks to the safer part of town where James waited with the coach and rode back to Grosvenor Square in silence. Gwen sat staring down at the coin, flipping it over and over, watching moonlight slide across the surface of the smiling man.

Constables recovered several of those coins over the years, though they'd never been able to track them back to the King. Now he knew why. The man was a spider, building his web one careful strand at a time. If they turned around and went back to the church, the catacombs beneath would probably be empty.

But he had no intention of going back.

When the coach pulled to a stop, Sally and Sam rushed through the front door and stood on the step holding hands, their faces white. Hadn't Gwen realized how much their lives would change if she was hurt or killed? She had responsibilities, now. Of course, she hadn't been in any state to listen to reason.

She climbed out of the coach, let the children wrap their arms around her, and disappeared into the house. He sat there for a moment, muttered, "Well, that was several orders of magnitude worse than I was expecting," then leaned out the window to call, "Would you mind taking me home, James?"

The man nodded and clicked at the horse. They drove past his parents' apartment so he could be certain they were safe, then James brought the coach around and dropped Tony off at his own flat.

It was spartan, cold, and dark. Every spare cent went to care for his parents, so there was no one to keep the hearth lit when he was gone, and no one to decorate the walls with embroidery, or the tables with dried flowers.

Tony trimmed and lit the oil lamp, built up a fire, pulled the blanket off his bed, and curled up in his armchair near the flames. It would take too long to heat the air enough to make his bedroom comfortable, and he had to be up and in the office in a few hours, anyway. He closed his eyes but saw Gwen getting struck again and again by bullets. Her face had twisted in pain and fury, so different from the clever, irreverent, good-natured expression he was used to.

He had seen Gwen in danger more than once and had seen her fight many times, but tonight was different. She had been cold and withdrawn, and while she was careful not to use lethal force, he got the feeling she would have liked to.

Now that he thought about it, he had seen more death and destruction in the nearly two years he'd known Gwenevere St. James than he had in his entire career, prior.

And, as far as he knew, he was the only member of the Metropolitan Police to have ever seen the Cutthroat King. He'd wanted to drag a dozen constables with him, to storm the damn place and root out the sickness infecting the city from beneath.

Instead, he'd gone on an unsanctioned raid, shot a man in the arm, and watched as the woman he cared about made a deal with the proverbial devil. He hadn't been able to let Gwen go on her own, and, if he was honest, he wanted a bit of revenge for Sam, too.

But standing there as the King threatened Gwen, her family, and his own, he'd seen no better way out than to keep his mouth shut and agree. All the Cutthroat King asked in return for his parents' lives was that he ignore her exploits. He didn't have much choice, and his honor was a worthy price to pay for their safety.

Wasn't it?

Tony was in his office less than a quarter of an hour before Sergeant Chen barged in without bothering to knock. He was broad across the chest and shoulders, like most dwarvish men, and walked with his hands closed into hammer-like fists swinging on the end of beefy arms.

"Hardwicke! Did you hear?"

"Good morning, Sergeant. Hear what?"

Chen narrowed his eyes. "About the explosion, of course."

Tony dropped his eyes to the case file he'd been reading and gave himself a moment to compose his features. He expected this, of course, but that wasn't the same as being ready for it. Though he knew going after the King had been the only course of action that might save Sam, guilt swamped him, both for leaving the man to preside over a kingdom of thieves and cutthroats when he should have been in jail...and for the lies he was about to tell.

"No, what explosion?"

Chen pulled up a chair and ran his fingers through his short beard. It was oiled and neatly curled and only about an inch long in keeping with regulations, but he pampered those whiskers as if they belonged to his favorite cat.

"A building on Carter Square by the old Christian church. Someone set off a bomb on the bottom floor and burned up everything that was flammable."

"Any injuries?"

"No, not so much as a soot stain on any of the residents."

Of course not. Gwen chose her target carefully. She never would have risked hurting an innocent bystander. "Any clues?"

"Nothing to speak of, yet. We have the elf squad down there right now, and if they can't find anything, there's nothing to find."

Apprehension skittered up his spine, but he ignored it. "True enough, with senses like theirs."

"Of course, the CI has a hunch of his own."

"Of course he does. What has he come up with this time?"

"Thinks it must have been a hideaway for the LER, and they burned it out so no one would know."

"Why would the League for Equal Representation use a secret meeting space? They're a public collective and well funded enough that they don't need to hide." In fact, Gwen was one of their biggest donors, and they had a rather nice building near the center of town.

"Who can say?" Chen said, standing up and stretching. "But once the CI gets an idea in his head, he's like a dog with a bone. The slagging man is still convinced Jack the Ripper is hiding somewhere in Buckingham Palace. Thought I'd give fair warning."

Tony saluted him in thanks as the sergeant saw himself out. Chief Inspector Mac Sweeney had been a good officer once, but he was one of those men who saw authority like a letter of marque: permission to do what he wanted. His nickname behind closed doors was The Birmingham Screwdriver because he was a hammer and looked at every problem like a nail.

So Tony wasn't surprised when, an hour later, a PC knocked at his office door to say, "The Driver wants you in his office, Inspector."

Tony closed the case file he'd been reading, thanked them, and made his way to the chief inspector's office, trying to think up reasons the explosion should not be investigated. He didn't come up with anything convincing by the time a gruff, broad Scottish accent said, "Who is it?"

"Hardwicke, sir."

"Come in, Tony."

Fergus Mac Sweeney was a small, thin man with a voice far deeper than he had any right to, and a black mustache so large and intimidating it deserved its own rank. He was a terrier in human form, with a personality too big for his body and no conception of his actual stature in the world.

"Have a seat," he said and gestured to a chair nicer than the one in Tony's office, and several inches shorter than the one Mac Sweeney sat in.

"What can I do for you, sir?" Tony asked.

Mac Sweeney leaned forward to rest his elbows on the desk and gave Tony a serious look. "You and I need to talk. And don't try to weasel out of it, either, alright?"

Did he know? It took all of Tony's training not to break out in a cold sweat. He could honestly say he had not been involved in the explosion, but he couldn't disavow knowledge of it, either. It was, absolutely, vandalism of the felony kind.

"It has come to my attention," Mac Sweeney said, "that you have been seen in the company of Lady St. James, the next Duchess of Wainwright."

Relief made his stomach watery. "Yes, sir."

"After a bit of digging, I discovered she was in the same village at the same time you were when that nasty affair took place over the summer."

For a moment he stood again before the families of the dead constables and explained their loved ones died trying to save the village from a rampaging vampire. He told those grieving families their dead fathers and sons were heroes...all while knowing their deaths were his fault. They never would have been there if he hadn't called them in.

Gwen warned him, but he thought he knew better. He would live with those grief-stricken faces in his memory, and his dreams, forever.

"I believe she was, sir," he said, trying to sound as casual as possible.

"And you're up for promotion, are you not?"

Tony took a slow breath through his nose and tried not to react. "Yes, sir."

Mac Sweeney leaned back in his chair and folded his hands across his stomach. "Here's the thing, Tony. Lasses like her aren't for men like us. They're above our pay grade, you might say. Don't see the world the way we do. And, unlike you and me"—he raised one finger—"they have the money and stature to sweep most problems under the rug."

Hot anger climbed the back of Tony's neck, but he decided to play dumb and force the man to say it outright. "I don't take your meaning, sir."

"It would be in your best interests to stay away from the woman, Inspector. You don't want to put your promotion in jeopardy, not with your parents to care for. A woman like that, with all her money?" He shook his head and made a cutting gesture. "She can do what she likes without need of you. Leave her to her business, and if she goes down, she can't drag you with her."

Tony stood abruptly, and the chair skidded across the floor behind him. "I wasn't aware the department gave relationship advice, sir. I appreciate your concern, but I will handle my relationships as I see fit."

Mac Sweeney sighed and stood. "I was afraid you might see it that way. She's not a sore sight, after all. And I've heard she's not very particular, if you know what I mean."

Tony clenched his fists, and Mac Sweeney raised both hands. "Don't get your knickers in a twist, Hardwicke. I thought it would be best to handle this man-to-man, but if you'd like, you can consider this an official order. Keep your nose out of the lady's business. You understand?"

"Yes, sir."

He had to force the word between his teeth, but couldn't stop himself from wanting to grab the little man by the collar and haul him into the air.

"Good enough. That will be all."

Tony stormed out of the room and back down to his office, slamming the door once, twice, three times for good measure. Who the hell did Mac Sweeney think he was? And why did command think they needed to be involved in his personal life...unless it wasn't him they were worried about?

Tony turned away from the door and ran his hands through his hair, thinking furiously. How long had they been interested in Gwen's affairs? Was this a result of her deal with the Cutthroat King, or something more insidious?

Gwen agreed to the arrangement late last night, or early this morning. If the King owned officers in the department, even high-ranking officers like the chief investigator, could they have learned about the agreement so soon? And why try to pressure him to stay away when he'd as much as promised to look the other way, already?

Unless someone else was pulling the strings and they were watching her for other reasons. This may be a not-so-subtle warning that he might get dragged down with her. His mind pulled up vivid memories of the small, bare apartment his parents called home, the bits of decorative embroidery his mother used to purchase her dignity, the cold hearth in the dining room, and threadbare clothes several years too old.

He was so close to giving them the life they deserved, not simply the one he could afford. Was he stupid enough to risk it all now? He had to speak to Gwen.

Given their exertion the night before, he expected to find her looking tired and haggard. But he ran into her, literally, on her way out the door. She was wrapped in the new jacket Percy made, as if it didn't sport several burn marks from the bullets, and wore a hat lined with fur that made her brown eyes look even darker.

"Tony!" she said, catching herself before she plowed into him. "You're here. That saves me a trip to the Yard, then. I wanted to apologize for last night and—well, are you out for a case? If not, can we chat in the carriage? I'm off to Delilah's shop."

He would rather have sat in the warm study with a glass of whisky in his hands, but he followed Gwen into the vehicle. The carriage had almost become more familiar than his own flat. James had prepared the little heater, which sat on the floor happily pumping out stored heat from whatever fireplace they left it in overnight. Gwen's townhouse was large enough to set aside an entire fireplace purely for heat storage.

"Have you thought about fitting up the townhouse with electric heat?" he asked, closing the door behind them.

She blinked at him, then said with a lopsided grin, "If you think that question will get you out of being thanked, you are mistaken, Inspector."

"No, I was genuinely curious."

"Then yes, I have thought about it. But it would require workmen and construction and wires and weeks of noise and strangers tromping about the house. It seems an unnecessary inconvenience when the fireplace and a few strategically placed heaters will do just as good a job. And a fire in the hearth is so much more comforting."

"That's true enough, I suppose."

"Back to the subject." She patted his knee with one gloved hand. "Because you can't put it off forever. I want to apologize. I dragged you with me last night—"

"I chose to go."

"And put your family in danger. Then I left you in the coach without so much as a goodbye or thank you. My only very poor excuse is that I was not in my right mind. I was so angry about Sam"—she shrugged—"I wasn't thinking clearly. I'm sorry, and I hope you can forgive me."

He sighed and looked down at his hands, folded in his lap. He couldn't bring himself to say it.

"Flabbergasted, Inspector?" she asked, leaning back and folding her arms across her chest with a smile. "I do not blame you. Don't get used to it, however. I so rarely have reason to apologize that this may be your only opportunity to hear the words. I suggest savoring it."

He rubbed a hand across his face and muttered, "Damn your disarming charm."

The amusement drained from her face. He regretted that. Gwen's sense of humor was part of the reason he loved her.

"Bloody fucking hell," he said, and dropped his face into his hands. How could he admit it to himself now? Now, of all the times to realize the extent of his feelings?

She put a hand on his shoulder. "Tony? Are you quite well?"

"No," he growled, "I bloody well am not." Then he sat back, away from her comforting hands, and pulled in a steadying breath to fortify himself. Bad news was best broken quickly, as his father said. "The CI called me into his office this morning and told me that if I didn't keep my nose out of your business, it would mean my job."

"What—why? Ahh." Her lips thinned into an unhappy line as realization stiffened her expression. Gwen's mind was quick, and she likely arrived at the same conclusion he did. "There must be money flowing from the underground to the Yard."

"That's my suspicion, as well," he said. "Word travels fast in the underground, I suppose. And if it is not that, then it's likely something worse and they are watching you for criminal activity."

She leaned against the wall, jaw clenched as she thought. "Either is likely, given my involvement in recent affairs. I suppose the fact that my wards inherited Claire Monmouth's estate after both she and her mother died might look just a little suspicious."

"Just a little."

"And I was at a country party where several PC's died."

"And it is no secret you donate significant amounts of money to the LER. It took all of my considerable powers of persuasion to convince the Post not to publish that photo of you at the last rally. You need to be more careful."

"Perhaps you are right."

"Good. I hope that means you will by keeping a low profile."

The corner of her mouth twisted into a grimace. "I can try. But I have to keep Sam and Sally safe, and right now that requires business with the Cutthroat King. I will accept whatever consequences follow."

"There are other ways to protect them," he said, leaning forward. "Leave the country. Spend some time on the continent. It would do all of you good and give this affair time to blow over."

"I do not walk away from my responsibilities lightly," she said, her voice growing hard. "There are consequences to breaking one's word. I cannot just wait for this to blow over."

"I know a thing or two about responsibilities, Gwen, and this isn't the same. It is coercion. He forced the agreement upon you. There is nothing dishonorable about reneging on a promise made under duress, especially when that promise may get us both killed. What would become of the children without you? Or of my parents without me?"

"I would be happy to set up a trust for them, Tony. They are worthy people and if you would let me—"

"No. Gwen, that's not the point of this conversation."

"What is the point?"

His frustration rose with every denial. Why did she refuse to acknowledge the danger? Was she truly committed enough to risk everything? "My point is: you don't have to do this. We can think of another way to protect Sam, something that doesn't risk your life or my job."

"If you have an answer, Tony, please share it because I have been up all night and have found none. The man knew too much about me, and if I try to walk away from this agreement, who will he threaten next? Delilah? Percy? My mother? You and your family? I couldn't live with myself knowing they were in danger because of me and I could have protected them."

"And what if he refuses to honor your arrangement?" he demanded.

"That's what the blood is for. He could not have made me a more binding offer, not knowing what witches can do once they have your blood, and all the more because he offered it freely."

"Then why not take the blood to them now and force him to relinquish his claim? It was made under false pretenses, anyway."

"Because I made a promise and those have power."

"And I made an oath to uphold the law," he replied, frustration reaching a peak as he threw his hands in the air. "An oath that becomes harder to keep the longer I know you."

Her eyelids flinched, and she looked down. "I see."

"That's not what I meant," he said, but the damage was done. He watched in helpless regret as the doors she left open for him closed one at a time, first in the line of her mouth and then in her eyes. It had taken him months to earn enough trust for her to be open with him, but her expression was now locked and barred.

He wanted to tell her that his feelings for her too often outweighed his desire to keep his oath, that it tore him apart because the thought of not being on her side made his guts hurt...but she wouldn't believe him, not now.

She had been abandoned and used falsely in the past, used in ways that made earning her trust a gift. And he just shit all over it because the thought of breaking his oaths and losing his job scared him. Because knowing her was changing him into the kind of man who might not have made such oaths in the first place, and he wasn't certain he recognized who he was becoming.

But even then, he never wanted to hurt her. "Gwen—"

"No need to explain, Inspector. You have a family of your own to protect, after all, and I have never pretended that my life was a safe one. Your oath and your family will be much more secure without me around."

"That's not what I meant, dammit!"

She smiled a gentle smile that raked his insides. "It was. And it is fair."

"It's not—" he started, then sighed and closed his eyes.

Maybe it was. Maybe, somewhere deep, he knew if he pushed her enough, she would be the one to make the final decision about their relationship, whatever it was, and he wouldn't have to bear the guilt of walking away when she needed him. It would be one thing if he was only responsible for himself. He could learn to deal with the guilt of breaking oaths for her sake. But for his parents?

His fingers closed involuntarily on the edge of the seat, squeezing hard. "This isn't how I wanted this conversation to play out."

"Things do not always turn out the way we hoped. Life has taught me that much, at least. If it makes your conscience any easier, I would not wish to be the cause of you losing your promotion, or damaging your ability to provide a comfortable life for your parents."

"I know."

"Perhaps we can visit this conversation again, when...well, we shall see, I suppose. But I hope I will not lose your friendship."

He barely forced the word past the emotion clogging his throat. "Never."

The coach stopped. Sulfur and smoke added a bite to the air that told him they had reached the Artificer's district. They sat for a moment in silence, but he could not force himself to say more and Gwen had never been good with waiting. She stood, leaned forward to kiss his cheek, then climbed out of the coach and called, "James? Would you be a darling and take Inspector Hardwicke round to Scotland Yard?"

"Of course, ma'am. Be happy to."

With a click and flick of the reins, Tony was headed back to his office alone with her kiss still burning on his cheek.

7

Gadgets

GWEN

"So, you're still alive, are you? Percy will be glad to hear it," Delilah said over her shoulder while hammering a nail into the wall of the reception area at the front of her shop. "He must have sent me three messages last night worrying that he'd killed you."

I gathered up the pain of Tony formally ending whatever our relationship was and stuffed it into a box in the back of my mind with everything else I did not have time to examine. There would be plenty of time to cry, later.

"Messages?" I asked, hanging my coat and umbrella on pegs near the door. "Is that finally working?"

She snorted and picked up a frame, measuring it against her nail. "Not well. The text is still garbled. One said, 'I slope the coat five pints'."

"Maybe Percy can't spell," I said, peering over her shoulder as she hung the plaque. "Three gold hammers, eh? I expected no less."

"They waited to send it until well after all of the other shops had theirs, the slagging bastards."

"Of course they did," Fleur said, striding out of the back with a handful of papers that ostensibly had something to do with administrative work, her red hair floating in a cloud around her head. She gave her fiancée a fond glance as she laid the papers out on the front desk. "They don't like admitting the lady dwarf has the best shop on the row. Especially not when they didn't want her in the guild in the first place."

"They can go chew on their beards," Delilah said, and stood back to admire her work. "I'm here to stay. And despite all of Percy's shortcomings, I can't blame him for that wonky bit of artifice. It's either the scrying spell we're using, or lining up the proper letters within the sentence that causes it to malfunction."

"Well," I said, "at least nothing has exploded. Yet."

"Small miracles."

We were working on a method of sending messages over long distances using a combination of magic and artifice, inscribing the spells and then powering them with runic sentences that funneled natural forces. If we succeeded, we'd be far more effective and efficient. All of them failed, some rather spectacularly, but that had not stopped Delilah.

She dusted off her hands and shouted, "Take your lunch, you lot!"

The background noise of ringing hammers, crackling fires, and pumping bellows died as the four apprentices cleaned their stations and filed out the front door chatting merrily. There were two female apprentices in that group. Soon the Artificer's Guild would have the same kind of equal representation they were fighting for in the courts, and Delilah would be the spearhead.

"Have I told you that I'm proud to be your friend?" I asked after the door closed.

"Off with you," she said, making a shooing motion, but her round cheeks glowed pink. "What are you trying to butter me up, for?"

Delilah Irons was the strongest and most stubborn person I knew. Like all dwarves, she was short of stature, somewhere just below five feet tall, but she was strong, with broad, capable hands, a button nose, rosebud lips, and a riot of black curls. Her light brown skin, a gift from her Brazilian father, was always a bit burned on the cheeks and forearms from time in front of the forge.

And she had an absolute weakness for compliments, something Fleur discovered early in their courtship.

"Can't a woman tell her best friend how amazing she is?" I asked.

"What do you want, Gwen? Since you bullied Percy out of your jacket, I assume it's gadgets you're after."

As quickly and succinctly as possible, I explained my position and what I needed to do. She watched me with narrowed eyes, her face turning pale every now and then, and when my story was over she shook her head.

Fleur joined us, her long, elegant fingers wrapping through Delilah's broad, calloused ones. "How you manage to get yourself into these situations is a mystery, Gwen. I would ask for details, but I don't think I want to know."

"We'd better help however we can if we want her to get herself out, again. Come on."

Delilah led us toward the back of the shop and through a corded-off area to what Artificers called "the Boom Room" but was, in fact, a separate testing facility.

Artifice, the art of inscribing runes into objects in specific orders and patterns to imbue them with power, was notoriously dangerous. If a rune was inscribed in the wrong place, at the wrong depth, the wrong size, too far away from or close to another rune, or a hundred other little details, it could have catastrophic results.

I had personally seen no less than thirty runic explosions, and caused a few, myself. Delilah was the best artificer in the West, and even she bore more than a few scars. But her Boom Room had never been rebuilt, and that, alone, was reason enough for at least one golden hammer from the Guild.

Along the south wall, several mannequins stood next to a peg board and a display table where the most recent inventions waited to be tested. Delilah passed the clothing, which was, no doubt, part of her collaboration with Percy, and walked straight to the table.

She picked up a small device, something like a bracelet, and held it up. "I think this one might be your best bet. Remember that invisibility spell we tried?"

My arm had disappeared during that test, along with all sensations from the limb. Delilah was forced to deactivate the device based on feel, alone, forcing me to be limbless long enough to get sick. Of course, I'd been obliged to wear a lead vest and helmet in case my arm exploded, so an invisible limb was, in some ways, a relief. Still, it was rather uncanny.

I shuddered and took a step back. "That was an experience I don't care to repeat."

"This isn't the same," she assured me. "I altered the function so it behaves a bit differently, but I think it might be the most effective tool for the job you've got to do. Here, watch."

She carried a mannequin to the center of the blast zone and started setting up the device. One of the tenets of traditional artifice was that it was not magic. Artifice was the art of using runes to capture and control natural forces, like electromagnetism or kinetic energy. But Cassandra Monmouth somehow discovered how to activate and control magical energy with altered runes that Percy claimed were fae, and not human at all.

We'd experimented with the technique for the better part of two years, learning by trial and error, but only managed a few small successes. I hoped this would be one of them.

Delilah fastened the device onto the mannequin's arm, turned a dial, pressed a button, and...it disappeared. That wasn't entirely true but explaining the experience was almost impossible. It was as if the mannequin didn't matter. It wasn't interesting enough to look at or remember.

Several times I caught myself asking Delilah what device we were going to try before remembering we were currently trying it. The only reason I didn't forget about the mannequin was that I knew it was there.

Delilah wandered toward the mannequin, and when it was close to her I found it difficult to pay attention to her, as well. A moment later, they popped back into existence. Or, at least, popped back into noticeability.

I held the table as a wave of dizziness washed over me.

"Give it a moment," she said, teeth gritted. "It will pass."

Once I felt a bit more like myself, maybe a minute later, I held out my hand, fascinated.

"Wait," Delilah said as she opened up a compartment on the underside of the device and pulled out a large diamond, perhaps the size of the tip of my thumb. It was dull, cracked, and looked burned on one side.

"God's breath," I said, peering at the ruined stone. "How much money have we spent on diamonds alone?"

"You don't want to know," she said, dropping the bracelet onto my palm. "The larger the diamond, the longer the spell lasts.

"How long would a diamond that size give me?"

She tilted her flat hand back and forth. "Five minutes, more or less."

"That's it?"

"You try making a magic spell work with a few scratches in some metal," she said, scowling.

"I only meant that, well, you'd think a stone that size would give you quite a bit of time."

"This is experimental, Gwen," she said, waving one arm at all of the artifice. "We can't bring any assumptions into this room. The technique is still too new. I might be able to make the spells more efficient in the future, but right now you should just be glad we can get anything to work, at all."

"I am," I assured her, and raised my hand to peer at the bracelet/device. "What do you call this?"

"A Sightscreen. At least, that's the working name Fleur came up with."

"How do I work it?"

"You see this centerpiece?" she asked, pointing to the circular face of the bracelet that resembled a large clock face with concentric circles of runic sentences and a button at the center.

"Yes."

"This is the spell, itself. And when you press this"—she pushed the little button down with one finger—"it meets perfectly with the other runes to activate the spell."

"It channels magical energy and uses the diamond as a battery?"

"That's the theory. Only way I can keep it small enough not to be noticeable."

"Will the button pop up when the diamond is spent?"

"At that point, it won't matter whether the button pops up or not. There is nothing left to hold the magic, so the spell is useless. Like shouting to the wind you'd like it to grind you some flour but having no mill."

"But I can choose to disengage the button to save energy?"

"Yes."

"Delilah," I said, turning the bracelet over in awe, "this is incredible work."

She beamed for a moment, letting me enjoy the warmth of her smile before she ruthlessly squashed the expression. "It certainly cost enough. Wait a moment."

From a leather pouch fastened to her apron, she pulled two smaller diamonds and placed them on my palm along with the

Sightscreen. Taken together they may have equaled the size of the first one.

She showed me how to load and unload diamonds, how to make certain the button was properly engaged, then set me about practicing. We waited for her apprentices to return, and I walked round the shop making a general fool of myself, but no one noticed.

Sometimes they would look at me, frown as if confused, then shrug and go back to whatever they had been doing. When I turned off the device, the same wave of dizziness washed over me. I wobbled to the wall, leaned against it, and slid down to sit and catch my breath.

"How much did practice cost us?" I asked.

Fleur, who handled all of the monetary aspects of the shop, looked a bit sick. "Unless you plan to change your working arrangement, you really don't want to know."

I sighed and shrugged. She was probably right. My late father's coffers were large enough to be embarrassing, and the properties and holdings I would inherit when I finally accepted my title would only add to them year after year. No one should have such ridiculous wealth, so I did my best to spend it as well—and as often—as I could. Putting it back into circulation in the hands of skilled people like Delilah and Percy was infinitely better than letting it accumulate.

"Do we have any other diamonds I can use within the next night or so?"

Fleur disappeared to a safe in the back room and returned with a diamond of similar shape and quality to the first one. It glowed on her pale palm. "If you wear this one out, it will be a while before we can get you another."

"Understood. May I ask a question?"

"So long as it's a good one," Delilah said.

"What would you use to channel the magic if gems were not available?"

She pursed her lips and rubbed her hands together. "I suppose...I might be able to make some kind of metal alloy and engrave it with property runes to try and trick the magic, but"—she shook her head— "gems have special properties. They're made deep in the earth with forces I can't replicate, not yet."

"Would something else, something of equal magical significance, work to channel the energy?"

"I don't truly know. Like I said, all of this is an experiment, and I don't know much about magic, yet."

"Fair enough."

"Why do you ask?" Fleur said. "Is money getting tight? I can make some adjustments, if so."

"No, just curious. Dammit, that's not true," I said, remembering the metal oath I had taken to always tell Delilah the truth. "I'm trying to think of other ways to power bigger spells. There isn't a diamond in the world big enough to power the spell I want to work."

Her dark brows shot up to hide beneath her curls, so I said, "It's nothing to worry about. It will be a long time before I can even attempt it."

I tucked the diamond into a hidden pocket in my skirt and fastened the Sightscreen to my wrist. "Is there anything else on this wall that might come in handy?"

"No," Delilah said, pushing me out of the Boom Room. "Most of that has at least two more tests and rounds of revisions before you can play with it. I'll not have you bully me like you did Percy. It would have served you right if that jacket went up in smoke with you inside it."

"You are a paragon of care and nurturing, Delilah," I said as she shoved me into the front room. "That is why I value your friendship so much."

She snorted, gave me one last shove as she said, "Get on with you," then pulled her goggles off her forehead to cover her eyes and shouted to her apprentices, "Let's get on, you lot! Daylight is wasting and you've only got two more months before you take your tests."

Fleur gave me an apologetic wave and closed the door.

Aristotle was waiting for me when I returned, pacing back and forth on my desk in the study. He croaked out, "Hello, pretty girl," and sailed across the room to land on my shoulder. After my painful meeting with Tony, the bird's affection was a balm on my emotional wounds.

"Good afternoon, sir. How was your day, praytell?"

"He made off with Mrs. Chapman's reading glasses," Sally said from her customary chair. "She was so mad she said she had to go have a sherry or pluck his feathers one at a time till he confessed."

"No wonder you looked so nervous when I came home," I told the bird. "You're just lucky she has a brand new duster and doesn't need any feathers. Bring back the glasses and I will find you something even shinier for your nest."

He tilted his head at me, as if weighing the offer, then jumped into the air and sailed out the door.

"Is that a new gadget?" Sally asked, pointing at my wrist.

"It is."

"What does this one do?"

"Makes one absolutely uninteresting," I said.

Her lips twisted in dismay. "Why would you want that?"

"So people don't notice me," I said as I hung up my jacket and umbrella.

"Does...that mean you're planning to leave, soon?"

I tugged the end of her blonde braid and said, lightly, "Only to make certain the Cutthroat King will never be able to reach Sam, again."

She bit her lip, closed the book in her lap, and said, "I know you're going to tell me no, but—"

"You have always been very clever."

"But I have to ask," she continued, taking my hands and gripping my fingers as if holding on tight enough would convince me to change my mind. "You and Sam have both put yourselves in danger for my sake. How can I let you do this without trying to help?"

"Darling girl, the best thing you can do to help me is stay safe. I can do almost anything if I know you and Samuel are safe. But if I'm forced to worry about you, I'm likely to make much more foolish decisions."

Her lips compressed into a thin line and she nodded unhappily.

"Can you fetch Samuel for me? I need to know as much about Lord Rutledge as possible."

She left her book on the chair and hurried up the stairs. I turned the book over, curious, and read the cover. Magical Tools and Their Uses by Dr. Ferringum Sewell. Sally was still trying to help me find an amplifier. I read Magical Tools several years ago, and didn't remember anything about amplification, but it was worth asking Sally what she learned so far. Perhaps she picked up something I did not.

I turned to the chemistry station on the back table and began mixing up more smoke grenades. White, this time, instead of green. If I snuck into the building at night I was far more likely to pass white smoke off as fog. I was nearly finished measuring out the sugar when Sam's footfalls thudded down the stairs.

It is a feature of young boys that they tramp on stairs with the enthusiasm of hungry elephants sighting food, so I was already drying my hands when he entered the study.

"You wanted to see me?" he asked, sticking both hands in his pockets. He must have been more nervous than his expression let on.

"Do you want to sit down?" I asked. "We can ask Mrs. Chapman to bring in some tea and cakes." Snacks always made Samuel more comfortable, as I had learned the first day I met him.

"Yes, please."

The distracting food arrived—sandwiches, cinnamon biscuits, and little flowers made of marzipan that Monsieur must have been experimenting with—and I gave Sam a moment to take the edge off his nervous energy by stuffing his mouth. Monsieur, our cook, was extremely talented.

"Very well, Sam. I need to know everything you've learned about the Marquis of Rutledge."

He paused halfway through a bite of one of the delicate marzipan flowers, then finished it in a single gulp. "Okay. Where should I start?"

"How about where the man spends his time?"

Sam wiped his mouth with a napkin, something he never would have done two years ago, and said, "When Parliament is in session, he spends all day in his offices. Sometimes he even sleeps there. He takes a walk through Hyde Park on Tuesdays and Thursdays just after lunch, and the rest of the time he spends in his townhouse on Brighton Street."

"Have you learned anything about his townhouse?"

Sam fiddled with the napkin. "You're asking me if I've burgled him."

"I am."

Watching him fight to hide the shame that turned his cheeks red almost broke my heart. I tried not to let him see my relief when he said, "I only watched from outside."

"And did you ever see the construct?"

Sam sat up at that and his eyes brightened, making him look much more like the boy he had been. "It's a dog. Well, it's not a dog

since it's not alive but it looks bang-on like one. It sat outside
his office door in Parliament, guarding it like any real dog. He
said it's name was, um...Ripper! He called it Ripper, and he
said it would only protect him if something went wrong."

"What sort of dog?"

"I thought it looked like those statues outside Lord Bun-
bury's house. The ones the hackney knocked over."

"A mastiff?"

"Yeah"—he snapped his fingers—"a mastiff! It wasn't as big
as the statues, but still big enough to scare me."

"I thought you didn't burgle him."

"I didn't! I saw it when I was in Parliament."

"When were you in the Parliament building, Samuel?"

He stood and brushed off his pants. "I don't—that's not
really important, is it?"

"Is it?"

"I don't think so."

We stared at one another for a long moment. "Does the
construct accompany the Marquis everywhere?"

"He doesn't take it with him on walks, or when he goes to
events or dinners. Just at his office and at home."

"Why would he need protection at the office?" I wondered.
Not taking the construct with him during normal daily business
was understandable. Smaller constructs were rare enough to draw
attention, and commissioning one was prohibitively expensive for
most people. I saw a few on the continent (the owl had been my
favorite) but never one in England or Scotland. So a large dog

would draw rather a lot of attention. And if it was stolen, as the Cutthroat King professed, showing it off would be dangerous.

Unless, of course, he was confident enough not to care. Or to be purposefully offensive.

"Was that all, Lady Gwen?"

I blinked and focused on Sam. "Is there anything else you think I should know?"

He thought about it for a moment. "You won't let me come with you, will you?"

"That would quite defeat the purpose, Samuel."

"I could sneak out and follow you anyway."

"Will you?"

His jaw clenched and unclenched a few times as he weighed his answer. When I returned from confronting the King, bruised, dirty, and covered in sweat and burn marks, he had wrapped his shaking arms around me hard enough to crack ribs.

Now he was questioning what keeping secrets would cost us.

"I suppose not."

"Good. That's settled, then."

He nodded while picking at his nails, as if he expected as much but still had to ask. "I guess the only other thing you should know is"—he took a deep breath, and looked me in the eye— "I love you."

Sam left me sitting in the study with unshed tears, chewing my lower lip and wondering how I had come to this place. I'd spent the last ten years traveling, learning everything I could in the hope that I would find something to lead me to Lia.

Now, here I was, back in England with two children to care for, about to commit burglary, and the only link to my sister was a spell I couldn't work. None of it made sense.

Once I'd gotten myself under control I said, "Did you hear all of that, Sally?"

There was a beat of shocked silence, and Sally edged into the study, shamefaced.

"I support the cultivation of at least a few bad habits—they make a person vastly more interesting—but eavesdropping is so gauche."

Her lips twisted into a sideways smile. "Can you steal something that big?"

"We are about to find out. But first, I've got a question for you." I picked up the book she'd been reading and asked, "Have you learned anything interesting about amplifiers?"

Her face lit up and she said, "As a matter of fact, I have."

8

Raining Dogs and Cat Burglars

GWEN

S tep number one? Reconnaissance. Sam's observations were helpful, but I needed specifics about each location to decide which was most suitable for a heist. Lord Rutledge's home would be the quietest, the most secluded, and also the best fortified. His offices at Parliament were surrounded by people, which was both a blessing and a curse; it was easier to disappear into a crowd, but also easier to be caught.

The third option was hijacking the construct somewhere en route between the two. But the Cutthroat King implied the construct was dangerous, and if it fought me in the open, anything might happen. I did not like the unpredictability of that situation.

Step number two: planning and organizing the actual theft. The most dangerous part and, ironically, the only part I looked forward to. Lord Rutledge was an avuncular type, with antiquated opinions, a thick streak of misogyny, the barrel chest and sinewy arms of a sportsman, and a soft midsection that spoke of years of good food and even better drink.

He was not the cleverest member of the House, and I disliked him almost immediately. During our first conversation, he was one drink short of accusing me of toppling the monarchy for refusing to bear children. Stealing from him would be the least morally reprehensible part of this job.

Step number three: escape with the cargo. This part made me the most nervous because it required hiding a highly visible and recognizable object long enough to transport it across the city. And I refused to involve James in such an affair. It would be too dangerous. In fact, I would be entirely on my own. The thought made my ribcage clamp down painfully upon my heart, but I ignored it.

Three simple steps that would be anything but easy.

But if it kept Samuel out of the Cutthroat King's clutches, it would be worth it.

As night fell, I slipped into a snug pair of black trousers, a black shirt and knitted sweater, a pair of soft leather boots with a reinforced toe and stiff soles, and a grey wool coat. I would rather have worn my Percy jacket, but the fit was a bit too constricting for cat burglary.

After braiding my hair and pulling a dark cap over my ears, I stood in front of the mirror. I looked like a poor excuse for a burglar, but I would, at least, be hard to see. Aristotle cocked his head and looked at me askance.

"What?"

He made a croaking sound that mimicked laughter and said, "Your legs."

"Yes, bird, I have two of them. Look." I did a little dance and shook my foot at him. "What did you think I hid beneath the skirt?"

He laughed at me, stomped a few times on the dresser, and turned in a circle, mimicking my dance.

"You," I told him, fondly, "are a naughty boy."

"He's a pretty bird," he countered.

I fetched the pretty bird a treat and left him in the study as I retrieved my bag of chalk and crept out of the house via the stables. Sam was waiting in the shadows, arms crossed over his chest, nose pink from the cold.

"Sam—"

"I know the way," he said, his voice conciliatory. "I know the patterns of the bobbies and the staff in his house. I won't do anything illegal, but I can help."

We stared at one another for a long time. I was unable to let myself say yes, but hesitant to dismiss any advantage I could get. A bit of shadow detached itself from the sky and soared down to land on Sam's shoulder. Aristotle waggled his tail feathers and tilted his head.

"Both of you?" I demanded in a whisper. "God's breath. Fine. But you will be silent and follow directions, no matter what they are. Am I understood?"

They nodded solemnly.

Lord Rutledge's townhouse was of the ornate variety, three stories of grey stone and scrollwork with a small garden on one side and pillars round the front door. We hid between a home and a parked carriage, slipping into the shadows.

"The basement is the last light to go out," Sam breathed. "The bobbies walk through in five-minute rounds."

I nodded. Though I would much rather have left Sam safe in his room, I certainly might have had worse companions. He was quick, quiet, and competent, which was an unnerving thing to recognize about my fourteen-year-old ward.

We sat in silence until they snuffed the downstairs light. Then we waited a bit more.

Once everyone was likely asleep, I crept down to the servants' entrance to peer through the window. Most of the larger townhomes were similar in design; the servants' entrance, storage, pantry, butler and maid's rooms, still room, and all the functional spaces in the house were in the basement. The entertaining spaces were on the ground floor, and the family rooms were generally on the second or third. That made my search easier.

After ensuring the downstairs was quiet, I rejoined Sam—Aristotle was in the air somewhere—and began searching for the best holds to start my climb. The edifice was composed of large, square stones that fit together neatly, but not smoothly. There was a ledge and corner on nearly every stone, some as wide as the pad of my fingers, and others about half that size. Perfect for climbing.

But to ascend safely, I needed the right balance of light: enough to see where to place my fingers and toes, but not enough to be visible in the light of the street lamps. If the construct's job was guarding his master, it would more than likely either be in his room or just outside.

So I would climb to the second floor, at least, and find myself an open window. Creeping through the basement and first floor without being seen was a risk I didn't wish to take, not during a reconnaissance mission.

Ghostly croaking echoed down the street. A series of high-pitched calls that made the hair on my arms stand up. Aristotle.

Sam and I dropped behind a bare hedge and held our breath as I peered through the branches. A constable strolled down the center of the street, swinging his nightstick by the cord and eyeing the houses with lazy conscientiousness. After all, what were the chances of a crime happening here, in the wealthy part of town?

Sam gave me a sidelong glance that said he understood exactly what I was thinking.

As soon as he was gone, I handed my thieves' lantern to Sam. "Point this at the walls, but never the windows," I said as I dusted my fingers lightly with chalk. "If I stop moving, turn it off until I move again. Keep it on the lowest setting no matter what."

"Are you sure you want to climb? Why not use the—that thing Delilah made you?" he asked, gesturing at my wrist with his chin.

"Because I do not know whether the magic works on a construct, and I would rather not have a metal mastiff tear into me."

Sam nodded and crouched behind the shrubs as I found myself a pair of good holds and began climbing. The stiff soles of my boots let me rest my weight on my toes, taking the pressure off my fingers and arms, so I made quick work of the ground floor.

The first floor had a series of large windows with wide ledges that were likely part of a ballroom or library. I edged toward the closest window, made certain my feet were stable, and crouched on the sill to rest my arms. The ballroom was dark and empty.

I found another solid hold and edged back onto the wall. The stone was cool and slick, the cold air stung as I fought to breathe slowly, and the weakening light made good holds harder to find. As I neared the second story and reached up for my next hold, legs tiring and toes screaming, I found the ledges on every potential stone only half as wide as the pads of my fingers.

Stay calm, I thought and blew on my fingers to keep them dry.

I placed my hand carefully, locked my grip by folding my thumbs over the top of my fingers, lifted my leg for the highest toe hold I could manage, and pushed myself up to my full length. My right toe slipped, making a little crunching sound, and I fell with a swallowed gasp. I caught myself and slammed into the wall with a huff of expelled air, clinging desperately as my full weight settled on my fingertips. My tendons burned, and the edge of the block dug into my skin as I dangled.

God's breath, I was going to fall.

The toes of my boots scraped along the stone as I struggled for a toe hold, gripping the wall so hard my arms shook. Just before my fingers gave out, my right boot caught on a protruding stone and I threw my arm out to clutch the closest window ledge. It was made of a different stone, smoother, but wider.

I locked my arm in place, swung the other hand over, scrambled up onto the ledge, and flattened myself against the window, breathing hard, hands shaking. Panicked adrenaline coursed through my body, making every muscle shake. Aristotle's warning echoed down the street, Sam flicked the light off, and the constable passed again.

After my heart stopped trying to pound through my chest, I turned to peek into whatever room I was next to and found myself sitting in a hall window. Moonlight turned the inside of the hall a pale blue. The wood wainscoting and sconces reflected enough light to see the figure padding down the corridor in the dark, its clawed feet sinking into the carpet.

The creature's head was large and stood a bit higher than my knees at the shoulder. It had a wide chest and powerful jaw, and the moonlight reflected off the runes etched into its brass skin. It prowled past the window, moving as naturally as any living animal.

My suspicion was confirmed. Rutledge kept the construct for safety, so it roamed the house at night. The construct would not need sleep or food and it would never experience fear, anger, or any other emotion. It was the perfect protector.

Breaking in to steal it while it was on guard duty would be a terrible idea, especially in a neighborhood such as this, where any kind of commotion would be noticeable. As much as I hated it, Parliament was probably a safer option. People wandered all over the grounds there without suspicion. What was one more person?

At least my reconnaissance was successful. I had narrowed my options. It was time to go.

Just as I turned to lower myself, the dog construct appeared in the window, mere inches away, its paws on the sill as it stared at me with black glass eyes, the light from the thieves' lantern reflected off its skin with an ominous glow.

I swallowed a surprised shriek and lurched backward by instinct, rolling off the sill. I threw my hands out in desperation, but the window ledge was slippery and my fingers slid off the edge.

I hung suspended for a breathless eternity before my stomach dropped. Night air rushed past me in an instant of free fall, and I landed hard in the shrubbery with a cry of pain I couldn't bite back. Aristotle screamed.

A wave of stunning pain broke over me and I fought to stand, wincing as my ribs sent out a distress signal that made my knees tremble. The constable would be here in moments, and I was too shaken to move quickly.

Sam ducked beneath my armpit and wrapped his arm around my ribcage to pull me to my feet. We stumbled toward the stables at the back of the house.

Lord Rutledge kept several horses, who whickered and stamped their feet as we crept inside, leaving pale plumes of breath barely visible in the cold air. The constable was sure to look in the stalls and shine his light into the auto parked off to one side.

"The back," Sam said, pulling me toward the tack room and a large storage cupboard. Hiding in a cramped space would give us no room to maneuver if we needed to escape, so it was the tack room or nothing. The constable would be foolish not to search there, as well, but we were out of options.

"Anyone in there?" a gruff voice called.

No time left.

Opening the door without making a sound took several stomach-turning seconds, all while watching the light of a torch grow closer.

"Get in," Sam breathed. I slipped inside and put my back to the wall behind the door to make room for him, but he closed it behind me. I made to grab him, but light shone into the stable, and crunching footsteps approached.

The light through the crack in the bottom of the door grew brighter as he neared the back, stopped to check a stall, and moved on.

"If anyone is in here, come out now and it will be better for you, see?"

I turned my feet as far to the side as they would go and squeezed myself against the wall as the steps stopped outside the door. A clicking noise, rummaging sounds, drawers sliding in and out.

The door handle to the tack room creaked. The door swung open, far enough to brush my nose. I held my breath. Light from a dwarven torch played across the rows of ropes, harnesses, and bridles hanging from pegs along the back wall.

Face turned to the side, I tried to make myself as narrow as possible. If he looked behind the door, I would have to knock him out and then run. My lungs burned.

"Oi! What are you doing in—oh, Constable. Sorry to startle you."

Samuel.

"What's goin' on in here?" the constable demanded.

"Lord Rutledge is taking these boys on a trip in the morning," Sam said to the sound of a few affectionate pats on a horse's neck. "I told him I'd make sure they had a good night. Can't have them getting cramps on the road tomorrow, what with it being so cold tonight."

"I heard a cry," the constable said, unconvinced.

A scuffing sound. "Slipped on a horse apple and nearly brained myself on the stall door," Sam said, sounding embarrassed. Had I not known the boy, I would swear he was a seasoned groom. "Didn't even know I could make a noise like that. Dangers of the job, eh? Can I do anything for you?"

One of the horses whinnied, the light stopped moving, and the constable said, "Have I seen you somewhere before?"

My heart squeezed so hard it stopped.

Sam laughed. "Not unless you like horses more than a normal man."

The constable snorted but sounded a bit more at ease. "You about finished in here?"

"Just locking up."

"Good. Get inside then."

"Yessir." The door swung shut and Sam said, "Go back to sleep, lads. All's well," as retreating footsteps became fainter. We were safe.

I slumped to the ground and gave myself a few moments to calm my buzzing nerves and ascertain the damage. I did not re-break my ribs, but my hip would be bruised terribly and I had at least one gash from the branches I broke landing in the shrub.

But I was alive and unseen, so I contented myself with that and opened the door to the tack room. The constable had opened the cupboard to check inside and left the bottom drawer ajar.

"Bloody hell, my lady," Sam said with a shaky laugh. "Are you alright?"

"I'll live. And watch your language, young man." He snorted and turned to keep an eye on the front of the stable.

Wincing at the pain in my hip, I crouched to close the cupboard and hide any trace of our entry. There, tucked in among a series of packages, was a weather-worn and spotted package tied with twine and stamped with several postage stamps from Greece and the continent.

If that had been all it was, I would have closed the door and left well enough alone. But the paper on the package was torn at one corner, and through that tear a pale green light shone, faint as a distant firefly. Had it been daylight, I never would have seen the glow.

The Cutthroat King's voice echoed in my memory. *The man is a great collector of items he has no business possessing.*

I shouldn't have done it. There was no excuse for my behavior except...I was struck with an overwhelming curiosity and found myself opening the package before I mustered the willpower to stop.

"Lady Gwen," Sam hissed, but I barely heard him. My skin was buzzing with a feeling I could not name.

Crushed on one side and soft with water spots, the rough wood shipping box wasn't doing a very good job of protecting whatever was inside. As I pried back the lid with the blade of my knife, the glow grew stronger. Inside was a wrapped and tied sphere, surprisingly heavy for its size, that glowed softly even through the paper.

I unwrapped it, hands trembling in anticipation.

An eye stared back at me.

Not just any eye, but one made of crystal, faceted to reflect light toward the iris, a circular opal around an inch and a half in diameter. The pupil was made of a rich, emerald green cabochon jade that lit up the small space with the green glow I'd noticed.

The crystal eye hummed with power. It was mesmerizing. Aristotle cried once, twice, three times. I jerked in surprise and fumbled the eye before trapping it against my chest.

"We have to go," Sam said.

There wasn't enough time to repackage the gem and escape the stable. Cursing my stupidity under my breath, I rearranged the packages and shut the cabinet door, then crept around the auto and slipped into the hedges on the side of the stable, Sam right behind me. Mere seconds later, two beams of light shone on the building from the front of the house.

Damn and double-damn.

Aristotle hopped around the crystal, turning his head to get a clear view from one eye at a time, making cooing noises.

"Ooh," he said, dropping his head till his eyeball was millimeters from touching the surface. "Ahh."

"I know you love shiny things," I grunted as I tried to extricate myself from my clothing without causing various scrapes and bruises to sing with pain. "So you had better enjoy it now. I must sneak it back as soon as possible."

He gasped at my suggestion, then gathered the eye to himself, pulling it under his chest with his wings as if he could hide it from me, like a mother hen with her eggs.

"We cannot keep the eye," I told him as I tossed the blood-stained sweater onto the top of the growing pile of ruined clothes.

"What eye?"

"Very funny. As of now, I am a thief by accident. I have no wish to become a thief on purpose."

He ignored me and continued to coo over his newfound egg (which was far too large for him, being roughly the size of my fist) as I doctored and bandaged my wounds. The scrape on my hip was deeper than I thought, just shy of requiring stitches, and dried the trousers to my skin with a thick layer of blood.

"God's breath, that hurts," I muttered as I peeled away the fabric after soaking it in water from the pitcher on my bureau. "Ouch! What kind of gentlemen keeps such rotten, bloodthirsty, fly-bitten, ill-bred shrubbery right below their windows? It should be illegal. Just look what it's done to my hip!"

Aristotle considered the injury, tilted his head, and said, "Oh la la."

"You," I said and bopped him on the beak, "are a little pervert."

Once my injuries were dressed and I swallowed a good deal of brandy to dull the pain, I fought Aristotle for the eye and sat to examine it properly. The crystal that composed the body of the eye was clear as glass in some facets, and very slightly milky in others. It was old enough that some of the faceted edges were smoothed by countless hands over hundreds, maybe thousands, of years.

I turned the eye, watching it refract the light. Script of some kind was carved into the side opposite the iris.

"It's not Greek," I said, turning the stone to catch the light. "It may be Mycenaean, or proto-Sinaitic, but I doubt it. The letters are too worn to identify. If it is Mycenaean or perhaps...it cannot be..." My voice slowly died away as an idea gripped me. "Is this the Eye of the Grey Sisters?"

"Mine?" Aristotle said as he hopped onto my arm.

"No, silly bird. I think this is a representation of the eye used by the daughters of Ceto. They were witches, the children of Titans, and Perseus stole the eye they shared to force them to reveal how to kill Medusa. Hecate and Ceto have been conflated in the past, and with the recurring symbol of three..."

My mind positively whirred with information, bits of knowledge spinning and slamming together with only one inevitable outcome.

My voice came out thin, high, and excited. "I think I can use this as an amplifier for the spell."

"Save the girl?" Aristotle asked.

"Yes. Save the girl."

He sidestepped down my arm to get close to the eye, stared longingly at it for a moment, then looked up at me, tilted his head, and said, "Mine?"

Falling asleep was impossible. Visions of Lia stepping through a spectral door filled my head. The force of my love would pull her toward me. We would wrap our arms around one another and never be separated again. But those visions were contrasted by the guilt of having stolen something invaluable and knowing that I would not return it until I knew whether it was the key to making the spell work.

What was the pompous Lord Rutledge doing with it, anyway? He could not know what it was, or the power it possessed. When I held it to the light, it focused the beam into the iris, making the jade pupil glow. If it channeled magical energy the same way it channeled light...then it may only be a matter of days before I wrapped my arms around my sister.

She would change everything, and I would no longer be alone. And Mama... Well, I almost could not bear to imagine what she would feel when she saw her daughter alive.

Of course, I could not move forward with the spell until I stole the construct and returned it to the blasted Cutthroat King.

And I learned tonight that stealing from the Marquis's townhome was not a good idea.

This meant my other option was to steal it from the House of Parliament, right from under his nose, while hundreds of people watched. I needed a really good plan...a really good, foolproof plan.

But I drank too much brandy and fell asleep before I thought of one.

9

Ripper

GWEN

Scaring the daylights out of Tony was the perfect way to begin my day. I already delivered the eye to Delilah, asking her to set everything else aside and discover if we could funnel magic through the crystal. Tony was the last stop I needed to make before taking my life in my hands and burgling a powerful member of the House of Lords in his own office.

To be fair to Tony, my disguise was most convincing, so when he yelped and jerked away from me, one hand sliding toward his pistol, I could not blame him. Just imagine the shock on his face when he realized the person beneath the workman's jacket and hat was, in fact, the woman he broke off a pseudo-relationship with.

Or had he? We'd never come to a proper understanding of the state of our relationship. A few stolen, desperate kisses and genuine affection did not a commitment make. In either case, his surprise was absolutely delicious.

"Bloody hell, Gwen," he growled as he straightened his jacket. "What are you doing?"

"Only giving you fair warning, Inspector. In case things go sideways, today."

He closed his eyes briefly, then said, "I don't want to know what you're about to do, do I?"

"You do not. However, I would rather have you arrest me than someone else, if it comes to that. And if the task requires recovering my body, you are the only one who could deliver the construct," I said, lightly.

"That's not funny."

"No. It's not. But I have to be prepared, for Sam's sake. I'm not asking you to help me do...what I am preparing to do. Just to help Samuel if he needs it."

Tony's jaw muscles clenched, and he looked away from me, trying to decide how to react. He stuck both hands in his pockets, a gesture Sam often used, and said, "Tell me."

I explained my plan and the route I planned to take, and he listened quietly. Once or twice he looked as if he wanted to disagree or suggest something else, but swallowed the words and only nodded to show he understood.

"Very well," he said when I finished.

We said uncomfortable goodbyes, Tony unable to make himself easy and me pretending he didn't put me off a couple of days ago for being a bad influence.

I waited for him to leave, then made my way from the street outside Scotland Yard to Westminster. Moving about the city dressed as a man, in my heavy work boots, thick trousers, jacket, scarf, and hat, was a novel experience. I never had a reason to hide my gender, but the inconspicuous nature of appearing like a male member of the working class was rather extraordinary...and tempting.

And focusing on that was a much pleasanter pastime than remembering being shoved off by the one person I managed to build a romantic interest in for years. In the end, I could not blame him for it. Wasn't it I who warned him we were not a good match? That I would only hurt him in the long run?

It was still true, but a part of me wished he had ignored the warning and stayed. Which was unfair and sadistic. I was not the woman to marry him, and expecting him to hang on to hope for a life he would never have with me when he could find the right woman was cruel.

So I pretended it did not hurt, and focused on my newfound freedom: traipsing about New London in trousers, without the hindrance of layers of cloth to obstruct my ability to stretch my legs. And the lightness of the garments! No corset, petticoats, no hip pads or drawers...just what Mr. Yates called long underwear, and wool trousers.

I must have been at least twenty pounds lighter if one did not count the toolbox I carried under one arm or the canvas cloth on my shoulder. The lightness and ease of movement reminded me of my travels on the continent and the thin, airy clothing I wore in the desert. Only now it was not far above freezing and my breath puffed out in little white clouds, despite the sun that melted the sleet from the sidewalks.

Traffic around Westminster was busy, as always, but I wove through the carts, autos, and pedestrians with an ease that made me irrationally angry at the clothes I was used to wearing.

My wristwatch said it was nearly noon, which meant Lord Rutledge would soon take his afternoon walk if Sam's observations were reliable—and they nearly always were. I waited in line at the delivery entrance with my forged work order and tried not to sweat. The guard leaned against the fencing and yawned, holding out one hand to the delivery boy two places in front of me.

"What's your business?" he droned.

"A letter for Lord Lockbridge, sir."

"Show me."

The boy held up the envelope, and the guard gave it a perfunctory glance before handing it back and waving him through. This was going to be easier than I thought. The same song and dance for the next man, and then the fellow directly in front of me stepped up.

"Handover, Cooper," said another guard, who joined the first from inside the fence.

Cooper turned, exchanged a handshake with the new man, and strode off toward the other side of the building as if he had nothing better to do than enjoy the walk. The new man held out his hand and snapped his fingers.

"State your business," he said.

The man in front of me, whose cap slouched over his ears, said, "I've a set of ten vases with flowers to be delivered for the Viscount Holbrook."

The guard snapped up the paper and looked it over. "You're missing the delivery instructions. Get them in writing or I can't let you in. Next."

"But, sir I—"

The guard's voice hardened as he leveled a gimlet eye at the delivery man. "Next."

Slouch-cap quailed under his gaze and slunk away, leaving me the next person in line.

"State your business," the guard said, holding out his hand.

I placed the paper in it, my palms sweating. He opened the work order, read it through, glared at me, then held the paper to the light, as if searching for something.

"Let me have that toolbox, and open the canvas bundle."

Heart pounding, I let the weight of the box drop into the man's hand and unfurled the canvas with a quick snap. He searched around the box, examining tools and dropping them back in amongst their compatriots. Then he grabbed my wrist and turned my hands over.

For the first time in my life, I was grateful for the calluses on my palms and stains on my cuticles. I mixed up several powders earlier that morning, and black sludge clung to my knuckles and wormed beneath my fingernails.

The guard examined my hands, then my face, and said, "You're in the wrong profession, lad. Here, go on. And see you're out by six."

My heart gave a relieved little flutter. Percy may scold me for time spent in physical training, but it just convinced this guard I was a workman. I gathered my supplies as quickly as possible while the boy behind me tried to explain the nature of his delivery.

The halls of Parliament echoed with my footsteps less than five minutes later. I strode down the marble floor as if I knew exactly where I was going, silently counting off the seconds.

Sam told me the location and door number of Lord Rutledge's office, but it took a few passes to orient myself. Once I was in the right part of the building, I found the hallway, positioned myself so that my back was to the door, laid out my canvas cloth, and started unpacking supplies.

Three minutes from the door to the office. Hopefully, I had the timing right. Otherwise, Lord Rutledge may already be on his walk. Several people passed my little farce: aides, page boys, servants of various stripes, visitors, and delivery crews, but no one seemed to notice me.

Was I too late?

A door opened and a male tenor voice said, "You are quite right, my lord, of course. I cannot believe I didn't see the truth of the matter until now. I hope you will inform your party that I intend to switch my vote?"

"Naturally, Cardiff, naturally," boomed the unmistakable voice of the Marquis of Rutledge. I heard a slapping sound and imagined him walloping the other man on the shoulder with his meaty hand.

"Are you off for your walk? Would you like a bit of company?"

"No, no, that's quite alright. Think better when I'm alone, you know. But I appreciate the offer. See you in chamber tonight, old boy."

The door closed fully; the lock snicked into place, and the decided clack-clack of Lord Rutledge's footfalls echoed down the hallway. I waited several minutes after the sound of his voice faded before I set the toolbox on the canvas, grabbed both corners of the fabric, and slid my pile of tools into the adjacent hallway next to Lord Rutledge's door.

Once most of the tools were stored in the box and the canvas was ready for transport, I withdrew a pair of long, thin metal tools from the inside seam of my jacket. One was slightly curved at the end, and the other had a series of wavy teeth. I slid the first tool into the lock and pushed the mechanism up to hold it out of the way while I moved the tumblers with the second rod.

It was fiddly work, but I was grateful Parliament had not yet seen fit to replace the doorknobs of the lord's offices with dwarven locks. Those were impossible to pick and would have left me standing in the hall for far too long. I leaned in close, wiggled the second tool to lift the tumbler, and felt the click as it slid to the right height.

"There you are, you little beauty," I whispered and turned both tools at the same time.

Before the door opened, someone said, "What are you doing?"

I flinched, my heart jumped into my throat, and the tumblers fell. I was so close to slipping in unnoticed, and now I would have to defend my actions to a stranger who might have the right to throw me out of the building. Or have me arrested.

By the accent, I judged my accuser to be a functionary, who often either came from a higher social level than the average worker or learned to school their accents to sound as if they had. But I couldn't be certain. That left me with two options: violence or subterfuge. Violence was a bad idea, so I followed Sam's lead and tried to brazen it out.

Throwing my arms up in frustration, I spun and said, in my best cockney accent, "Look what ye've done! I almost 'ad it. Who'd ya think you are, sneakin' about?"

The man blinked, taken aback, and searched for something to say. "—what? What are you—"

I didn't give him the chance to get his legs back underneath him. "You want to tell 'is lordship why the knob ain't fixed when he gets back? Cor, blimey, you're a thick one, ain't ya?"

"His lordship—"

"Who d'ya think has me down here? Now, scapa flow, eh, and let a bloke work."

"What?" he demanded, confused by my rhyming slang. He was from the upper classes, then, and not used to being spoken to by someone with a bit of confidence.

So I laid it on thick and said, "Piss. Off."

The young man's confidence withered. He said, "Ah. Just see that you clean up afterward."

I dismissed him with a wave of my hand and turned around to work on the lock again, pretending my fingers weren't shaking. After a moment, I glanced over my shoulder to find him gone. With a sigh, I began working the tumblers, heard the satisfying click of the lock as the door swung open, and grabbed the corners of the canvas to drag it into the room.

I was betting, perhaps foolishly, that with the traffic and strangers in the building, the construct would not attack me right away. Even so, the hairs on the back of my neck stood at attention as I closed the door. Percy's wondrous jacket didn't match my disguise, so I was as vulnerable as I'd ever been when I turned to examine the room.

To my surprise, I did not spot the construct right away. I expected it to be crouching and growling at my intrusion, prepared to rip my throat out. But there was a wealth of relics, antiques, and curios displayed with purposeful ceremony, as if they weren't mere items of personal interest but something to be flaunted.

Every appointment in the room was expressive of the owner's opinion of himself, not only the velvet chairs and mahogany desk, but the mounted animal heads, antique rifles, and smoking jacket thrown carelessly over the back of the tufted chair. And I suspected he didn't have a right to own more than half of the items on display. In fact, a sacred dwarven relic that never would have been given to a non-dwarf was displayed on a shelf.

The hammer was worn down too far to be of use, so the artificer retired it, carving it with the runes of their clan and a record of their accomplishments before dipping it in gold. Those were always given to the next of kin once the artificer died, and it was sacrilege for the hammer to be here, in this tobacco-scented room. Everything here screamed of pompous entitlement, including, if the Cutthroat King were to be believed, the brass dog sitting at attention next to the desk.

It watched me with emotionless black eyes, but stood perfectly still. In terms of pure quality, it was everything I had seen through the window and more. Rows of runic sentences were carved into the metal skin and appeared to extend inside the creation, where gears and belts clinked and whirred in a quiet symphony.

It had everything a living dog might have: ears, eyes, teeth and a tongue, a tail, even dew claws. But it had none of the personality. It simply stared at me. Despite that, even standing still, it was the single most complex and impressive piece of artifice I had ever seen. Workmanship of that quality would earn the artificer a government sponsorship in any country in the world.

No standard artifice could have made such a thing, because intelligence and will are not natural forces that can be harnessed by runes in the way force or sunlight can. How in the world had this been made? Perhaps with the same magic used in the bracelet strapped to my wrist.

"What a good boy," I said, trying to make myself believe it. It ignored me.

I fished the key from my trouser pocket and held it up. "Do you see this? It is your key, the key owned by your true master. Would you mind terribly if I used it? It won't hurt," I said, inching forward.

The construct opened its mouth to reveal two rows of very dog-like teeth, including some particularly shiny canines. Would it hear me if I gulped?

"There we are, Ripper," I said, remembering the dog's name. "That's a good lad."

Its head tilted to the side, like a living dog, but with no emotion. It was more like watching a snake than a mammal. I was only a few feet from it now, and it did nothing but watch me. No growling, no barking. Given that it was a rare and dangerous bit of artifice, I suspected it was ordered to attack only if Rutledge was in danger, but I didn't want to get my fingers bitten off finding out.

"Look, here's the key," I said, sliding up next to the desk, using it for balance as I leaned forward. There was, in fact, a keyhole on the back of the dog's neck. Just a few more inches and I could slide the key in, turn it, and...there!

The clinking and whirring stopped, the dog faced forward, and a circular platform raised up out of the back of its neck. The surface of the platform opened with a little click to reveal a device nested inside. The device also raised with the quiet turning of gears, and a long needle snapped into place.

It was wickedly sharp and caught the window light like a little star at the tip. I sighed, and feeling somewhat like Sleeping Beauty, jabbed the tip of my third finger. It hurt enormously, far more than it had any right to hurt, and drew more blood than a small wound should have.

"Ouch," I muttered and stuck my finger in my mouth.

But the bleeding didn't stop.

The wound wasn't that deep, but a stream of blood trickled down my palm. What blood the needle captured flowed down a channel in the needle's front, then split to run in a curving pattern around the device in the construct's neck.

Gears and belts began moving, the device lowered and locked into place, and the metal dog turned its head to look at me. Honestly, I hadn't thought I would get this far, so I gave little thought to what to do with the dog once it was under my control.

I'd expected to have to battle the thing, knock its parts around hard enough to misalign the runic sentences, and carry it out in pieces. But here it was, standing and offering me a doggy grin.

I cleared my throat and said, "Ripper, stand."

It's little—or not so little—metal bottom rose.

"Sit."

It dropped.

"Down."

With a few clinks and scrapes, Ripper the construct lay down.

"Good boy," I said, getting into the spirit of the thing. "Sleep."

It didn't move.

"The word you are looking for is *cease*," came a deep voice from the doorway.

I nearly jumped out of my skin but caught myself before I actually leaped onto the desk.

"No need for all that," Lord Rutledge said, waggling his fingers at me while his white mustache flapped. How had I missed his approach? A man his size and so loud? I should have heard him halfway down the hall.

Time to brazen it out. "I see you are back early from your walk."

"A bit too late." He laughed, closing the door behind himself before locking it and ceremoniously dropping the key into his coat pocket. "But we'll get all that sorted out. Admiring my dog, are you?"

"It is impressive."

"So it is. Bought it at great cost, you know. Only one of his kind."

"Bought it? Or stole it?"

"Is that what he told you? Conniving bugger. I'm the one who commissioned it, how can I bloody well steal it from myself?" He crossed to the table against the opposite wall and began stuffing a pipe from a gold box.

"That," I said, edging toward the door, "is for the two of you to work out. I am only the messenger."

"Ha! Messenger," he said, taking a few puffs. "Thief, you mean."

"Think of me as a repossessor."

Lord Rutledge turned and leveled a pistol at me. "I could think of you with your brains all over that window behind you. But you are awfully pretty for that, even if you are an unnatural creature."

"Unnatural?" I demanded, insulted. I leaned into the anger so the fear wouldn't make me incompetent. There was nothing to protect me now, no umbrella, no coat of armor. Only my wits, unless he closed the distance between us.

"Of course you are. Look at you. A spinster traipsing about town as if you had the right to live like a man. And that ain't the only reason."

"I am as competent as any man," I said.

He grinned, his mustache pulling up at the corners, then gestured at me with the barrel of his gun. "It don't appear that way, now, does it?"

"Ripper," I said, "attack."

The construct didn't move, and Lord Rutledge laughed.

"You should learn a bit more about the job before you take it, Lady St. James. Ripper won't attack anyone he has bonded with. That was part of the commission, you see. A bit of a safety mechanism, just in case. You would have known that if you were as capable as you claim to be."

Insulting him would not improve my position. Neither would flinging the smoke grenade in my pocket at him, and the real grenade would kill us both in such close confines...though it might be worth it. So I played for time.

"You recognized me, even in this?"

He snorted. "'Course, I did. You've been quite a headache for me, over the past year. Been watching you rather closely. In fact, I think we need to have a serious conversation, but this ain't the place for it. Come along." He lifted a long wool greatcoat from the coat rack and tossed it over his arm, hiding the gun, which never wavered from my chest.

"I'm not going anywhere with you," I said, though I was very much afraid that was exactly what I was about to do.

He crossed the room in a couple of strides. "You see these lovely trophies I've got? I didn't buy them from a shop. I hunted and killed 'em, and I wouldn't mind making a trophy out of you, lady, except that I've got a few questions I'd like answered. So tell Ripper to follow, and let's be about it. Unless you'd rather die right here?"

I could hit him. I was faster and more agile. But where would I go? I couldn't get through the door and the leaded window would be impossible to break unless I sent Ripper through it. But I'd likely be dead before I had a chance to follow.

So I gritted my teeth, gestured to the door, and said, "After you, my lord mustache."

He slapped me. The blow wasn't meant to stun. It was a warning: *if you don't do what I say, I will hurt you.*

"Now, dear girl, tell Ripper to follow us. We're going for a ride."

10

A Change of Heart

TONY

Standing outside his parent's door in the cold was becoming a bad habit. So was his hesitance to see them. Why did it have to hurt so damn much every time? The only thing worse than seeing them was not seeing them. He didn't think he could ever forgive his brothers for that.

"Soonest begun," he muttered, and knocked on the door.

A moment later, his mother answered. Her hair was in a neat bun and her mouth popped open when she saw him. "Anthony! Why are you hours early, my darling? Come in, get yourself out of the cold."

He stamped his feet on the mat, hung his coat and hat on the rickety stand, and followed his mother into the sitting room. She bustled around, cleaning sewing supplies off the chair so he could sit.

"Today is a good day for your father," she said as she set her embroidery basket on the small table. "I'm so glad you're here early because one never knows how long these episodes will last."

"That's why I'm here, Mother. I can't stay for supper tonight."

Her face fell, but she rallied and hid her disappointment behind a mask of contentment. "Well, you're here now, and that's what matters."

She would never ask him why he couldn't stay, because she believed it was none of her business. But he wished she would.

His father trundled out of the back rooms, dragging his slippers along the uneven floorboards with a whooshing sound. "Well hello, boy! What are you doing here so early? We weren't expecting you till supper time."

Tony blinked at the old man. He was always jovial but his eyes were clear and sharp, as penetrating as he remembered them being when he was young and trying to get away with sneaking sweets from the kitchen. Nothing got past those eyes.

"I can't stay for supper, so I thought I might stop by a bit earlier."

"Oh? What's so important it would keep you from our weekly appointment?"

His mother made a delicate little noise of discomfort, but Tony smiled. There was his father, bluff and frank. "I've promised to help someone with an important delivery."

His father sunk into the worn chair. "You must have judged it a worthwhile cause, or else you never would have given your word. I suppose we'll have to sacrifice you. "

"In truth, Father..." Tony began, then shifted in his chair as if making his body more comfortable could make his soul rest easier. But doubts swirled inside of him, bumping off every tender surface. "Sometimes I wonder if my judgment isn't more faulty than I would have liked to believe."

His father laughed. "That is the sort of nonsense good men say."

Tony squirmed. "Lately I question whether such a word applies to me."

"Anthony," his mother began, her tone distressed, but his father held up a hand and said, "Let me ask you a question, boy. Do you think a villain ever asks himself if he is a bad man?"

"No, I suppose not."

"Well," his father threw both hands in the air. "You have your answer."

"But how can I be a good man when I feel myself pulled in two directions at once? When I joined the Yard, it seemed so much easier. The law was the arbiter of what was right, and I devoted myself to serving it because it protected people."

"That's because you were young and wet behind the ears. Young people need something to believe in with their whole hearts because they haven't learned the truth yet."

"What is the truth?" Tony asked. He felt as if it was the most important question he would ever ask, especially under the knowledge that these precious moments with his father were so terribly fleeting.

The old man sat forward and rested his elbows on his knees. "That many things can be true all at the same time, and sometimes it is only circumstances that decide whether an action was good or bad. Good men can do bad things, and bad men can do good things. People are more complex than simply good or bad."

"Then consequences don't matter?"

"Of course they matter, my boy. But when you look back at the consequences in the years after, they look different from what they did when you first experienced them. Did you know that your mother and I were never meant to marry?"

Tony leaned back, as surprised as if he'd been slapped, and looked between his parent's faces. His mother blushed prettily but said, "It is true."

"Then how did the marriage come about?" Tony asked.

"I compromised her," his father said, a touch of humor in his voice.

This time Tony blushed and immediately felt that he should not like to hear any more about the subject, but seeing his expression made his father laugh.

"Not truly, though I wouldn't have regretted it if I had. It was a misunderstanding but caused quite a scandal. She had to beg off from her previous engagement and we were forced to marry. At the time, our situation seemed completely unfair, as if nothing worse could have happened to either of us. But looking back after thirty years..." He turned to look at his wife, and the affection between them glowed as warmly as the fire. "I would do all of it again. Even face the months where she hated me for taking her away from her true love."

Tony saw no trace of the pain or struggle on his mother's face, no regret for the years lost since her husband's injury. And he could imagine how she must have felt that her entire life and future were being torn away from her, because they had been.

"So would I, my love," she said and reached out to press his hand.

It was heartwarming and uncomfortable all at once, so Tony said, "The happy ending didn't take away the pain. You both suffered greatly, and I'm certain your fiancé suffered, too."

"No, it did not erase the suffering," his father said. "But it put the suffering in perspective, making it only a small part of a beautiful story. Maybe even a necessary part. We bought our happiness, and the cost was worth the prize."

"The promise of a different outlook in the future unfortunately does not make my current choices seem more tenable," Tony said, frowning.

"Then let me ask you this question: if everything went wrong for both choices, if they both ended in failure, which one could you live with yourself for having chosen?"

Tony sat back, flummoxed. He built his career around believing that the law was the immutable center of rightness. And he still believed that, in part. But the systems that served the law were systems made of men, men who were as imperfect as himself.

And if those laws could be manipulated to fire someone like himself for his personal affairs, or to put someone like Gwen in prison for trying to save the life and honor of the young man who depended on her, why did he still treat it as infallible?

More, if he were to be fired for doing something he believed to be right, would that sit on his conscience easier than succeeding in a field because he bowed to corruption?

A vision of Gwen in chains or dead on the street while he wore his Chief Inspector's badge with pride made his stomach twist into a knot. He swallowed back bile and said, very quietly, "What if my decision impacts my ability to care for you and my mother?"

She knelt beside his chair, held his face between her cool hands, and said, "My darling. You will live with your conscience long after your father and I are gone. Make the decision that allows you to be more like the man you want to be, one that lets you admire the person you are. That is all your father and I have ever wanted for our sons."

A rogue tear slipped down his cheek. Tony took his mother's hands and kissed them both, then wrapped the old man in a hug. Fate denied him a father for most of his adult life, only allowing bits and pieces of the man he remembered to slip through the cracks of his injury. Tony knew it may be a long time until his father was this lucid again, if he ever was.

And instead of staying here and reveling in the moment, he was about to leave them and put himself in danger.

Despite great technological advances over the past twenty years, there was still no faster way to cross the city than by horse. Tony hired a nag from the closest livery and took to the street, guiding his mount between slow-moving carts, hansoms, and autos with a sense of urgency he could not ignore.

He'd promised Gwen to wait along her escape route so he could be sure she made it safely away, but she wouldn't pass that way for another hour, and he wasn't certain he could wait. If he hadn't buggered everything up, she would have asked for his help instead of merely his oversight.

And he meant to give what he could.

He stopped in front of Westminster, paid a newsboy to hold the reins, and jogged around to the visitor's entrance. He ignored the outraged exclamations as he pushed to the front of the line.

"Scotland Yard," he said, flashing his badge to the guard. "Has the Marquis of Rutledge gone out for his walk yet?"

"Um, I—well, I can't rightly say, sir. He doesn't leave by this gate."

"Fine. What is his office number?"

The young guard blinked, looked down at his boots, and mumbled, "I just started last week, sir, I don't—"

Tony brushed past him and entered the echoing building. Someone inside should know, even if it was some functionary. If Gwen was in the office now, he didn't want to spoil things for her.

"You," he said as an elf in uniform passed holding a silver tray. "Has the Marquis of Rutledge left for his customary walk?"

"Who is asking?" he demanded, looking down his long nose in that way only servants of the very wealthy were capable of.

Tony showed the fellow his badge and watched his expression change from haughty to hesitant. "In fact, sir, the Marquis returned some time ago, and has since quitted the building."

Tony's heart stopped. "Was he alone?"

"I am not privy to that information."

"Shit," he spat, hands clenched into fists. He might already be late for the rendezvous.

Without bothering to even thank the fellow, Tony turned and sprinted out of the building. He bulled through the gate, to the shocked dismay of the visitors, and flicked a coin to the newsboy as he leaped onto the horse's back. Traffic had grown heavier and maneuvering through the crowded street without causing an accident was trickier.

At that rate, he wouldn't get anywhere close to Spitalfields before dark. There had to be a way through. Tony stood in his stirrups and tried to pick a path through the crowd. Perhaps if he could squeeze between—was that Rutledge's coat of arms?

The black carriage with the silver shield and leaping stag on its doors fought clear of the press and turned right onto Vauxhall. Tony had a choice: continue forward toward the meeting where he'd promised Gwen to be, or listen to his gut and follow the Marquis.

He pulled his horse's head around and exited the street sideways, jumping the curb and nearly unseating a couple of women on bicycles. A traffic officer blew his whistle and shouted, "Oi! You, there!" but Tony ignored him and cut across toward Vauxhall Bridge Road, eyes flying to the place the coach should have been. But the Marquis vehicle had disappeared.

"Come on," Tony urged the horse, which was a recalcitrant nut brown mare who was too jaded to be affected by much of anything, including Tony's heels. She wasn't happy about forcing her way out of traffic. It took considerable patience and a few kicks that were rather harder than Tony would have liked, but soon they were plugging down Vauxhall as Tony searched for the Marquis's carriage.

If Gwen got away cleanly, Rutledge would be suitably incensed and probably head off to file a complaint about his stolen goods. If she hadn't, he would know. Besides, the man was here, now, and his intuition said—the carriage door opened, a slouchy cap emerged for an instant, as if the wearer were about to leap from the open door. But the hat and wearer were dragged back inside and the door slammed shut.

That was the cap Gwen had been wearing when she'd ambushed him outside his office. Suspicion confirmed, he kicked the mare into a trot and started closing the distance between them.

"Halt! You! On the brown mare!"

Tony gritted his teeth and looked over his shoulder. An officer on horseback cantered up the road behind him, mustachioed face set in grim lines of determination as he cut a swath through traffic.

If Tony ignored him, the constable would give chase, but he didn't have time to spare, so he simply continued the trot and waved an irritated hand.

"Cease!" the constable ordered as he pulled up alongside.

"Stand down, Constable," Tony began, "I am Insp—"

The constable jerked his horse's head to the right and plowed Tony off the road, nearly crushing several pedestrians who screamed in fright and leaped out of the way.

"You are in violation—" the Constable began as he reached for the reins of Tony's horse.

With a quick jerk, Tony turned the mare's head aside, grabbed the constable's lapel with his left hand, and slapped him. The blow was only hard enough to break his attention, but the young man leaned backward with a blink of surprise and slid off his horse as if he'd been punched.

Tony jumped down, walked around the front of the stamping horses, grabbed the man up by his shirt front, and said, "Do you see this badge, Constable? Perhaps you should identify your perpetrator before you threaten him and nearly kill innocent pedestrians!"

The young constable's eyes were dazed as he blubbered about how he didn't know and the traffic officer said, but Tony didn't have time for that.

He shook the man, and said, "I am in pursuit of a criminal. I am commandeering your horse. Take this one back to the livery and give them"—he pulled the ticket stub from his pocket—"this receipt. You understand?"

"Y-yes, sir. Yes, sir."

With a last, hard look, Tony threw himself onto the back of the spirited bay, grabbed the reins, and kicked the horse into a ground-eating lope. The carriage had advanced too far up the road, and Tony squinted against the icy wind that made his eyes water as dozens of black-topped carriages filled the lane.

He forced his fluttering heart to calm as he searched each coach, trying to find the coat of arms or Gwen's slouch hat. If the Marquis turned off Vauxhall, he would miss them both entirely.

"Use your brain, man," Tony told himself as he passed the next pair of vehicles that did not belong to the Maquis of Rutledge. "If I had Gwen St. James in my coach, where would I take her?"

That was the wrong question to ask. If the Marquis found Gwen stealing from him and forced her into his carriage, where would he take her, and why? She'd already tried to exit the carriage once, and she was a dangerous person. If the Marquis knew that, he'd likely want to get her someplace private, and quickly.

The Marquis's estate was in Regent Park, so if he was bold enough to take her there, they'd pass Hyde Park on the way. If he had violence in mind, there was more than one out-of-the-way corner nearby, and certainly more deniability.

With that horrifying thought in mind, Tony kicked the bay into motion and cantered down the road searching every carriage he passed, finding nothing. He pulled to a halt at the corner, his mount dancing in place as he tried to decide whether to search Hyde Park or plow on toward the Marquis townhouse.

He'd trusted his gut this far. Tony turned toward the park and cantered his horse down the lane, his cheeks stinging, fingers numb, blood thrumming in panic. At least, until he came to his senses. If Gwen was in trouble, there were bound to be loud noises.

Pulling the bay to a stop on the grass, he slowed his breathing and listened. Horses, carriages, laughter and chat, whining bicycle chains, and...was that the sound of snapping wood?

Orienting on the sound was tricky because distance and echoes made the noise appear to be coming from at least three different places. He strained his ears, not breathing for fear of missing it.

Crack! Crack, crack!

Tony turned the bay toward the sound of gunfire and kicked it into a full run, flying across the grass to the north side of the park. Ignoring the lanes, he cut a straight path toward the sound, leafless trees passing in a blur. The horse's hooves dug up great clots of frozen earth as it thundered on, breathing in deep gasps. Wind roared in his ears and pulled Tony's coat out behind him like a cape.

They rounded the outside edge of a meadow bordered by trees and entered a path enclosed by evergreen hedges on each side. He stood in the stirrups and pulled the reins back, making his horse sit and skid to a stop.

At the edge of the hedged path where the road turned back toward the open lawn, perhaps two-hundred yards away, a disabled carriage sat at a precarious angle. A bronze shape the size of a hound shot across the grass and plowed into the right front wheel like a wrecking ball, shattering the wood and making the horses scream and leap to the side.

A body tumbled backward out of the carriage in a controlled roll, hit the ground on its feet, and leaped aside. Two more gunshots sounded with a crack, sending grass and dirt spraying into the air where the figure had been just seconds before. When the figure stood, hat having fallen off in the tumble, a wealth of shiny brown curls tumbled down their back. Tony's heart nearly stopped in relief.

Gwen was alive.

And that brass shape zipping across the grass for another run at the carriage must have been the construct. Tony climbed off his horse as a large white-haired man leaped from the coach, hit the ground, and rolled.

The following explosion took the two of them off their feet and sent pieces of the carriage tumbling through the air. Both horses screamed and bolted, dragging the smoking bits of carriage and harness behind them.

Tony drew his pistol and started running.

11

It's Called an Armbar

GWEN

Fifteen minutes earlier

My mind raced as Lord Rutledge walked me down the corridor and toward the exit with the construct following obediently. He kept the gun trained on me beneath the jacket while he had a smile or laughing greeting for everyone we crossed paths with. No one noticed anything out of the ordinary.

I could have screamed, leaped aside, or engaged in any number of shenanigans to bring this hostage situation to a close. But I had two problems: while I doubted Lord Rutledge wanted to compromise his political position by being part of a fracas in the middle of Westminster, I could not absolutely guarantee it.

He could, in fact, be ruthless enough to fight or kill me at the center of British politics, which meant the innocent people going about their daily activities would, by extension, be in danger.

The second issue was a bit deeper and more problematic: if I escaped now, I would not learn what he meant about my being a problem for him over the last year. I had my suspicions, of course, but unconfirmed suspicions are dangerous.

So, I allowed myself to be escorted from Westminster, appearing for all purposes like a compliant victim, so I could enjoy the look on his face when I showed him exactly how problematic I could be.

"Don't bother running when we reach the out-of-doors," he warned before we entered the antechamber. "Despite what you might believe, I will happily shoot you."

I doubted that, but I had no intention of running. Not until I had more answers, anyway.

Lord Rutledge led me toward his carriage, a black four-seater with his family crest on the door, similar to my own clarence but without the extra frills of artifice to make the ride smoother or ease the burden on the horses. He spent his money in other places, as evidenced by the mechanical dog padding silently behind us.

The coachman jumped down to open the door, and Lord Rutledge said to me, "If you don't mind?"

"I certainly do mind," I groused. "The only reason I am participating in this charade is for the pleasure of the look on your face when I break your arm."

Lord Rutledge climbed in behind me, sat opposite me with the gun pointed at my chest, waited for Ripper to leap into the carriage and the driver to close the door. Once we were safely ensconced, he leaned forward and slapped me again. This time, he meant it, and my head snapped to the side, cheek burning, eyes watering.

"At some point or other you must learn that the natural balance of power always leans toward those who have the strength to take what they want," he said genially as if he hadn't just struck me. "I am stronger than you are, so you will cease making threats you cannot possibly carry out, or I will be forced to teach you a lesson your father clearly didn't bother with."

Certain I had been taught my lesson, he pounded one meaty fist on the roof twice, and the carriage jolted into motion. I sat back to let the momentary dizziness pass, swallowed the blood from where my teeth cut the inside of my cheek, and folded my arms.

"And what makes you think he did not try, sir?"

"If he put any real effort into it, you would be obedient and meek, as is proper. He had a good head for business, but he was weak. I, Lady Gwen, am not. Though I would rather not kill you if I don't have to. The mess, you understand."

"You believe your right to strike me was granted by greater physical power?"

"That is not simply my belief, it is an immutable law of nature: the hierarchy of strength. The strong can take what they will and can protect what they take. The weak can do neither, and so need the strong to protect and provide. If you would learn to accept this as the natural order of things, perhaps you would not have cost me so much time and effort and ruined so many of my plans. Now you will pay for your actions."

"Pray, who will make me pay, my lord? Surely not you."

"I will not be drawn into a pointless verbal sparring match. You will answer my questions as I ask them, or I will cause you pain until you do. Am I understood?"

I allowed myself a moment to sulk. Lord Rutledge was several orders of magnitude cleverer than I had given him credit for, but he had a weakness I could exploit when the time was right.

"I asked you a question, Lady."

"So you did."

His walrus mustache made his frown look far less sinister than it should have, and his lazy lips took the verbal bite out of his words. But he was willing to commit violence, so when he said, "Am I understood?" I knew the threat in his voice was a real one.

"Perfectly," I replied, suitably cowed by his manly intimidation.

"Very good," he said, his natural joviality reasserting itself in his tone. "What have you done with the eye?"

I stopped breathing for a heartbeat. "I'm sorry?"

"Don't play dumb with me, lass. I know you stole it. I want to know where it is."

"How do you know?" I asked, then flinched and covered my mouth with both hands.

He chuckled. "You think the dog and the constable are the only protections I have? I thought you cleverer. When you stumbled across Cassandra Monmouth, I wrote that off as an accident. Wrong place, right time, and all that. But when you discovered Ashcroft's relationship to the vampire, I thought, here is a woman with uncommon intelligence, for her sex. Don't make me reassess my opinion of you."

"You knew about Monmouth? About Ashcroft?"

He snorted. "'Course I did. Who do you think arranged it all? Ah, there. I can see by the look in your eyes you are beginning to recognize who you are dealing with. I hope you will believe that I mean what I say, and that there are consequences to crossing me. Now, unless you'd like me to perform a thorough search of your home for my property, tell me what you have done with the eye."

I made a mistake and misjudged this man badly. My mask of indifferent fear slipped, and he saw the recognition and anger in my eyes. I was going to have to do something dangerous, more dangerous than I'd planned.

I leaned over, opened the carriage door, and made to jump. Rutledge's fingers clamped on my upper arm, hauling me back inside faster than I anticipated. The door snapped shut.

He flung me across the inside of the carriage, and my back hit the other door, jamming the handle into my spine and making the back of my head bounce off the lacquered wood. White stars flashed before my eyes.

The construct remained seated, but our positions had changed and there was a bit of distance between us; Rutledge on one side near the right-hand door, and me on the other. That gave me time to move before he could strike or catch hold of me.

"You're a madman," I panted, rubbing the back of my head.

"No, I simply have more information than you do. And if you try to escape again," he thumbed back the hammer on this revolver, "I will be forced to do something unpleasant. Where is the eye?"

"I gave it to the Cutthroat King."

His eyes narrowed, the pouches beneath them shaking like loose pillows as the carriage turned and began crunching over gravel instead of cobbles. Gravel? A park? He wanted privacy. Good.

"You are lying," he said, regaining his seat on the bench.

"Am I? How can you be certain?"

"Because I have had Scotland Yard watching you for months."

Tony.

"Why am I still alive, if I have been thwarting your plans at every turn?"

"Because you are a notable public figure and I thought, perhaps, your arrest would send the right message. But I see that was wishful thinking. You are much better off out of the way, permanently. I will find the eye, myself. Perhaps take over conservatorship of those two lovely children. They may come in handy, at least."

White hot rage seared my insides, but my voice was only disgusted as I said, "All of that information and you still failed to learn the most important thing about me. Amazing."

"And what is that, pray tell?" he asked as he sighted down the length of the barrel and aimed at my chest.

I squeezed the ignition packet on the grenade I'd been hiding since folding my arms over my chest. The gunpowder ignited with a sharp snap. The Marquis flinched at the sound as I held up the grenade and said, "I don't care much if I live or die."

He froze in shock for a few precious moments at the sight of the live grenade smoking on my palm.

I ordered, "Ripper, break the coach wheels!"

All hell broke loose.

Ripper smashed through the wood of the lower panel in a single violent leap. Less than a full second later, the coach jerked to the side as the first wheel went down.

The Marquis's arm swung upward as he tried to regain his balance, taking the barrel off my chest. He fired once in surprise, the shot splintering the wood just above my left ear, then twice in reaction. Little bits of ceiling rained down on my head. I used my free hand to push myself up and lashed out with my right foot as the Marquis tried to correct his aim. The toe of my sturdy workman's boot connected with the Marquis's wrist and sent the pistol clattering against the carriage wall as he yelped in pain.

I tossed the grenade between his legs, unlatched the door, and rolled backward out of the cab in the same motion. There was a stomach-dropping lurch as Ripper took out another wheel, and I landed hard on both feet before leaping to the side.

Two more shots rang out and kicked up dirt not far from where I landed. The man was quick for his size. Ripper's metal feet dug into the earth as he flew by for another go at the coach, passing between me and the driver, who climbed unsteadily to his feet.

Before Ripper could blast through the final wheel, the Marquis leaped free of the carriage and my grenade exploded. I rolled backward, away from the blast, but debris still rained down on my face and torso as my ears rang.

The Marquis appeared above me, his face red with anger as he wrapped both huge hands around my throat and squeezed.

I generally wore skirts while at home, in part because it was expected and proper, and in part, because I enjoyed the swishing sound they make. But trousers have several advantages. One is the lack of weight, as I noted earlier in the day. The other is the freedom of movement, which was particularly handy when executing martial arts maneuvers.

The Marquis of Rutledge, like most men, assumed his greater size and strength assured him victory against someone like me. So, instead of covering my legs and torso with his weight, which would have effectively immobilized me, he locked his elbows out and leaned into his shoulders, leaving space between my body and his.

I fastened my hands around his right wrist, used my feet to push my hips to the side, kicked my legs up so that my left calf hit him in the neck and my right leg wrapped across his chest under his armpit, leaving his elbow pressed against my hips. When I arched my back and thrust upward with my pelvis, he lost his balance and toppled to the side.

I took a great gulp of air as I arched my back. His elbow strained backward over my hips and a high-pitched "ahh," escaped beneath his mustache as he thrashed. But he was not strong enough to break away.

"This," I said through my teeth, pulling harder, "is called an arm bar."

"Stop," he panted, his own body arching with pain. "Stop!" He tried to wriggle out of my hold but the man had no technique.

"Your strength doesn't matter now, does it?" I growled.

"Gwen!" a voice yelled.

"Help!" the Marquis cried.

I jerked his wrist backward, tight against my chest as my hips thrust upward. The Marquis's elbow held for a strained second, then popped. He screamed. I let go and rolled to my feet, panting and glaring down at the red-faced man who tried to kill me and been responsible for so much death and suffering.

"I warned you that I'd break your arm," I said.

Something cold and hard rested just behind my ear, sending a shiver running down my back. I froze, cursing myself for having

forgotten the driver, and fought the urge to cough away the stinging pain in my windpipe so he wouldn't shoot me for moving.

"Stop!"

Tony stood not ten feet away, panting, his pistol raised. The
driver took a handful of my hair and jerked me backward, using
my body as a shield between Tony and himself.

Unfortunately, I didn't have any techniques to save myself
from this. Just anger and fear.

"You're going to put your gun away," said the driver in a
smooth, carefully cultured voice. "Unless you'd like to see what
the inside of Lady St. James's head looks like."

"Drop your gun and step away from the woman," Tony countered, and his voice was like hearing thunder on the horizon that
promised a coming storm.

Click. A cold rush of primordial dread slid down my spine at
the sound of a gun hammer locking into place behind my ear.
Despite what I told the Marquis, I didn't really want to die, at
least not yet. Not when Lia was so close. Not when Sam was still
in danger.

"Enough," the Marquis gasped. "Stop this. Jasper, that is an
inspector from Scotland Yard."

Which meant his death will be much harder to explain.

Rutledge rolled to a sitting position, then struggled to his feet
while cradling his broken arm, his once red face now pale with
pain and beaded with sweat. "The inspector would like to protect
his friend, naturally. And he is sworn to do his job, just as all
good public servants are. He won't shoot either of us, will you
Hardwicke?"

"Put the gun down," Tony growled, not taking his eyes off the driver.

"Put it down, Jasper. You see I am in no danger. The inspector is behaving rationally."

Tony's jaw clenched, and the cold barrel dropped away from my head.

"There, you see, Inspector? No harm done. Just a misunderstanding after a nasty accident. Hot tempers and all that. No need to put your career in jeopardy over a trifle, not when you have people to care for."

"Ripper, to me," I said.

The construct left the wreckage of the carriage and limped to my feet. The explosion damaged some part of it, but I didn't have time to check what it was. My eyes were fastened on the Marquis's face.

"You had better get your master to a surgeon," I said with mock concern. "His arm is already swelling. If they don't set the bone soon, he may never regain proper use of his arm, even with elvin medicine."

The man's small, dark eyes fixed on me with a hatred hot enough to make my skin burn. I had surprised him, challenged his assumptions, and come out at least marginally on top. He was down an expensive carriage, an expensive construct, and one arm.

"I'm glad you survived the accident with no harm, Lady Gwen. Your mother will be glad of your safety, and the children. Inspector," he said with a nod.

The driver, a pale, waxy-faced man, passed me and helped Lord Rutledge onto one of the coach horses that wandered back after their first panicked flight. It danced sideways, unused to having a person on its back, but the Marquis never would have walked out of the park without passing out.

We watched them disappear into the park in silence, the driver giving us a single backward glance before rounding the bend in the path. Tony didn't say anything, just gathered his horse and reached down to lift me. I climbed on behind him, wrapped both arms around his waist, leaned my head tiredly against his back, and said, "Ripper, follow."

Tony walked the horse out of the park, then turned toward Grosvenor Square.

After we rejoined traffic, he asked, "What happened?"

"The Marquis was expecting me. He's the one responsible for Lady Monmouth, and the vampire that enthralled Lord Ashcroft."

Tony blew out a long breath.

"You need to get your family out of town," I said. We both knew the Marquis's veiled threats had been serious ones.

"And take them where? I can barely afford to keep them in their current residence."

"Take them to Wainwright. I'll pay for the ticket. Mama would love to have them."

"Gwen—"

"Damn your pride, Tony. Your parents are in danger now because you came to help me. Let me do this. It is not charity, it is a debt. I'll send them north on the train with the children."

Tony was silent for a long time.

We turned into the square, and each clop of the horse's hooves echoed like a hammer striking a gavel. Knowing I had been right, that something bigger than we suspected was connecting these dangerous supernatural events, didn't feel very gratifying given what that information cost us.

Whatever sense of safety either of us had, less for ourselves than for our families, had been destroyed. The Marquis was a pompous, condescending ass, but he had significant political power, and apparently, his fingers were also deep in the pockets of important people in Scotland Yard.

Tony reined in at the front door.

"We'll take them to Wainwright together," he said.

"I don't have the time, I need to return the—"

Tony dismounted in a rush, then grabbed me by my waist and lifted me from the horse's back in an easy motion. His eyes were implacable as he said, slowly, and without removing his hands, "We will take them to Wainwright together. They will be safer that way."

I looked down, unable to hold his gaze. "Can your parents be ready to leave tomorrow afternoon?"

"I'll be certain of it." I nodded, and Tony remounted. "You'll tell me the rest of it on the train," he said.

I agreed.

He kicked the horse into a trot, leaving me standing in the square with the construct at my feet, and not much time. I had to fulfill a promise, retrieve the artifact that was currently putting Delilah in danger, schedule a train ride, and hope that I was still alive to escort the children in the morning.

12

Going Home

GWEN

Standing before the Cutthroat King without Tony at my back was an entirely different experience than blasting our way to the questionable throne room. This time I simply found a likely looking criminal, showed them the coin, and followed as they led me to the King's lair. We entered through the basement of a foundry and wound through underground tunnels like rats.

I stood in the same room, but without fury to bolster my confidence. Despite being armored with my jacket, leather corset, umbrella, and several other dangerous weapons stashed about my person, I felt significantly more vulnerable, even with Ripper standing next to me, awaiting orders.

Perhaps that was also due to not being mindlessly enraged, but whatever the cause, my defiance merely percolated instead of boiling over. Which made the man sitting on the throne several times more intimidating than he had been, and me about five times more likely to say something stupid to cope with the stress.

The King, still in black and looking as if he stepped out of the late Middle Ages, lounged across this throne and said, "I did not expect to see you back successful so soon, my lady. And with a black eye, no less. You appear to have had a rather exciting few days."

"Is it black already?" I hoped the bruising would give me the benefit of at least an evening's respite but I suppose it was too much to hope for. "I see you are still here, sitting uselessly on your arse while other people work."

The King raised a dark brow. I forgot how shark-like his eyes were. One point for my runaway mouth. Luckily, the room was empty save for the guards who escorted me here and the King, himself. Otherwise, he might have had to do something unpleasant about my impertinence.

But he only raised his arms to the sides and said, "The benefit of being king. Now, if you will, please give the construct the key and order him to come to me."

I pulled the key from my pocket, bent to give it to Ripper, then stopped and straightened.

"You know," I said, considering the key as if I'd just had an interesting thought. "Rutledge told me he was the one who commissioned the construct. It is extraordinary. I have never seen anything like it."

"Nor will you."

"What makes you believe you have a claim to it? I only ask because I've become rather fond of the creature over the last few hours."

The King sat up slowly, every movement as deliberate as a dance performance. He leaned forward, looking down at me from this throne, and said, "Because I made it."

I had given the artifice a thorough once-over between arriving at home and nightfall, taking notes for Delilah with Sally's help. I had not lied; it was an extraordinary piece of artifice far beyond what most artificers were capable of. I stopped fiddling with the key and narrowed my eyes at the man who ruled New London's underground. He was a human, handsome in a dark and sharp kind of way, and graceful as a predator.

I turned the key over in my hands a few times and said, "You are no dwart."

The King leaned back with a self-satisfied smile and rested one hand on his thigh—high up on his thigh. "I'm glad you noticed."

"You really should reconsider the snug fit of your trousers, but that is not what I meant and you know it. In fact"—I took a few considered steps forward, piecing together information—"I'd say you're not human, either."

The amusement faded from the King's face. He made a dismissive gesture, and the guards left the room, closing the door behind them.

"I'd say," I continued with another step, "that you chose a very clever glamour. Did you kill the old Cutthroat King? Or has it always been you?"

He stood, glaring down at me with unreadable eyes beneath the crown of silver spoons. An apt metaphor, that crown.

"What would make you ask such a foolish thing?" he purred.

"I prefer to be on equal footing when I am in business with someone. Makes the working relationship run so much more smoothly."

"Equal footing? My lady, the only relationship we will be engaging in is one where you complete your promised task and hand over the construct. Unless you would prefer to change the nature of our association, in which case, I will still be the party on top."

He had no interest in me, that much was clear. But he did think innuendo would make me uncomfortable enough to throw me off balance. I might as well disabuse him of that notion.

"Ripper," I said. "If the King takes another step toward me, or threatens me in any way, you will destroy yourself."

The dog stood and locked eyes on the King's feet, still as a cat before leaping after a bird

The Cutthroat King froze. "What are you playing at?"

"Merely protecting my investment. Since this"—I pulled a folded piece of parchment from another pocket and held it up—"is useless. Is it not?"

One corner of the King's mouth tugged upward ever so slightly. "You cannot think me such a fool that I would give you my blood?"

"Oh, this is your blood. But human-channeled magic will not target the blood of a fae creature. Isn't that right? I suppose it is a good thing I managed to get my hands on the Eye of the Graeae. That should help the targeting spell."

The poorly worn glamour melted away like chalk in the rain. The King did not have wings or pointy ears or other physical characteristics mortal creatures expect from the fae—an unfortunate result of having read too many fairy tales—but he was lithe, powerful, dark, and elegant, like a weasel given human form. His eyes were a bit larger than humans or elves, his face more delicately built, his torso longer, and his canines sharper.

He showed them to me with a predatory smile. "You are clever, Lady St. James. But are you wise enough to recognize the danger you are in?"

"I suppose time will tell. You know, you really should have specified what condition the construct was to be in when I delivered it to you. A poor oversight from one of the fae, a race so renowned for making deals. Pity."

I pulled a grenade from my pocket and handed it to Ripper, who took it carefully between his teeth and continued to watch the King.

"What are you doing?" he demanded, panic lacing his voice for the first time.

"You've probably spent too much time around humans," I chided him, lighting a match with delicious theatricality.

"Stop!"

I pressed my advantage, knowing that by his very nature, he was bound to the letter of our agreement, knowledge the other humans he dealt with had not been able to benefit from. I leaned down to light the fuse. "It is a pity. But I'm sure you'll be able to repair it...in time."

"Wait!"

I stopped mere centimeters from lighting the grenade and turned my head to look at the King, widening my eyes innocently. "Yes?"

"I will allow my guards to kill you for this."

"True. But not until after Ripper's head has been blown to pieces."

I lit the fuse.

The King's body jerked as if he'd like nothing more in the world than to leap forward and tear me apart, but his desire to save the construct was too great. His mouth worked, and his hands flexed.

"Unless, of course," I said as if a thought had just occurred to me. "You'd like to renegotiate the—what did you call it—nature of our relationship?"

The King glared at me, and I pinched off the lit end of the fuse with a smile.

"The Cutthroat King is fae, then?" Delilah asked as she rubbed sleep from her eyes and unlocked the door to the Boom Room.

"As fae as Percy," I said. "But quite a bit more dangerous. I believe he may be weaselkin of some kind. A mink or a marten, perhaps. Some kind of mustelid. A fierce predator, in any case. That aside"—I brushed that off as I followed Delilah into the back room—"I was damn lucky that gamble worked."

"Aye, you were," Delilah said over her shoulder as she unlocked the enormous safe. "If he'd been any less arrogant, you'd be dead. And then who would commission me and Percy? Who would care for the children? What would your mother do with both of her daughters gone?"

My spine stiffened.

Delilah pulled a wrapped bundle from the dark insides of the massive safe and held it out, glaring at me. I glared right back. "I do not need my mother thrown in my face, thank you."

"But maybe you do. Because you seem to have forgotten that there are people who rely on you now. You have responsibilities, ones you chose. You don't simply get to run off without a word, anymore. If something happens to you there are conseque—"

I did not want to have this argument; I didn't have time for it. So I pulled a copy of my notes on the construct out of the leather satchel on my shoulder and held it in front of her face. She stopped chastising me and snatched the papers.

"What is—Gwen where did you—? I've never seen one so complex! Look at the alteration of this runic sentence, it seems to be converting kinetic energy to—I mean, that's never been done. And here!" She stabbed the paper with one blunt finger. "There would be at least a rudimentary level of intelligence. But how would it generate energy? Stone and hammer, Gwen, where did you find this?"

"Consider it an apology for putting your meal ticket in danger."

She looked up, snorted, said, "As if I wouldn't be just as successful on my own steam," and laid the schematics on the table before flipping down the magnifying glass on her goggles to examine my sketches more carefully. She ran a finger across my notes, muttering, "As if you weren't more than a meal ticket. Slagging idiot."

"Before I leave you to your research," I said, putting one hand on the papers to distract her. "I need to know what you've discovered about the eye."

She blinked as if to physically force her mind from one subject to the other, her single magnified eye looking four times the size of the other.

"Will it work?" I asked. "Will it power the spell, once the circle is closed?"

"That's a complicated question," she hedged.

"D...please. I need this."

She looked down and shook her head. "Does it have the capability? Yes, I think so. I think you could channel a significant amount of magical energy through that artifact. It is as if it were made for the purpose. But that spell is many times bigger than anything I can replicate in the shop with the knowledge we've gathered so far. If it cannot hold...you may take out an entire city block."

"If the spell is properly completed," I clarified, "and the final sentence calls the magical forces, the eye will trap and channel them?"

"Didn't I just say that?"

I breathed a long sigh, closed my eyes, and let it sink in for a moment. Lia. The promise of my sister was so close my chest ached.

"Yes," I said, "but I'm slow. And you wrapped it up in a bunch of warnings about blowing up."

"That's a real danger, Gwen," she said, putting one broad hand on my forearm. "Like I said, it has the ability. But we won't know if it has the capacity until we test the spell in a space large and safe enough."

"Large and safe," I repeated. "Somewhere like the moor?"

She shrugged, her eyes darting back toward the scattered notes on the table. "Something like. Just so there's enough room that we don't kill anyone or blow ourselves to slagging pieces when we test it."

I grabbed Delilah by both round cheeks, kissed her once, and left her standing near the notes in stupefaction. I had plans to make, and a train to catch.

Tony's parents, both kind and grateful but confused by the whole affair, were safely stowed away in a sleeping compartment at the end of our private car shortly after we boarded. Sam ran from window to window as if he would see something different six feet in the opposite direction, while Sally sat at the table with a sketchbook and began recording the trip before we left the station.

Tony gave me a dirty look when he realized I'd rented a private car, but I had no intention of making an eight-hour ride in discomfort. And I most certainly would not subject his aging parents to the stink, cramped seating, and general discomfort of the standard passenger car. I hated traveling by train, so it might as well be as comfortable as possible.

As we boarded, I leaned in and said, "Try, for a moment, imagining Samuel in cramped second or third-class seating, and then tell me I was too extravagant."

No doubt imagining the same scene I had, of Sam squeezing between strangers, leaning to see out of other windows, and generally making a pest of himself, Tony shrugged and accepted the upgrade with grace. I did not tell him that this was the children's first long train ride, not including the trip back from the Chatsworth estate, which was rushed, and I wanted them to enjoy it without restriction.

Once everyone was settled and the train was well underway, I told Tony about the Marquis of Rutledge and what he'd revealed during our conversation. His eyes kept resting on my left eye, which was nicely blackened and only marginally concealed by the careful application of cosmetics, and frowning.

"God's breath, stop," I said, at last. "It is only a bruise. It will heal."

"It might not have happened if I had been more loyal to my friend than my job." He looked out the window, jaw clenched.

I touched his knee, which was bouncing as he stared. "Your career and your oaths matter. Your job is important, not something to simply throw away because you have a troublesome acquaintance."

He placed his hand over mine, licked his lips, and said, "Is that what we are to be? Mere acquaintances?"

"Tony—"

"I should not have said what I did, in the carriage that day. It was wrong and unfair. Any burdens I feel are my own, and not yours to bear."

This time I looked down, away from his earnest brown eyes, and tried to relieve some of the pressure in my chest with a deep breath.

"I appreciate your saying that," I said, meaning it more deeply than I had anticipated.

Tony would not wound me on purpose, but it was impossible not to think of my ex-fiancé and his assurance that I should share my body freely since no man would ever desire me more than he desired my estate and title.

The sense of betrayal I had felt was so acute that I had destroyed his family sitting room—during our engagement party, no less—before I was even conscious of what I'd done.

"You must know," Tony said, leaning forward, his voice low. "You must know how much I care for you."

Men had told me they loved me, often in the pursuit of passion or at the peak of it, but this was different, and I wasn't certain what to say, or how to respond properly.

"Hey."

I froze, mouth half open, then scowled. Had I truly heard a disembodied voice or was my mind playing tricks on me. "Did you hear that?"

"What?" Tony asked.

"Hey," the disembodied voice called. "Help."

Tony shot to his feet, declarations forgotten, as he searched the cabin. "What was that?"

"Murder. Fire. Help."

I recognized that phrase and that voice. With a sigh of resignation, I walked to the end of the car, and pulled my luggage out of the bin. I was a bit cagey when it came to my luggage, particularly when I was traveling with magical antiques, and it was a good thing, too.

The zipper slid across the hardened leather with a buzz and a black head poked out of the opening, feathers rumpled, blinking at the bright lights.

"Ooh," Aristotle said, then hopped out of the suitcase and onto my arm.

"You sneaky, fiendish little stowaway," I said, every word dripping with exasperation. "How did you manage to get in there without my noticing?"

"I'm a clever bird," he said, puffing up his chest and tipping his beak back.

"You're lucky you didn't get smashed, or worse. What am I supposed to do with you now, eh?"

"Feed me."

Aristotle didn't leave my side for the rest of the train ride. He hopped across my shoulders, picked at my hair, and chattered away, repeating some of his favorite phrases. The newest one, taught to him by Sam, I suspected, was, "Scarper off, you toe rag!" which he seemed to enjoy saying to Tony, most of all.

We arrived at the station well after dark to find both carriages waiting for us. Footmen stood outside, ready to bundle us and our luggage into the waiting vehicles.

Tony took the first carriage with his parents, and I followed with Sally, Samuel, and Aristotle, who preferred to ride on the roof despite the frigid air. I hadn't been to Wainwright in years, and wouldn't have been there now if the Marquis hadn't threatened the children.

I should have broken both of his arms.

It was colder this far north, so close to the border with Scotland, and a light dusting of snow turned what could be seen of the landscape into something magical. The children rode with their faces plastered to the window, watching as the forest around Wainwright swallowed up the moonlight. Now and then a frost pixie lit up its tiny corner of the forest, glowing pale blue for a moment, then winked out, like a firefly.

When the manor came into view, my throat closed with unshed tears. Wainwright was, in fact, a castle, one of the oldest in the North of England. Austere, built of red stone and covered in vines, it might have sprung from some dark gothic romance novel where the tortured hero brooded in tortured, broody loneliness. In truth, it was a busy working manor that oversaw the village and farms nearby and served as the seat of adjudication for the countryside.

My father had it renovated when he and my mother were affianced, and what had been cold stone and drafty halls was now much less cold and only moderately drafty. There was only so much one could do to modernize a castle built as a fortification without destroying its character. But now there were carpets, electric lights, an updated kitchen, and the other important modern conveniences that were required to comfortably entertain.

I had never cared about that, even as a child. What I loved was the romance and mystery of the old place. The dusty hidden rooms no one ever used, the turret windows that looked far out over the countryside, and the library...oh the library. Sally would be over the moon.

Those out-of-the-way corners full of cobwebs and mystery were home.

But as we pulled onto the gravel drive, it might as well have been a haunted castle from a story, full of secrets and abandoned hopes and dreams.

Except that Mama stood in the doorway in a heavy dressing gown, her hair braided, a dwarven lamp in her hand that shined on her smiling face. She was petite, elegant, and charming, but possessed of an indomitable will. That combination made her one of the most dangerous people I had ever known. You could not tell her no because you did not even realize you wanted to.

The children flew across the drive and flung themselves into Mama's arms.

"Hello my darlings," she cooed, kissing both their heads, though Sally was fully as tall as she. "How did you like your trip?"

I climbed down and crossed to the second carriage, offering Tony's mother my arm.

She smiled tiredly at me. "Thank you, my lady. We have not had a trip in so long, I had forgotten how tiring they are! Not that your lovely car was not the peak of luxury, of course, but even a few hours of sitting can wear on one, with time."

"I understand, completely," I told her, pressing her hand as Tony led his father toward us.

"What is this place, my love?" he asked Mrs. Hardwicke in a tremulous voice, eyes wide as he took in the sheer size of my childhood home. "Looks like a castle. Why are we here? Where is my chair?"

"We are having an adventure, darling," Mrs. Hardwicke said. "The duchess has invited us up for a Yule visit. Was that not kind of her?"

Tony's father frowned and followed his wife toward the door, one elbow secure in his son's hands.

"Mr. and Mrs. Hardwicke, welcome to Wainwright! I am so pleased you accepted my invitation to come stay and keep me and the children company. There is nothing like a house full of friends to make winter less dreary," Mama said.

"We are honored, Your Grace," Mrs. Hardwicke said, patting her husband's hand. "Aren't we, my dear?"

Mr. Hardwicke still frowned, trying to understand what was happening.

"Mr. Hardwicke," Mama said, catching his attention. "I hear you are a connoisseur of pipe tobacco. We have far too much in storage, and I would be so pleased if you would try it while you stay and tell me what you think. We imported only the finest varieties, I am told, and I am afraid they are going to waste here, with no one to smoke them."

His eyes brightened at Mama's lie—my father had smoked smelly cigars—and he said to Tony, "New tobacco to try in my pipe, how about that, Tony? But I am tired. Where is my bed?"

With a bit of coaxing, the Hardwickes were taken safely upstairs to a suite of rooms already prepared for them. Hannah, Mama's maid, took the children to their rooms, leaving Mama, Tony and I standing in a little circle in the great hall before the massive wood staircase.

Servants carried luggage inside, bringing with them the biting winter wind.

"Come into the parlor," Mama ordered, her charm having been spent on those that deserved it.

We followed her to the hearth, crowding against the warmth of the fire.

"Now," Mama said, turning a gimlet eye on Tony and me. "Explain."

Out of long practice, I managed to hide my discomfort at being spoken to like an unruly teenager, but Tony winced.

"The less you know, Mama, the safer you will be."

"Gwenevere," she said, turning her ire on me. "Do not patronize me. Ignorance helps no one, and I will know why I am protecting the children and the Hardwickes if you please. Now."

I took a deep breath, exchanged a fortifying glance with Tony, and launched into the explanation we had concocted. Mostly truth, as far as was safe, leaving out everything to do with the eye, the grimoire, and the possibility of bringing Lia home.

"The Marquis?" Mama demanded when my tale was done. "But he has always been such a—well—" She caught herself before she could say something demeaning, but I had no such scruples.

"An ass."

"How could he have been so machiavellian all this time?"

"He fooled everyone. And I do not know what his plans are, but he threatened the children and the Hardwickes to keep Tony and me quiet. I will not risk their safety and I could think of nowhere better than Wainwright."

What I meant was, I could think of nowhere more secluded and no one more competent, but I suspected she already knew that. I'd seen four of the estate's hunters positioned in the woods as we drove through.

Mama glanced at the staircase, where the four people in question had disappeared not twenty minutes ago, and shook her head. "Well, they will certainly be safer here than in town. I shall set additional watches, as well, and have their rooms guarded at night."

"I cannot thank you enough, Your Grace," Tony said.

Mama's expression softened. "You have done your best to keep my reprobate of a daughter safe, Inspector. It is the very least I can do."

"Reprobate?" I demanded.

She turned on me. "Do you have a better word for it?"

I considered that. "I suppose not."

"Your room is on the first floor, first on the left, across from your parents," Mama said. "I'm certain you are tired. Shall I have tea or brandy sent to your room?"

Tony knew a dismissal when he heard one, and he had the good grace to take it without question. "No, Your Grace, thank you."

Then he gave both of us a polite bow and hurried up the stairs. Mama sighed and seemed to deflate, shook her head at me, then opened her arms.

13

Open Doors

GWEN

B y breakfast, Mama had everyone eating out of her small hands.

She presided over the table, teased the children, complimented Mrs. Hardwicke's dress, and made certain Mr. Hardwicke was as comfortable in his seat as he would have been in his own home.

"They are already in love with her," I said in an aside to Tony.

He nodded between bites of sausage, but the symptoms were there in his eyes, too: a softening of the expression and warmth that kindled when looking at her, as if he were right on the edge of smiling.

I sighed and attacked my breakfast. This was why I had run away. Or, at least, an important part of why. When in Mama's company, it was impossible not to desire to please her. One wanted to be whatever version of oneself would make her proud, whether that version was who one truly wanted to be in the secret corners of one's heart, or not.

Perhaps the children already knew who they were, so her presence would only bring them joy. But I had spent most of my life either trying to figure out who I was without Lia, or to put myself back together. So, while I desperately loved her, Mama was something of an unknowing prison guard who imposed her rules on my life without ever realizing how badly they fit.

And I could never tell her that, because it would hurt her deeply, and that was not an option. So I sat in silence, eating my breakfast like a workman at the end of a long day's labor, listening to Mama charm everyone in the room.

After breakfast, she gave the grand tour, showing everyone the most important and usable parts of the house. I grabbed Sally's hand and whispered, "I've something to show you."

We snuck out of the line and ran off, giggling beneath our hands like a couple of schoolgirls. The halls of Wainwright were high and supported by huge exposed wood beams that always played host to at least one or two sparrows and uncounted spiders. I counted the beams as we hurried off, five, six, seven, to turn right at number eight and push open the huge oak doors.

Sally caught her breath, and my heart leaped in recognition, like seeing an old friend on the street after many years apart.

The room was two stories, with a carved wooden staircase that spiraled up the second-floor walkway. Enormous windows punctuated floor to ceiling bookshelves, and the cushions on the low sills turned them into perfect reading nooks. Old tufted chairs and couches were scattered about the room, but never too far from the fireplace, which was large enough to sleep in, if one didn't mind the soot.

Long ago, some romantically minded Wainwright had commissioned an artist to paint the ceiling. So, when one looked up, a pastel sunset sky smiled down. The study on Grosvenor Square was large and full of books, but the manor had a proper library and Sally stood in the center of the room, spinning round, her eyes wide, fingers stretched out as if she could gather them all to herself by sheer force of will.

"There are so many," she breathed. When she stopped and looked at me, her heart was in her eyes.

"What are you waiting for?" I asked. "Go explore!"

Sally grinned and ran to the first bookshelf, her fingers tracing the spines of the books with careful reverence. When I left her, she had curled into a window nook with five books piled on the nearest table. I had hot chocolate sent in for her.

Samuel didn't need my guidance. As soon as the tour was complete, he disappeared, only to be discovered in the stables with the other boys his age, his trousers already half caked in what I told myself was mud, despite the frozen ground.

I could wander all day, checking on my family and getting reacquainted with the house, but that was just a distraction from the eye. It was in my luggage, along with the Mordegant Grimoire, waiting. And, after all, Delilah said I needed open space.

Mama had prepared a guest room for me last night, but I found myself wandering the halls, drawn to the one place I had not seen in nearly a dozen years. The handle was cold. How long had it been since anyone touched it?

The door swung open, groaning on its hinges like an old man standing up from a low chair. The hearth was empty and grey. Our beds bracketed the window, close enough for whispering in the dark. Watercolors painted by childish hands were tacked willy-nilly to the walls, and dried flowers hung crumbling in the corners.

On the dresser next to my bed was a pile of twigs, rocks, and acorn caps, surely meant for some noble purpose. On Lia's, paper and ink and postcards.

"I could not bring myself to change it," Mama said, slipping her small hand into mine. "Nor to box up her things. When I open this door, it seems, even for just a moment..."

I squeezed her fingers. She had let us live in the nursery for too long, but we hadn't wanted to be separated, to sleep in our own rooms so far away from one another. Looking at it now, I saw our ghosts, jumping back and forth between our beds at six years old, covering the floor in papier-maché at ten, whispering secrets at fifteen when only the moon was close enough to hear us.

The door was a portal to the past.

"Mama? Do you ever wonder...if there was some kind of magic, or—"

"Don't," she said and squeezed my hand. "Don't do that, dearest. It's not fair."

To whom? To her or me? Our father had noticed little change, aside from being required to shake hands at the funeral. And he'd been dead for years; dyspepsia, the physician said.

Mama closed the bedroom door.

My favorite thing about large houses is the freedom of movement. There are a million places to hide, paths to take, and corners to slip round when no one is looking. The ideal time to take advantage of this freedom is after lunch, when everyone is full and content and puttering about their own hobbies until dinner.

I strapped myself into my leather corset vest, gathered supplies, wrapped myself in the magic jacket, pulled a fur-lined wool cap over my head, took my umbrella, and slipped out the kitchen door when no one was looking.

Like most manor houses, the front of Wainwright comprised lawns, strategic trees, and a fine gravel drive. To the back and sides of the house were the stables, the head gardener's cottage, the chapel, the steward's house, several other functionary buildings, and the formal gardens.

But, beyond that, was the wood. Wainwright did not groom the forest for hunting, as many estates did. It was, perhaps, one of the few things my father had done well. While the huntsmen managed herd populations, the forest around Wainwright was as wild as one could hope for, full of mature old trees, pixies and sprites, and generations of squirrel families.

The wood bordered the moors to the north, where shepherds grazed their sheep in all but the coldest months. That was my destination. Lia had been taken in the forest, and it seemed right that I try to get her back as close to the spot as possible. Legends and tales of people trapped in faerie lands all spoke of time and memory passing differently there. If I brought Lia out, perhaps seeing similar surroundings would make the transition easier for her.

If I could get the spell to work, of course.

I followed the edge of the forest toward the north, ignoring the cold and the wet ground, visualizing creating the circle, casting the spell, and using the eye. A spectral door would open and my sister would be standing on the other side, as she had been that fateful night when Cassandra Monmouth tried to sacrifice five children to save her daughter, Claire.

Only this time, I would not break the circle. I would finish the spell and pull Lia through.

Under a low overcast sky, the moor stretched like a series of waves rolling to the horizon. Bits of snow clung to the shadows beneath scrubby bushes and low-cropped grass, and the wind raced over it with a mournful cry.

I found as level a spot as I could and began preparing the spell by digging the first circle. As I dug, my muscles warmed, and my mind floated away to daydreams about what life would be like when she was finally home.

Setting up the spell was harder than the digging for one reason: the moor is not flat, and the symbols had to be laid out with precision.

"This would have been much easier on a slab of concrete," I muttered, dribbling the white sand through the pinched opening of the leather bag.

Cassandra's circle had been large enough to fit herself and five children inside. My circle would be considerably smaller, only big enough for one. Over the last months, I had spent so many hours studying the spell that I recreated it mostly by memory, only checking the grimoire to be certain the symbols were correct.

By the time I finished, my fingers were red from the cold and my nose was ready to run off of my face, but I didn't notice. I was a single circle away from activating the spell, from getting my sister back. I carefully slid The Eye of Graeae out of my pack, unwrapped it, and set it in the exact center of the circle.

All that was left was to finish the second circle, the ancient fae runes that controlled magical energy the same way modern dwarvish runes controlled natural forces. The runic sentence was, essentially, a workaround that allowed non-magical creatures, like humans, to harness and shape magical forces. When Rutledge had given Cassandra that spell, he hadn't just given her the ability to open a door through the wall, he'd given her Pandora's Box.

Anyone could work magic if they learned how to marry the sentence with the spell. Delilah and I had been working on that relationship for more than two years and had only managed a few working spells. Roughly half of them had exploded, giving the Boom Room its nickname.

And I was about to join the two spells on the fly with no experimentation and pray they worked. My hands trembled, which was not ideal for rendering perfectly shaped magical symbols, but I could not stop them, and I was too close to give up.

Now just the outer circle, the one that would contain and force the magical energy into the symbols to power the spell.

"Gwen, stop!"

I flinched but continued pouring and didn't look up. If Tony meant to stop me, he was too late.

A long, forlorn cry made the hairs on my arms stand at attention. That was Aristotle.

"Stay out of the circle," I yelled, only a foot from closing it.

"Don't do this!" Tony yelled. His voice was closer, but not close enough.

The last grains of sand dribbled out of the opening, closing the circle.

But nothing happened.

I stood near the eye, panting, sweat dripping down the tip of my nose, staring at my symbols. But there was nothing.

Tony stopped just outside the circle, hands on his knees as he recovered from what must have been quite a run.

The circle was dead.

"What did I do wrong?" I asked, and my voice was small and querulous. All this work, the late nights and hours of study, for what? For Lia to be just as far from me now as she was the moment she disappeared.

"What did I do wrong!?" I threw my hands up to the sky for answers.

I had been so certain this would be it. This was the key to Lia. My sister's laugh, her hugs, her trust and belief in me, even when I didn't deserve it. The way she always smelled like parchment and lemon.

It should have worked. The spell was correct, the activation runes were correct, the circle was unbroken, and the eye sat in its place of honor, ready to channel the energy directly into the...I knelt down and examined the crystal.

How could I have been so stupid?

I turned the ball slowly until the jade pupil pointed at the spell itself. Then I unbuttoned the jacket and slipped a knife from the sheath at the small of my back.

Magic, all magic, came with a cost. This spell had demanded the life of both Cassandra the witch and all five of her sacrifices. Of course, it would not activate without a commitment. I dragged the blade of the knife across the side of my hand and turned it so the pooling blood dripped to patter on the runes.

Energy hit the circle like a lightning strike, Aristotle cannoned into my chest, and a wall of blue light shot into the sky, separating Tony and me.

"No!" Tony yelled, but the sound was muffled by the energy swirling in the light. He raised his hands to hit the barrier but remembered what happened to him the first time and growled in frustration, hands balled into impotent fists.

Blue light from the outer ring of fae runes struck the back of the eye, which began glowing with first a pale light but was soon so incandescent with magical energy it would have blinded me if I looked at it. When I thought it might explode, power blazed out of the pupil to be sucked up by the inner ring of magic symbols that came to life one at a time.

"Gwen...Gwen, please don't do this." Tony's voice sounded weak and far away.

Aristotle dug his claws into the fabric of my jacket and beat his wings hard enough to send my cap flying off my head, as if he could somehow pull me away from the circle. The cap hit the outer barrier and snapped, like a strand of hair in a flame, and went up in smoke.

A door slowly appeared, first a weak rectangle of translucent light, but it gained solidity with every passing second as a new rune lit with power. My heart beat so hard it was the only thing I could hear, and my whole body shook with the force of it.

Aristotle bit my ear, cawing and pulling at my clothes, but I simply stood and stared, waiting for Lia to materialize in the door as she had the first time.

Two symbols left.

One symbol.

No Lia.

Where was she?

"Gwen!"

The final symbol lit. Blue light flowed toward the door frame and spiderwebbed across, making the door shimmer, then fade. No, not fade. It was like watching frost melt from a window pane. The light that had created the door faded and pulled back toward the glowing frame. The portal was empty, and beyond it was a country that defied description.

"Lia?" I breathed.

She wasn't there.

Aristotle released my jacket and dropped like a stone with his claws extended toward the eye.

"No!" I shouted, reaching toward him, panicked, but it was too late. He struck the crystal on one side; the pupil shifted and the spell began to lose power. I picked up the bird, determined to shake him until his tail feathers fell out, but something else happened.

The pressure building inside the circle was too great. It needed somewhere to escape, and the open doorway was the only path.

The grass inside the circle bent as if under a strong wind. Both handles on my satchel were picked up and pointed at the door. My hair dragged itself loose from the few remaining pins and flew toward the door like a flag, along with the edges of my jacket and the hem of my skirt.

It was something like being sucked up by a tornado. And I couldn't run, because the power hadn't yet dissipated from the outer circle. The suction increased, pulling at me until I had to brace myself against it, clutching Aristotle against my chest and digging into the turf with my walking boots.

"What's happening? Gwen, what is happening?!"

The last thing I saw in the mortal world was Tony's grief-stricken face, distorted through a haze of blue light, as the vacuum pulled me off my feet and sucked me backward through the magic door.

It was like breaking the surface of the water when you swam too deep, combined with the painful tingles of heating your frozen hands by a fire. All of the air was sucked from my lungs, my entire body convulsed, heat washed over me, and I landed with a painful jolt on my back.

How long I lay there gasping as the world spun I could not say, but I held a weakly squirming Aristotle against my chest and said, "You"—pant—"are a very"—pant—"naughty bird."

14

You

GWEN

When I opened my eyes, I found myself lying on my back staring at a blue sky through leaves rustled by a warm wind. I was cushioned on fragrant moss, and the air was sweet. Was I still in Wainwright, or was I dead? The longer I stared, the more uncanny the place felt.

I sat up, wincing at the dull, body-wide soreness, and ignored Aristotle as he hopped back and forth while making distressed noises. This was his fault, after all.

I ran my fingertips across the moss, soft as a feather mattress with little white flowers poking their heads up at intervals, and realized suddenly what was wrong: I had created the magic circle in the dead of *winter*. This wood was at the height of late spring.

It both looked and felt like the Wainwright forest, but the birdsong was more musical, more harmonious than I was used to. And while it was near twilight, the air was warm enough to make me want to remove my jacket.

"Oh alright," I told Aristotle as he picked at my sleeve with his beak. "Come on."

He climbed up to my shoulder and hid his head beneath my hair, which hung in a tangled mess down my back. Lovely. I made to stand, stretching sore muscles as I did so, and realized something else about the wood that eluded me: it was alive.

Of course, you might be thinking, *forests are alive, Gwenevere,* and you would be right. But this forest was *alive.* The sound of the wind in the leaves was purposeful, an echo of soft voices, not merely noise. And the trees were not dumb vegetation but ladies gathered to whisper behind their fans about the newcomer to the party.

I expected the usual sense of the organic chaos of life in a wood, the imperfections and random course life takes when it grows, changes, and dies. But every twig and leaf had been planned with harmonious purpose. This was not a place where life fought and adapted until it was slowly overcome by entropy. This place was created to sustain indefinitely at the peak of beauty.

It was less like a forest, and more like a painting of a forest. An idea, not reality, yet enchanting nonetheless.

Forgive me if I did not do the description justice; it is difficult to translate the experience of being in a different world.

It was that feeling, more than anything else, that convinced me I was in the Sunset Lands. I had made it to the other side of the wall.

And Ophelia was here, somewhere.

That thought sobered me enough that some of the sense of confused wonder evaporated and my brain jumped back into more practical thinking. I found my pack nearby, but neither the book nor the eye had been sucked through the door with me. Was that comforting or worrying?

Aristotle wormed further beneath my hair, disappearing almost entirely, but he was warm against my neck so I didn't mind. If I had to be stuck in the Sunset Lands, I was glad he was with me, even if it was his fault. When I pulled the pack onto my back, he stood on it instead of clinging to my jacket.

Now that I was here, I needed a plan. Could I find Lia and get the both of us home? Every bit of information about the fae that I read, heard from old storytellers or saw in person floated to the top of my mind like lily pads on a pond.

Perhaps I would need none of it, and everything I learned was a garbled, mistranslated version of the past. But anything that could help me, even a bit, was worth remembering. I refused to think about Mama or the children, pushed Tony's grief-stricken face from my mind, and set off through the faerie woods.

Before long, it was clear this was, in fact, Wainwright forest. It was too familiar to be anything else. I found trees and rock formations where I expected to see them, only perfected when compared to their mortal counterparts. Was some alternate version of the manor also nearby?

It was worth a look. As I headed in the general direction of the castle, I exited the less traveled part of the forest, expecting to find a footpath in short order. What I found was not like any footpath I had ever seen. In the forest I was familiar with, the paths were all packed dirt. Small, round, white flowers carpeted this path, and arching bluebells lined it, glowing like tiny lamps.

I wanted to pull off my shoes and feel the cool petals against the soles of my feet. Which, if I had learned anything about the fae, was likely dangerous. Would I be bound to take the path as soon as I set foot on it? Or was it only what it appeared to be: a more comfortable way to navigate the wood?

Should I follow the path and take whatever appeared at the end, or beat my way through the undergrowth and remain in hiding until I learned more? Obvious answers may be traps in fae lands, but the wood itself was likely equally dangerous.

When I saw Lia through the magic door what felt like ages ago, she was dressed as a medieval queen surrounded by soldiers. That suggested she was not making a secret living in the woods. I gathered up my courage and stepped out of the brush and onto the path.

Aristotle bit my ear.

"Ow! Aristotle, this is not the time for a tussle. Come out of there."

But he was on my back with his claws dug into my pack, and it was impossible to reach him, tangled in my hair as he was.

"I do not have time for this, you little beast," I growled as I bent backward and fought to untangle him with no luck.

"Don't go," he whispered in my ear.

I froze. "What do you mean?"

"Don't go to the castle."

I spun, trying to get a look at the bird's face. He always had something of a masculine voice, likely from whoever had first taught him to speak, but this was a man's voice, not a bird's.

Had being in the Sunset Lands done something to him?

"Why not?"

"It isn't safe for you. Stay in the woods. Hide."

"God's breath, Aristotle. How would you know that? Wait. Here, come out."

I managed to get hold of one ankle and pry the bird off his desperate grip on my pack. He spread his wings wide, as if he meant to intimidate me, and eyed me sideways. I could have laughed at him if his human-like warning hadn't scared me so much.

"Why isn't it safe?"

The bird didn't answer but kept his wings flared. I rubbed his chest with my free hand to see if I could calm him, but his posture never changed.

"I cannot hide in the woods. I wouldn't know what was safe and what to avoid. Something that might be safe for us in mortal lands may kill us here."

"I will help you," he whispered.

I snorted, partly at him but mostly at myself for having this conversation with a bird. "You are as mortal as I am," I said, chucking him under his bird chin. "I don't see how you would be of any help telling the difference."

Aristotle's wings dropped to hang limply at his sides, and he looked down like he was ashamed.

I brought him close for a cuddle. "It's not your fault you don't...unless it is."

I held the raven at arm's length. My hand was shaking, and he still would not look at me.

"No," I whispered. "No, I am being paranoid. That is expected in extraordinary circumstances. I am assigning meaning to things that are mere coincidences. Aren't I?"

My heart pounded so hard it was all I could hear, and I couldn't catch my breath. With a small sound of protest, I sank to my rear on the pathway. Aristotle hopped off my arm as I dropped my head into my hands, but they started to tingle and go numb.

"Breathe," I told myself. "This place is playing tricks on your mind. You are not hallucinating. You know who you are. You remember your past. This is real. And you will not throw up, by god. Get it together, Gwen. Get it together."

"You're fine, Gwen. Stop. Stop, just breathe."

"I'm fine," I repeated.

"Just breathe."

"Breathe," I said, and pulled a slow breath in through my nose, held it, and let it out through pursed lips.

Pale, elegant, long-fingered hands closed around my wrists. I stared at the familiar hands as if they were the only solid things left in the world. The last time I had seen these hands, they were holding cards.

I leaned back and my eyes followed the hands to wrists covered in fine black wool, wide shoulders, a broad chest, a snowy waterfall of a cravat, a stubborn chin, a mouth turned down in distress, but as beautifully carved as a statue. A straight, narrow-bridged nose. Black curls falling over his forehead. Thick brows drawn up in the center. Eyes as dark as coals.

"You?" I breathed.

He shrugged. "I'm afraid so."

Every time I had seen this man in the past came rushing back to me: at Mama's ball, at Lady Chatsworth's party, and afterward on the balcony when I had practically assaulted Tony. He'd given me the necklace that led me to Cassandra Monmouth, and told me the poem that unlocked the truth about the Reavers, letting me save both Percy and Thistle Honeycutt, the missing housekeeper.

He crouched in front of me, watching me remember, reading the changing expressions on my face, and winced at the knowledge in my eyes. I jerked my wrists out of his hands and stood, but he followed suit and towered over me.

"You!"

He raised both hands in a calming motion. "Look, keep your voice down, alright? I can explain everything, but"—looking over his shoulder toward the castle—"not here."

He reached for my hand, but I jerked out of his grasp and backed away. "Don't touch me."

"Lady St. James—Gwen, please—"

"And don't call me by my first name, you...you..." I could not think of a curse strong enough and settled with the clever and cutting insult, "You raven!"

He dropped his hands and rolled his eyes. "That was beneath you."

"You cannot decide what is beneath me, you lying wretch!"

"Gwen," he warned, "keep your voice down. We need to get out of here. Do you understand me? We are both in great danger. We have to leave."

"I am not going anywhere with *you*, and I am certainly not leaving without my sister."

"You will regret it if you go to the castle. There is nothing for you there."

But I was not in the mood to be intimidated or coddled. Anger was so much better than fear, and both were preferable to the panic I felt moments ago, or the grief trying to settle on my shoulders when I thought about my life with Aristotle, every private moment, the tears, the laughter, the way I had been more honest, more exposed to that bird than to anyone else in my life.

"No." I shook my head and flexed my hands. "You do not get to tell me what to do. How dare you think that you have any right to—"

In a flash, the man was on top of me, one hand clamped over my mouth and the other at the small of my back, pressing me against him from chest to hips. He leaned down until his face was inches from mine and warned, "Be. Quiet. Now, you can come with me of your own free will, or I will pick you up and carry you, but you cannot stay here and you absolutely can not go to the castle."

I froze, but it was not because his body was warm or his breath smelled inconceivably like red wine. It was because stillness looked like submission. After a moment of searching my eyes, he nodded and stepped back, thinking I had seen reason. But reason fled and all I saw was a chance to attack.

"Gwen!" He barked, but it was too late.

I unleashed every bit of fury I had, throwing punches, kicks, and other moves I had not had the chance to practice in ages. He side-stepped, parried, or ducked every attempted attack as if I were an untrained child, which only infuriated me more.

"Gwen, stop," he grunted, parrying a jab and leaning out of the way of a cross. "There is nothing for you in the castle, and we don't have time to—" The right hook nearly hit his self-assured chin, but he caught my fist and held it. I swung the other, but he caught that, too, and said, "—this. You are not safe here."

With almost no effort, he spun me by my fists until my back was to him, wrapped one arm around my waist, and picked me up like a toddler, pushing all the air from my lungs. I didn't have the strength or the speed to stop him.

I had been right the first time I saw him. He was dangerous.

"There," he said, taking a deep breath and adjusting the fit of his jacket with his free hand. "Let's get out of here. I'll explain everything once we're safe."

But I, naturally, did not go quietly. I was too angry to think straight, so I wriggled like a landed fish, kicked, and unleashed a string of invectives that would have made Mrs. Chapman blush from shoes to hairline.

"Put me down you wretched, poxy-faced, lily-livered, son of a flea-bitten goat and a—"

He turned around, ignoring me and my struggles.

"Mangey donkey! You long-faced, lying weasel! You—"

"Gwen—long-faced?"

"Crusty, pustule-filled—"

"Halt!"

He froze, I stopped cursing, and he heaved a resigned sigh. I raised my head to see two breathtaking creatures in shining armor standing on the path, one with a silver spear and the other with a crossbow, both leveled at us. They might have been human if it wasn't for the long, lean lines of their limbs and the backward bend of their legs. Their elongated muzzles peeking beneath helmets fashioned like canine faces.

I suspected, in mortal lands, they would have been hounds.

We turned, or I should say that he turned with me dangling in a very undignified way from one arm. "Lovely, Gwen. Now look what you've done."

"You're one to talk," I muttered.

The guards lunged, Aristotle said, "Shit," and I was free, tumbling onto the path on hands and knees.

"Stop him!" one guard barked, but they were not fast enough. A raven disappeared in a whir of feathers, leaving me alone.

Alone.

He left me.

I was too stunned and tired to fight.

They bound and gagged me, dropped a sack over my head, and led me away as a prisoner. Which was not at all what I had planned.

Nothing sounded as it ought. Footsteps didn't echo properly, and silence wasn't only the absence of noise but a kind of low, melodic background hum. Smells were similarly unexpected. I had not noticed until my eyes were covered, but the odor of decaying vegetation did not exist in the forest. Instead, the rich scent of green things and the light, powdery aroma of flowers perfumed the air.

But, as we walked, those scents gave way to richer, wilder smells that had no mortal counterparts. Some things were familiar but not in the right combinations. The guards, who were also hounds of some kind, smelled of wind, rain, and the coppery tang of blood, but also of...coffee?

They jerked to a stop, and the guard holding my elbow in one oddly shaped hand cleared his throat.

"What do you have there, Harl?" a feminine voice asked. The sound of it made a shiver run down my spine, but I couldn't say why.

"A trespasser, lady. We caught her fighting in the forest." His voice sounded like the words were growled between clenched teeth.

"Fighting? Truly? How delicious. Who was she fighting?"

"The Raven."

A beat of surprised silence. Her voice was not so confident when she said, "The Raven? You are sure of this?"

"Sure as I can be."

"Lock her up until the King calls for her," she said, at last. Even I could not miss the apprehension in her tone.

Harl grunted and the dragging continued.

We stopped walking a short time later, and someone untied my wrists. I ripped the bag off my head in time to see Harl disappear, but not behind a closed door. I was not in a room made of stone, as I expected a cell to be. It looked like the inside of a tree, with walls of living wood and a floor of the same soft moss I noticed in the forest. Instead of a door of iron bars, the wood simply grew back to cover the passage.

It was as if a door had never been there.

If I hadn't been gagged, my mouth would have hung open in shock. This was a prison inside a tree, one that responded to the guard's wishes. Was that magic, or simply a property of the world, here? And where was the light coming from?

Luminous mushrooms, something like wood ears, grew along the ceiling and cast a soft, pale green light about the chamber. It would have been magical if it wasn't a prison cell. It was also silent and lonely.

I did not even have a window.

How long I stood in pure stupefaction, staring at the blank wall, I could not say. There was no way to mark the time unless I counted breaths or heartbeats, and that required more focus than I could muster.

I'd abandoned Sam, Sally, Tony, my mother, and everyone else I cared about to bring my sister home, and instead, I was stuck in a faerie prison with no means of escape save what I brought with me and the words of a woman I hadn't even seen.

Lock her up until the King calls for her.

How long would I wait?

Would they feed me in the meantime? Faeries were notoriously absent-minded where mortal needs were concerned. What would my family think or do when Tony told them I was gone? A picture of Mama's face, as it crumpled in grief, flashed across my mind.

I sank to the floor and dug my fingers into the moss in frustration. It was as thick and soft as the carpets of Wainwright. I stretched out, defeated, buried my face in my arms, closed my eyes, and tried to sleep.

An indescribable sound made me shoot upright, bleary eyes struggling to focus as a shock of adrenaline electrified my limbs. Still too sleep-addled to trust my vision, it took a moment to believe what I saw; the wood on the opposite wall melted away into an arched door. It was like watching a tree grow but in reverse.

The creature who entered my cell was thin, swarthy, with long limbs and knobby joints. The tips of its ears poked far out to the sides of its head, and its pale eyes were huge, goggling above a long, slender nose. The simple garments of homespun wool—long socks, a belted smock, and pointed shoes—hung on a thin frame.

I was fairly certain that I was looking at a brownie, but I suspected it would be rude to ask for clarification.

It carried a garment tossed over one arm, a little embroidered velvet bag in the other, and crossed the room with a jerking motion that was something like watching a fawn learning to walk.

The brownie stopped in front of me, held out the garment and the bag, and said in a voice like crumpling paper, "Wear these."

I tucked my hands behind my back. "No."

I had to choke off the impulse to add thank you to the end of that sentence. Proper English manners would likely get me in a lot of trouble, especially if I indebted myself to a faerie simply by sharing my appreciation.

The brownie blinked as if my single-word statement had been confusing.

"My own clothing suits me just fine," I clarified.

The brownie wobbled forward and tossed the gown at me. I caught it on instinct. The little velvet bag was left on the floor, and the door closed up behind the brownie as it left.

I dropped the dress, for that's what it was, on top of the velvet bag and stomped to the other side of the room, muttering, "Wear these, indeed."

It took a good bit of grumbling and pacing to calm my nerves, perhaps twenty minutes as well as I could judge. The most logical explanation for being given such clothing was a presentation before the King. Were I to wear the dress, I would appear biddable and less dangerous...which would also make me appear weak. Worse, I would have no protection.

But if I refused, I would likely insult the King and start my foray into the Sunset Lands on dangerous footing. But I would, at least, be physically safer. Though wearing several knives and grenades in the presence of a fae monarch was a foolish political decision, even for me.

I was stomping down the last bit of moss over my hidden trove of weapons when the creaking startled me again. This time I watched the wood grain thin and compress, shifting like wet clay sculpted by an invisible finger.

The hound guardsmen entered, looked at my dirty coat and disheveled hair—not to mention my glorious black eye courtesy of Lord Rutledge—and gave me disapproving glares.

"You are not ready," one of them growled.

"I am perfectly ready."

They exchanged uncertain glances, shrugged in a way I interpreted to mean *it's her own fault*, and escorted me from the room by spearpoint.

I was going to see the King of the Faeries.

15

Royal Introductions Part 2

GWEN

My stay in the cell did not prepare me for the wonder of the fae court.

Both eyes nearly rolled from my head as I tried to take in every detail. We were not in a mere tree, as I suspected, but a palace, and one that had been grown, not built. Someone had coaxed trees and vines to grow in corridors with moss-covered floors and arched doorways. Instead of sconces filled with oil, electric, or dwarven lanterns, there were lamps made of blooming flowers that glowed from within, casting soft, luminous light.

Unlike the rough bark of my cell, these walls were smooth as granite and grey as the skin of a myrtle tree. Subtle wood grain caught the light and shimmered as we passed, like a tigers-eye stone. And that wasn't the worst of it.

The throne room was grand on an imperial scale and so deca-
dently luscious that I took deep breaths just to pull as much of it
into myself as possible.

White-barked trees grew in regular, matching pillars down each
side of the room, reaching all the way to the vaulted ceiling and
stretching their branches across it like exposed rafters. The ceiling
itself was a canopy of silvery leaves that overlapped so that no light
penetrated.

Dark vines curled down from the rafters to end in spectacular
chandeliers covered in wild roses. Each flower glowed from within,
as if a firefly rested in its heart, bathing the vast room in subtle
pink light and a fresh, sweet smell of wind and sun-warmed grass.
Beneath our feet was the same carpet of moss, but it was laid out
in repeating patterns of varying greens, like a mosaic, all the way to
the throne.

There was still more to see and process, to smell and feel, but it
was impossible to concentrate on the room, as spectacular as it was,
once I saw the people gathered on either side of the aisle.

Describing what I saw, even to myself, was possible only in vague
impressions because it was too overwhelming to comprehend:
dryads, nymphs, and gnomes, tall and regal, small and delicate,
round and full as an apple, curving as a river rock, soft as pussy
willow or lamb's ears, sharp as thistle and thorns, all creatures
gathered to watch as the human was paraded down the aisle.

Nearer the throne stood the Aes sidhe, the kings and queens of
the Sunset Lands, and they were something too fine to be called
merely beautiful. Just walking past them made my knees weak. I
had to call on every lesson, every battle I had ever fought, not to

sink to the ground and weep. None of my theoretical knowledge from years of study prepared me for the sheer, overwhelming presence of them.

In form, they were as humans, elves, or dwarves, but perfected, as the wood outside had been a perfected version of mortal woods. Whether their skin was dark or light, their bodies thin or round, their lips delicate or ripe, each one looked as if they had reached whatever form of perfection they had been created by the gods to celebrate.

Deep in my soul, I felt ashamed to stand before them in my imperfection, and blessedly grateful to have seen even one of them, just once. Tears stood in my eyes, but I did not bother to blink them away. It was too wonderful for words...and too terrible to bear. I regretted not wearing the faerie gown, simply to look a bit less like a dandelion in a rose garden.

At the head of the room rose a dais of smooth stone, and on it sat an elegant throne made of what looked like bone carved with vining flowers. When I saw the King, my first thought was of a sunset with horns. His skin was a golden bronze, like a tanned sportsman who spent all his time out of doors. His hair and beard were red-orange and shining, his eyes warm amber, and the translucent robe he wore over a bare chest was a rich magenta that faded to deep blue-black at the bottom.

He wore no crown, but the antlers rising from his head were decorated with dangling golden chains and jewels that caught and refracted the light into spinning rainbows. Had I seen nothing and no one but him, I would still have been spellbound.

The guards stopped us a dozen feet from the foot of the dais, the crowd of spectators murmured (even their harmonic mutters were goosebump-inducing) and the King tilted his head, sending rainbows cascading across the floor.

"So," he said in a voice like distant thunder, "this is the trespasser. A strange creature to violate my borders. How did you come to be here, human child? Answer me truthfully, for your life is at stake."

It took every bit of willpower and all my presence of mind to answer the question while remaining upright. "I had no intention of violating your borders, your highness. Only of trying to find my sister."

"And you thought to find her here?"

"I saw your folk take her when we were young."

He leaned forward and narrowed his eyes. That simple gesture made me want to prostrate myself and beg forgiveness, though I had done nothing wrong. "Did you, indeed? How did you see such a thing?"

The pain of the memory came flooding back, and it was somehow bracing, like a strong cup of coffee or being dunked in freezing water. I settled a bit more into my body, and said, "She stepped into a faerie circle in the wood near our home."

The King scoffed and waved a hand. "Stepping into a circle where the wall is weak is an invitation, human child. This is known."

"But she did not know it, your majesty. Your folk have been gone for so long that my people regard your stories as myths and tall tales."

"Misunderstanding the truth does not change it. Now, tell me how you came to be in my lands."

I wanted to push further, to ask if my sister had passed this way, but his command weighed on me with unstoppable force. So I took a gamble. "I used a spell hoping to locate her, but as you can see, it did not have the intended effect."

The crowd muttered, and the King stiffened ever-so-slightly. "You are no witch. I'd set my oath on it."

He hadn't asked a question, so I didn't answer. Explaining the techniques Delilah and I had worked out would be a bad idea, especially since they were based on the combination of fae symbols, human magic, and artifice. Faeries were notoriously curious and covetous of information and novelty. If they thought I could give them that, they'd never allow me enough freedom to escape and find Lia.

"How did you cast the spell?" he asked after a moment.

"I asked a witch to cast it for me," I lied.

That seemed to satisfy him, and provide me with an important piece of information: I could lie and get away with it.

"You find yourself here, then, by a whim of fate," he said, opening both hands to the sides. "What think your human eyes of the Fae Court?"

I knew a bid for flattery when I heard it, so I gave him what he wanted, even though it was nothing more than the truth. "It makes my soul sing to see it, Your Majesty. There is nothing in the mortal lands to compare."

He sat back, the hint of a pleased smile on his face. "How did you come to be in the presence of the Raven? It is a shame you found such a poor guide, child. Though my guards tell me they discovered you fighting him"—the crowd tittered at that—"so perhaps your judgment is more sound than you deserve credit for."

"The Raven, sire?"

His amusement faded. "My guards report seeing him with you in the forest."

"I do not contest their testimony, sire, but I know nothing of The Raven."

"She lies."

The female voice was clear and cold, like church bells in the winter, and seemed to echo off the vaulted ceiling and reverberate in my chest.

"Please join us, General," the King said, "and expose this lie if it be so."

The crowd parted, and a woman in green stepped onto the path. She strode forward, her steps firm and decided, her blonde hair braided intricately down her back. When she reached the foot of the dais, she turned and faced us.

All the air rushed from my lungs so fast I saw stars. The guards caught me before I wobbled to the ground, but every time I tried to take a breath, my lungs squeezed closed again.

"Perhaps you are most suited to deal with this matter," the King said, tilting his head toward the woman.

"You honor me, my king," she said.

Another spear of pain nearly sent me to the ground.

She turned hazel eyes on me, and the world stopped. Those eyes belonged to my sister, but the woman staring down at me was not smiling and fiery. She was carved of ice disguised as spring. It wasn't

Lia, and yet, it was. The soft roundness of her childhood face sharpened into womanly beauty, but the edges were dangerous.

"Why do you lie to His Majesty?"

I opened my mouth, but nothing came out.

One blonde brow rose in derision. "If you will not speak freely, we will drag the words from you. Where is The Raven?"

The only word I managed to push past my numb lips was, "What?"

"Restrain her."

Guardsman took me by the arms in bruising grips.

"To her knees before the King."

My knees hit the moss floor, and still, my brain would not process what was happening.

"You were seen in company with The Raven, a servant and asset of the King, who disappeared these many years. Why were you in his company?"

I tried to speak, but words eluded me.

Lia with flowers in her hair. Lia laughing and blushing as I read her passages from a recently pilfered romance novel. Lia punching the stable boy in the nose when he pulled my braids. Lia holding my hand and saying, "Sisters protect each other."

"Harl," she said, lifting her chin and glaring at me down the length of her nose. Her hazel eyes were so cold, like spring grass locked beneath the last frost of winter. "Let us see if we can loosen her tongue. Five lashes ought to do it."

Somehow, between her orders and my next breath, my coat had been pulled down over my shoulders, exposing my back and trapping my arms. Yet I could not drag my eyes from her face. She would not do this. She couldn't. Not my Lia.

Harl shook out a lash, the leather whispering as coils loosened and rubbed against one another in anticipation. It was a dry, hungry sound that sent a chill of fear slithering down my spine.

"With your permission, Majesty?" she asked.

Permission must have been given, because a cruel smile curled one corner of her lips, lips that had, once upon a time, whispered secrets to me in the dark.

Harl raised his arm, and I squeezed my eyes shut.

The crowd held its breath.

Thunderous flapping echoed through the hall. Leather whistled, someone gasped, and I grunted as I was struck from behind. It was like getting hit with a pillow the size of a cart. At the same time, a crack split the air...but there was no pain.

A familiar scent, wild as the wind across the moors, made me open my eyes to find long arms wrapped round my chest and a body pressed against my back.

Aristotle.

"Welcome home, Raven," Ophelia said, her voice cutting. "I am so glad you decided to join us."

"Don't move. Don't speak," he whispered in my ear. Then, louder, "That makes one of us, lady."

"How dare you come back to me now, and in the company of my kin? Is there no treachery beyond you?"

"I thought you enjoyed my treachery," Aristotle said, his voice heavy with innuendo. "Was that not your motivation for employing me in the first place?"

"To serve my needs, cur, not your own pathetic desires." She flicked her fingers in my direction without even looking at me and said, "Is this how you have been spending your time when you should have been serving your king? It is a pity the wall did not destroy you, as it has so many other cowards."

"A pity indeed, my lady. For if it had, I would not be forced to listen to you complain."

A shocked gasp rose from the crowd, and Ophelia's face—my sister's face—twisted into a mask of fury. But her voice was absolutely calm when she said, "Why do you force me to hurt you?"

She flicked her fingers and the whip fell again. Aristotle flinched against my back.

"Lia," I breathed, able to speak for the first time. "God's breath, what are you doing?"

"Silence," she snapped without looking at me. "Do not think our shared blood will save you."

The whip fell again. He jerked, and his arms tightened as if he had to use me to keep himself upright.

"Stop it!" I shouted, my thundering heart echoing in my ears. "Lia, stop this!"

Another crack. And another.

Aristotle panted against my neck, his whole body shaking, but he did not let go.

Another crack. I tried to wrench free but the guards had grips like manacles.

"Ophelia!"

She relented, turning her flinty gaze on me. "You should not have come here. This is no place for a powerless, plain human. What gifts do you bring the King that he should allow you to roam his lands? Neither great power, nor great beauty, nor skill worth the name. Better the King kill you now than allow you to continue to profane his court with your presence."

A keening sound pushed up my throat, choking me in its desperation to escape. Aristotle shook, but his arms were the only things holding me together.

"You are fierce, my general," the King said, approvingly. "But the Raven may yet be of use to us in the coming campaign, and to kill the human without cause would be a discourtesy to your blood. Are you certain she does not bear a gift like unto yours?"

"I am certain, Your Highness. She possesses nothing that makes her fit for your court."

"I see." The King sat back and stroked his red beard, staring at me like I was a riddle he would like the answer to, but not quite enough to put too much effort into figuring it out.

"Very well," he said, sitting straight and looking over my head to take in the entire court gathered in the hall. "We will test the human to see if her blood breeds true. Your family is owed that much, General. Three trials shall she be given, and if she fails to impress us—" He tilted his head, and the crowd made an excited, hungry noise.

"If it pleases your majesty," Lia said, "let these two be jailed together so my foolish sister might see the cost of her impertinence and intrusion."

A malicious grin curled one corner of the King's mouth beneath his mustache. "Perhaps it will teach her what to expect if she fails.

And remind The Raven of his place. Let it be done. Give them time to heal, and we will begin the trials."

Aris released me as guards hauled us to our feet, and the crowd cheered. Here was something exciting, something new, and the room fairly reeked of bloodlust. What would the trials entail, and would they kill me if I did not pass?

I should have been worried about those things, but my eyes and mind clung to Lia like she might disappear if my attention wavered. She stood beneath the king, her golden hair shining, a circlet of silver on her head, her eyes hard and her lips tight.

She was alive.

She was here.

And she hated me.

She did not even look in my direction as the guards dragged us out of the hall. I noticed nothing of the wonders of the fae court after that. The glamour of the place had been broken. My feet dragged with every step, and my breath came in jerky little hiccups that would turn into full-out sobs if I couldn't control them.

But I refused to collapse, not in front of those strange, staring eyes and beautiful faces. I raised my chin, clenched my jaw, and rode a wave of sorrow out of the hall like the duchess I was supposed to be.

But when we were shoved into the prison and the door of our cell grew back, turning the room again into a perfect circle of bark and moss where there were no listening ears or staring eyes, I let the weight of my pain drag me to the floor and pin me there.

"Well, that could have gone better," Aristotle said in a rasping voice.

He, too, was lying on the floor, his cheek pillowed on the moss, forehead covered in sweat. He had abandoned me and then saved me when my own sister would have had me whipped. How many times had he saved me, this lying raven? She even punished him for protecting me. Was he a liar or a hero?

What gifts do you bring to the King that he should allow you to roam his lands? Neither great power, nor great beauty, nor skill worth the name. Better the King should kill you now than allow you to continue to profane his court with your presence.

Sisters protect each other.

Aristotle shifted, and a groan pushed past his white lips. My grief was so heavy it was impossible to stand, so I crawled to him. The whip had shredded his shirt, leaving ragged strips of bloody fabric plastered to his back.

Jaw clenched, I tore the rest of his shirt to the hem and carefully peeled the strips away from his skin until his back was bare. His flesh was red, swollen, and torn. He needed stitches. He needed a doctor.

How was I supposed to clean and dress his wounds without water? Perhaps that was part of the punishment leveled on both of us. Ophelia's face as I last saw it floated in the back of my mind, her lip curled in a sneer.

Numb and too overwhelmed to think, I tore strips from the bottom of my skirt and mopped up as much of the blood as the fabric could retain. My hands shook too much to try mending the flaps of torn skin.

"I have to bind these," I warned him.

"Do it."

He winced and sucked air through his teeth as I tied the dressings in place as tightly as the thick fabric allowed. There was nothing else to be done after that, so I lay next to him and closed my eyes.

"Thank you," he said.

I didn't answer.

There was no reason to answer. There was no reason for anything.

16

Everything Ends

TONY

G wen was gone.

She was just...gone.

There was nothing left but a shovel, the cursed grimoire, the crystal, and a smoking circle of magic symbols. His legs began to shake.

She hadn't intended this; the panic on her face as the door sucked her backward made that much clear. But she had set herself up for it in this foolish attempt to retrieve her sister when she didn't even know where the woman was!

How could she have been so stupid?

She was supposed to test this spell with Delilah, to prove it would work the way she expected before...he sank to the turf and threw up on the grass, retching until everything he'd eaten for lunch sat in a steaming pile in front of him.

Tony fell backward and scooted away from his sickness. Cold air stung his lungs as he gasped in great, bracing breaths, trying to regain his composure. God's breath, he had to tell her mother and the children. His stomach threatened to revolt again, so he dropped his head between his knees and breathed through his teeth until he was composed enough to push himself to stand.

His feet.

Looking down at them, solid brown leather shoes on the wet turf, he knew they were supposed to be doing something. It took a moment to remember what. He lifted first one foot, then the other. At some point, he recovered the book and the crystal, leaving the shovel on the moor alone, and told his feet to carry him back to Wainwright.

Darkness blanketed the forest and lamps glowed on the porch when he stood outside the manor door, his arms full of proof Gwen had once existed. What could he say? How could he explain what happened to a woman who already lost one daughter? And the children...

Damn, he was cold.

Following Gwen's footprints without a jacket was stupid, but when he realized she left, he'd somehow known what she intended to do. There hadn't been time to gather his coat or his wits, only to bolt out the door and follow her with his heart in his throat. Now that he stood shivering on the doorstep, his brain didn't seem to want to cooperate. Gwen simply ceased to exist in the mortal world. Was she even still alive? Percy would know, wouldn't he? He should find Percy.

"Anthony?"

Tony looked up. He had wandered into the dining room. Five shocked faces stared at him, ten round, unblinking eyes boring into his chest. The duchess grabbed his elbow and dragged him toward the fire.

"Sally, dear, bring the whisky. Samuel, fetch a blanket, please. Here, Inspector, sit."

He swallowed the alcohol in a single gulp and the warmth settled like a burning coal in his stomach. Painful needles prickled his skin as he warmed beneath the blanket next to the fire. His mind swam back into motion, clinking and grinding like a claggy millworks as it picked up steam.

His mother held his face between her hands, searching his eyes with her own. "Are you well, my son?"

He swallowed, then croaked, "I'm fine, Mother, but I am not well."

The book and the crystal were heavy in his hands.

"Here," the Duchess said, "let me hold those while you drink this. Then you can tell us what happened."

She took Gwen's things before he could stop her and set them on the table like old mail not worth reading. He drank the tea. It was hot. Then he dropped his head into his hands and rubbed the sleet out of his hair, giving himself time to think, time to come up with a way to tell the Duchess of Wainwright her only living daughter was gone.

A way to tell Sam and Sally...

"Gwen is gone," he blurted, choking on the word as bile traced a stinging finger up the back of his throat. Sally gasped. His mother made a distressed sound. But the duchess said nothing. Lady St. James only watched him, her face grave and composed.

"Where has she gone?"

He forced the words out through the tightness in his chest, in his throat. What to say? What would keep them all safe but still be something close to the truth? Was she dead? Did that matter if she could never come back?

"She went looking for her sister."

The color drained from the duchess's face in a rush. She stood like a statue in a dinner dress, her trembling lips the only sign she was alive.

"What does that mean?" Sam demanded. "Sally, what does he mean? Where's Lady Gwen?"

Sally answered the question Tony could not. Clasping her hands so hard the tendons strained against her pale skin, she raised her chin and ignored the tears standing in her eyes. "My lady knows what she's doing. If she went to look for her sister, she will find her, and she will bring her back."

The duchess began to cry.

Tony found Sally in the library the next morning. Her skin had always been pale, but now it was transparent, purple veins showing at her temples, and dark smudges lining the undersides of her eyes. Strands of blonde hair escaped her messy braid, and the air around her chair smelled like stale tea thanks to the used teacups that littered the floor and table next to her.

"How long have you been awake?" he asked.

She looked up, glanced at the clock on the wall, and shrugged, making the book wobble in her hands. Fair enough. He wasn't certain if he had slept, either.

He gestured at the book with his chin. "I don't know if it is wise to read that."

"Why?"

"I was given to believe it was dangerous."

"It is. But Lady Gwen said—" She paused, cleared her throat, and continued. "Lady Gwen said we should learn the most about the things that are the most dangerous. Besides, this book helped her get through the wall, so it might help her get back."

"How did you figure that?"

She glared up at him and closed the book with a decisive thump. "I'm not stupid, Inspector. And I was helping. It wasn't hard to work out."

Tony nodded and stuffed his hands in his pockets. So Sally felt as responsible as he did. She was too young to bear a burden like that, but if he couldn't believe himself blameless, he doubted she could, either.

"She was supposed to test everything with Delilah first," was all he could say.

"I know. It's just that...if Sam was gone, and I thought I could find him..."

Tony pursed his lips to keep from frowning. He didn't want her to see or feel his disapproval. That was the last thing she needed.

"Will you make me a promise?" he asked.

She blinked up at him, blue eyes wide. Sally was truly growing into a beautiful woman. He hoped Gwen would be there to see it. "Don't try to cast any of those spells or do any of the magic, alright? If something happened to you, I doubt Sam would bear it well. And I have the feeling the duchess will need you very much until Gwen comes home."

Tears gathered in her eyes and spilled onto her cheeks. She needed to hear that someone else believed Gwen would come back. "I promise."

"And you will tell me what you learn?"

"I will."

He gave her a weak smile, patted her arm, and left to find Samuel.

The boy took longer to locate than his sister, but Tony wasn't surprised to spot him sitting on the lowest branch of a leafless oak, his long legs dangling.

"Hullo, Sam. What are you doing out here?"

"Couldn't stay inside," Sam said as he picked at the bark with one fingernail. "Too sappy in there."

Dishwater hair a shade or two darker than his sister's fell in his face, shielding his expression from Tony's gaze. But he saw the boy's mouth working, pursing and curling as if he had so many things to say that his lips couldn't form the shapes for all the words at once.

Tony tried to put as much confidence into his voice as he could when he said, "She'll be back. You know that, don't you?"

The boy shrugged. "Why should I care?"

Tony's brows lowered. What did that mean?

"Me and Sally are rich now, and we never have to go back on the streets, so what do I care if Lady Gwen leaves? I got what I need."

Tony looked down at his hands, trying, and failing, to formulate a response. "The duchess said you and Sally can stay here as long as you'd like."

"So? We don't need her, either."

"That's beneath you, Sam. The duchess is a kind woman who only wants to help."

Sam raised his head, his eyes bright with anger and wet with unshed tears, jaw clenched so hard the muscles stood out. He dropped from the tree branch, pointed a finger at Tony, and said, "Everyone wants to help the poor orphans, don't they? Until something better comes along. Well, we don't need the duchess, or Lady Gwen, or you!"

Sam pushed him with both hands, baring his teeth and panting as he shouted, "Maybe we just want people to leave us alone!" And pushed him again. "We don't need her charity or your pity!"

"Sam—"

"No!"

The boy made to push him once more, but Tony caught his wrists and jerked him forward, wrapping him in a tight embrace that he couldn't wiggle out of no matter how much he fought.

"Let me go!"

"No."

"Get off me! You rotten, self-righteous, bastard!"

Tony just squeezed harder, waiting out the storm as Sam fought the emotions battering him.

Finally, he went limp, though his chest heaved. He said softly, "Let me go."

"Nope."

The shaking started in his chest, radiated out, and soon Sam convulsed with sobs. He wrapped his arms around Tony, gripping fistfuls of jacket as he buried his face against Tony's neck.

There was nothing left to do but hold on.

The eight-hour train ride back to town was much less pleasant in third class. The duchess offered to buy his ticket, but he declined. She already cared for his parents. It felt wrong to allow her to do more, especially with Gwen gone.

That thought soured his stomach, even though he hadn't been able to eat anything since watching her disappear.

Sally remained steadfast, believing Gwen would come back, but how? According to Gwen, her sister was kidnapped at sixteen and had never made it back through the wall, though she must have tried. Of course, he'd heard it said people lost their memories in faerie and that time passed differently. Perhaps Ophelia had gotten lost in the magic.

Perhaps Gwen would, too.

Then again, Gwen was...well...Gwen. If anyone could come back from the other side of the wall, it was her. He'd never met anyone so frustratingly determined.

But he still saw her in his memory, Aristotle clutched to her chest, panic twisting her face as magic pulled her backward through the door and out of this world. She might have expected to blow herself up, but she had not anticipated *that* which made it hard to believe anything. Or perhaps, made it easier to believe everything. He wasn't certain which was worse.

He was certain that the Marquis of Rutledge was a criminal and a danger to the realm and to those he loved. And now that his family was as safe as possible, it was time to do something about the man responsible for so much death, responsible for bringing back the book that made it possible for Gwen to be stolen from everyone who loved and needed her in their lives.

But first, Tony had a few questions.

Sleet and soggy piles of dirty, half-frozen snow lined the edges of the streets as Tony made his way to Scotland Yard. He carefully avoided the worst puddles, but his shoes were wet, nonetheless. Hiring a hansom would have been smart, but he needed the exercise to take the edge off his temper and the cold air to clear his mind of the dangerous thoughts swirling there.

Killing Lord Rutledge was not the right answer to his problems. Even if it would make him feel better.

Probably.

The Yard was abuzz when he entered, people scurrying back and forth like ants, whispering and gesticulating, eyes flashing everywhere to make certain no one was close enough to hear.

What on earth?

Tony's hand flashed out to catch the lapels of a passing constable. The man flinched and turned an angry expression on Tony, only to see the look on his face and shrink away.

"Inspector Hardwicke, sir. What can I do for you?"

"What has happened?"

"The disappearances, sir. Have you not heard?"

Tony's fist tightened, making the cloth creak beneath his fingers. "Would I be asking you if I had?"

The constable swallowed. "I suppose not, sir. Ah—several members of the House of Lords have disappeared overnight, all members who opposed the new legislation. You know, the Equal Representation—"

"Yes, I know. Get on with it. Who has disappeared and how do you know they've not simply left town?"

"Because they told no one of their plans, were seen the day before yesterday going about their normal routines, went back to their houses, and then haven't been seen since. No signs of a struggle, no notes, nothing. And the telegrams we sent to their country estates have come back with no answers. The lords aren't in residence."

Tony dropped the man, took a deep breath, and surrendered to his investigative instincts. "Who?"

"The Lords Hargarave, Blumshire, Rutledge—"

"What?"

"...What?"

"Did you say the Marquis of Rutledge is among the missing?"

"Yes, sir."

"Have the detectives already gone out to the townhouses?"

"Of course, sir."

Tony swore and strode away, leaving the constable standing in shock as the rest of the officers swirled about him. He only stopped in his office long enough to secure more ammunition for his pistol before heading back out into the cold. If this conspiracy extended as far into the government as Gwen suspected it did, he might be too late.

Constables swarmed the townhouse, taking notes, asking the servants questions, carrying bags of evidence, and generally making the entire place unfit for any proper investigation. If there had been any footprints or other evidence worth considering, it was gone.

"Who is in charge of this investigation?" he demanded of the first constable he saw.

"I am."

At the sound of that voice, Tony's jaw tightened and his hands curled into fists. Before he turned to face the man, he took a deep, steadying breath and forced his shoulders to relax.

"Chief Inspector Mac Sweeney," Tony said with admirable self-control.

"Hello, Tony. What are you doing, here?"

Tony raised his hands as if it should be obvious. "I thought you might like another set of eyes on this case, given all the attention it's getting."

"And you thought your eyes were the ones I needed, eh?" Mac Sweeney said as he folded his skinny arms over his chest and waggled his mustache, unable—or unwilling—to hide the amusement in his voice.

"I've got one of the best track records in the region," Tony said reasonably.

"Aye, you do, that. Unfortunately for you, you don't have the right."

Reminding himself that breathing was an important aspect of keeping one's temper, he took two whole breaths before he responded. "You can assign me to the case."

The man laughed, his small dark eyes twinkling the way light glinted off the edge of a blade. "No, I can not."

"Why?"

"Because you don't work for Scotland Yard anymore. Do you not check your mail? Oh don't look so surprised," Mac Sweeney said, disgusted. "You knew this would happen. I did warn you, after all."

Hitting the man in the face would not be a very good idea, even if the sight of his nose split down the middle made a warm little glow flicker in Tony's chest. So he said, instead, in a low, vicious whisper, "How long have you been under Rutledge's thumb?"

"What a thing to suggest," Mac Sweeney scoffed, but his smile was full of spite. Proof that he was fired for helping Gwen escape

Lord Rutledge. "You can pick up your last month's pay from the bursar. Have your office cleaned out by next week."

Unless he really was going to punch the man, here in front of half of the PCs in New London, he needed to leave. Now. But he couldn't resist leaning down and leaving the corrupt CI with a final thought.

"You realize, Mac Sweeney, that all you've accomplished is to take the leash off a dog who bites."

Mac Sweeney clearly wanted to say something clever about Tony comparing himself to a dog (the opportunity was too tempting to pass up) but the expression on his face must have reminded the man that dogs have teeth and Tony's were sharper than most.

Mac Sweeney, however, couldn't let a subordinate have the last word. He rallied, puffed up his chest, and said, "Firing you was a mercy, Tony. Go find something useful to do and keep your head down. Dogs who bite get shot. Remember that."

Tony stared down at him long enough to make a promise with his eyes, and then turned and walked away without looking back.

He spent his entire career operating under the rule of law, making his decisions based on what was right rather than what was expedient, believing law enforcement stood between the innocent and those willing to do harm. And while that allowed him to catch too many offenders to count, it also stopped him from realizing that the real corruption didn't lie with the common thieves and lowly criminals.

Those were the symptoms of the problem, not the cause.

The rot was thickest at the root, and it started with men in power; men like Rutledge and Mac Sweeney. Knowing he had been part of that system, had supported it for years, made his gorge rise. It didn't matter that he was unaware of the corruption. He probably could have found it if he'd bothered to look. Instead, he'd kept his head down and done his job.

He'd served the law.

But rules written by men like Rutledge could never be just, not when they corrupted the very systems meant to protect people. Sickness swirled in his gut as his mind replayed every arrest, every pat on the back he received for bringing in another criminal. He'd joined the Yard to protect families like his. Instead, he'd become a knife in the hand of a broken system.

Tony didn't know how many sleepless nights of regret were waiting for him, but he did know one thing: he no longer had to answer to the law.

He would cut out the rot one swing of the axe at a time and pray it was enough.

17

The Raven

GWEN

"Gwen?"

The line between awake and asleep blurred so far that time and place lost their meaning. I thought while I slept and dreamed while awake. The past twelve years rolled through my mind like a breaking wave, drowning everything in its path: the traveling, the hours of study, the near-death experiences, and the endless searching for a way to bring Lia back.

I wanted to feel whole again, to feel less alone, to mend that broken part of me that called her name over and over. Now I knew that wound would never heal.

The hole would never be filled.

"Gwen?"

To survive after losing Lia, I dug a deep pit in my soul and walled myself inside. While I had never given up trying to find her, testing everything from standing in faerie circles and leaving offerings near faerie mounds at twilight, to following will-o'-the-wisps into the woods, the fae would not take me.

Perhaps Lia was right and nothing about me made me worthwhile enough to steal. Perhaps I had dug my pit so deep that no one could see me at the bottom of it. No matter the cause, I was used to my pit and the walls around it. At least, until the spell changed everything.

The grimoire had given me the most terrible gift of all: hope. Which had become a set of stairs. Now I stood on the top step with the pit behind me, staring out into sun-drenched lands, only to realize I would never enter them or feel their warmth on my face.

Lia didn't want me.

The pain was so sharp that I did not feel the cut. I only knew that I was bleeding.

"Is it safe to say that I told you so, or should I wait until after you've had a good cry? It is always so difficult to tell with humans."

I would not cry. There was nothing left inside me. Crying was for people who still had a bit of their soul left to leak out of their eyes. I was just...empty.

"You will recall that I warned you about this. I told you that you would regret coming here. Your sister has been changed by her stay in the Sunset Lands. She cannot help it if she is a bloodthirsty shrew."

I closed my eyes and squeezed them shut.

"You saw her. She is an absolute monster. Imagine what the woman is like when no one is watching. She probably peels off that gorgeous face to give the monster underneath a break from the lies."

My hands clenched into fists, and I pressed them against the sides of my head.

"I would say it was a miracle the King hasn't had her killed yet, but I suppose being a vicious termagant has its benefits. It made her a general, after all. She will captain the forces of Faerie when they finally invade mortal realms, so I suppose she must have at least some brains in that pretty head."

In a single, fluid motion, I rolled to my feet and slapped him as hard as I could. His head snapped to the side, and a bright red handprint bloomed on his cheek. I stood with my fists balled at my sides and spat, "If you open your mouth once more, you vile, treacherous bastard, I will plant my fist so far in your guts—"

He smiled at me, the corners of his eyes crinkling, and said, "There's my girl."

I stood for a moment with my mouth hanging open, cheeks still hot with righteous indignation. If I could not have the numbing grief, I needed the anger. I needed something to hang onto.

Then I realized he was standing. "What? But, your back! Your wounds! You should be—"

"Faeries heal fast," he said with a shrug. "Your sister knew it when she ordered me whipped. She's a wily bitch, that woman."

I growled and raised my hand, but Aristotle only smiled a satisfied smile. He was baiting me, and he saw the exact instant I recognized it.

"Did you expect me to stand around while you lay there and wallow in grief? It has been two days, Gwen, and I've barely coaxed water into your damnable mouth. Would you rather starve?"

He gestured to a tray covered in a white cloth, and the smell hit me like a runaway cart, making my stomach growl. When was the food delivered?

"You have already spent too much of your life grieving that woman," he continued. "She doesn't deserve your tears."

"What, and you do?"

He looked over his shoulder at his back, which made the muscles across his stomach tighten. "Well, this did hurt considerably."

"You brought that on yourself with your clever mouth," I snarled, remembering the way he baited her, too.

"Are you telling me I deserved to be whipped?"

I opened my mouth to say that yes, he deserved it for lying to me for years and keeping secrets and...and then I remembered the way he'd enveloped me in the throne room, and how he flinched when the whip fell.

"And now you are angry at me for trying to keep you alive," he said in an infuriatingly reasonable tone. "I only used words, but you've slapped me, screamed at me, and you are about to punch me. Clearly, violence runs in the family."

"I am not violent," I said through gritted teeth.

"I can tell."

My fingers curled into fists. He was still baiting me, but he didn't deserve the response of my anger. Emptiness crept back in, pushing my fury out with a desolate sigh. God's breath, I was so tired. I just wanted to sleep.

My voice came out sounding far too childlike. "Why won't you just leave me alone?"

He lifted my chin and forced me to look up into those familiar dark eyes. "Because I will take your anger, your fear, your pain, even your hatred. But I cannot let you despair, Gwen. It would be the end of you, and I will not allow that."

But I wanted the end of me, and he saw it in my eyes.

"I have many more insults all stored up for such an occasion," he warned. "If it takes a few bruises to keep you alive, you are welcome to have a go at me."

And he would do it. No one knew me as well as he did, knew which buttons to push. He would drag me back from the edge, kicking and screaming. But all I wanted to do was fall.

"Don't take this from me," I breathed. "It hurts too much."

His expression softened, and he tilted his head. The gesture was so much like Aristotle that tears pricked my eyes, but I dashed them away with the heel of my hand. If I could not cry for Lia or myself, I would not cry for that damnable bird.

But the tears did not stop.

I opened my mouth to tell him to stay away from me, but what came out was, "You stole him from me."

Aristotle was my friend, had comforted and protected me, made me laugh and saved my life more than once.

I loved him.

And now he was gone as surely as Lia was gone. When I asked, "Was it always just a glamour?" hope and sorrow mixed in my voice.

"No, it wasn't a glamour. Shape-shifting is part of who I am. It was always me. It has always been me."

I wasn't certain if that made me feel better or worse, but it did make me cry. My knees gave out. I sank to the moss and wrapped my arms around my stomach as the keening I'd swallowed in the throne room clawed up my throat and forced past my lips.

Aristotle sat next to me and pulled me into his lap.

That made me cry harder.

The flood toppled every stronghold left inside me. Amidst the raging waters, there was no room for self-pity, anger, or betrayal. And, somehow, even the hole in my chest proved not to be endless once it was filled with tears.

Exhausted at last, I sat up and scooted away from Aristotle. The numbness got me nowhere, and I refused to accept defeat so easily. My insides were still raw and bleeding, but that meant I was alive. *Dum spiro, spero*; while I breathe, I hope.

And I would not give up hope of bringing my sister back to me.

"What is your real name?"

Aristotle blinked at my sudden return to life, then raised a black brow. "What a bold question, my lady. We barely know one another. Alright." He laughed and raised his hands to ward himself from my angry expression, a relieved light in his eyes. "Alright. You can call me Aristotle, or Aris, if you prefer."

"Is that your real name?"

"It is the best name I have."

"That was not my question."

His voice turned solemn, and he said, "You know better. No faerie gives away their real name."

I had read as much, but I needed to know it for certain. The reality of my situation, a prisoner in a castle I'd never even seen, in a country I knew next to nothing about, meant I needed every weapon I could muster. Especially if I was going to survive the trials set me by the King.

"Fair enough," I said. "Can you tell me what you are?"

"What I am is smitten, my lady."

I ignored that. He was no more serious now than he had been in the ballroom so long ago. Flirting was probably second nature for him. "Are you—sidhe?"

"I suppose I have that distinction, though there are those who would disagree."

"On what grounds?"

"You saw the sidhe in the court of the King. They are beautiful enough to make one weep. I do not share that blessing."

I snorted. As if he was not the most handsome man I had ever seen. "Must you answer every question in such a roundabout way?"

"It is in my nature," he said with a mischievous smile.

"Is it in your nature to be infuriating?"

"To obfuscate."

"You," I said, "are a liar."

His head tilted to the side again, sending a little arrow of pain through my chest. I needed to think of him differently in this form, because losing my friend hurt too much. So, I decided to take his suggestion and think of him as Aris.

"If I keep things from you," he said, every hint of amusement gone, "it is because I believe ignorance will keep you safer."

I huffed. "Shouldn't that be for me to decide?"

"No. Not here. Here, you don't know enough to keep yourself safe. And knowing too much could be equally dangerous. I'm going to be walking a very fine line to keep you alive and sane."

"Then why did you stop the spell?" I blurted. "I would still be safe in England if you hadn't."

He tore a chunk of moss into tiny pieces and refused to look me in the eye. "Because I thought it would shut the door. I didn't expect the power differential. How could I? I'm no witch."

"No, but you are a faerie. You should have at least some knowledge of magic."

"Magic, yes. It is part of my blood. Magic is fickle, and unrestrained magic has a mind of its own, but it obeys us because we are its children, the natural vessels for the expression of it. But that spell is something else, an unnatural blend of both worlds.

"So far as I can understand it, when witches were given access to magic, they created rules that bent it to their will. They enslaved it. That is why it destroys their bodies. The magic *that* spell calls upon is feral. I could not know how it would behave, only that I wanted to stop it and get you out of that circle."

"And your ability to turn into a raven is not magic?" I asked, remembering his earlier assertion that the raven form was not a glamour.

"Not in the way you are thinking of it."

Looking at him now, long-limbed and broad-shouldered, I wondered how he compressed so much into such a small space. "Was it hard? To be a raven for so long, I mean."

Pain flashed in his eyes but disappeared so quickly I was not sure I had seen it. "You have no idea."

"If it was so hard, why live as a raven in my home so many years?"

"There are benefits to being a pet," he said, and his eyes flicked down my body. My cheeks flushed, but he clarified, "I'm not talking about watching you change clothes, although that does rank very high on the list of—"

He laughed and caught my hand before I could slap him, then kissed my palm, moving so fast I didn't even have time to be shocked.

"Being close to you was the best way to help."

I thought back over every conversation he was present for, every time he gave me a clue or threw himself in harm's way. Every time he comforted or watched over me while I broke apart and dragged myself back together. "But, why? Why would you want to help me? Who am I to you that you would care?"

He locked eyes with me, eyes that I knew so well even in this unfamiliar form. How could I have missed it all those years?

"You are a good person," he said. "Isn't that enough?"

No, it wasn't. Not only because I was clearly not a good person—my numerous fatal flaws stood witness to that—but because being a good person wasn't sufficient motivation for a stranger to devote themselves to helping one. Those thoughts were difficult to communicate, however, when one was being gazed at in that manner by a man as handsome as Aris.

Which made me ask, "How did you make me forget you?"

Being in his presence now, I could not imagine forgetting him. Aside from those aristocratic features and burning eyes, he was magnetic, charming, clever, and infuriating. Yet I had forgotten him every time, as if he slipped into the cracks in my mind as soon as I was out of his presence.

The lazy, self-indulgent expression returned, and he waved a hand. "Oh, that? It's a parlor trick. All the sidhe can do it. Think of it as another aspect of our glamour."

"But your raven form is not a glamour?"

"No. It's... a manifestation of my personality."

"Are there others?"

He looked down. "A few. But the raven is my favorite."

"Because you can steal things and people expect it of you?" I asked with reluctant amusement. How many times had I caught him with jewelry, beads, buttons, spoons, or anything else that was small and shiny?

"That," he agreed. "But ravens are also shockingly intelligent animals. Which makes it much easier to speak. You have no idea how hard it is to keep your thoughts to yourself all the time."

I was, in fact, very familiar with keeping my thoughts to myself; my true thoughts, anyway. Those would rarely have been welcomed or accepted by the people closest to me. At least, since Lia was taken.

And we were now in the same world, the same building, close enough to touch. "I must find a way to save my sister."

Aris rolled his shoulders, something he often did with his wings, but I doubted he realized it. "I know you don't want to hear this, but...you cannot save her, Gwen."

I glared at him. "Why not?"

"Use that brilliant mind of yours. She has lived here for what? A dozen years? She has been changed by her time here."

"Nothing could change her enough to make her stop being my sister. And changes can be reversed. She does not have to stay what she is. I can break through to her."

He ignored the belligerence in my voice. "The Sunset Lands are not like mortal lands. You don't understand the effect this place has on you, let alone on other people. Let me ask you a question: how long do you think you have been in this cell?"

I looked around the room, trying to gauge time. "Perhaps three days?"

"So, you have been a prisoner for three days, by your guess, and you have not even tried to conjure us a plan for how to escape."

My brows drew together. He was right. In fact, I hadn't even fought the guards. I had accepted being arrested and walked sedately alongside them as they led me heaven knew where or for what purpose. "Is it magic?"

"Not in the way witches do it. It is simply the nature of a cell to keep people in, so people never—well, rarely, anyway—think of trying to escape."

"That makes no sense."

"That's the point," Aris said. "It doesn't make sense to you because you are not fae. Why do you think, of all the faerie stories that exist in your world, the rarest are stories of people who people come back? Listen to me." He rolled to his knees and took both my hands in his. "When you were taken before the King, you saw things you did not expect, and people so beautiful it made your heart want to fly apart in your chest. Am I right?"

I nodded.

"They do not have only their beauty to aid them in getting what they desire. They have—damn, there is no name for it in your language. Let us call it charisma. If they use it against you, you will want to give them your name, to eat their food, to do anything they ask simply to experience the pleasure of pleasing them."

I snorted. Pleasing other people, particularly those holding me hostage, was not only the least of my concerns but the polar opposite of my instincts.

He read my expression and closed his eyes with a frustrated sigh. "You don't believe me."

"It's not that I don't believe you, but I cannot imagine myself behaving in such a manner. Not under any circumstances."

"Can you not? Very well, it is time for an object lesson, then. Stand up, this is important."

I could say that Aris stood, but uncoiled would be a better description of what his body did. Something fundamental changed in him. When he moved, it wasn't the ordinary shifting of bones and flexing muscles; it was the movement of water or wind or fire, a force of nature; effortless and absolutely perfect.

He still held my hands, still looked like the dangerously attractive man I met several times, but now he looked *more*: more graceful, more elegant, more intense. The force of his gaze was physical, a stinging heat on my face, lips, neck, and breasts. My nipples puckered at the sensation, even under layers of clothing, and he had done nothing more than look at me.

"Come to me," he said in a voice like warm honey wine.

One thumb rubbed over the back of my knuckles, sending fire tingling up my arm and down to the base of my spine. That simple gesture felt better than any night I had ever spent in any man's arms. My knees were so weak that if he let go of my hand, I would have sunk into a drunken puddle on the moss.

He pulled me into a closed dancing position so that our bodies touched from chest to knees—a stark reminder he was still shirtless. One hand ran from my shoulder blades to the base of my spine, making heat pool between my legs. We had danced this way once, but dancing was the last thing on my mind.

Aris leaned down until his breath was warm on my neck. Full body shivers ran from the base of my skull to my toes and back. My body was languid, heavy, and yet crackling with potential energy as if I were coals waiting for a spark.

"If I told you to kiss me," he said, the bass in his voice vibrating against my skin, as intimate as a caress, "you would do it, wouldn't you?"

"Yes," I breathed.

His fingers tightened on my hip. "If I told you to spread your legs for me, you would."

I would. I wanted him to ask me. Even to force me. Breath of god, to do anything to me.

The slightest pressure from his nose and lips at my neck made my head fall limp to the side, giving him access to whatever he wanted. He leaned forward until his breath was hot on my skin. Gently, almost reverently, he pressed his lips against the arch in my neck.

A helpless moan slipped between my lips.

Aris let go of me and retreated until his back hit the wall. He stood there, chest heaving, hands clenched at his sides.

Only my bones kept me standing.

"You have no way to protect yourself, even from me, and I am the least of my brethren," he said in a strangled voice. "Tell me how your sister would have fared, alone, at only sixteen. Tell me their influence over her, used for their own purposes, did not change her. You saw evidence of it yourself. And you think you are safe? That you can defy them for her sake?"

I blinked several times, then tore my gaze from him. My hands shook and my stomach was tight with need. If he hadn't broken contact, I would have thrown myself at him. I was still tempted to. "What did you do to me?"

Aris had the grace to look ashamed. "Nothing. I was simply myself, with no mask, and no pretense. I know what you expect a human to look like, so I can become that for you. It makes you more comfortable to see what you expect. It is a kind of mindless glamour I have become used to producing. But my kindred will not offer you the same concession, and I do not believe they offered it to your sister."

I thought of Ophelia alone in this beautiful world with no knowledge and no power. If Aris dazzled me without even trying, to the point of wanting to throw myself at him, what would she have experienced? And she had been so young.

"This," I began, then swallowed to clear my throat. "This ability is not only sexual?"

"No. It is charm. Influence. In all areas. And do not forget, fae morality cannot be equated with human morality. Your politics are a mere shadow of ours, but power is still the golden ring everyone reaches for. If they believed they could gain power or influence by using her, they would. And they will do the same to you."

Ophelia would have survived here by her wits, and if she rose to the rank of general, she'd been smarter and more cunning than her rivals. True, she was not the same girl I knew. That much was clear. But that wasn't her fault.

Aris saw my expression and sighed. "How can you hope to reach her, Gwen? Everyone in this castle will have more sway over you than I do, and your sister has dealt with them for a dozen years. If she had not hardened herself, she would have died."

I ground my teeth together, thinking. It would be foolish to deny the effect this stupid bloody faerie had on me, one I noticed from the very first time I saw him. But I had no intention of losing my free will. Finding a way to combat that intoxication was paramount, especially if I intended to escape with Lia in tow.

So what if I embraced it? Was inoculation by exposure a possibility? If I knew what to expect, if I was prepared for it, could I fight it?

Mama held unreasonable influence over me my entire life, and I'd learned to throw that off. Perhaps, with enough practice, I could do the same to the influence of the fae.

"No," Aris said, again holding up both hands as if to ward me off. "I know what you're thinking, and the answer is no."

"How do you know?"

He backed away from me, sliding along the wall and keeping as much distance between us as possible. "Because I know you. Maybe better than you know yourself. You think you are being clever, but you are just looking for an excuse to feel the pull again. Like an addict."

"No, I'm not," I said, continuing to advance. "I'm testing a theory."

"I won't drop my mask for you."

"You aren't the only one with wiles."

Aris closed his eyes, his lips white with strain. "Gwen. Stop it."

It was a tortured plea torn unwilling from his chest, and it froze me.

"Don't ask me to do that," he said. "I don't think I can take it."

Why should it hurt my stomach so much to hear his voice sound like that? Or to see the way his forehead pinched together between brows drawn down in pain? Perhaps he was right. Maybe I wanted a distraction. And, if I was honest with myself, knowing I made him uncomfortable was a small, petty revenge for years of lies...and for stealing my best friend.

Creaking broke the tension and made me spin toward the door growing in the wall. The brownie stood in the portal with another gown draped over its arms. My stomach dropped.

It was time for the first trial.

18

A Trial of Magic

GWEN

To my relief, the brownie was not there to escort me to the trial. It merely looked me up and down, lifted the fabric pointedly, and left the dress and a little velvet bag on the moss before retreating. Giving me time to prepare? I stared after the creature as the door closed, thinking.

Aris lifted the abandoned dress and examined the fabric, turning it back and forth to catch the dim fungal light emanating from the ceiling.

"You might as well wear this," he said.

"Why?"

"Do you want to appear for your first trial in that?"

I looked down at my blue jacket. It was a bit worse for wear, but it would also protect me, and that was not worth giving up. "Yes, as a matter of fact, I do."

Aris shrugged and opened the velvet bag. "You are either wise or incredibly foolish. If the king feels you are trying to offend him"—he pulled out a gold armband in the shape of a snake and examined it—"he may decide to have you killed, outright. It is a miracle he did not kill you on your first presentation, looking like that. At least your black eye is mostly healed."

"I am not so easy to kill as all that," I said, offended.

"Oh, yes you are, my lady. Or do you need another demonstration?"

That stopped me. Yes, I wanted one. Wanted one enough that the mere thought of the power Aris held over me made my knees weak. And that was terrifying. "I can do without your overbearing charms, thank you."

He snorted. "They won't protect you the way I do. They will seduce and beguile and push to see how far you will go before you break. And your anger will only make breaking you more entertaining."

"We will see how entertaining they find me," I muttered, cracking my knuckles even though I knew I had no chance in a fair fight.

"Know this, Gwen; here, one only risks openly offending someone they believe they can beat in a duel. Insults are taken as seriously as blows, which is half of the reason for the stories about faeries speaking in riddles."

"What is the other half?"

"Truth is power. If you tell someone the truth, you give them power. And faeries guard truth more closely than anything else."

I hesitated and unwillingly remembered seeing Thistle Honeycutt in her true form, and then Percy through the hag stone, his sleek dark body and huge eyes both strange and familiar at once. The stone was stored safely in a locked desk in my room. I should have brought it with me.

There were many things I should have done. At least I had been smart enough to bring a few tools with me. Hopefully I would not need to use them, but it was comforting to know they were accessible, should worse come to worst. I needed a plan, and for that, I needed knowledge.

I considered the shimmering fabric he held and tried to strategize.

For this first trial, at least, my options were to protect myself physically by wearing the jacket, or to try to make nice by wearing the dress. One was an outright declaration of hostility or suspicion, and the other was both a symbol of goodwill and obedience.

My goal was to survive long enough to bring Lia back with me. Which of those options would get me closest?

"Aris? What is the fae opinion of humans stumbling into the Sunset Lands?"

"It does not happen often enough for there to be a general opinion. Think of it this way: if a unicorn appeared in your townhouse and asked for a treat, what would your response be?"

I sighed. "They are going to make a spectacle of me, aren't they?"

"That is a definite possibility."

"But only if they do not think I am dangerous enough to kill. So, what is more effective: a show of force, or subterfuge?"

Aris stood up, alarmed. "A show of force? Did our little tussle in the woods prove nothing? You are a very skilled human, Gwen, but the fae are faster than you, stronger, and they've lived long enough to master any skill they care to learn. Unarmed combat is an area in which you cannot best them."

I shook my head at him in disgust and began unbuttoning my jacket.

"What are you doing?" Aris asked.

Not smiling at the panic in his voice was difficult, so I focused on the buttons.

He grabbed my wrist before I could do anything untoward, such as reach into a hidden in a pocket, and said, "You cannot attack the fae court."

"I can't?"

"You certainly won't get your sister back if you make yourself too dangerous to keep alive."

Sarcasm dripped from every word when I said, "That is a very creditable point, well done. Do you truly think me so stupid?"

He raised an eyebrow.

I rolled my eyes and pried my wrist out of his hand. "I cannot wear the fae dress if I am still cinched into all of this, can I?"

Relief washed over his face, and he backed away with his hands up. I could have told him my true weapons were already hidden beneath the moss, but it was more fun to let him flounder. Apparently, I had not exhausted my need for petty revenge.

"To be clear," he said, "I support your tendency toward mayhem, but attacking on uncertain ground is not—" His voice choked as I pulled my shirtwaist off and dropped it onto the moss. "Is not the best first move. If we are going to survive, we must—must play this"—I unbuttoned my corset, and it joined the harness and jacket on the floor—"like a game of...like...like a game of chess," Aris finished, his Adam's apple bobbing as he stuffed his hands in his pockets.

"What?" I asked him, innocently. "Why is your mouth hanging open? You've seen me do this at least a dozen times, haven't you?"

He swallowed again. "A dozen times, at least."

"Would it make you more comfortable if you changed into your raven form?"

"Moon and stars, no," he said, finally turning away as I dropped my skirt onto the growing pile. Beneath was nothing but my chemise, and that was practically transparent.

It was cruel to get a bit of revenge that way, but a lady uses what weapons she has at her disposal. I only hoped my weapons would be as effective against the other fae as they appeared to be against Aris.

"What can I expect from this trial?" I asked as I pulled the dress over my head.

"Impossible to say. You have read enough faerie tales to get the general idea, I am sure. Spinning flax into gold, retrieving golden fleeces and all that."

A shiver of unease ran down my spine. Most of the tasks given in faerie tales were rather horrendous. Weaving coats of stinging nettles came to mind. "Is there any way to prepare?"

"Only the chamberlain knows what the trial will be, and he will not reveal it."

"At least they do not intend to kill me."

"What makes you think so?"

I paused. "There are three trials. If they want maximum enter-
tainment, does it not make sense to keep me alive through the
third?"

Aris turned and regarded me, his expression sober. "These are
the Sunset Lands, Gwen. You must stop making mortal assumptions. You cannot trust anything here to make sense or be as it
seems."

When the guards collected me and dragged me back to the
throne room, the response from the court was, if not gratifying,
at least not insulting. While the gown was simple, similar in style
to medieval houppelandes, with long, bell-shaped sleeves and ex-
pansive fabric, it certainly left me looking better than my battered
coat had.

The gown was something like the formal attire one might wear
to a ceremony or religious rite, plain and unadorned. And as this
was a ceremony of sorts, it fit well enough. I simply had to maintain
my composure. Which was a thousand times more difficult as soon
as I saw my sister again.

She stood at the right hand of the King, chin high, an expression
of haughty disdain on her face. How many times had I seen that
face creased with laughter? Watching her made ignoring the intoxicating scent of wild flowers and the domineering beauty of the
King much easier as the guards and I walked down the flower-lined
path to the throne.

Before it stood a simple wooden table with three objects placed at equal distances across the top: an unlit candle in a silver candlestick, a bulging leather sack as large as my joined fists, and two gold coins.

On the opposite side of the table stood a sidhe man with eyebrows like storm clouds, a hawkish nose, and a sweeping black beard that spread across his chest. He might have been in his late sixties, or several thousand years old. His blue-gray robe faded to an obscuring mist before reaching his feet and turned into a train of clouds that billowed as he moved.

The cloak made the man appear to be floating several feet off of the ground. His eyes, the clear blue-green of a shallow sea, crinkled around the corners as he smiled kindly at me. Since I was not gibbering in a puddle, I had to assume he was using the same simple glamour Aris used that protected me from his true aspect.

He leaned in and took me by the hand, kissing it as if we were at a ball somewhere in New London, and not in the court of the faerie King, taking part in a trial that might end with my death. He nodded once in respect, and I reciprocated with as elegant a curtsy as I could manage.

"You have been assigned three tasks by Obyrron the Mighty, King of the Sunset Lands," he said in a voice like crashing waves. "I will judge your performance."

Unsure of how to respond, I nodded.

"The first task is before you." He gestured to the table with a sweeping motion of one hand, stopping over the gold coins. "Turn these coins into songbirds."

I swallowed the objection that rose to my lips and fought to keep my expression serene. I had no magic, but letting them know that might be a fatal mistake. Best to keep my proverbial cards close to my chest. In faerie stories, some circumstance always arose to change the fate of the hero or heroine when confronted with an impossible task.

Was that more fiction, or a truth carefully concealed?

I took a coin and examined it, flipping it between my fingers and feeling the cool weight as it sat on my palm. It could be a bird, if I wanted it to. A small bird might weigh as much as this gold coin. With a deep breath to center myself, I imagined the coin melting, shifting, rising to form a small, fat bird that would open its mouth and trill a beautiful song into the scented air.

Of course, nothing happened.

I focused harder, pushing my will at the coin until sweat beaded on my upper lip.

Nothing.

Closing my eyes, I imagined gathering all the energy from my body, drawing it toward my hands, shaping and forming it. My hands grew hot. The edge of the coin bit into my skin.

"She cannot do it," Lia said with cold disdain.

I blinked and looked down. The coin lay on my palm, unchanged.

The crowd tittered and my cheeks went up in flames. I had not truly expected anything to happen, but to have my failure thrown in my face, and by my sister, made anger sit like a rock in my belly.

"Perhaps," Lia said, a bit of malice entering her voice, "she simply lacks motivation. With your leave, Chamberlain?"

The dark-haired man nodded, once.

"Bring him."

Everyone turned to see two more of the hound guards escort Aris into the room. He strolled between them as if he were walking in the park, a sneer on his lips as he regarded the staring faces of the crowd.

"My lady," he said, widening his arms and giving Lia a mocking bow. "To what do I owe the honor of being dragged back into your presence?"

Lia turned to the King, who gave her a nearly invisible tilt of the head.

"Guards," Lia said. "Hold him."

They took Aris by the upper arms, gripping hard enough to turn his skin red. Dread ran down my spine on tiny, cold feet. Lia left the stairs and stalked down the aisle, put both hands on his chest, and ripped his shirt neatly into two pieces.

"Well, that was unnecessary," he said, releasing the glamour and standing before the crowd bare chested.

She walked around him in a circle, examining his skin. "I see you have healed from my displeasure rather quickly. Good. I want you healthy for our demonstration." Then she patted his cheek, turned, and strode back to her place before the King.

His eyes never left her, and his expression never changed.

"You have the honor of assisting us in His Majesty's test," she said once she resumed her place. "Our subject needs motivation, and it would appear you still need a lesson in manners. This demonstration will serve both purposes. Therefore, know this: if she fails the next test, I will hurt you."

"What?" I heard myself say.

Lia ignored me and spoke only to Aris. "If she takes too long to complete the test, I will hurt you."

"How can you do this? Lia, what has made you so cruel?"

"Cruel?" she asked, finally turning to me. "He should be flayed alive for his betrayal. I am merely hurting him and using his pain to help you complete your trial. I am merciful. Now, let us not dawdle and leave our whipping boy waiting in apprehension."

"Very well," the chamberlain said with a slight bow.

He opened the sack and emptied it onto the table. Seeds spilled across the wood, bouncing in every direction, even skittering so far as the feet of the crowd behind me.

"Return every seed to this bag without touching them, or moving from that spot," he said.

I gaped at the seeds. There must have been hundreds of thousands scattered across the room. My mouth went dry. Not even with a broom and pan could I be certain of returning every seed.

Perhaps there was a way around the test, something clever. I doubted a godmother would appear to save me, and I did not speak the language of animals to call upon ants to do my bidding. My wits were all I had left.

Could I use a runic circle to draw the seeds together? No, that would require knowing what type of seed it was, how far away they might have traveled, giving specific directions for movement and knowing which natural force was most likely to be molded for such a purpose. That required subtle artifice far beyond my skill. I was more likely to blow up the palace than move a single seed.

Besides, revealing this new magic to the fae could be more dangerous than letting the humans have it.

Lia sighed and said in a bored tone, "She appears distracted. Perhaps a demonstration is needed." She raised one hand and green fire kindled at her fingertips, running down the edges of her hand and lighting her face with a lurid glow.

My breath caught in my throat.

Magic. Lia had *magic*.

Part of my mind spun off into the past, searching to see if any hint of that gift manifested itself when we were children, but discovering nothing. The other half searched within me. If Lia could use magic, the gift may be in my blood, as well, just waiting to be unlocked. Could that be her true goal, to use stress to force a latent ability to manifest?

Lia's flames curled and writhed with a dry hiss, like snakes waiting to bite. I did not have time to wrack my brain for a clever solution, so if magic was the only way out of this problem, I had to try.

I turned to the table and focused my attention on a single seed. All it had to do was move a few inches. Just a few. Move, I thought at the seed, picturing it fly across the table. Every muscle tensed as I channeled all of my will, demanding the air molecules gather and propel the little black seed across the table.

Nothing happened.

I blew a stray hair from my face in frustration. If I did possess some of the magical talent Lia displayed so indifferently, how could I unlock it? My sister did not give me a chance to find out.

She pointed at Aris with one finger. A line of fire shot across the intervening space and struck him in the stomach.

"No!"

My scream echoed off the walls as he wrapped his arms around himself and fell to his knees.

When the fire died, Aris knelt with his head hanging, black hair covering his face, his skin scalded like a boiled lobster. But he was breathing.

"Should you move from that spot," the bearded man said as I made to rush to his side, "the trial shall be concluded, and you will fail."

My leg froze before my foot hit the ground. Aris raised his head, his gaze pinning Lia like an arrow. Sweat poured down the sides of his face at the temples and his lips were white, but he said, "If memory serves me correctly, your fire has lost a bit of its kick, lady."

Lia flicked a finger and sent sparks dancing into the air. The moss sizzled when they landed. "Do not worry, Raven. I shall revive your memory when this human fails."

Helpless rage burned in my chest, hotter than Lia's fire. Crouching, I tried to ignore the fact that my sister was a magic wielding general who tortured people and bent all of my concentration on the single seed. Move, please. Move!

My heart jumped. The green flames sizzled, and Aris sucked in a pained breath through his teeth, grunting as he braced himself on the moss with both fists.

"I haven't failed yet!" I cried.

"I did say he was here for a dual purpose, did I not? Continue. Unless you cannot move the seeds, of course."

Furious, I turned all my will, frustration, longing, and desperation on the seeds, drawing strength from every failure and insult and injury. I clenched my fists, gritted my teeth, held my breath, and pushed.

Nothing happened.

"Yet another test failed," Lia said, false sadness coloring her voice.

I spun in time to see her level her hand at Aris, the crackle of her flames drowning out my cry of, "Aris!"

He arched backward, his muscles strained, but he did not cry out. The flames did not burn him, but sank into his skin and glowed beneath his flesh. He threw his head back, veins bulging in his neck as the pain clenched every muscle in his body.

When it was quiet, Aris hung suspended for several long moments as smoke rose from his skin. Then he took a deep breath and stood, muscles shaking, raising his chin in defiance.

"The final test, if you will," Lia said, turning to the bearded chamberlain with an expression as calm as if she had just spent a morning in the garden, not burning a man from the inside.

What had become of my sister? What could have turned her into this?

The chamberlain gestured at the candle and said, simply, "Light this."

The little candle was innocuous, as mundane as the seeds or coins. I stared at the wick. To light it, I simply needed to produce enough heat. But how? Without much effort, I recalled seven different spells a witch might use to produce heat...but I was not a witch. I could not use the runes, and I had no tools for what small artifice I did know.

Fine. Magic, it must be. I imagined heat from my blood, from the air, condensing at the tip of the wick. In my mind, I saw the molecules vibrating faster, creating heat. With gritted teeth, I willed it into existence, but not even a trail of smoke appeared.

Lia raised her hand.

Instead of watching Aris writhe in pain, which made my throat close and tears sting my eyes, I watched Lia's face as the flames roared. Her expression was absolutely immobile, cold, distant.

She looked down at the fingernails of her opposite hand, bored.

I could no longer stand by, failure or not. Dodging the guard who reached for me, I lunged toward Aris but was stopped by Harl, who wrapped his arms around me and growled in my ear.

"Stop!" I screamed at my sister, but she only raised a finger and coaxed the fire higher, till it burned his chest instead of his stomach. I wrenched my arms and shoulders but gained no purchase as Aris's face contorted in agony.

At last he cried out, a furious shout of pain and anger. And Lia flinched.

She flinched.

Her eyes were hard, but she flinched and released the fire. That single motion was a light in the darkness, small and sputtering but still there.

Lia, *my* Lia, was somewhere beneath that hard exterior. She had to be.

Aris collapsed. My knees wobbled, but Harl held me fast as Lia turned toward the King.

"This woman possesses no magic, your majesty," she said. Her voice was tired.

"Very well, General. We shall wait for the next test, then, to see if your blood runs true."

The chamberlain bowed low. "If I may speak, my King?"

"Speak."

"This human woman has quite caught my eye. Might I have your permission to escort her to tonight's festivities?"

Obyrron smiled, and the crowd burst into excited chatter. "It has been many years since a human has joined the dance. Very well, bring her if you like. I am certain she will be entertaining, if nothing else."

After a bow, the bearded man turned toward me and smiled again, kindly. "I shall call upon you at the proper time, madame."

I was sweating and still so furious that it was hard to see straight, so I only gave him a stony glare.

"Take them back to their cell," Lia said. "Leave the coward to the tender ministrations of my talented sister."

19

Upping the Tension

GWEN

The hound guards let Aris slide to the floor on his stomach and left us without a word. I knelt beside him, mind whirling as I wondered how to treat magical injuries. His skin was flushed, but there was no outward sign of a wound. I lay my hand against his back and jerked it away, scalded by the heat.

A fever that high would kill a man.

"God's breath," I murmured. Was there even a way to care for...whatever this was? Aris made a noise of agreement and turned to lie on his side, curled in a ball.

As carefully as possible, I sat next to him and pulled his head into my lap, brushing the sweat-soaked hair off his brow.

"I'm sorry," I said. It seemed like a pitifully small offering after my inability to stop Lia from hurting him.

"It wasn't your fault. She would have done it, anyway."

"Why? What are you being punished for?"

He didn't answer for so long that I thought he must have fallen asleep, but he finally said in a raspy voice, "Not doing my job, I suppose."

Should I keep him talking or let him sleep? How did one treat magical internal burns?

"What was your job?"

"I was a spy. I gathered information for the general so she could strategize."

"Who did you spy on?"

"The other courts, mostly."

"There are others?"

"Several. But I spent most of my time in Queen Titania's court. She is the only true threat to Obyrron."

I rolled my eyes. "Be serious."

"I am deadly serious, my lady."

"Obyrron and Titania? From A Midsummer Night's Dream?"

"Where do you think Shakespeare learned their names?"

"Are they married, too?"

"Of course. But they hate each other."

"How long have they been estranged?"

"Since the Great War."

My jaw dropped open. That was thousands of years. "Are they so old?"

"They are immortal, Gwen."

It was difficult enough to grasp the idea of infinity as a concept, but knowing I met someone that long-lived was impossible to come to terms with. "What happened between them?"

"Queen Titania is a traitor. Don't they explain that in your stories and histories?"

A traitor? It clicked into place. "She was the one who taught mortals magic so they could defend themselves against the fae!"

He yawned. "Among other things."

"Will you be alright? I don't know what to do for you."

"There is nothing to be done. I will heal. It is only pain. But"—he wriggled a bit, curling into my lap—"this is nice." Then he yawned again.

I left off the questions and watched as his breathing depended, becoming steady and rhythmic, and his long, dark eyelashes fluttered closed to rest against his cheek. His skin was still so hot that just pillowing his head on my lap made me sweat.

And Lia had done this to him with a cruel smile on her face.

Reconciling the general of the fae armies to the girl I had known was even harder than meeting an immortal. I simply could not accept that the cold, malicious woman was the smiling, teasing girl I grew up with. But she *had* flinched. I hung on to that, no matter how insufficient a comfort it was.

Aris warned me not to believe anything I saw, and all of my research confirmed his warning. But if I could not believe what I saw, how might I solve the mystery of this place and get myself and my sister out of it?

Absently brushing my fingers against Aris's forehead, I let my mind work.

The man I knew as Aristotle had been a spy for my sister, snooping on the court of Queen Titania, who supported mortals in the Great War.

Ophelia was the general in charge of invading mortal lands, so seeing her standing in the door Cassandra tried to open finally made sense; she had been waiting to cross with a dozen fae soldiers at her back. That could only mean she knew the door would open. I didn't want to think about how she knew, or whether she had a hand in planning it.

But how did Lia earn such a position when the other contenders must have been hundreds if not thousands of years older and more experienced? She was either as clever and ruthless as she appeared to be, or more powerful than the others who could have held the title.

True, her life as a human made her uniquely qualified to plot our downfall. But would she? I lay back on the moss and let my thoughts come together as they would, drawing lines between bits of information until they began to form a recognizable structure.

How long I lay in a daze with Aris's head on my lap I cannot say, but it felt like only moments before the wood creaked and the door appeared in the wall. Aris shuddered, sucked in a pained breath, and groaned as he sat up.

I brushed the hair out of his face. "Your color looks a bit better."

"Huzzah for me."

I would have responded to his sarcasm, but three otherworldly creatures entered our cell and stopped my breath. Nymphs had been described, painted, sculpted, and rendered in various forms of art all over the world, but none of it did them justice. And despite never having seen one myself, I knew what they were.

Their large, round eyes were entirely black, the bridge of their noses was flat and almost blended into their cheekbones, and their greenish skin shifted to silver in the light. Each of them moved with the grace of swaying trees, and their gauzy garments appeared to be woven of spiderwebs. They had the otherworldly appeal of dark ponds and mossy banks when one has been too long in the sun.

One carried an armful of fabric, the other a tray with combs and several bits of jewelry, and the third what I assumed to be soaps and bath oils. The last had thick hair the color of autumn leaves swept back and decorated with beads and cuffs of gold. With infinite grace, the nymph bent to press fingers into the moss in the center of the floor.

The wood peeled back, much like our cell door, revealing a clear pool. Tendrils of steam curled into the air, and my skin broke out in goosebumps at the mere thought of sinking into the hot water.

"Manannán Mac Lir has called for you, lady. We are here to assist with your bath."

Manannán Mac Lir? The Irish god of the Otherworld and the sea? My hands went cold and my throat tightened in surprise. A veritable god was escorting me to a dance? Coherent thought tried to flee, but I managed to choke out, "I do not need assistance, but I appreciate the offer."

They traded confused glances and Aris sighed. "It would be an insult to deny his minions, Gwen. Besides...you smell."

"What, and you don't?"

"I am not attending the festivities with a god."

I closed my eyes. "Don't remind me."

"Just get in the bath."

"But you...they..."

"Since when are you a shrinking violet? Besides"—he raised a mischievous brow despite still being pale with pain, and eyed me from foot to crown—"dozens of times, remember?"

He needed a good kick to the shin. My hands balled into fists remembering how many times I changed in front of that raven, told him secrets, and cried into his feathers. I would have liked to scold him, but the nymphs decided I was taking too long, so they set down their burdens and began helping me out of the faerie gown.

"Turn around," I ordered Aris over my shoulder.

"You did not seem to mind putting on a show earlier, my lady. Or does your bravery only extend to flustering me when we are alone?"

I narrowed my eyes, and he turned until his back was facing me. But he was right. It was one thing to embarrass him when we were alone, and yet another to be stripped bare. It was the difference between power and vulnerability.

"You are awfully brave while there is company in our cell, bird," I grumbled at him.

"One must be brave while one can," he replied.

The nymphs handed me down into the water, and as the heat licked up my calves and thighs, I moaned in involuntary pleasure. It had been years since I'd gone so long without a bath and my muscles responded by going limp as a full-body shiver ran up from the soles of my feet.

"Gwen?" Aris asked.

"Hmm?"

"Please don't make noises like that."

I smirked and sank beneath the water.

The nymphs lathered and combed and oiled with a professional efficiency that rivaled that of any Parisian bathhouse. I might have let myself enjoy it if I couldn't feel Aris's eyes on me. He turned his back when I asked him to, but I doubted he stayed that way. If he could tease me, he would. I expected that much. But I did not expect how strangely sensual the experience was.

Soap bubbles popping and water lapping at my stomach were the only noises as they scrubbed my hair, massaging my scalp with strokes of long fingers. The oils they rubbed into my skin were fragrant, like honeysuckle and sandalwood, and conjured images of wild gardens ripe in the sunlight. And since the water was only waist-high, the cooler air of the cell gave me goosebumps that made my nipples pebble.

Every time I glanced in his direction, Aris's eyes were sliding away, as if he were watching me seconds before. I never caught him at it, but I felt his gaze like a brand on my skin.

By the time the nymphs finished, my mouth was dry and my fingers trembling. They handed me out of the pool and began toweling the water from my steaming skin.

"You may use the bathwater, Raven," one of them said while sliding a gold armband onto my biceps.

"I think I shall wait," he replied, voice thick.

"That would be unwise, as the general has commanded your presence."

Aris had a way of obeying that made it seem as if he were conferring a favor rather than fulfilling an obligation. It was a personality quirk I associated with Aristotle. While I knew they were the same person, each time I was forced to confront the fact it had the strange effect of making the man both more familiar and more improbable.

I stood immobile as my hair was combed and styled, watching Aris cross the room with an easy stride despite the tension in his shoulders. His skin had faded to its normal pale hue, and the muscles of his abdomen shifted in a rather distracting manner as he walked.

He gave me a cheeky grin. "You don't have to turn your back, if you'd rather not, my lady."

I snorted, then jerked in surprise as his trousers disappeared. My breath whooshed out as if I'd been punched. The damnable man was utter perfection. I refused to feel guilty for looking. After all, I had a duty to do thorough research as the first human to spend time amongst the fae.

It was strictly professional curiosity.

For posterity.

The nymphs did not lavish their hygienic attention on Aris, leaving him to make do on his own. He sank beneath the surface with a similar groan of pleasure that made my cheeks go up in flames.

When he stood and reached to take the cake of soap from where it lay on the moss, I held my breath. Blue-black hair was plastered to his head and neck, dripping onto a lean form so lovingly sculpted the gods must have wept while making him.

He sent me an amused, knowing look from beneath long lashes, and I dragged my eyes away, clenching my fists until the moment passed. Determined to make it through the rest of this farce with my dignity somewhat intact, I trained my eyes on the translucent fabric pooling at my feet and did not move them until the nymphs finished with me.

When they left, I was properly covered in the new fae gown, complete with accompanying jewelry. Of course, whether the words *covered* and *proper* truly applied to the scenario depended upon one's perspective.

Either the sidhe had very a different definition of the words than modern Europeans, or they truly planned to make a spectacle of me, because while the sleeveless dress was pinned at the shoulders with exquisite brooches and did extend from my collarbones to my ankles, it was so sheer that it left absolutely nothing to the imagination. At least, not when seen from the right angles.

A jeweled belt caught the dress into a series of aesthetic gathers and pleats that I tried to arrange for maximum modesty. Judging by Aris's expression, I was somewhat less than successful.

When taken with the ostentatious jewelry: two beaded anklets, a torque with a ruby-eyed serpent head on one side and curling tail on the other, a hammered armband—all of which were likely solid gold—and a pair of jeweled ivory combs, the entire effect was meant to showcase the body, not to hide it.

A spectacle, indeed.

I had never been overly modest, though I bowed to the fashionable rules of the day, but this ensemble pushed even my limits. Worse, it left me nowhere to hide any of my weapons.

Aris cleared his throat, then folded his hands behind his back and walked round me in a circle, eyeing me as if I were a statue he was considering purchasing for his entryway. He tugged on a lock of my hair which, down and combed, reached to the small of my back, then dropped it as he completed his perusal.

"You'll do, I suppose," he said, then dodged a slap, laughing.

"This coming from the man who is still mostly nude?"

"And here I thought you enjoyed the spectacle of my manly physique. I left the shirt off just for you, and now you want me to cover up? To what lengths must I go to please you?"

I swallowed the response that jumped to mind and said, "You might try keeping your eyes off my breasts, to start."

He allowed his gaze to linger a moment longer, then held out his arms and changed. The plain black trousers he preferred shimmered and shifted, flowing over his skin like water. His ensemble mirrored mine except that his tunic boasted billowing sleeves and was belted so the embroidered hem reached only to mid-thigh, leaving a distracting amount of muscled leg open to ogling.

The fabric was equally sheer. It caught the light from the mushrooms above us, and let it shimmer over acres of sculpted muscle. He wore a golden torque as well, only his sported a raven's head.

"Showoff," I muttered.

"A fellow must dress to match his lady. Can't be outdone by a mere human, after all. And if I do not glamour myself some clothing, I would be dragged bare-assed before your darling sister."

Aris must have truly wanted to be punched.

Besides, I never could have competed with the man in terms of sheer physical beauty. Attired in a series of potato sacks he would still be unnaturally attractive. My training and general level of activity kept me healthy and in good shape, but I enjoyed a scone as much as anyone and sported the jiggly bits to prove it.

Being seen next to him was certain to destroy whatever confidence I had, but being seen was not my goal in wearing the dress. I was more likely to learn valuable information if they saw me as biddable and unthreatening—at least I hoped so, or else I was about to show far more of myself than I was comfortable with for no good reason.

"You might enjoy my public exposure, given your lascivious nature," he continued in a teasing tone, despite the fact that I had not responded, "but I assure you I would not."

"Aris?"

"Yes, my lady?"

"Shut up."

"I live but to serve you."

That conjured some interesting thoughts that I did not get to ruminate on because the strange, wood-creaking sound of the appearing door made me bite my tongue. Before it opened, Aris grabbed my wrist—his skin was warm now, not uncomfortably hot—leaned down, and said, "Do not believe anything you see or hear. Do not thank anyone, or accept any gifts. Do not drink the wine or eat the food. And do not get so caught up in the dancing that you cannot stop. Faeries can dance for days and they're likely to drive you to exhaustion or death if you give them the chance."

"Despite what you may think," I said as I wrenched my wrist from his grasp, "I am not a complete nincompoop."

"I am in earnest, Gwen. And don't—"

"I know, don't make any promises."

One corner of his mouth curled. "I was going to say, don't kiss anyone. But, yes, that part, too."

I doubted anyone would try. Even the lowliest faerie was more graceful and beautiful than I, and as I was a prisoner. Who in their right mind would find a dalliance with me desirable?

Two of the hound guards appeared, Harl and one whose name I had not learned. Their paw hands rested on their weapons and their eyes were alert and hard.

Harl said, "The lord Manannán and the lady await you. Raven, you are to wear this."

He held a gold collar dangling at the end of a length of chain. It was too thin to be of much use containing a faerie, but it was not meant as a means of physical control...it was a symbol of power and subjugation, and Aris knew it.

The muscle in his jaw flexed as he ground his teeth. His knuckles turned white and his weight shifted. God's breath, he was going to punch the guard. Cold sweat ran down my spine. If he attacked Harl, I would have no choice but to support him, and in an ensemble this flimsy, I was guaranteed to get pummeled if not killed outright.

I'd have to be fast.

I shifted my weight as if impatient or nervous, but in truth, I was preparing to lunge or dodge, if necessary. The guard on the right watched Aris, not me, and he was close enough that I could take out his legs if I moved with all possible speed.

If that did not work, my secret cache was close enough that it might do us some good. My back foot shifted, toes digging into the moss for leverage.

Aris let out a slow breath through his nostrils and raised his chin, defiant. His body language said he would not resist, but if the hounds wanted him in a collar, they would have to put it on themselves.

Harl's eyes shifted warily to Aris's hands. "Graowh, restrain him."

Graowh hesitated, then circled at arm's length until he could press the tip of his sword to Aris's spine from a safe distance. Only then did Harl raise the collar. It locked around Aris's throat with a metallic *clink*, and both guards sighed in relief. But seeing the collar around his throat made my stomach twist in revulsion.

Harl and Graowh retreated to the door and gestured with flicks of their ears. "Come."

People certainly liked issuing orders here.

I took a deep breath, called upon my mother's training as the future Duchess of Wainwright, and sailed into the hallway with Aris at my back.

20

To the Ball, Cinderella

GWEN

The long hallway was less like a corridor and more like an aspen grove. Delicate trees lined the hall like pillars and stretched arching branches to support the roof, an architectural detail repeated throughout the palace.

Carved stone doors were evenly spaced on either side, each one representing a unique scene that was a work of art. We stopped and waited outside a door carved with the head of a mighty horse, its mane flowing into crashing waves. Manannán Mac Lir opened the door before the guards knocked. A single glance into his room was all I managed before the five of us set off down the hall, but I could have sworn gently lapping water covered the floor.

My escort—a literal god, according to legend—waved his hands at the guards, who slowed to lag several yards behind us. He held his forearm out to me with a smile, then patted my hand when I accepted it.

"I am sorry for the result of the trial this morning," he said in that rumbling voice, "but more for the cold reception of the court. It must be rather disorienting."

How does one comfortably converse with a god? "I appreciate your concern," I said, thinking through my response. "I, too, wish the outcome would have been different. I hope you did not have to pick up all of those seeds?"

He laughed, and the sound was as merry as a gurgling brook. "Only in a manner of speaking, and it was the work of a moment. You must be wondering why I asked for your company?"

"In truth, I assumed you hoped to be entertained by my clumsiness."

"Never think so, my dear. No, I asked for your hand this evening for two reasons: the first is that I dearly miss the mortal world. I was hoping you might bring a bit of it back for me, in a manner of speaking."

"Is that why you are so carefully glamoured?"

He looked shame-faced at that. "You noticed, eh?"

"Your consideration is very kind."

"Bah," he said, waving his free hand. "Not a bit of it. How else can I lure you into my confidence?"

I laughed at the conspiratorial wink he gave me and realized how difficult it would be to navigate this world when clever old gods were so charming.

"You haven't told me the second reason yet," I reminded him.

"We will get to that soon. Has anyone told you what to expect tonight? No, of course, they haven't. What am I thinking?"

"Beautiful creatures that will dance so skillfully and for so long that I might die if I join them?"

"Of course, that. But these gatherings have a more important purpose"—he raised one finger—"political machinations."

"Ah, the glorious sport of the nobility."

He lay one finger alongside his nose and winked again. "There is much to learn at events like these if you have the stomach for them. And violence of one sort or another is always certain to make the evening interesting."

"I have had enough violence for one day," I said, remembering Aris's face as his back arched under Lia's fire.

"And so you have," he said, patting my hand again. "But, as objectionable as brutality may be, it is, at least, educational. And anything educational is a benefit to you."

The hall ended in a set of enormous white double doors covered in flowering vines that perfumed the air with the scent of honeysuckle. A pair of guards in full, decorative plate armor with helms resembling coursing hounds stood barring the way with crossed spears.

When they saw us, they snapped their spears upright, pushed the doors open, and announced in booming tandem voices, "Lord Manannán Mac Lir and his guest, the Gaelethsdaughter."

I leaned in and murmured to Manannán through the smile locked on my face, "What did he just call me?"

"A mere title, pay it no mind. It is what they'll call you until you give them a name of your choosing."

He led me inside but pulled me almost immediately to the edge of the foyer, where there was still a modicum of privacy. Graowh continued past us with Aris. Despite being led by chain and collar, Aris strolled with lazy grace and a raised chin, as if conferring an honor on the gathering by his mere presence.

Other guests turned to watch him pass, their expressions either wary or darkly amused. Scorn curled one corner of his mouth as he ignored their whispers, the only act of defiance he could offer. An act I recognized too well, having performed it more than once myself.

Before they disappeared through a hanging veil of wisteria that separated the foyer from whatever lay beyond, he turned his head and winked at me over his shoulder. I hoped that bravado—real or not—would serve him. There was something profoundly wrong about seeing anyone degraded with chains.

That was likely the point, and knowing my sister was capable of it made me sick.

"We shall wait here a moment," Manannán said, drawing my attention back to him and leaning in as if to whisper a secret. "Take this time to fortify yourself, for you will not get the chance once we engage in the party. Now smile prettily, so our esteemed companions believe I am a clever lover."

So, he was giving me time to prepare for the walloping I was sure to get when confronted with so many faeries at the height of their revels. Did that make him an ally, or was he disguising some more nefarious motivation I had not guessed at?

Either way, it was good advice. I fluttered my lashes at him obediently, and he laughed. I caught the very edges of his true nature, as if it slipped for a moment past the edges of his glamour, a friendly puppy slipping its collar to frolic.

Only it wasn't a puppy. It was a stallion breaking its lead to thunder down a beach, hair flying in the wind, reveling in the wild freedom and salt spray of the breaking waves. The power of it rolled over my body like a summer storm. I had never fawned over anyone in my life, but the desire was nearly impossible to ignore.

If the mere edge of his influence was so compelling, I was in trouble.

Pain broke the spell the last time I felt such a compulsion. I called to mind every bit of the grief that had almost broken me, Lia's cruel words and hard eyes, and let it all become lemon juice in my open wounds.

Fortifying was not a strong enough word to describe the sudden abyss that opened at my feet. Not too far, I told myself, tightening my grip on Manannán's arm as he nodded and led me through the curtain of fragrant purple flowers. Had he not given me time to prepare, I might have found myself deeply intoxicated by the scent, alone. But the sights and sounds beyond the veil were utterly spellbinding.

If you were wondering, faeries *do* sweat, and it smells like spring rain.

We stood along the edges of the circular ballroom shaped by a series of soaring white trees. Their branches wove a fragrant domed roof some fifty feet high in the center. Instead of the chandelier that would have hung from that point in an English ballroom, a tornado of fireflies danced and spun in a murmuration that lit everything with a soft green glow.

If a leaping brook could play the waltz with dew on the grass as chimes and wind in leaves as woodwinds, it might sound like the fae orchestra that played alien instruments in a circle at the center of the moss-covered floor.

They are overly fond of moss, but it is very nice on bare feet, and I had yet to see any fae creature in shoes. More to the point, most faeries, Aes sidhe included, wore nothing at all. Watching the bend and stretch of perfectly formed limbs as they danced with inhuman grace was hypnotic. It would have been a shame to hide such bodies under something so mundane as clothing.

A woman swirled by us, her breasts, stomach, hips, and thighs as lusciously round as a ripe peach. A crown of apple blossoms and butterflies adorned the red hair that trailed behind her on an invisible breeze. Every movement of her feet and hands held all the wild grace of a deer in flight.

"The music is as dangerous as the dancers," Manannán warned with a downward gesture. "Perhaps more so, because it goes straight to the blood."

I looked down to find my feet moving, as if I were about to let go of his arm and join. Stilling them was an act of will, not only because the music sang in my blood, but because the dancers were surpassingly beautiful. Each one interpreted the music as best suited their form, twisting, spinning, dipping, and leaping, and yet they each complimented the others.

It was a kaleidoscope of beauty in every color and shape; sharp and cutting, curved and soft, gnarled, smooth, ripe, and everything in between. It was impossible to look at any of them for too long without being drawn forward, but Manannán kept a firm grip on my arm.

The dance lasted far longer than any English dance, and, yet, the dancers did not appear to be winded in the slightest. When they stopped to applaud, a stab of sadness made tears spring to my eyes because it was over.

No wonder mortals rarely survived such encounters.

But my sister *had* survived it. I scanned the crowd to find her standing near the bank of windows in another green dress, watching the event with careful neutrality, Aris's gold chain clasped negligently in one hand.

He stood stone-faced and hard-eyed. No one approached either of them.

"It was difficult for her, at first," Manannán said, following my gaze.

"You were here when she was—when she arrived?" I asked.

"Oh, yes. She enchanted the entire court with her fire. But mortal fires smother quickly in the air of the Sunset Lands, and she had much to learn to survive."

"Did the trial not confirm her as a member?"

"It did. And if that was a guarantee of safety, she might have kept her spirit. But the politics of court life has made her quiet and careful. After all, she is the only half-mortal member."

I closed my eyes to retreat from the overwhelming visuals so I might have a moment to calm my emotions. He had just confirmed yet another hint of our parentage that I didn't want to examine, so I locked it away in the back of my mind with everything else I did not have the strength to face.

How severe had her suffering been to snuff out a light so great as hers was? Did she resent me for not finding a way to her sooner? If she did, could I blame her?

Manannán patted my hand and said, "Look alive, my girl. Now that there is a break in the dancing, it is time to socialize. Which is the second reason I desired your company tonight."

We were approached by fae of all sorts, each more dazzling than the last, with voices that sounded like bluebells or ringing swords, and eyes and skin of every imaginable shade, tone, and texture. And all of it happened beneath the watchful gaze of the King, who sat apart on a throne raised at the center of the circle of musicians.

An extraordinary man and woman approached us before the music resumed. She was as dark and elegant as an otter, with huge eyes and long lashes, and he as pale and long-limbed as a birch tree. Their nude bodies were adorned with silver chains and bells that sang with every movement, and little gems winked in their hair.

The pale man inclined his head to my escort. "How thoughtful of you, Manannán, to bring the human creature so we can enjoy her presence. It is rare we have such a novelty in court. Do you speak, child?"

The desire to answer him, to smile and fawn until he was pleased with me, was so overwhelming it nearly bent my knees. But Lia managed somehow, and I would never escape this place with her and Aris at my side if I allowed myself to be bent so easily.

I needed to establish my relation to the court as quickly as possible, so I clung to the pain that was never far from the surface in this place, wrestled back the desire to please him, and said, "Well and truly, sir, though you may not be pleased by what I have to say."

He laughed and clapped his hands, as one might when seeing a dog do a trick.

"How lovely," said his dark-eyed partner. "Does it dance, as well?"

"Oh, you must lend us a dance, Manannán," the man said, his leaf-green eyes alight with desire.

Manannán glanced at me, saw the heat of anger in my eyes, and said, "Only if you return the lady to me as soon as she wishes it."

"Surely you would not wish us to cut the fun short!"

"What I wish is of no moment," Manannán said. "I am but the Gaelethsdaughter's escort. It is her wishes I choose to honor."

The pale man leaned toward his partner and said, "It is sweet how he treats the human as if it is a real person. He is such an old dear."

Then he straightened and held his hand out to me. "Come, human, and let us see if you dance as well as you speak."

Manannán raised a brow at me, though not, I thought, to ask me if I wanted to accept. He told me much was to be learned from these events, if one had the stomach for it. And I could return to him any time I wished.

So I took the man's thin fingers in my own, gripping harder than I should have. He glanced at our joined hands with surprise, then pulled me away to the floor where other couples were already waiting for the music to begin. If the last song had been a waltz played by a spring morning, this one sounded like wolves on the hunt: drums and claws and pounding hearts.

The birch-man pulled me off into a whirling tempest, our feet flying over the moss, my hair whipping around us both as we spun.

Of all the polite skills Mama had drilled into me, dancing had always been my favorite. It did not require the constant attention of conversation with someone you did not care for. One could simply feel the steps and follow the music.

But there were no steps to this dance. It was a chase, and everyone in the circle was part of it. My heart thundered less with effort than excitement, as if I was a wolf running down a hind and my body was capable of days of exertion without rest.

"Do you give away your favors as freely as your dances, Gealeths-daughter?" Birch-man asked as he spun me.

"I give away nothing, sir. Even my words have a price."

"What did The Raven pay then? For I can still smell him on you despite the rose water."

"His heart," I lied. "I will take it from him and hold it in my two hands whenever I choose. If you will offer yours on a platter, as well, I will happily take it from you."

He barked a laugh and spun me faster. "No one values their heart less than The Raven, so I am afraid you have made a poor deal."

That was an insult to us both. Could I make him pay for it without committing myself to some kind of duel? I tightened my grip on his hand and jerked him into a counter spin, making him stumble. He swiftly corrected, but everyone had seen it happen.

Ugly color climbed the slender column of his neck. "Clever," he said, pulling me against him and leaning in close for a series of complex turns.

"It is a shame I cannot say the same for you."

"What is a shame," he said, glancing back at his partner who watched us with large, heavy-lidded eyes, "is that The Raven has been the first to plow such fertile fields when there are many more valuable partners with far sharper plows."

I was not stupid enough to believe he desired me. At least, not in any meaningful way. He saw me as a novelty, something to play with. Perhaps something to take from Manannán, a way to gain social capital at the expense of someone powerful.

Worse, he clearly thought using me would be a blow to Aris. And while he did not bother to hide his true, intoxicating nature from me, I was now too angry to feel much of the effect of it.

Aris had bowled me over when I wasn't expecting it and, were I honest, I was already attracted to him. The same could not be said for this creature. So I bared my teeth at him in something not quite resembling a smile and said, "If you happen to see any, be sure to point them out."

His expression shifted into something ugly, and his grip on my ribs tightened until pain made it hard to breathe. We had been dancing long enough that I was already winded, but I was not about to give this worthless creature the gratification of making me give up early.

With a flourish, he spun me into a blind turn at arm's length, and I somehow knew his goal was to send me crashing into another pair of dancers. A bit of embarrassment to add to the pain for my insult, and I did not have the strength to turn aside. I pivoted into it, instead, trying to at least see what was coming. A pillar. He wasn't merely trying to embarrass me. He was going to crush me against a pillar, and I did not have the benefit of healing as quickly as Aris.

If I hit, my bones would break, and that would make passing my trial impossible. I pulled back, but his hands were like manacles.

Another hand grasped my wrist and hauled me backward inches before I struck, in a maneuver I could not have pulled off on my own. Aris? I turned to stare directly into the hazel eyes of my sister.

Lia held my wrist in one hand and the Birch-man's forearm in the other, having stopped us both cold near the outside of the circle.

She looked the man up and down with slow contempt and said, "You are gracious to let me cut in, Shiverback."

He winced, and when she released his arm, leaving a smoking handprint on his pale skin. Lia pulled me back into the crowd of dancers. As we turned away, his expression twisted with impotent fury. But I had no attention to spare for him.

Lia had saved me. My heart thundered so hard my chest hurt.

"What do you think you are playing at?" Lia demanded, though her lips barely seemed to move, and I had to strain to hear her through the mad music. "Are you hoping to start a fight at the King's feet? How could you be so foolish?"

My throat stopped up, making it impossible to answer. Had she truly rescued me, or was she trying to ensure I did not embarrass her?

The music thrummed, breaking into a crescendo, and we stomped and turned and chased, holding hands like we had when we were girls spinning beneath the trees, our hair streaming behind us and tangling together, gold and ash, with the scent of wildflowers in the air.

Then it stopped.

The dancers cheered.

The world spun.

I fought for breath as lights danced at the corners of my vision. Lia released me and clapped her hands, once. Heavy, expectant silence settled over the room and hundreds of eyes bore down on me as I tried not to faint.

"It seems we have found something our human guest does passingly well. Since her first trial was so disappointing, I believe she owes us a demonstration. What do you say to a dance?"

The crowd roared.

Lia raised her eyes to the King, who was haloed in the shifting rainbows cast by the gems dangling from his antlers. He nodded once, and colors danced on the walls like autumn leaves falling.

"Give us the wild hunt," Lia ordered the musicians.

The crowd gasped.

"She is not suited to the Hunt," Aris's voice rang out. He'd pushed his way to the edge of the circle formed around Lia and I, his eyes hard. "I've been forced to spend time in her company. She will shame the music."

My heart, already withered in my chest, shrank in on itself.

"If she was such a trial to you, traitor," Shiverback called from the opposite side of the circle, "why did you risk your hide to save her from a whipping? Unless you've gotten something out of the deal you'd care to share?"

Lewd laughter.

"I do not believe in torturing weak things," Aris said, his voice thick with disdain. "But you are counted among the strong, are you not? I have no compunctions where you are concerned, yew-man."

"Enough of this!" Lia barked. "The King has spoken. Clear the floor."

Aris locked eyes with me as the crowd left me standing in an empty circle. His dark eyes pleaded with me, but for what? His jaw worked as if he wanted to speak but could not. And I did not have time to wonder why, because the first strains of music lit up the air like lighting on the horizon. A frisson of energy ran down my spine and through my limbs.

A storm built, filling the air with tension, fear, and hunger; the hunger of lightning for something to strike, of wind for trees to snap, of teeth and blood and the wild passion of desire.

Without my direction, my feet pounded the moss in time to the drums. The storm of music whirled around me, inside me, thrumming in my blood until I was spinning, chasing, mindless of anything but the need to move.

The wild hunt, she'd called it. And it was wild. The energy caught the crowd as well. Hot eyes followed me, bodies undulated, feet stamped, couples fell down upon the grass or entwined standing, giving themselves over to the madness that demanded sex or blood or death or all of it.

My body moved in ways I had never imagined, with grace I did not have, with speed I never earned. Sweat poured and breath sawed and my heart beat fast. Too fast. How long had I been dancing? Stars burst at the corners of my vision.

This would kill me.

Manannán was there, scooping me up and leading me through intricate steps. He took my weight on his arms and breathed on my face. The salt freshness of his breath brought air streaming back into my lungs, and I nearly fainted with relief.

Dancing with Manannán was like being carried by an ocean wave, powerful and inexorable, but his eyes were gentle. The music did not abate, but the crowd no longer noticed me. They were occupied with...other things. We slowed to a stop before the King.

Lia stood at his right, her eyes like agates, holding Aris's chain as he knelt at her feet. If I had been capable of feeling anything but exhaustion, I might have thrown myself at the both of them in fury.

"Permission to escort my guest back to her room, Your Majesty? If she does not rest, she may not be suitable for her trial, and as your chamberlain—"

"Take her," he said, hungry eyes surveying the crowd. He had already dismissed me from his mind.

"Take this one, as well," Lia said, thrusting Aris's chain at Manannán. "I want him out of my sight."

"Wait," Aris said, raising his head. "Give me a different cell. I will accept any other punishment."

Was I even capable of feeling more pain? It appeared so, because it crushed me like falling bricks.

"I will choose your punishment, Raven. Do not forget what you owe me. And remind that one to clean herself. She stinks of yew. Chamberlain."

Manannán took the chain to lead Aris and me from the festivities. We left the faeries in a state of bacchanalia...and my heart in shattered pieces on the moss.

21

Escape

GWEN

Compared to the madness of the dance and the blood-boiling magic of the wild hunt, the silence of the castle halls was soothing. I may have appreciated the peace if turmoil was not boiling in my guts and twisting my mind into tangled Euclidian knots. We stopped outside the bare wall of our cell, and Harl pressed one paw hand against the bark. Wood fibers slid backward and into themselves until the door appeared.

Manannán walked us into the cell and unclasped the collar from Aris's neck. Aris nodded in respect, and though he didn't rub the red marks away, he clearly wanted to. I did not blame him.

"I believe this belongs to you now, lady," Manannán said, and carefully placed the chain on my palm. "Thank you for accompanying me. I hope you found the experience enlightening."

Enlightening? Was that the word to describe my current state of near collapse?

He winked, then floated out of the cell like a retreating storm cloud. The door grew back. Aris and I stood in silence as I gripped the chain so tightly the links bit into my palms. For days after arriving in the Sunset Lands, the abyss of grief had claimed me. What reached for me now was something else, something darker and more dangerous.

If I did not tip into despair, anger was my only outlet, and I'd fought far too long to let despair win. I turned to Aris and pinned him to the spot with my eyes. When I spoke, the words came rasping up my throat, dry and raw.

"You will accept any other punishment than being stuck here with me?"

"Gwen—"

"Don't try to tell me you did not mean it. You must speak the truth, must you not?"

"Our chances of escape are better if—"

"Must. You. Not?"

Aris's jaw muscle clenched, and he flexed his fingers as if they were claws. "The truth about what? About whom? Do you have any idea how the truth can be twisted? Did I not warn you not to believe anything you saw or heard?"

I was brittle, and my voice cut the words into glittering shards I threw at him like daggers. "Don't pretend you said it to protect anyone but yourself."

"I don't have to pretend, you stubborn fool. Of all the things you could blame me for, and the list is long, this is the only one I will not accept."

"I blame you for lying to me!" I screamed. "For keeping all of this from me for...god's breath! You have known my sister was alive, known where she was for years, and said nothing! You've let me drink myself into stupors when you could have told me she was...that she was..."

She was, what? Not the girl I remembered? A powerful, angry woman who wanted nothing to do with me? An enemy? With a few simple words, he could have saved me from this pain. And he'd chosen not to.

"How could you?"

Aris winced, his lashes flinching as if I had slapped him. He dropped his eyes, swallowed, and clasped his hands behind his back.

"How can you refuse me an answer now, when I already know the truth?" I asked, bewildered.

His gaze lifted, and the pain in his eyes stopped the breath in my throat. Aris looked like a man falling and watching as the ground rose to meet him. His jaw worked as if wanted to speak but could not.

Perhaps...he truly *could not*.

I stumbled backward a few steps as the combined knowledge of half a lifetime of searching and study smashed into what I had just experienced like a wrecking ball. Everything shattered, and my brain scrambled to pick up the pieces and put them together into something resembling the truth.

Hesitant, not daring to believe it, I asked, "Aris, are you under a geis?" Hope flashed in his eyes but he didn't answer, so I changed my question. "If a faerie were under a geis, could they speak of it?"

"No."

"Not even to confirm or deny it?"

"Not even then."

"If I were to ask a faerie questions adjacent to their geis, could they answer them?"

"That depends upon the question."

"Does the geis extend to every form of communication or only speech?"

He didn't answer, which was answer enough. Perhaps I should approach the question even more obliquely.

"You used to work for my sister?"

"Yes."

"In her capacity as general, or for another reason?"

A moment of silence. "I was her chief spy...and assassin."

I paused. Assassin? My mind whirled, and some emotion I did not care to inspect slammed against what was left of my insides until I was tender and bruised. If I examined that too long, I'd find myself back in the pit of grief that yawned hungrily beneath my feet.

Better to focus on things I could use to get us out of here, and to cling to them like a lifeline until the worst of this passed.

Aris was under a geis, a magical injunction that could not be broken on pain of death, which meant I would learn nothing helpful from that angle. When I had asked him earlier why he helped me, he'd said, *because you are a good person*. That had to have been the truth because faeries could not lie, but as he said earlier, that did not mean it had been the *whole* truth.

And he was plenty talkative until I asked him why he had not told me about my sister, so the geis extended to her. But he had spoken of her earlier, so it didn't extend to her purely as subject matter. Or, rather, he had shared possibilities related to her. Which meant the geis was more specific.

If my reasoning was sound, someone made Aris swear a magical oath that he would tell me nothing of my sister or why he had come, or been sent, to me. But he'd been a spy: Lia's spy. An assassin for my human sister, who had become a general of the fae King. She wielded magic unlike anything I had ever seen. My sister, who once held me when I cried and told stories with me in the dark beneath our blanket forts.

She had spies and assassins and used magic to hurt and control people. Thoughts and emotions spiraled like debris hurled by a cyclone, and while I tried to catch them as they flew by, they slipped through my fingers and left me empty-handed.

If I could not focus on something other than the pain, it would kill me. I knew it. Yet the storm would not be held at bay by anything so simple as trying to save my own life.

Because, it turned out, there wasn't much to save. Not my sister. Not my best friend. Not even my ancestry.

"Everything has been a lie," I breathed.

All the air whooshed from my lungs, squeezed out by the building whirlwind inside me. Ophelia—my Lia—was a lie I created to deal with the disappearance of my sister, and the real woman was nothing like I imagined her to be.

Aristotle was not my friend, but a fae spy sent to me for reasons I could not even pressure him to reveal.

Percy was not a talented elvin hat maker, but a selkie who escaped the Sunset Lands.

And, if I were to follow the threads of several circumstances I brushed off, from the vampire to the Cutthroat King, and add them to Lia's magic and position in the court—not to mention the title they used in relation to me—everything would reveal another truth I did not want to confront.

My mind shied away from it, pushed it far back into a dark room, and closed the door as the storm picked up and flung all of my carefully rebuilt fortifications to the far corners of my soul, leaving me bare.

To rescue myself from paralyzing grief, I'd hung onto the hope of escape, of bringing Lia home. But my fingers were bare and bloody. I was losing my grip.

"Gwen," Aris said. He sounded almost as tortured as I felt.

I held up one hand to keep him away and choked out, "Don't."

My legs wobbled. He lunged forward to catch me, and I attacked him. There was nothing else to do. I had to act, and violence felt better than whatever slimy blackness was wrapping around me. But there was no cohesion, no technique in my attack, just flying fists, sobs, and tears that burned down my cheeks to my neck.

"Gwen, stop," he said, fighting to grab my wrists and pin them together at the small of my back. The motion pressed me hard against his chest, so I jerked my knee up between his legs. He turned his hips, and the blow fell ineffectually on his thigh. He sank down, dragging me with him, and I hit the moss floor on my knees, straddling his thighs with my arms pinned behind my back. Strands of hair stuck in the tear streaks on my cheeks.

"You are right," Aris said, his chest heaving from the exertion of trying to capture my arms without hurting me. "I have seen you drink yourself into a stupor. I have watched you study late into the night, and sip laudanum to chase away the memories, knowing I could do nothing to help. Stars, the helplessness was the worst. I could not comfort you or even pick you up and carry you to your bed."

He brushed the hair off my face with his free hand, dark eyes tracing the tracks of my tears as he wiped them away with the pad of his thumb. "So many times I thought death might be a worthy price to pay to take away your pain. But, and I must be honest with you...I could never bring myself to do it because you might send me away if I did and...torturing Mrs. Chapman was simply too much fun. I could not give her up."

An unwilling laugh that was also a sob broke through my trembling lips. How could he tease me now, when a storm of conflicting, uncontrollable emotion raged inside me? When that storm broke, it would either destroy me or turn me into a person I did not recognize.

I had nowhere to run and I could not sit here and wait it out, or I would go mad. My body, my very soul, shuddered with the force of it.

"Shh," Aris said and brushed a cool palm over my forehead. "It will be alright, Gwen. We will find a way out of this somehow." His touch was tender, consoling, and not enough. Not *nearly* enough.

Maybe I did not have to weather the storm alone. "Aris?"

"Hmm?"

I swallowed and blurted before I could stop myself, "Will you kiss me?"

He jerked away as if I had slapped him, releasing my arms and dislodging me from his thighs. "Don't ask me that."

"Why? What is wrong with me? Is this something else you cannot do? Are all your flirtations and sideways glances just another lie you don't tell?"

"No," he rasped, scooting away.

I watched him go, feeling the loss of his presence like a physical blow, leaving me alone against the storm. Alone, again. Unsure whether I spoke to him or myself, I asked, "Are you such a coward?"

"Yes! Yes, damn you, I am a coward." He surged to his feet and glared down at me, eyes burning. I felt in memory his body jerk as the lash fell, saw Aris hit the standing stone as Cassandra hurled him through the air, and remembered the comfort of his small body as I cried myself to sleep. I was being unfair to him and I could not bring myself to feel sorry for it. I was past feeling anything besides the turmoil. But Aris did not seem to notice.

He was too angry.

"For years I wished I could speak to you, or touch you. I accepted the crumbs of your kindness as if they were ambrosia because I knew you could never see me as anything other than a pet." His mouth twisted around the word as if it tasted sour. "And now that I stand before you in my own skin, I find that I do not have Tony's strength. He is a better man than I will ever be. If anyone ever deserved your affection, it is him.

"But I cannot turn you away, not even for your own good or my pride. If you tell me you need to cut me to ribbons with the broken pieces of your heart, I will let you do it. I cannot watch you destroy yourself. I am not strong enough for that. So do not ask it of me. Not unless..."

Somehow, between the beginning of his speech and the end, he closed the distance between us and pulled me to my feet. We stood facing one another, chests touching with every breath, the air between us alive with heat. My body shook to the rhythm of my heart, telling me to attack, or run, or scream, the adrenaline demanding that I do something—anything—to release what was building before it destroyed us both.

Aris cupped my face with both hands, his thumbs brushing my jaw as his fingers tightened on the back of my neck. "Is that what you need, Gwen? Someone to hurt? Or—" His eyes dropped to my lips, and he took a shuddering breath. "Someone to punish you?"

Warmth flooded my body, a shocking and distracting counter-point to the storm of emotions battering my insides. Had there been a bottle available, an herb, a potion, a spell, a knife, anything other than moss and wood, I would have used it gladly. But I had none of those things.

I had only Aris. If he offered an escape, I would take it.

"Yes," I heard myself say. "Can you...can you take me away from myself? I can't stand to be alone inside my body anymore."

His hands slid from my face to my neck, then down until he gripped my upper arms, as if he could trap me or keep me still while his eyes searched my face for something. "Once more," he said, his voice raw. "You must ask me once more."

His hands shook.

I could not form words, so I threw myself at him, wrapped my arms around his neck, and kissed him blindly.

Aris froze in shock. For a moment I thought he would not respond, but he growled into my mouth, reached down to grip my bottom, and lifted me from the ground. I wrapped my legs around his hips and squeezed, wanting to be closer, to get outside myself and as far into him as I could. My back hit the wall, and he pinned me there with his chest and hips, his tongue dipping into my mouth, not to sensually tease, but to demand a response.

I answered, throwing myself into the kiss with tongue and teeth, curling my fingers into the silk of his hair and locking him in place. He rolled his hips against mine and the thin fabric of our fae clothing did nothing to stop the hard length of him from pressing against my sensitive flesh, making pleasure shimmer down my legs in a liquid promise.

I moaned as need pooled low in my belly. He pulled his head away from mine, tearing out some of his hair in the process, and bit my neck hard enough to make me gasp. The contrast of the pain and pleasure heightened every sense, dragging me away from the last vestiges of my conscious mind until nothing existed but a desperate, slick need between my thighs and a hunger that made me wild.

His teeth raked against my skin, the caress hot and demanding as his fingers curled into a fist at the base of my skull. He twisted my head to the side and bared more of my neck. His other hand supported me from beneath, fingers splayed wide enough that the tips brushed against the most sensitive parts of me.

I had no restraint or self-control left, nothing but the need to feel anything that wasn't my pain. Writhing against his hand, against his mouth, I raked my nails down his back in a warning and a command. Aris pulled me away from the wall and fell to his knees on the moss floor, with me sitting astride his thighs. He ran his hands down my shoulders and to my chest, at first cupping my breasts so gently that I barely felt the touch.

His eyes were heavy-lidded, and the pulse at the base of his neck beat almost as fast as my own. His sensual mouth opened as he stared at me for so long that I thought I might burst into flame. When he bent to pull my nipple into his mouth, I cried in relief and arched against him, my head falling back and my hips grinding against his.

He froze, released me, then dragged me upright to look at him. "Say that again," he ordered.

What? Had I spoken?

He must have seen the confusion in my eyes because he tightened his fist in my hair and repeated, "Say it again. My name. Say it."

"Aris," I breathed.

For a moment he seemed spellbound, his eyes on my breasts, my throat, my swollen lips...and then he broke. He jerked up the hem of my dress to bare my thighs and slid his thumb along the wet length of me, circling the knot of my need with one finger as he lifted and positioned me with the other hand.

I hadn't realized he was naked, but he must have released whatever glamour allowed him to manifest clothing because, when I looked down, there was nothing to hide his body from me. I reached between us and wrapped my fingers around him, sliding from base to tip and testing his fullness. He bucked against my hand, making a deep sound of need that nearly dragged me over the edge.

I couldn't wait any longer, despite the growing tension of his thumb circling and teasing. I gripped him at the base, pulled myself forward, and sank down in one smooth motion that filled me so deeply I gasped and threw my head back.

Aris groaned and surged upward in an involuntary spasm that seated him to the hilt. I felt the throbbing of his need in the center of me, full and *finally* not alone. Cradling his face in both hands, I kissed him as I rocked my hips back and then forward, feeling the silken pressure of him slide all the way out before he filled me again.

Tension built as I rode him, coiling tighter and urging me faster. I bit his shoulder till he gasped in pain, then lifted myself and dropped back onto him hard, once, twice, until his head fell backward and he had to brace himself with his hands to stay upright.

There was nothing tender in our joining, nothing loving in our caresses, merely pure need and desire so sharp it made each stroke and pleasure an agony I held onto with every shard of my consciousness.

In a dizzying move, he twisted and dragged me beneath him, pinning me with his chest and thrusting once, hard enough to make our bodies slap together.

"You cannot know how many times I imagined this," he said against my lips. He raised himself to grab my wrists and pinned them above my head. But he wasn't moving, and I could not stand it. I pulled at him with my legs, locking them around his hips and dragging myself against him.

"I dreamed of making love to you," he said as he looked down at our joined bodies, hair falling over his forehead, lips wet from my mouth. "I wanted to cherish you, dreamed of the moment I entered you, and imagined watching your eyes widen as I filled you. But that's not what you want, is it?"

My eyes were wet with frustrated tears as I writhed, desperate for more of him, but he held himself still and watched, eyes hot. I turned my head to bite his wrist, but he pulled our arms farther to the side until I was splayed beneath him and locked in place.

"Please," I begged.

"Sun and moon," he breathed. "You are the most beautiful thing I have ever seen."

Had I been more than a mindless ball of need, I could have disputed that fact. But he was still inside me and if he didn't move soon, I would kill him. I just could not force the words out to say so.

"You don't want my tenderness, do you? You want *this*." He pulled out and thrust home in a powerful stroke that tore an incoherent noise from my throat. He bared his teeth in a feral smile before repeating the motion again and again, setting a punishing rhythm and driving himself so far into me that I began to break under the strain.

Aris freed one of my hands, which I immediately used to sink my fingernails into the straining muscles of his chest. He growled, leaned back, and said, "Wrap your legs around my hips again."

I obeyed without thinking. He gripped my hip with one hand to keep me in place, then raised himself on his knees until only my shoulder blades touched the ground. With his opposite thumb, he began the torturous teasing once more, holding my body rigid, impaled, as he circled the bundle of nerves, watching me come undone with strained cries.

Shimmering waves of pleasure tightened every muscle until I saw stars and my breath sawed in ragged, sobbing gasps. Finally, I broke, shuddering as a tidal wave of pleasure swamped me, my legs shaking so hard I couldn't keep them locked in place.

For a moment I sank into darkness, my strength spent. I could have slept then, and gladly. But Aris wasn't done. When I opened my eyes, he stared down at me with possessive satisfaction and unspent hunger, our bodies still joined as he held my hips locked against his.

"Now it is my turn." He grabbed one leg from where it lay limp and twisted it across his body so that I lay on my side with him still inside me. "That is a beautiful sight," he said, almost to himself, and moved experimentally.

The change in angle dragged him against me unexpectedly, making me gasp. He thrust a few more times just to watch me squirm, then grabbed my hips again and turned me. I went willingly as the need built once more, shifting until I was on my hands and knees before him. He spread my knees farther apart, baring me to his gaze, and made a little noise of approval before sinking his fingers into my hips hard enough to add a frisson of pain to the pleasure.

"Now I'm going to take what you offered me," he said through his teeth, squeezing harder. "Because that's what you want, isn't it?"

He retreated and thrust.

"Yes!"

One hand fisted in my hair, dragging my head back, the other controlling my hips, Aris thrust hard, harder, driving himself into me as if he could split me up the middle. I cried, grunted, made noises of need I had never heard myself make, and still wanted more. I needed him to take me away from myself until I was so far from Gwen and her troubled thoughts that I did not remember my own name.

I pushed back against him, and when he let go of my hip to slide his fingers around my throat, holding just firmly enough to make me feel the pressure, I gave myself up for lost. I took everything he had to give until I was bruised from it and still wanted more.

He arched my body back like a bow, reached one hand around until his fingers again found the center of my pleasure, and teased me as he thrust.

"One more time," he said. "Come for me, Gwen."

He sped up, sliding in and out, fingers circling, hand squeezing, until there was nothing left—no Lia, no Sunset Lands, no feeling but the tension and the pleasure and his body. Something terrifying built inside me, something wild and feral, a part of myself I'd kept under control for years. Aris stripped away the careful facade I built one thrust at a time, until the lady, the heiress, the woman was gone and all that was left was a creature I barely recognized.

I bared my teeth and arched my hips backward, meeting him thrust for thrust. My vision blurred as the creature inside me roared to life, ready to kill or die, desperate for the pleasure that shimmered just outside my reach.

When I looked over my shoulder, Aris was behind me, his face a mask of desire, sweat dripping from his temples, his muscles flexing in a sensual dance that sucked the rest of the breath from my lungs. He was so beautiful it hurt.

But it was his eyes that flayed me, dark as the night sky and hot as burning coals. The possession in them was as wild and feral as the need driving me.

"Fuck," he grunted, leaning back and sinking deeper, as if he'd grown inside me, stretching beyond what I thought my body was capable of. Blackness teased the corners of my vision and reality blurred until Aris grew raven's wings and trapped me with claws that drew beads of blood from my hip.

"Yes," I whimpered as my body tightened impossibly and oblivion tugged at me with velvet fingers. "Please."

"Now," Aris commanded.

I flew apart into a thousand pieces as he arched into me with a cry, his body tensing in long, wracking spasms that locked us together as we shook and panted.

We fell onto the moss, loose-jointed, spent, breathing hard, and too tired to move. The world spun in a kaleidoscope as gravity pulled me down, and down. Aris cradled me against his chest and curled around me as I fell headlong into the empty, blissful darkness of exhaustion and slept without dreaming or feeling.

22

Job Offers

TONY

The little apartment looked desperately empty without his mother's needlework hanging on the walls. Workmen carried out boxes and what few pieces of furniture his parents owned and loaded them into the cart he hired to take everything to the train station.

Mr. and Mrs. Hardwicke were moving in with the duchess for the foreseeable future, by her express orders, and no one was brave enough to gainsay her, least of all Tony. He would not be able to afford to keep his mother and father even in this small place for much longer. The balance of his accounts was dangerously low.

His parents, the duchess, and the children spent the holiday warmly ensconced in Wainwright doing whatever happy people did during holidays. Tony spent it searching for evidence tying the Marquis of Rutledge to the vampire and the kidnappings. So far,

he had failed to turn up anything concrete, just as he had failed at
nearly everything else.

"That's all of it, sir," the burly foreman said, gesturing to the
loaded cart outside.

Tony handed the man a few coins. "Can you see the cart is taken
to the yard and properly loaded and tagged? It's Hardwicke with
an e, going to Wainwright."

"You can count on us, sir. We shouldn't have no problems, now
the riots have died down. It was hairy work for a while, trying to
get shipments down the streets. Never knew when you might run
into a closed street or folks throwing bricks and bottles an' all. But
it seems like the cold weather took the fire right out of 'em."

"So it seems."

"Let's hope it holds, eh? Alright, you lot! Look lively," the foreman called as he pulled on his cap and joined his crew.

Tony stood on the stairs as they departed. Was it the cold weather
that stopped the demonstrations from turning into riots, or was it
the absence of the marquis and his cronies? The League for Equal
Representation still organized protests and demonstrations, but
the riots abated shortly after he disappeared.

And Gwen had seen the vampire last year, just as the riot broke
out that spilled into the zoo. The vampire had access to members
of the House of Lords, so it was possible Rutledge was responsible
for that connection, too.

The rioting turned public opinion against the movement,
which, Tony suspected, was the purpose. What he still didn't understand was why the marquis wanted to subvert the movement in
the first place.

Humans, elves, and dwarves should be equally represented, both in Parliament and in the peerage. Land and titles—and therefore, power—should not be exclusive to humans. And he could not make out how the marquis would benefit from keeping it so.

The man would not lose his title and had no investments in industries competing with either the Artisan's Guild or the Artificer's Guild. At least, none Tony had discovered. But he wasn't done looking.

Absently, he locked the door to his parents' home for the last time. He'd have to turn the key over to the landlord soon, but, in the meantime, there were more important things to do. Sighing a puff of white breath into the air, Tony turned up the collar of his jacket and set off down the street with his hands in his pockets.

He had an appointment to keep.

Two blocks later he turned down a side street and hopped into a waiting hansom. Unlike most cabriolets, which had open faces, this one was equipped with a pull-close and curtain for privacy. These *Sneaky Sams* were generally reserved for well-to-do ladies of ill-repute, which made it the perfect disguise for the Cutthroat King.

The lord of New London's underworld sat on the right-hand side of the bench with a fur blanket over his legs and an incongruous pipe between his teeth. He lifted the corner of the blanket and patted the seat encouragingly.

I must be mad, Tony thought.

But there was nowhere else to sit, so he clenched his jaw and swung himself into the cab. He pulled the folding window closed and tucked himself between the most dangerous criminal in England, and a little window that would allow neither escape nor rescue if something went wrong.

"Mr. Hardwicke," the King said around the pipe as his dark eyes glinted merrily. "I must admit, I was intrigued to receive your message. Though it was unfair of you to use the coin reserved for her ladyship."

"Her ladyship is not here to use it, and it was the only way I could guarantee my message would reach you. I have a proposition for you."

The man—or faerie, as the case may be—sat up and raised one eyebrow. "Do you, really? That sounds like fun. One so rarely has the chance to corrupt bastions of integrity."

"Spare me the act. I am not here for games."

"Oh, but you are, Inspector."

"I am no longer an inspector, as you certainly already know."

"Of course you are. In your heart, you still have not let go of the man you were when you wore the badge. But you will, in time. When that happens, I shall refrain from using the name. Perhaps then we can come up with something more fun to call you."

Tony's hands closed into fists in the fur. Which was, he hated to admit, soft and warm and welcome after the chilly walk. He focused on the sensation of the fur and fought to control his temper, which had been balancing on a knife's edge since Gwen disappeared.

The King was needling him, testing his boundaries, and if he reacted, the man would have won and gained valuable information about how to manipulate him. So he forced himself to respond in an even voice.

"I will give you the Marquis of Rutledge if you furnish me with the information I need to catch him."

The humorous expression dropped like a discarded mask. "Why would I want such a thing?"

"Because you hate the man. He wronged you, and you want revenge."

The King stared at him as if he could dig the thoughts out of Tony's head after those dark eyes bored a hole in his skull. "What makes you think I cannot have his head delivered to my lap on a platter any time I choose to call for it?

"Because you have not yet done it."

The King leaned back and chewed the bit of his pipe for a moment, looking less like a criminal and more like a nobleman. "I am patient."

"I am not."

After a moment of thought, the King smiled, sharp and predatory. "Very well, Inspector. Ask me what you will. But I'll have your word, first. The marquis will be delivered to me, and not to Scotland Yard or another law enforcement agency: me. As soon as it is in your power to do so. Alive."

"You do not say unharmed?"

"Oh, harm him, by all means."

Tony remembered Gwen's black eye and swollen lip, and the children laid out for sacrifice thanks to a spell Rutledge gave Cassandra Monmouth. He cracked his knuckles. "I intend to."

"I have one additional condition. A small one."

"What?"

"I need to find someone, too."

Tony narrowed his eyes. Who in New London would be beyond the reach of the Cutthroat King? Rutledge was an extraordinary case, a man with the contacts and the means to disappear. Anyone else was likely fair game. "Who?"

"No one important. An inventor."

"Why do you need this inventor? I will not deliver an innocent person to be harmed."

An ironic smile curled one corner of the man's mouth, but his eyes were hard. "A pretty bit of morality coming from a member of the Yard."

"I'm not a member. And if you do not answer my question, our deal is off."

The King sighed. "I mean no harm to the man. Neither will I restrain his freedom. That debt has already been paid."

What debt had been paid, and by whom? Beyond bringing Rutledge to justice, it really was none of his business but... "Alright. Tell me what you can."

"Shall we shake on it? You find the inventor for me, I tell you everything I know about Lord Rutledge, and you deliver him to me. When you're done with him, of course. So long as he is alive and conscious, I have no other demands."

A fist of guilt closed around Tony's heart. Was he truly about to go from being a law-abiding member of the New London Police to making a deal with the ruler of one of the most powerful criminal syndicates in Europe?

He remembered the tears trapped on Claire Monmouth's lashes when he carried her body back to her home; the traumatized expressions of the children meant to be sacrificed on her behalf; Cassandra Monmouth's desperation, the determination of a mother to save her child.

And Gwen, her eyes wide and full of fear as magic sucked her backward through a portal.

None of those tragedies would have occurred without the damned grimoire, a book Rutledge purposefully loosed upon the world. He held out his hand, and the Cutthroat King took it.

The man had a smile like a shark. "So glad to be working with you, Inspector."

Snow blanketed the ground when Tony stepped off the train. How could it still be winter when so much had happened? The Wainwright coach and four were waiting for him, heater blazing away to keep the cab warm. As soon as his parents' belongings were loaded onto the cart, he climbed inside and watched the frosty world pass by through the window.

Wainwright loomed over the landscape, its red towers glowing with the warm, steady light of dwarven lamps. His mother no longer had to squint by firelight or flickering candles to sew. Another blessing he owed to the women of the St. James family.

Tony now had at least two debts to settle, one paid to the duchess for caring for his family while he was destitute, and one owed by the Marquis of Rutledge. One he would pay in blood.

But first, he had to deliver his parent's possessions so he would be free to find the missing Mr. Beauregard. The inventor was the key to locating more missing puzzle pieces regarding the Marquis's disappearance.

Find the inventor and turn him over, find the Marquis, wring every bit of information out of him, and turn him over, as well. And then?

The carriage pulled up and Tony shoved that question to the back of his mind. He hopped down and jogged up the steps, pulling off his hat and gloves as he entered the foyer.

"Watch out!" a high-pitched voice called.

He ducked in time to avoid the little white birdie as it whizzed above his head and bounced off the wall, hitting the carpet and rolling to a lopsided stop against his shoe. With two fingers he plucked it off the floor and turned to see his mother, the duchess, Sally, and Sam standing in groups of two at opposite sides of the parlor, each holding a badminton racket.

They'd pushed the furniture out of the way and strung a table-cloth between them like a net. His mother was radiant with a combination of embarrassment and joy. Her cheeks were full again, comfort and a good diet softening the bones in her face the way the snow softened the landscape outside.

"Anthony!" she cried, hurrying across the room to embrace him.

He kissed her cheek and held her at arm's length for a moment. She looked happier and healthier than she had in years. He hadn't been able to give her that. Guilt chewed at his guts like a rat in the walls, trying to get free.

But none of that showed in his voice when he said, "Hello, Mother."

"Your father is napping by the fire," she said, pulling him into the room. "We thought we had better get a bit of exercise, as it has been too snowy to walk out of doors of late."

"No need to explain yourself to me. I think it looks like the perfect way to spend an afternoon."

She handed him off for greetings. Tony did his best, maintaining a semblance of joviality as long as possible. He took the duchess aside while Lawton, the butler, carried in refreshments for the players.

"The cart was right behind the carriage," he told her. "They should unload it within the half-hour."

"How was your trip?"

"Long. How have the children been?"

She glanced over her shoulder, eyes soft with affection and worry. "About how one would expect. Sam closed himself off, though his personality sneaks through every now and then. And Sally...well, Sally has taken the burden as if it is hers to bear. She comforts everyone, is solicitous to everyone, and then disappears into the library each evening. I think she believes she might find something that can—some way for Gwen—well—" She cleared her throat and touched his arm. "You must be tired. I'll hold them off if you would like to rest."

He took advantage of her offer and retreated to the room set aside for him. A thick mattress, warm blankets, and soft pillows were luxuries he denied himself for years because his money had more important places to go. But even his privations hadn't mattered in the end.

With a grateful sigh, he sank into the bed and let the world go dark.

The duchess cornered him in the drawing room after dinner.

He thought he had successfully escaped with a glass of whisky in one hand and a book in the other. The rest of the family was roasting chestnuts in the sitting room, but she'd followed him with a determined expression that reminded him so much of Gwen it hurt to look at her.

"What can I do for you, Your Grace?"

"Tony?"

"Yes?"

"Kindly stop calling me that. Unless we are in a formal setting where other ears would be shocked, I would prefer it if you called me by my given name."

So this was where Gwen inherited her distaste for formality, though the duchess normally had manners that put royalty to shame. "Evelyn," he conceded. "Is there something I can help you with?"

"Yes, as a matter of fact, there is. Though I have a feeling you will want to sit down."

He better than to argue with the duch—with Evelyn. Choosing a chair by the fire, he set aside the book he was clearly not going to be given the chance to read, and waited.

Evelyn didn't sit so much as alight on the settee. Ankles crossed, hands neatly folded in her lap, perfectly arranged blonde hair going grey in that way only blonde hair did—simply getting paler and more delicate—she was a picture of aristocratic perfection. So different than her daughter, and yet their hearts were two of a kind.

"I'll cut right to the chase, shall I? I want to hire you."

Tony nearly spit out his whisky. "I'm sorry?"

"Have you seen the size of this estate, Tony?"

"A chunk of it. It's quite large."

Evelyn sighed. "You have not seen half of it. Not even a quarter. There are holdings, trusts, investments...men's work, my husband used to say. But the truth is that managing all this takes a keen business mind."

"I'm certain of it," he agreed, not quite sure what she was getting at.

"I have managed this estate for the last decade and learned many valuable things, not the least of which is that a large part of success in business ventures is recognizing a good investment when you see one. And I believe you are a good investment."

He downed the rest of his drink and welcomed the burn that slid down his throat. "I have nothing to invest in, as you well know."

She brushed that off. "Of course you do. You have yourself."

"I'm not certain I follow, Your G—Evelyn," he corrected when she glared at him.

"I would like to finance a private investigation agency, based in New London. And I would like you to run it."

A hollow pain shot through his stomach as if he'd just been punched, and he couldn't stop himself from saying, "I appreciate your intentions, but I am not a charity case and I do not want your pity."

She snorted. It was such a Gwen-like response that it brought him up short.

"Do you believe I would disrespect you in such a manner? I am making a business decision. There is no agency in England that can properly investigate supernatural and magical"—she waved her hand as if none of the words she wanted to use would fit—"mysteries. Scotland Yard has a monster department if you'd like to call it that, but they are not equipped for the kind of mysteries I would like solved. If there had been such an agency, perhaps we might have found Ophelia, and Gwen would never have...my daughters might still be here if someone knew where to look, and how."

The guilt succeeded in chewing through his stomach and moved on to his heart. He hadn't been able to stop Gwen. Evelyn would be wrong to trust him to try.

"I know nothing of the occult or of magic, beyond what I have learned at your daughter's side. And that wasn't enough to stop her."

Evelyn's mouth thinned, but she said, "You can learn. You can hire those who do know. I am well aware of the books Gwen keeps in the townhouse, and I know what Sally has also been studying, though she tries to hide it from me."

"Evelyn—" he began, but she spoke over him.

"I will fund the business for the first five years, or until you begin turning a profit. Once the business is profitable, I expect twenty-five percent of the yearly income until my investment is paid off, and ten percent of it afterward. You can choose the location of the office, supplies, and employees. You may also set the budget. All I ask is that mine is the first case you take."

Her hazel eyes might as well have been moss-covered granite for all the give he saw in them. She wanted her daughters back, and she didn't want any other parent to be forced to give up on their children because the constables did not know how to look for them.

He could search for Gwen, he could continue to help people, and he could do it with what amounted to carte blanche. With resources like that, he might also be able to bring down the marquis and his ilk.

Besides all of that, she watched him with the desperate, furious hope of a mother burning in her eyes. How could he tell her no?

When he pushed open the library door, he found Sally exactly where he expected to: in a chair near the fireplace with several books and papers spread on the table before her. In the two years since coming to live with Gwen, Sally had grown from a scrappy orphan to a proper young lady, making every change in her power to become powerful in her own right. She even sounded like a young aristocrat.

But watching her pore over the books, her brows drawn in concentration, she looked so young and vulnerable. She did not deserve the pain of Gwen's absence or the sense of responsibility she'd drawn on herself.

"How is the research coming?" he asked.

She squeaked and jerked upright, one hand over her heart. "Can't you warn a person before sneaking up on them?"

"I did not sneak," he said. "I even knocked."

Her cheeks turned pink. "Oh. I suppose I was...absorbed."

"I suppose so," he said, leaning over the table and shuffling the papers about. There were alchemical symbols, patterns, texts in languages he didn't recognize, and the open grimoire at the center. "Have you learned anything useful?"

Her mouth flattened into an unhappy line. "No. I don't know what makes me think I can find something when Lady Gwen looked for years but..." She shrugged.

"You can't stop?"

"The life Sam and I have now, we have it because of her."

"You have it because you are a good person, Sally."

She shook her head, her lips pinched together in a thin line. The girl was riding the ragged edge of self-control. How many hours had she spent researching? Finally, Sally swallowed and admitted in a ragged voice, "I love her."

A little arrow of pain pierced his already wounded heart. "And we are going to find a way to get her back," he said, in that moment promising her as much as himself. Sally and her brother were good people who deserved to be cared for by someone who loved them. They deserved Gwen, and Evelyn deserved a daughter she could fuss over and worry about.

If there were a way to bring his father back, to fully return him to the man Tony had grown up loving, wouldn't that search have been worthwhile?

Sally's eyes filled with tears. "You promise?"

He touched her cheek and she closed her eyes, one tear slipping from beneath her lashes. "I promise."

The next day, Tony set off for the moor with a sack full of supplies, and enough paper and ink to catalogue the entire site of the spell that stole Gwen from them.

23

Telepathic Jewelry

GWEN

When I woke, Aris was still curled around me, one arm thrown over my stomach and wrapped beneath my ribs. His breath warmed the back of my neck and stirred the hairs there, making goosebumps run down my arms. My first instinct was to snuggle backward and press my bottom against his hips, but we lay naked on the moss floor of the cell and the door could open at any moment.

It was difficult not to think, not to remember how easy it was to lose myself in his arms, and harder not to want more of him, even with the threat of discovery. Aris had given me the relief I had so desperately needed to exorcise the storm raging inside of me. Now the sky was calm, and while my soul still hurt in ways I did not have the words to express, even to myself, the bone-deep urge to run or fight had dwindled.

But the desire to find more satisfaction had not.

That was an urge I had probably better control. As much as I felt like I knew him from years of his company, even if in another form, his geis made it clear there was much more I did not know. And this was one of those peculiar situations in which ignorance was not bliss. Ignorance might, in fact, be deadly in the long run.

I rolled out of his grasp and slid the fae gown back on, making the mistake of glancing down at him over my shoulder as I tied the girdle.

He lay propped on one elbow, dark hair mussed, gazing at me with a pleasure I had never seen in the eyes of any man, not even Tony; as if merely watching me made him happy. Which made the idea of joining him on the moss ridiculously tempting, never mind his muscled torso and other, more distracting bits of flesh.

He smiled a slow, sensual smile that turned my brain to mush, so I turned resolutely away to fasten the damn belt before my body got the better of my common sense.

"You are a cruel woman, Gwenevere St. James," he said, but his voice sounded relaxed and pleased.

"Glamour some suitable clothing onto your naked hide, you bloody Corinthian."

"Only if you retrieve the plate of food left for us by the door."

A plate of food covered by a napkin sat lopsided on the moss. When had it been delivered?

When I turned, he was suitably clothed again in black trousers and a black shirtwaist open at the neck, sleeves rolled up over the taut muscles of his forearms. Bloody damned hell in a handbasket. This had to stop. Every little glance and detail should not have the power to turn me into a lusty glutton. It hadn't been so long since I was intimate with a man...well, I suppose it had.

Tony and I had never formalized our relationship, but it still felt wrong to bring someone else to my bed while the possibility existed. And that was what? Two years? No wonder my mind kept replaying the feel of Aris's hands on my body. A shudder made me clench my jaw and search for a distraction.

Food. Food was good. As soon as I settled on the idea of eating, my stomach drove everything else from my mind. Before I sank my teeth into a roll, I raised my brows and made a little questioning noise.

"It is safe," Aris said, popping a grape into his mouth. "They will not try to feed you fae food now that the trial is underway. They won't want to contaminate the outcome."

"Can faerie food really bind you to the Sunset Lands?"

"Not in the way the stories tell it, no. It is simply ridiculously tasty and makes enjoying mortal fare nearly impossible. Imagine giving up your bread and eating a bit of this moss, instead."

I plucked a bundle of moss and twirled it thoughtfully. "It might be edible with a bit of marmalade."

"You cannot eat marmalade on everything."

"Would you care to make a wager on that?"

"I would not. You'd pretend to like it merely to spite me."

"That is a baseless accusation and entirely true. How do they get mortal food if they do not grow it?"

He waved his fingers. "Magic."

I swallowed a mouthful of very fine cheese. "Can you tell me anything about the next part of the trials?"

"Unfortunately, I cannot. They are exceedingly rare, from what I understand. Then again, I am not so old as some in the court, so *rare* is a matter of perspective."

"How old are you, if it is not a taboo question?"

"It is, but I have lived long enough among humans that I do not feel the sting of it. Reckoning time between the Sunset and mortal lands is tricky because there are no concrete rules on how time passes, but if I had to hazard a guess, I would say somewhere around forty or fifty years in human terms."

"Still a young man, then," I said, but I wasn't really thinking about his age. My mind was already on the next logical question. "How much time has passed in the mortal world since we have been here?"

Aris sighed and glanced at me from the corner of his eye. "There is no way to know. An hour. A week. The magic separating our worlds doesn't behave according to logic. But our perception of the passage of time is equally dubious. Time feels slower here."

A little arrow of pain pinned my fluttering heart to the inside of my ribcage. I had been born exactly ten minutes before Lia, and somehow she had always behaved as if she were the older sister. Now she may be years older or younger. Yet one more small, intimate detail of our connected lives this place stole from us.

"What did the king mean the other day about my blood breeding true? Does it have anything to do with my sister's magic?"

Aris thought as he ran a grape over the backs of his knuckles. "Something like. They say some mortals exhibit supernatural abilities when they spend enough time in fae lands. This place was created by magic, after all, so perhaps it makes the manifestation of it easier."

When I fought the vampire, he told me he smelled power in my blood, though I did not possess any magic. And he called me—my mind skittered away from the memory. I did not need to track down the truth of that claim right now, particularly when it would not help my current situation.

But I did need to know something else. "Might I manifest it?"

"If you have not seen it yet, then I doubt it. Though there may be other—" His mouth snapped shut, teeth clacking together. He winced.

"Are you alright?"

He nodded and loosened his jaw, wincing, but did not finish his thought.

"May be other *what*?"

His lips thinned, but he did not answer.

"The geis?" I asked.

A sigh.

Right. So he could not speak directly of my sister, his geis, or any possibility that I might have...what? Some other ability in my blood. That painted a very interesting picture. Who would benefit from forcing Aris to keep this knowledge to himself?

To answer any of those questions, I would have to ask the one thing I had been avoiding thinking about for many months. "Aris. Can fae and humans truly have children?"

He choked on a bit of bread, then said, "What a question, Gwen. Thinking of starting a family, are you? I'm flattered, but I have never seen myself as a father."

I scowled at him. "Can they?"

"Yes."

"And those children may inherit the qualities of either parent."

"If the stories are to be believed."

"Ophelia's magic is not human magic." It was not a question, and he did not answer.

I plucked more moss and tore off small chunks to give my hands something non-violent to do. Firmly pushing the image of my unnaturally beautiful and persuasive mother out of my mind, I focused on finding answers that could help me now.

I'd have to phrase my next question carefully. "If a—" My voice died, but I forced the word out with a ruthlessness borne of necessity, "if a changeling bore the gift of their fae parent, wouldn't they know it?"

This must have been safer ground, because Aris said, "Mortal lands tend to...what is a suitable word? Dampen, I suppose, the gifts of non-faerie children. More than that, people tend to overlook what they take for granted, especially if their gift is not extraordinarily visible or distinguishing."

"Can you tell if I have anything of the sort?"

He looked at me helplessly. Dammit. I reworded the question. "Are there any common non-magical gifts inherited by changelings?"

It was much easier to ask that question when I could pretend it did not affect me.

"I don't know if the word common can be applied. There are not enough humans in the Sunset Lands to make a judgment. Perhaps asking Percy would yield more results, but"—he leaned forward and stared at me—"magic is not the only quality separating faeries and mortals. Faeries are stronger, faster, and have keener senses. It would be unsurprising if a changeling inherited such traits from their fae parent."

My heart galloped and my head felt like it was about to detach and float up toward the ceiling like a balloon.

"A changeling might notice," he continued, voice soft and slow, as if he knew the answer would hurt, "that they can hear things other mortals cannot. That they are stronger and faster than their peers. They may distinguish details other mortals miss or heal faster and sustain less damage. They may even age far more slowly."

I wanted to say I didn't do any of those things, but the words dried up before they reached my tongue. How many times had I heard Mr. Yates or Mrs. Chapman long before they entered the room despite the thick carpets? Several days ago, I bent the Cutthroat King's crown with a negligent squeeze of one hand.

You may not have any magic, but your blood is full of power. Is that what keeps you from my thrall, delicious changeling child?

In an instant, I was back in the clearing, trapped by the grey-faced vampire as he whispered in my ear while my blood dripped from his chin. Darkness closed in at the edges of my vision.

"Breathe, Gwen."

I sucked in a shaky breath. Apparently, one could only bear so much truth before one's nervous system shut down to protect itself. Hundreds of questions bubbled to the surface of my mind, but the only ones that mattered were ones that brought me closer to escaping with Lia.

So I ruthlessly ignored everything else my heart was burning to know and asked, "Being faster or stronger than average humans will not be enough to gain me entry to the court, will it?"

He chewed thoughtfully, a wrinkle appearing between his brows. "The value of a gift is defined by what you do with it. So, if you fail? Likely not. Unless one of the lords or ladies takes a shine to you and makes a servant or plaything of you."

I remembered the heartbreaking beauty of the fae, the control Aris had over me when he stopped masking his true nature, and shuddered. To be a willing, grateful slave?

"I think I would rather be dead."

His mouth twisted, but he said, "Some humans find the experience...rather enjoyable, I've heard. While they live, anyway."

"Because they are mindless slaves to the pleasure of it."

"You certainly did not seem to mind the pleasure, if the noises you made were any indication."

"That is beside the point." I sniffed.

"I'd say it was right on point, twice at least."

I threw the remaining bread at his head, but he batted it out of the air, laughing. It hit the pile of chains I'd thoughtlessly discarded the night before, which shifted with a musical tinkling. Something silver toward the bottom of the pile caught my eye, peeking between clumps of moss. I twisted to get a better look. Hadn't all the links been gold?

"Who gave you the bruise on your ribs?" Aris asked.

Distracted, I glanced down at the spot Shiverback had squeezed and saw a purple bruise as large as my palm through the sheer fabric.

"Was it me?" His voice was sharp and hard, like a blade held against his own throat.

Had he not noticed it last night? Perhaps it was too early for the bruise to show or he had his mind on...other things.

"No," I said. "No, it wasn't you. It was Shiverback, who seemed to think I made a mistake in seducing you. He was a few hours too early on that guess."

Aris didn't smile. He did not even blink. He was as still as a spring loaded with force, or a cat about to pounce. "How did he do it?"

Seeing Aris so still with his eyes flat and his jaw clenched made it much easier to believe he was an assassin. "I am not certain I should answer."

"If you don't tell me, I will find out for myself."

I needed to distract him, because the darkness in his voice was, quite frankly, rather frightening. So I stood and crossed to the pile of chains. "And what do you propose to do about it while trapped in here with me?"

"They will not keep me imprisoned forever."

"So certain, are you?" I asked, bending to fish the silver from the moss.

"I am too valuable to kill. The King will want to use me eventually."

Instead of focusing on the threat implicit in his statement, I lay the object on my palm. It was a silver ring, plain and perfect. Turning it over, I watched the soft glow of the mushrooms above travel across the smooth surface. Where had it come from?

"Did I not warn you about accepting gifts?"

I jumped, clutching the ring in a surprised fist, and glared at him. "Must you always be sneaking up on people? It wasn't a gift. I just found it here."

He took my hand, turned it over, kissed my wrist, and snatched the ring from me. "In the pile of metal Manannán gave you."

"Yes."

Aris returned his attention to the ring, leaving me free to wonder why Manannán would hide a ring in the chains he gave me when he could easily have used his influence to force me to accept it.

Aris tilted the ring to catch the light. "Words have been engraved on the inside."

He read them in a musical language full of rolling R's and sibilant sounds. His eyes widened. "How did she manage this so quickly?" Then he grabbed my hand and slid the ring onto my index finger.

"What does it mean?" I asked.

"Say your sister's name. Her full name."

"Isn't that dangerous?"

"The power of your name is partly in the giving of it. She has not given it to anyone, and I already know it, so you won't be giving me any power over her."

"How do you know?"

He pursed his lips and raised an eyebrow.

"Right. The geis. What will happen if I say it?"

He blew out a frustrated breath. "What must I do to earn your trust? Shall I save your life a few more times? Will that do it?"

How much more must he do? Aristotle had been my friend for years, had made me laugh, comforted me, kept me company, and yes, saved my life many times. But Aris, The Raven of Obyrron's court, who had lied to me for years? I wasn't so certain.

The geis alone was reason enough to distrust him because I had no way of knowing what it forced him to do or keep from me. But I did not have any other allies, and I needed every scrap of information I could get.

"Alright." I settled myself, took a deep breath, and said, "Ophelia Magnolia St. James."

Thank the moon and stars! What took you so long? Never mind. Gigi, listen to me. If he is there with you, and if you trust him, take the Raven's hand and hold it so his skin presses against the ring.

Lia's voice in my head was as clear as if she stood in front of me, but it was so disorienting that I flinched in surprise and nearly fell over. Aris caught me by the arms to steady me, his eyes concerned.

Can you hear me? Lia? I thought at her.

For the love of—don't yell! And we don't have time for questions, just do as I say or tell me if you cannot.

Heart pounding, I looked at Aris and considered his dark eyes, eyes I knew so well...then grabbed his hand and threaded my fingers through his.

He's here, I thought.

Raven, Lia said with absolute command in her voice, *you must take my sister from this place immediately.*

Aris rolled his eyes, and his mental voice was just as sarcastic as his expression. *Oh, thank you for that insight, great and wise General. I should have thought of that before, but, well, there's this cell, you see, and—*

Unless you'd like several more lashes, shut your beak and listen: the next two trials are of strength and beauty, to begin tomorrow tonight. I convinced the King to give her a day of rest to prepare. When my sister passes, the King will hold a great feast to welcome her to the court. During the feast, you must create a distraction to cover your escape. Take her then and escort her through the rift. You have my permission to use any means necessary to complete both instructions.

You have much more freedom to create a distraction than I.

If you only knew, Lia thought, and what passed for her mental voice was thick with frustration. *I have done what I can, but any additional help you can provide will make it easier to get her out.*

After a moment of silence, Aris said, *You realize what this means for me?*

If you are not willing, now is the time to tell me.

His gaze slid to mine, eyes searching. Then his jaw clenched. *I am willing.*

Good. Gwen—

Willing to what? Wait, how are you doing this? Lia I—what if I don't pass? I blurted the mental thought, feeling swept along in a current I could neither stop nor swim against.

You will pass, Lia said, as if the question was ridiculous. *The important part is that you must listen to The Raven. He is the only one who can help you escape. Now, prepare for the trial in whatever way seems best to you and either hide or destroy this ring by any means necessary.*

Then the sense of her presence faded.

Lia? Lia! Wait, come back!

"She's gone, Gwen."

"Ophelia Magnolia St. James," I said.

Nothing.

"Ophelia Mag—"

Aris grabbed my face in both hands. "Gwen. She. Is. Gone."

I stared down at the silver ring for so long that my vision blurred. When I could no longer see, I looked up and said, with swimming eyes, "She doesn't hate me."

An entire world fell off my shoulders. I was so light I might crumble to dust and float off on the breeze. Everything holding me together, the stubborn determination, pain, and hope, burned away, leaving me in disconnected pieces.

I shook so hard my bones ached.

Aris pulled me into his arms and cradled my head against his chest as I fought for self-control.

How could I make sense of all this? The deception, the cruelty, the politics? My mind was too scattered to bring the gears grinding into place. I wanted to fall apart and cry until I was nothing but an empty husk, until the strange mixture of joy, pain, and relief burned itself out.

But I did not have time to fall apart again, and it wouldn't help me in this moment, in any case. For a while, I let the comfort of Aris's body, the warmth of him and the sound of his heart beneath my ear, become the anchor tethering me to sanity.

Soon my breathing and heartbeat slowed to match his, and the shaking subsided. I mentally hauled myself back into order, stepped out of his embrace, dried my eyes with the heels of my hands, and pulled the ring off of my finger.

"What does the trial entail?" I asked as I crossed the room to the folded remains of my clothing and tucked the ring into one of the many secret pockets Percy had sewn into the coat. "Will they expect me to lift something heavy?"

"Strength of arms. As in combat."

I faltered. Aris had proved to me, in a rather humiliating fashion, that my chances of fighting a faerie and winning were laughably slim, despite my newly recognized advantages. I would have had more luck with magic. But I swallowed my misgivings and asked, "How does it work?"

"The King chooses a champion to face the challenger in single combat. The challenger chooses the weapon, and the duel ends with submission or death."

"That's comforting. I don't know what makes Lia think I can win, but it won't hurt to show up in a bit of armor."

I stripped out of the fae gown, tied up my hair, and began applying layer after layer of thick British winter wear, topped by the jacket Percy made for me. When I was done, I raised a brow at Aris and said, "Next time remind me to charge for the show, if you cannot keep your eyes to yourself."

He grinned a slow, sinful grin, and my insides turned to jelly.

"Never," he said. Then his expression slid back toward neutrality and he gestured to the pile of translucent fabric I'd left on the floor. "That's a gamble, Gwen. It is likely the King will be insulted by your appearing before him improperly attired."

"A bigger gamble is fighting a more skilled opponent with no protection."

"Fair enough. Just be prepared if he orders the guards to strip you."

"So long as there are weapons nearby, he can order the guards to try anything he likes."

"Gwen—"

"Oh calm down, mother hen. And what will you be doing while I fight for my life?"

"Only the moon and stars know. The stars and your sister, anyway."

"She seems to keep a lot of information to herself."

"It is probably safest."

"She said to prepare, but aside from this"   I looked down at the buttoned jacket—"what else can I do?"

He gave me another smile, but this time it was dangerous. A mischievous glint made his dark eyes sparkle and he glided toward me, hands up.

"Practice," he said, and attacked me.

I collapsed sometime later, soaked with sweat and panting. The jacket saved me from broken ribs, but it was so hot from absorbing Aris's blows that overheating was a distinct danger.

"How did you learn to fight like that?" I asked, struggling out of the soggy coat like a snake shedding its skin, and mopping my forehead with a sleeve.

For a moment, I thought Aris would not respond. His expression was empty when he said, "My father."

While sparring, he'd had to slow down significantly not to take my head off, so learning more about his technique would have helped me prepare for my trial. But the tone of his voice warned me not to push for more details.

Besides, choosing unarmed combat would almost certainly be a mistake. An equally skilled opponent who was also faster and stronger would win. The rapier may be my only chance of success if winning against such creatures was possible.

Lia clearly thought it was, unless this was all some convoluted plot to continue scraping out my insides. I had to believe it was not. I had to believe I could win and somehow get the three of us out of there.

I dropped the jacket onto the moss to give the heat time to disperse so it would be ready for my duel, and asked, "What does it mean to become a member of the fae court in practical terms?"

"The same thing it means to become a member of any court: you are subject to their laws and expected to participate and obey."

"Is it a bond that can be broken?"

"Not without becoming a traitor."

In most cultures, the penalty for treachery was death. I stared down at my hands while running a series of calculations. I thought becoming a member of the court might give me time to find Lia and escape, but it appeared it would also keep me prisoner here. If I trusted Lia, and I did not appear to have much choice in the matter, then this was the only way out.

"Can we escape through the same hole in the wall you used when you came to mortal lands? Is that the rift Lia referred to?" I asked.

"If we can make it out of the castle and past the guards? Possibly. I made it through once, but I cannot be certain the magic would not kill me if I tried it a second time. It may not even be open."

"How can we get out of the castle?"

"That will depend upon what your sister has planned, and what kind of distraction we can contrive."

What your sister has planned. There wasn't time to solve a mystery so opaque. But a distraction? I glanced at the mound of moss I'd carefully constructed to hide the gear I brought with me.

"I have an idea for that," I said, and smiled.

24

A Trial of Strength

GWEN

"This is mad," Aris said, folding his arms. "You do realize this is mad?"

Of course, I did. The entire affair was ludicrous from beginning to end. I was proceeding on the assumption that my sister, the general of an antagonistic nation who had already proved herself willing to physically and emotionally harm me and those I cared for, had secret beneficent plans for my escape.

That she was, in fact, playing both sides. She meant for me to trust her on the authority of a single, hurried conversation held in secret. The truth was that I was being manipulated on every side by multiple parties. Not even Aris was free of the stain of it.

But I had no other allies, no knowledge of the layout of the palace aside from the hallways that led from my cell to the throne room. And no other viable plan.

"I thought you supported my tendency toward mayhem?"

"Not necessarily in a castle filled with enemies and long odds of escape."

"Do you have a better idea?"

"Sneaking. I am very good at sneaking. Even made a career of it, you know."

I narrowed my eyes at him and continued buttoning my jacket. "How do you plan on sneaking with me in tow? Can you fit me under your glamour?"

"No."

"If we sneak out, can we get to a door in under five minutes?"

His expression was flat. "Unlikely."

And that meant my Sightscreen would not last long enough for me to escape unnoticed. "Can you turn me into a raven?"

"Are you trying to be insulting?"

"If I intended to insult you, dear bird, you would know it. I am quite serious. How far is it from our cell to the closest exit?"

"Several hundred yards and stories."

"And all of that is empty?"

"Of course not."

"Then how do you plan to sneak the both of us out of the palace without resorting to mayhem and before I fail the last trial?"

He leaned back against the wall and crossed one ankle over the other, for all appearances totally at ease. Yet the muscle of his jaw feathered and his eyes were tight at the corners. "I am willing to admit this is uncharted territory. I have never planned such things with anyone other than myself in mind. But Gwen, listen: turning traitor once you are accepted to the court is one thing. This is another, entirely. It will be tantamount to declaring a personal war against Obyrron. If I had more time, perhaps—"

"Well, you don't," I interrupted, my voice cutting.

His eyelids flinched, but I couldn't bring myself to feel guilty. I was nearing the end of my reserves and had little patience left for trying to manage anyone's emotions, least of all my own. I sighed and closed my eyes.

I could not afford to fall apart now, not so close to the second trial.

Warm hands settled on my upper arms, and Aris pulled me against his chest. The steady beat of his heart beneath my cheek was ridiculously comforting, and the sweep of his hand up and down my back made me want to melt into a puddle.

"I am sorry, Gwen. Sorry you are forced to trust people who have lied to you. You have every reason to distrust me. But I will do everything in my power to get you out of the Sunset Lands, even if it means slaughtering every soul in the castle in the process."

The sound that escaped me was half sniffle, half unhinged laughter. "That was both melodramatic and macabre. Well done."

"A fellow does what he can."

For a while, I enjoyed the sensation of being held and the warmth of another body. But the reality of my situation would intrude soon, and I had better be prepared for it.

"What will happen to you after all this?"

"When your sister is done shaming me in front of the court, you mean?"

A lump stuck in my throat. "Mmm."

"She will either have me killed or consider me suitably chastised and reinstated."

"As a spy and assassin?"

He shrugged as if those titles meant nothing, but I'd seen the way people reacted to him. They kept their distance and watched with expressions both wary and intrigued, as one might stare at a tiger in a zoo.

"You must have had quite a reputation," I said carefully.

"Mmm."

"One you earned?"

Aris released me and strode to the other side of the room. "When your trial of strength begins, your opponent will likely try to finish you quickly. You are only human, after all, and they won't want to take the chance of being shamed by a lucky strike. The longer you last, the better your chances of being able to capitalize on a mistake."

"I see."

"Do you? Good."

We stared at one another for a long, breathless moment. Unspoken words polluted the air like stench rolling off the Thames, hanging for just long enough that we both knew they were there. But the moment passed, the words faded, and Aris cleared his throat.

"You will need to take full advantage of every opportunity, every mistake. You are a clever fighter and you have good instincts, but your mind is sharper. Use that. And remember, don't trust—"

"Anything I see," I finished, feeling as if a little hole had been carved out of my chest, but unsure why.

Gasps accompanied our entrance to the throne room. Aris had been dragged along with me, and the court did not seem to know who to stare at with the most dismay.

I was attired in dirty, creased clothing that was absolutely unsuitable for court, and the guests weren't simply shocked at my wardrobe, but excited to see what the King would do about it. It was blatant disrespect, and they were already hungry for a spectacle.

Aris abandoned his show of sardonic amusement and stalked into the room like a hunting dragon, eyes sharp and expression hungry. He moved like a predator, smooth and calculated, and the crowd unconsciously leaned away from him as we passed. Given the pull of his presence, I suspected he must have let his glamour slip, and it took every bit of my concentration to ignore him and focus on the room.

As soon as I allowed the atmosphere to touch me, the overwhelming presence of the fae and their heightened energy smothered me. My knees went weak and my breath caught, but I refused to kneel or ogle. I would not give in to the desire to cry and prostrate myself. So I pulled my pain around my shoulders like a cloak and locked my eyes on the sand circle before the throne.

Harl and Graowh hauled me to a stop just outside the ring and glared at me until I offered the King a respectful curtsy.

"Have I not provided proper court attire that you appear thus before me, human?" the King asked without preamble. The jewels and chains hanging from his antlers quivered with irritation, casting trembling rainbows on the floor.

His displeasure settled on my chest and dragged me toward the ground. My heart stopped for a moment and cold sweat prickled at the base of my spine, demanding I make amends for my grave misdeed. I clenched my fists until my fingernails bit into my palms, holding onto the pain as a shield against the compulsion of his emotions.

"Your Majesty has provided everything I could possibly need," I said, sounding far more in control of my emotions than I felt. "But one is often most comfortable in those raiments to which one is accustomed, especially when facing a trial."

He stared at me down the length of his nose, eyes narrowed in thought.

"And, if I may," I continued, hoping to head off any other complaints, "the strange garments might make the trial more exciting for your subjects to watch."

The spectators murmured, and the King, being a politician, recognized the benefit of appeasing the crowd. "If she does not have the magic of your blood, General, she certainly has the temerity. Very well," he said, "so long as the garments are searched, first."

I curtsied, but my breath caught. The mortal weapons had been stuffed beneath the moss in my cell but Lia's ring and the sneaky bracelet Delilah made were in the hidden pockets of the coat. Percy created them to be seamless, but would that pass a fae inspection?

The King waved a hand, and the guards began searching me, unbuttoning the jacket and running their hands over me with impersonal efficiency. When they searched the coat, I realized something important: they were so unaccustomed to mortal clothing they did not realize the myriad of places a clever person could hide things, much less a master tailor such as Percy.

"Nothing but fabric, Your Majesty," they said.

I took a shallow breath.

"These coarse human garments are offensive, but we shall see if they help or hamper you," the King said. "Chamberlain, you may begin."

Lia raised her chin, face as cold as I had ever seen it, as Manannán said, "Thus begins the second trial of the human who seeks entrance to the court of King Obyrron, the Lord of the Sunset Lands and High King of all Faerie. Challenger, choose your weapons."

I had thought this over during the long walk from the cell to the throne room and settled on the one weapon that made sense. "Swords."

A hum of approval rose from the crowd.

Manannán raised his hands to quiet them before he continued, but my eyes were on Lia's face as he said, "To act as King's champion for this duel," her mouth curled into a grin of pure malice, "we call upon The Raven. If you would earn back your title and honor, you will win this fight for your King."

My stomach dropped so fast it made me dizzy.

Aris showed no surprise, only bowed to the King as if he had spoken instead of Manannán. "I am willing."

"Then bring forth the weapons."

Mind racing, my gaze flashed between Lia, Aris, and Manannán. They chose the only person I stood a chance of beating, not because I was stronger or faster—we established that on my first day in the Sunset Lands—but because he was the only soul in this entire land who might hesitate to hurt me. And even that was no guarantee.

To earn my way to the banquet and my chance to escape, I would be forced to hurt him. I imagined slicing through skin I touched less than an hour ago and shuddered in disgust. How could I bring myself to do enough damage to force a believable submission? What would they do to him if they suspected he lost on purpose?

What would I do if he fought me in earnest?

I was going to be sick. Aris's expression was impassive, his dark eyes cold as he unsheathed a rapier with casual skill and swung it a few times to loosen up his wrists. A buzz of appreciation hung around the spectators as they whispered and pointed at him. Several faeries shot pitying glances my way.

The man who held me until my body calmed, who cradled me against his heart mere moments before, now appeared distant and cruel. He sneered at me with such disdain that tears stung my eyes.

"Enter the circle to begin the trial," Manannán said.

Aris gave me a mocking bow. "Ladies, first."

My toes brushed the edge of the sand. Once I stepped inside, it would be to engage in combat with Aris. Could I truly hurt him? Would I forgive him if he hurt me?

"I beg your indulgence, Your Majesty," said a voice from the crowd.

I nearly cried in relief. At least, until I saw the speaker. Shiverback strode out of the crowd and toward the ring, then knelt before the King.

"I humbly petition for the honor of taking The Raven's place in this duel," he said.

"On what grounds?" the King demanded.

"The Raven was the faithful servant of the General for years," he said. "And the human is her sister. It may be difficult for her to watch as they try to kill one another."

In the single moment of shock, before she controlled her features, Lia's face paled. So this was her doing. She had planted the ring with Manannán and arranged for me to fight Aris, but she had not anticipated this eventuality. How could she guess Shiverback would bid for such public revenge?

The King held up one hand, silencing the uproar. My heart squeezed itself into a knot as his amber eyes flicked between Aris and Shiverback, who leered at me from the other side of the circle.

"It is very interesting for you to champion our general so suddenly, Shiverback. Very interesting, indeed."

"She has served your kingdom and your people well, Your Majesty. After all she has given up, it seems a shame to make her watch as her assassin kills her sister."

"I can assure you, yew-man," Lia said in a voice that rang like steel upon steel, "that I do not care who steps foot outside that ring so long as His Majesty's will is served."

"You have always been such a loyal servant," Shiverback said, dropping his head in a mocking bow.

The King observed this byplay with a cruel gleam in his eye, one finger tapping rhythmically on the armrest of his throne. "Enough chatter. This substitution pleases us."

"Your Majesty," Lia began, but he raised a hand to silence her.

Her eyes flashed toward me, then she folded her hands and dropped her head in submission.

The guards took the sword from Aris and handed it to Shiverback, who spun the blade in a complex pattern. His eyes dropped to my ribcage, then met my gaze with a cruel smile. His wrist still bore the black handprint of Lia's fire.

He would exact upon the both of us at once and within view of the entire court. Unlike Aris, Shiverback had already proved his willingness to hurt me. An ugly sneer marred his beautiful face as he stepped into the ring.

I would not walk away from this battle. He would not allow me to submit. The couriers gathered close, their breath bated, eyes wide. Tension filled the air until it hummed against my skin like electricity.

I was fighting for my life, and all of us knew it.

"Challenger," Mannanàn said, his voice gentle.

My sword whispered as I unsheathed it, the familiar feel of the hilt bringing back a hundred memories of training dummies, clashing metal, dozens of small cuts, and the first time I killed a man. My mouth went dry. I took a deep, steadying breath, and stepped into the ring. There was no going back.

Manannán raised both hands. "This trial will last until one party has either surrendered or died. And there will be no use of glamour or magic of any kind. This is to be a trial of naked strength."

Shiverback scowled first at Manannán, and then at me. He must have planned to use glamour to his advantage, then. My fingers tightened around the hilt as I silently prayed that the fae would not sense the magic sewn into my jacket.

"If either of you step foot outside the ring thrice, you will be disqualified. If you surrender, the fight will end. There will be no respite. Are these terms understood?"

Shiverback voiced his response, but I could only nod.

Manannán looked between us, giving me a glance full of pity, then turned to the King. "Upon Your Majesty's pleasure."

King Obyrron sat up straight, his eyes boring down on us. "Begin."

I expected Shiverback to attack, to rush across the space in the blink of an eye and skewer me. Instead, he strolled toward me as if he were walking down a garden path. I set myself in a defensive posture, blade held high, but he only smiled at me.

And then he *smiled* at me.

The power of his unfettered presence hit me like a lightning strike. Aris had let me feel his presence, and I realized only now that he had protected me from the full force of it. But Shiverback had no such compunction. He wanted to bring me to my knees without ever landing a blow.

And why shouldn't I kneel before him? He was wind in the branches, sunlight on leaves, a part of nature as immortal and immovable as an oak tree. If he desired my obeisance, who was I to deny it?

"On your knees, mortal," he said. His voice rushed over my body demanding surrender. My joints unlocked and the tip of the blade dropped as my fingers loosened.

If any creature deserved obedience, surely it was he. Surely he would be pleased with me. He would reward me for being so dutiful. Just the thought of seeing him smile down at me made pleasure ripple up my spine. To kneel would make him proud.

Make him proud?

I'd been fighting for so long to make my own way in the world, to free myself from the expectation of those around me: society, my peers, Mama. Why did I fight so hard? When had it ever been worth the struggle? How many times had I avoided a room, pretended not to hear the whispers, told myself I was happier alone?

Instead of going my own way, I could release the burden and let someone else be in control. Breath of god, it would feel good to lay down my arms and know that, for once, someone was proud of me.

Shiverback watched me with dark amusement making his eyes burn. Such beautiful eyes. "I believe you may have been right, General," he said lazily. "This one doesn't share much of your blood."

General? Ophelia.

Was this what she felt here, at only sixteen? Did they descend upon her with their selfish desires and bend her, break her for their own pleasure? The thought of my smiling, laughing, ferocious sister kneeling before the likes of Shiverback as he used her for clout, for fun, made my lip curl in fury.

Pain rose from the well in my gut and stole through my veins like ice water, chasing the insidious pressure of his influence out of my mind and sending it flying like crows from a tree.

Sisters protect one another.

My fingers tensed, my jaw locked, and I straightened. Surprise flickered in his eyes, a tightening of his shoulders that said he had not expected resistance from a lowly human. He thought he could force me to become what he wanted me to be: compliant. Not even my mother had managed that.

I would not be broken by the likes of him.

Before I could think, my blade sang as I swung an overhand cut with every bit of speed and fury I could muster. Shiverback leaped away, but not quite fast enough, shock twisting his features as the crowd gasped and applauded. A red scratch ran down the length of his bicep, not deep enough to do damage, but proof damage could be done.

First blood.

I set myself and raised the tip of my sword. Words tumbled out of my mouth, sharp as broken glass. "When this fight is over, you will kneel before me."

An angry sneer turned his face into a grotesque mask. "When this is over," he spat, "I will drink a goblet of your blood to toast your sister's long life."

I charged.

25

At Swordpoint

GWEN

Shiverback lunged, trying to take advantage of my rush, and the tip of his blade blurred as it shot for my chest. I parried on instinct and slipped to the outside to gain my footing, dropping the point of my sword and leveling it to create some distance.

My father had been a poor excuse for a parent, but he paid for fencing lessons from the time Lia and I were ten years old, and I had never stopped training. Despite my skill, only time would tell if I could hold my own against Shiverback long enough to save my own life.

He was stronger than me and fast, as evidenced by his dancing, but was he skilled? Hard to tell from a single thrust. One thing he certainly was: confidently eager. He had no reason not to be.

When we trained for this, Aris defended every attack I threw at him with ridiculous ease, which meant skill alone would not save me in this fight. I had to be clever, so I decided to play defense long enough to learn what kind of fighter my opponent was before I committed to a course of action.

He circled toward my weak side, forcing me to turn, and flicked a couple of probing cuts toward my ribs. He was forcing me to guard my injured side, thinking the damage he'd done to my ribs during our dance would impede my movements. But I had already healed enough not to notice, and too much adrenaline flowed through my veins to feel much pain, anyway.

When he stepped in for a proper exchange, it was so fast I almost missed the tensing of his shoulders and set of his feet. Lunge, parry, riposte, counter-cut. We swirled around one another in a series of blinding moves that I only reacted to thanks to years of training.

He disengaged, his sneer replaced by a look of calculation. The rest of the court rushed in from all sides, pushing for a better view now that it was clear I wouldn't be dispatched so easily. Even the King leaned forward.

I was afraid they were about to watch me die.

Shiverback was fast, and his technique was perfect. He feinted toward my left, then twisted his arm and turned the motion from a lunge to a cut. I raised my blade and angled my shoulder to slide the cut aside, but he followed immediately with a counter that threw me off balance.

I staggered to the side as the crowd tittered with excitement and managed to fend off another flurry, but only just. My arm muscles burned, and every eye bored into me like needles, making my skin prickle. Shiverback grinned and raised his arms to the sides. The crowd cheered.

I used the opportunity to lunge, forcing him to defend, then feinted left. When he parried, I stepped into his guard and lashed out with a front kick that buckled his forward knee. He hissed and leaped back, retreating to the edge of the circle and glaring at me with bared teeth. Judging by his surprise and anger, his perfect technique did not include fighting dirty. I smiled in return.

Because mine did.

Circling to his left, forcing him to retreat, I harried with constant advances, forcing him to defend himself and put pressure on his knee.

I lunged, but he parried and advanced, using the motion to kick a handful of sand into my face. Coughing and blinking, I jerked to the side and raised my elbow to shield my face, narrowly avoiding his first cut but not the counter-swing. The slashing blow slid up the outside of my arm and would have disabled the limb, if it hadn't been for Percy's miraculous jacket.

His grin of triumph disappeared when I shook off the hit and set myself for the next exchange. Wide green eyes flashed from my arm to my face, looking for blood or signs of pain and finding nothing.

Taking advantage of his momentary surprise, I answered with a flurry of strikes, trying to see through the sand that made my eyelids scrape every time I blinked. The world swam in a watercolor blur as my eyes watered, forcing me to rely on instinct to defend myself when countered.

Shiverback landed another cut, this time along my ribcage when I couldn't see well enough to parry his strike. With a shout, he tried to close, thinking it had been a disabling blow. My ribs ached but weren't broken, and I was winded and sweating, so I let him inside my guard.

A gasp went up from the audience, but I barely heard them as I turned into his body, wrapped my free arm around both of his wrists, and used the hilt of my sword to punch him in the temple. He broke my grip, dragging the edge of his blade along the side of my jacket with all his strength.

We jerked apart, both staring and panting to see what damage we had done. My coat was hot from the stored energy, and that last cut left a shallow hole in the side. I did not feel the sting of the wound, but warmth trickled down my ribs and to my waist.

The heat warned me that the jacket could sustain perhaps two good hits before the embroidered runes no longer had the capacity to divert the kinetic force of his blows. Two more hits before I caught fire and blew up in the middle of the trial.

But Shiverback was also bleeding from a cut on his temple and another on his arm. I had drawn first blood, and the gasps rising from the audience made his face twist into a rictus of fury. More importantly, I'd learned something about his fighting style.

It was perfect.

If I had a chance of winning, it wouldn't lie in greater strength or speed, it would be in controlling my emotions and inflaming his. So I took a deep breath, grinned, and gave him a mocking bow with a little flourish of my sword.

He shrieked, the noise like the shrill cracking of a snapping tree trunk, and charged.

Anger only made him faster, and he flicked cuts at me from what felt like half a dozen angles at once. I tried to take advantage of the angles to strike him with my feet or to push in close, but he was always there, harrying with his sword point.

I sustained another shallow cut, this time across my belly, making a button pop off and sink into the sand. The crowd cheered as I leaped backward, sweating. That was the third time I should have been dead, but no one else knew it. I appeared to be shrugging off what should have been disabling injuries.

Disguising my fear with bravado, I said, "Well played, sir. You've lasted longer than I expected. Though your blade does seem to be a bit dull. You may want to have that sharpened."

He sneered and spat, "You'll find out how sharp my sword is when I gut you with it, human." He would do it with a smile. And soon, if I didn't end this quickly.

"Is he always this overconfident?" I asked the crowd.

They gasped and laughed behind their hands, either enchanted or infuriated at my temerity, but Shiverback was enraged. He growled and rushed me. The light of the hanging flower chandeliers gleamed off the metal like sunlight on water. He was too fast, too precise.

I was on the defensive, constantly moving away and trying to avoid the next blow that would bring me a hair's breadth from explosion. My heels inched closer to the line. Shiverback pressed in, baring his teeth as victory flashed in his eyes, his sword singing as it sliced the air.

My muscles burned and sweat poured into my eyes and down my neck as I defended, my movements growing less practiced and more desperate. He was angry. Furious in fact, but not careless. He wasn't making the mistakes I needed him to make. And I wasn't fast enough to take advantage of an opening even if he'd given me one.

My stomach sank as I responded to another series of strikes, slashing and ducking to avoid a kick. He was using my own tactics against me, and I could not fend him off. Aris's voice came back to me, insinuating that I may be stronger and faster than other mortals, if my guess about my bloodline was true.

I would likely have been skewered already, otherwise. Death breathed down my neck, and the fetid stink of it made me faster, sharper than I would have been otherwise, but even that was not enough.

Then it hit me. I knew exactly what I had to do to win, as if someone held a magnifying glass in front of me, bringing the problem into focus.

I was afraid of death.

Every mortal was. We were weaker, slower, less skilled than our immortal brethren, always walking the edge of our own destruction; one foot in the grave, one might say. And Shiverback knew it just as surely as I did.

But he was immortal. He had probably never feared for his life. He wouldn't be accustomed to dealing with the fear, as I was. A cut would only make him angry, not make him recognize his mortality.

So he assumed that being so close to death, I would always try to protect myself. And, until this moment, he was right. But I had a magic coat with at least one good blow left. Grunting with effort, I engaged him in a series of exchanges I had practiced since I was a child.

He responded with a textbook lunge that would have taken my eye out if I hadn't parried. The tip of his blade sliced across my cheekbone just beneath my left eye, and blood ran down my cheek to drip onto the shoulder of my jacket. If I had any sense, I would break off the exchange and reset myself.

Instead of retreating to put more space between us, I attacked.

Blazing in as if death held no fear, I pressed him backward and screamed while advancing. Taken off guard, he retreated to regain his position, but I didn't give him the benefit. I lunged, lunged again, then started a series of forms that would end with a high slashing cut toward his neck, but would also leave my right side open.

Whether he was familiar with the pattern, he was a good enough swordsman to recognize where the exchange was headed, like a chess player seeing several moves ahead. Knowledge and victory blazed in his eyes. Shiverback parried, then set himself up for the killing blow that would slide between my ribs when I inevitably left myself open trying to block the final strike.

Trying to save my own life, as any mortal would.

His body slipped into the proper position, the twist of his hip and shoulder setting him up for a winning blow. His blade fell, and I ignored it to lunge past his guard. It was too late to stop, and fear broke across his face when he realized I'd sacrificed myself for an advantage he could not guard against.

The sword struck, my ribs cracked with shots of fiery pain, and the jacket sent a blaze of heat from my right side across my torso as it tried to cope with the huge amount of force it held.

I took the blow and leaped.

I should have been dead. Instead of having a sword buried in my chest, I was still coming. His eyes widened in disbelief, and I watched the realization cloud his features, the understanding that our relative positions and my speed left him no room to maneuver out of the trap I laid.

I hit Shiverback with the full force of my charge and drove him, surprised, to the ground. I landed on his chest, pinned his knees with my arms, and pressed my blade against his throat. Sweat dripped off my nose to patter on his forehead.

"Yield," I panted.

He grimaced and made to shake me off. He was strong enough to do it. So I slid the blade along his windpipe, making him yelp as the shallow cut bled.

"Yield!"

I didn't see it, but I heard the dull thump as his sword hit the sand, dropped by nerveless fingers. The crowd erupted in shocked cheers and I fell backward, gasping as the pain in my ribs shot cold arrows through my lungs.

A pair of hands caught me and hauled me to my feet, by my vision swam as blackness crept in at the corners. I couldn't pull enough air into my lugs and my head swam, but I was alive.

I owed Percy a substantial raise.

As it turned out, I had more than a couple of broken ribs. Several of the cuts made it through the wool, and I bled into the hot water

of the spring while the nymphs fussed over me. I had, in fact, passed out on the way from the throne room, and had to be carried to a grotto that served as a bathhouse.

These nymphs, pale as birch trees and water lilies, hummed as they worked, and gentle sounds lulled me into a daze and, soon, to sleep.

A crone entered shortly after I woke to press something hot into my hands. She appeared to be at the extreme end of decrepitude, bone-thin with skin as frail as wet tissue paper, but there hung about her an aura of wisdom and knowing. She would not have been better, or more beautiful, had she been in the spring of youth. Looking at her made me feel that the woman was precisely as she ought to be, and that engendered a sense of trust I didn't question.

Aris would have warned me not to drink anything she gave me, but he wasn't present and I was too woozy to know anything other than that I was thirsty and in pain. The tea warmed me from the inside and dulled the sharp stabs that shot through my chest when I breathed deeply.

On a level deeper than understanding, her presence reminded me of Mrs. Chapman. Comfort stole over me along with the easing of the pain, and that was enough for me. At least, for now. I floated as weightless as a feather on the wind.

My coat and other assorted paraphernalia sat folded on a carven bench near the bath. Nothing was required of me but that I rest and allow myself to be prepared for the celebratory banquet. The nymphs bandaged my wounds with a salve that smelled good enough to eat and wrapped me in thick blankets. I grabbed my clothes before they bundled me out and escorted me down the hall to a room, rather than my cell.

I didn't pay attention to the room itself, since I planned to escape before spending much time in it. Instead, I played the possibilities of the evening over and over in my mind, trying to picture how the escape might take place, and work out backup plans for any eventuality. There was not much to go on, of course, but nothing else was pressing enough to occupy my mind.

The nymphs left me perfumed and shining, wearing a new sheer gown of pale blue with my hair in a thick, intricate braid woven with pearls. A sign of Manannán's favor? I stood and waited, listening, until their footfalls disappeared down the hallway. Then I rushed to my jacket and fished out the ring and bracelet.

"Lia?" I whispered after the ring was securely on my finger. "Ophelia Magnolia St. James?"

Nothing.

How was I supposed to know whether my distraction would help with no idea of what her plans were? I pressed my ear to the thick wood door, closed my eyes, and listened. For a while, no sounds vibrated through the wood. Perhaps I could sneak out and do a bit of...the faint clink and rub of armor stopped that thought.

Guards. So, despite being invited to join the fae court, I wasn't quite trustworthy enough to be left to my own devices.

With a sigh, I abandoned the door and slid the bracelet on, hoping it would appear to be just one more bit of jewelry amongst the other chains and bangles the nymphs had placed on my wrists and ankles.

I could turn the Sightscreen on and try to get a better understanding of the palace layout, but I had only one diamond, and
wasting it on an expedition that may give me no useful information
felt like a waste of resources. As far as I knew, Delilah had never
tested the device with other gems, so breaking my current jewelry
to power the spell would be foolishly dangerous.

I was left with nothing to do, forced to rely on people who either
spent years lying to me or had actively tried to harm me. For a
moment, I wondered whether brazening it out and striding into
the hallway was a good idea. What could the guards do, after all,
but return me to my room?

But getting into a tussle with my guards was the last thing I
needed. So I paced the room instead, from the enormous window
to the door, back and forth, back and forth until I wore a thin street
in the mossy carpet. Having nothing to do, no way to exercise my
anxiety, made all of my uncertain energy build until I was ready to
burst with it.

Every doubt, every worry, every secret fear woke up to prey on
my mind. I had no book to escape into, no Sally to teach, no Sam
to tease, no Chapman or Yates or Percy or Delilah, no key to the
secret bottom drawer of my desk...and Mama was as far from me
as she'd ever been.

So, when a heartbreakingly familiar flapping sound made me
spin toward the window so fast that white-hot pain sunk into my
chest, my vision went blurry.

Aristotle stood on the windowsill, his head tilted to the side,
bead-black eyes shining in the late afternoon light.

"Save the girl?"

I did not realize I was walking until I stood before the window with tears streaming down my face, my hands clenched at my sides, pain shooting across my ribcage with every breath.

"Stop it," I said in a voice that barely escaped my lips.

Aristotle hopped off the sill and down to a chaise that lay beneath. His form shimmered, like heat waves rising from the desert floor, and Aris lay in his place in his fae form. He was stretched out on his right side, holding himself up on one elbow in a caricature of seduction.

He waggled his eyebrows suggestively. "You prefer me in this form, my lady?"

But then he saw me, truly saw me, and appeared before of me a heartbeat later. Holding my face between his palms as if my skin were made of glass, he brushed my tears away with the pads of his thumbs.

His brows were drawn down, eyes hot with some emotion I didn't care to examine. "I'm sorry. I forget that we are still not the same person to you. I did not mean to cause you pain."

I allowed myself to enjoy the caress, to revel in the warmth of his body for just a moment, just long enough to feel as if I was not alone. Then I stepped purposefully backward and stood out of reach.

Aris dropped his hands and stuffed them in his pockets.

"Why are you here?" I asked.

His Adam's apple bobbed, but his expression was carefully neutral. "I have carried out the first part of your plan, my lady. It was not easy, but it will work the way you hoped. Though I still think it is mad."

"Thank you."

He bowed, but at least half of the motion was ironic. "There is nothing I would not do for a St. James girl," he said, and the words were more cutting by what they implied than by the way he said them.

I flinched, though I did not know why. Instead of pressing for more information, one of the questions plaguing me leaped to my lips. "Did you—did you know they would call upon you to duel me?"

A beat of silence. "I suspected they would."

"Why?"

He looked down at his shoes. Very English shoes in black leather. Black trousers. A black shirt open at the neck and rolled up past his forearms. Black hair that shone blue in the window light. Dark eyes that bored into my soul when he raised them to mine. But he did not speak.

"I see."

"No," he said, "you don't. But maybe someday you will."

Something had changed, something I had not been present for or could not trace. We were no longer trapped together to face whatever was coming next as a team, even if we were an unevenly matched, hesitant team.

"What happened to you?"

He stiffened. "What do you mean?"

"Between now and the end of my fight."

Aris looked down and dug a chunk of moss up with the tip of his toe. "I had a battle of my own."

"Were you—did you—"

"I don't want to talk about it," he said, rubbing his palms on his trousers.

"Would you have fought me?" The question crept out of its own accord.

"I would have had no choice in the matter."

"Would you have fought me?"

After a tense moment of silence... "Yes."

My heart skipped a beat. "Would you have killed me?"

"Gwen." He said my name like a prayer, but one for patience and not of contrition. "Do you believe I could so much as say a cruel word to you and mean it?"

Did he think keeping the truth from me for years, lying about who he was and why he stayed with me was not cruel? I wanted to pull those questions out like swords and run him through with each one, but the answers would not help me, not now.

Focus. Be rational.

"Are you reinstated in the court?"

He snorted. "Not quite. Not entirely. I have not been properly humiliated yet. But that does not matter. I don't intend to stay long enough to earn forgiveness."

It was my turn to swallow. "Are you leaving, then?"

"Of course."

"Very well. Can you give me directions to the rift you used to escape?"

A line formed between his brows. "Why would you need to—oh, for the love of the great tree, Gwen, you cannot be that smart and so stupid at once."

I blinked. "I'm sorry?"

He closed the distance between us in a single stride and lifted me into his arms so that our noses nearly touched. I was too shocked to move.

"You have no idea how many times I've wanted to do that just to shut you up," he said. Then rubbed the tip of his nose once against mine.

The wild smell I associated with him, bitter air and grass like the wind and rain on the moors, filled my nostrils. For a while, he simply held me there, looking into my eyes. Finally he said, "I promised to get you out of here, and I meant it. But I have already stayed too long."

He kissed the tip of my nose, set me on the floor, and strode to the window. "Be prepared to carry out as much of your mad plan as possible. I'm not certain when the distraction will start so keep your eyes and ears open. And Gwen?"

I did not think I could speak, so I raised my brows.

"We are going to save the girl."

Then he leaped out the window, shimmered in midair, and soared into the sky.

26

Dinner with the King

GWEN

*S*ave the girl.

Save the girl.

That refrain had colored my life for years and played in my mind over and over after Aris left me. For some time I sat on the chaise and stared out the window across the forest canopy. The palace soared above hundreds of acres of woodland that stretched to the horizon, undulating in a mesmerizing, wind-blown dance as the sky turned orange.

Save the girl.

Could I? Could I truly get myself and Lia out of the Sunset Lands? The longer I thought about it, the less likely it seemed. We were counting on a cobbled-together plan that could fall apart at any moment. As soon as one unforeseen circumstance arose, we would be in the dark.

And if they caught us? I doubted there would be any second chances.

Three sharp raps on the door had me leaping to my feet, my melancholy thoughts fleeing. Manannán stood in the open doorway, and this time he did not appear as the older gentleman I was used to. The black beard still sat on his chest, but he now appeared closer to a hale forty years, with gold cuffs across the corded muscles of his forearms and well-developed shoulders. But he smiled at me with the same kindness.

"Would you care for an escort to the banquet, my lady?" he asked.

"Your voice suits this form much better," I told him, taking the arm he offered.

"Let us hope this form also suits my purpose much better. Your duel was well-played. How are your injuries?"

I took a deep breath, winced, and said, "Bearable. A couple of cracked ribs, and a few shallow cuts that did not require stitching. Still, I do not think I will dance tonight."

"That is advisable. You will have more important things to use your energy on, in any case."

If Manannán was in my sister's confidence, which I surmised from his careful hints, was it safe to speak openly to him? I glanced at his profile, the firm line of his nose and lips, and decided against it. If he was content to speak in riddles and suggestions, I would be, too. "It is kind of you to mask your nature on my behalf."

He snorted. "My influence is the last thing you need to worry about, with so much at stake."

I shuddered thinking about how hard it would be to focus if Manannán were to unleash himself upon me. Resisting Shiverback had been difficult and I hated him. But Manannán was considerate. I would probably be lost.

"May I ask why you have been so generous?" I asked.

"I suspect we have the same priorities, you and I. And I owe a great deal to your...family."

That was a powerful admission. I nodded deeply to show that I understood him, and tried not to think too hard about the implications of his statement. Instead, I said, "Any wisdom to share about the banquet tonight?"

He glanced at me from the corner of his eye. "You have made enemies today. Keep a close eye on them."

"Enemies?"

"You did not think a mortal could force a fae warrior to submit and not suffer the consequences of their damaged pride, did you?"

"Warrior?" I asked, my heart sinking.

"Did you not know?"

I pursed my lips, and he laughed. "No, I suppose you did not. The Raven was a bad enough choice, though he is at least clever and has restraint. Shiverback is another matter. Had you been a mere human, you would have been dead in the first few seconds, even well trained as you are."

"But I am not fae," I said.

"Not enough to matter, not to him and his cronies. As far as they are concerned, you have insulted us most grievously. At least your sister had the good sense to have magic, which is an insult to no one."

"A lowly mortal woman shamed them, eh?"

"Do not be deceived, lady. Your sex has nothing to do with the matter. Many of the most capable warriors in the court are women. But you are half human, and you not only scorned his advances but shamed him publicly. Twice."

I sighed. "Warning noted, sir. Tha—" I stopped before I could say thank you. "Ah...you are kind to offer such advice."

He chuckled. "Smoothly done, miss."

We joined the rest of the crowd in a part of the castle I had not yet seen, filing into the banquet hall by twos and threes. Passing through the white arched double door was like entering another world. The banquet hall was a conservatory that jutted out from the side of the castle like a peninsula, so the walls on three sides were open to the night air through arched floor-to-ceiling pillars.

Sunset light turned the space into a pale pink confection of spilling flowers and rich, jewel-toned tablecloths. The tables themselves ran down either side of the peninsula, leaving an aisle in the center, and joined at the head where the King's table sat.

Manannán led me to the head table, next to the royal table on the right, and handed me into my seat with a bow. A place of honor, one I certainly had not earned and did not deserve. One that put me on display for the eager eyes of the rest of the court.

The tables filled, and it was just as hard to maintain my sanity as it had been the first time I'd walked into the throne room. I found that, to avoid being overwhelmed, I had to unfocus my eyes a bit and stare into the middle distance.

Lia entered with Aris, her hand on his forearm, and my heart squeezed hard enough to make me clench my teeth. They were beautiful together, gold and dark, day and night, both of them too graceful to bear. Had he been suitably shamed, then? Had his battle, whatever it was, allowed her to readmit him to his place as the dagger beneath her cloak?

I dropped my gaze and focused on my hands as he led her to the King's table and sat her at the right-hand of the throne-like chair reserved for the King. Aris sat on her right. I forced my fists to unclench and managed to give Manannán a forced smile when he took the chair next to me.

The King entered once everyone else was seated. I had yet to see him move beyond adjusting his seat on the throne, and it was impossible to look away from. He walked like a setting sun, slow and deliberate, his translucent robe trailing the ground behind him, the gems hanging from his antlers catching the light and burning with inner fire.

He stood before his seat, raised his arms, and said, "Tonight we welcome the Lady Gaelethsdaughter to our court, and celebrate her martial prowess as she becomes the strength of our arms, adding to our glory. When we retake the mortal lands, she will stride forth in honor beside us, an example of what mortals can become when blessed by faerie blood."

A shout rose, loud enough to make the floor shake, and my stomach heaved as if I stood on a boat during a storm.

"We also welcome back to us The Raven, our most capable spy and assassin."

Another, less excited, shout followed, this one filled with distrustful glares and halfhearted cheers. One corner of Aris's mouth curled, but he made no other acknowledgment.

The King took his seat, and servers of every description filed into the banquet hall with trays, platters, and trenchers of food that smelled so good my mouth watered. I risked a glance at Aris...Aris the assassin. Why I trusted him now was beyond me, but he saw my glance and shook his head with only the barest hint of motion.

So, I filled my plate but didn't eat, despite the way my stomach screamed. Instead of filling his own plate, Aris chose food and placed it on Lia's as she spoke with the King. He even cut the mutton into bite-sized chunks. My fingers tightened around my knife, but I did not throw it at him. Or stab anything. Not even once.

Fae approached my table in ones and twos, bowing and welcoming me to the court I was about to escape from, a court I fully intended to destroy, if given the opportunity. Responding with gracious nods seemed to appease them, and as it was all I was capable of, I was grateful.

So, I sat in silence and growing apprehension, nodding and smiling and waiting for whatever distraction Lia had planned, hoping my own did not deploy too soon.

Shiverback and his partner approached the table wearing smiles that poorly disguised their hatred and disdain. After a bow that was only as deep as necessary, he straightened and said, "The court is overjoyed to welcome such a gifted warrior to our ranks. It must be a relief to know you can protect yourself when the inevitable political spats break out. After all, the court is a dangerous place, is it not, my love?"

"Very dangerous. Enemies may come from anywhere. Best to sleep with one eye open."

I gave them a poisonously sweet smile and said, "What a thoughtful warning, but I won't be losing any sleep. By the way, how is that cut healing?"

His fingers went to his throat, and the false smile faltered. "So kind of you to ask. I see the little knick on your cheek has closed. How fortunate it is not still bleeding for the festivities."

Aris cleared his throat.

Shiverback blinked and shifted his glare to the other table, only to falter and blanch at something he saw in Aris's expression. He backed away from the table a few steps, pulling his partner with him, then shot me a furious glare before turning to stalk away.

"Despite their motivation, the advice is sound," Manannán said around a mouthful of food. "To survive here, you must keep your eyes open."

"I like the advice much better coming from you," I said.

He smiled and popped a bit of bread into his mouth. My stomach gurgled at the crunching sound of the crust. To distract myself, I said, "May I ask you a question?"

Manannán glanced at me from the corner of his eyes. "You have not seemed to require permission thus far. Though I would suggest adjusting the previous advice to encompass other senses, and not just sight."

Don't ask implicating questions too loudly. Noted. "You have experience in strategy and tactics?"

"When one lives for such a long time, one develops certain skills."

"Why would an army abandon a superior location to acquire a lesser position? One that is heavily defended, and with less"—I looked round the room—"resources."

He stopped chewing for an instant, then continued as if I hadn't asked anything out of the ordinary. "One must consider the motivation of the commanders to answer such a question: greed, revenge, resources, pride, a misplaced sense of justice. Once the motivation has been sussed out, the action does not seem so incomprehensible."

"Then it would be wise of the defending army to learn as much as possible about the motivation of the invader."

"Indeed, it would."

"Have you ever visited the court of Queen Titania?"

The corner of his mouth twitched. "I lived there for a number of years. Of course, now I live here in the court of the King, and I would not care to be anywhere else."

"Of course."

"I'm pleased to see you understand the situation," he said and popped a strawberry into his mouth. "Intelligence seems to run in the family."

"One can only be bashed over the head so many times before examining the object doing the bashing."

He snorted. "Many people accept the pain as part of life and never question it. That is often easier than looking about to realize it is your own hand holding the club."

I paused. That was an insight I hadn't expected. We were speaking in riddles of the coming fae invasion. How had we ended up on psychoanalysis? "You...have never heard of a man by the name of Freud, have you?"

A line appeared between his thick brows. "Who?"

"Only checking," I said and plopped my chin into my hands.

Psychoanalyzing myself could wait. There were more pressing matters to consider, such as how I was going to escape this place and what the consequences would be once I did.

Over the last few days, I had pieced together bits of information, and this conversation confirmed my suspicions. The fae were not united in their desire to invade the mortal world. Turning to look out at the miles of ravishing woodland beneath a glowing sky, it was difficult to understand how anyone could give such a thing up in favor of the imperfect, blood-stained mortal world.

Or, perhaps, not so difficult, after all.

I had fallen into a complex web of faerie politics, where every truth spoken had three meanings and only illuminated part of the bigger picture. King Obyrron wanted to invade mortal lands, and while he may justify that action in any number of ways that did not make sense to me, the goal was still the same, as Aris had said: power.

Even my appointment to the court was a move designed to solidify power. As a human, I was both a valuable source of information and a trophy of sorts. Another reason I could not stay in this country, no matter how beautiful it was. So, if and when they invaded, I would be a highly sought-after enemy.

It would be worth it to bring Lia home. I could worry about warning the other mortals once we were safely back on the other side of the wall. A flash of light beneath the canopy caught my attention and smothered my boiling thoughts.

Several more flashes—yellow, green, and orange—lit up the leaves of the trees below us like pixies waking up in the hearts of flowers. I squinted as dark shapes began to move between openings in the foliage, barely visible from this distance under the shadow of early evening.

A popping sound, sharp as gunfire, echoed through the hall and onto the balcony. The clinking of silverware died and silence fell upon the festivities as every head turned toward the castle interior.

Familiar green smoke billowed out of the double doors, thick and smothering, making the diners closest to the door stagger back in surprise. My heart leaped into my throat and my chest squeezed closed behind it. Was this the distraction Lia promised?

Hound guardsmen ran in through the smoke, coughing and waving their hands.

"The castle is under attack, your majesty!" one of them yelled. "Enemies have been spotted in the Wylderwood!"

Chairs and tables were shoved aside as faeries leaped up to fight or to flee. The King surged to his feet, vaulted the table with the grace of a stag, and held out one hand. A sword the length of my body condensed out of the air and burst into flame as he raised it above his head, bellowing, "To me!"

A few faeries changed shape. A bear roared and charged into the smokey castle, and hawks, swans, and owls soared off the balcony and into the sunset sky.

Lia dropped, covered her head with her hands, and yelled, "Get down!"

Aris and I followed suit, and a second later the balcony shook, the explosion so close that my ears rang from it. A sound like buzzing followed, and six or seven fae dropped to the floor, screaming.

Most of the diners searched the air for arrows, but I knew what felled the people writhing on the floor. My second grenade, the one filled with small iron beads. The one Aris snuck back into our cell to retrieve and plant.

"It's iron!" Lia screeched. "Treachery!"

The King roared in fury at this desecration of his realm. Half of the diners followed the King as he set off at a run, and the other half fled. It was absolute madness...and our best chance to get out of the castle.

We were four stories up, and the canopy stretched for miles beneath us with no moor in sight. More figures ran through the trees, hundreds of them, and the blades of their weapons caught the last vestiges of dying light.

How on earth would we make it to the rift through all this madness and with so many witnesses?

The three of us stood, exchanged a glance, and made to follow the King. I leaped over the form of Shiverback, curled on the ground as his mate tried to pry one of the iron balls from his thigh with a silver table knife, and held my breath as we broke through the smoke.

Once we were inside and the air cleared, I nearly tripped over the crater left by my grenade. Several pitted marks in the stonework were mute proof of the efficacy of the iron balls. Faeries ran in every direction, some with weapons and others with their arms curled protectively over their heads, but a stream of bodies joined the growing wake of the King to defend the castle.

"Who is attacking?" I asked as we joined the stream.

Lia gave me the look that said, *Use your head, Gigi.*

I should have asked her where Manannán was. He'd been at my side during dinner, and I had not even realized he wasn't there when the ruckus began. I wondered if anyone had seen him leave and doubted it.

Lia led us through the palace, following the King as if we, too, were off to do battle. Extraordinary sight after extraordinary sight passed me on either side, things I knew I would only remember in snatches of memory—statues carved with such loving detail they might have been real creatures, fountains dripping down living walls and singing with voices of heartbreaking beauty, murals of such realism and grandeur they must have taken hundreds of years to paint—but if I looked too long I would become entranced, so I pressed on with my eyes forward.

It had been quite a long time since I'd run any distance, and my lungs burned. More faeries joined us, compelled by the call of the King. His desire to protect his realm leached into the air around him and spread like fog, thicker than smoke and stronger than a river current. My thoughts and emotions drowned beneath his call, and I found my blood running hot as a sense of outrage stole over me.

Invaders had dared to desecrate this place. We would remove them, destroy them, punish them for their audacity. We would demand blood and ruin for this insult.

When we reached the main floor, we had to dodge the wreckage of the front gates, which had been blown open...from the inside. I hadn't smuggled in any explosives strong enough to do that.

A message was scrawled on the stone above the doors in an archaic form of English.

Down with the pretender king.

Had Lia staged an entire coup to hide our escape? No, that wasn't possible. Was it?

We struggled through the press at the door till we stood in the evening air, part of a milling crowd searching for enemies to fight, but finding nothing. Whoever was in the forest had not approached the castle. The King stood at the foot of the stairs, conferring with several warriors who had either manifested armor or changed faster than any can-can girl.

"Where is my general?" the King bellowed.

Lia turned to me, grabbed my face between her hands, kissed my cheek, and whispered, "Go. Now."

But we needed to fight, to end this threat to the realm and redress the wrong of—my head snapped to the side, and stinging pain made tears gather in my eyes. Lia's face was hard, but her eyes were worried. That expression, more than the slap, cleared the last vestiges of the King's influence over my mind.

She was right. This chaos was our only chance to have our disappearances make sense. But I couldn't stand to leave her, not now, not when I knew there was a chance she still loved me.

"Go with The Raven," she said, spinning my shoulders till I faced him. Despair sat like a rock in my belly.

Aris glanced at me, the worry in his eyes hardening into resolve. He snatched Lia's wrist, spun her around, and pulled her back against his chest, trapping both of her arms with one of his. Before I could blink, he pressed a knife to her throat.

Her eyes flared with surprise. "How dare you! Put me down, you blithering idiot!"

His grip around her upper body tightened, neatly pinning her arms to her sides as her feet dangled from the ground. "The instant you call upon your magic, lady, I will slide this blade into your skull, right here, behind your lovely ear. You may burn me where I stand, but we will both die. You understand me?"

She nodded, and her struggles stilled, but her face was red with anger.

"Have you gone mad?" I demanded, trying to keep my voice low enough not to draw attention.

Aris gave me a hard look and said, "Shut up and run, Gwen," then turned and sprinted into the trees, covering the ground at a surprising pace for someone carrying an entire person.

There was nothing left to do but pick up my skirt and follow.

27

Race to the Rift

GWEN

Trees and bushes flashed by as we jumped roots and dodged low-growing branches, running hard enough to make every breath a struggle. Aris somehow ran more swiftly than I, despite the extra burden, but ducked to the side with a shocked gasp when the first invader appeared.

It was twice as tall as Aris and wider around, with leathery skin the color of sandstone and legs as wide as tree trunks. A pair of five-inch tusks jutted from its lower jaw, but it completely ignored us as it lumbered through the trees, carrying a spiked club in one massive hand.

"Is that a—a troll?" I gasped.

"It's—an—illusion," Lia grunted between strides as Aris's grip forced the breath out of her lungs.

"Shut up, General," Aris ordered, skirting the next troll and turning sideways to fit between two trees.

If that was an illusion, whoever created it was a master craftsman. In my studies, authors described the act of creating a phantasm as one of the hardest arts to master. One must not only hold in their mind the details that make something look real, such as eyelashes or dirt under fingernails, but also the way the illusion interacted with its environment.

As the illusory troll stomped through the forest, its feet spread to absorb the impact and weight of its body. It left footprints and reflected light. One would have been a work of genius, but dozens of similar figures were scattered through the wood.

I tried to imagine what it might be like for English soldiers to fight illusions that real, and my blood ran cold. The fae might not handle iron weapons or shoot modern firearms, but if they could convince a regiment that their neighbors were enemies?

I tore my eyes away from the retreating phantasm and followed Aris into a darker, thicker part of the forest. My eyesight was better than good, but it was impossible not to stumble.

"This way!" a voice called, and the thunder of running feet sounded behind us. It must have been at least a squad of faerie soldiers.

"Aris, slow down," I said in one of those yelling whispers.

"Can't," he said. "They'll catch us."

"I've got a solution for that. Just let me catch up, you bloody Corinthian."

I reached them a second later, pushed aside the meaningless bangles on my wrist, and prepared to press the button on the Sightscreen.

"Gwen," Aris growled, but I held up my hand. I didn't want to press the button until I knew I needed it, because once I pressed it, we only had five minutes—if Delilah was correct—until the diamond gave out.

When the bushes started shaking, I engaged the runic spell. A wave of energy rolled out of the device and hovered in the surrounding air. I edged backward, getting as close to Aris and Lia as possible. Four fae soldiers leaped through the gap in the trees one at a time, elegant as coursing hounds on a scent. About five feet from me, they stopped, losing track of our footprints, their eyes glazed and confused.

I motioned for Aris to move and stayed close to him. We ghosted through the trees, making as little noise as possible as three other patrols crossed our path. Their eyes skimmed over us as if we were bushes or trees, and no more interesting.

It became clear the patrols were hunting us, and not the illusory invaders, as phrases like *the traitor* and *kidnapped the general* echoed between the trees.

Two minutes passed.

"We have to hurry," I warned Aris, pushing his back with both hands to make him pick up the pace. "We only have three more minutes, if we're lucky."

"One of Delilah's devices?" he asked.

"Yes."

He sighed. "You know, that knowledge might have come in quite handy earlier in our visit."

"I had other things on my mind," I said tartly.

He scoffed and pushed into a quick jog.

Three minutes. We had to get far enough away from the patrols that they would lose our proverbial scent. They may actually be following some sort of scent or magical trace I could not sense, but if they were, there was nothing to be done about it.

"How far away is the rift?" I asked.

"Another mile."

Horns rang out, sharp and brassy, sending birds fleeing from the treetops in a panic of feathers and falling leaves. The chase had begun in earnest.

"Let me go," Lia said. "If you let me go, I can divert them."

Aris leaped a fallen log, making Lia grunt when they landed and his forearm pressed into her stomach.

"Not a chance," he said. "You are our only insurance if we cannot get through the rift."

"Do you think Obyrron will hesitate to kill us both if he believes you have wronged him?"

"Yes, I do. You are irreplaceable, and the best hope"—he ducked a tree limb and pushed into a closer thicket—"he has of successfully invading. Too much has changed since he was last in the mortal world, and changelings are much rarer than they used to be. Use your head, General."

"I am using it, you great, bloody idiot! They will continue to chase us as long as you have me."

"They will chase us anyway, and you know it. If I am not a member of the King's court, I am too dangerous to be left alive. Besides, you ordered me to use whatever means were necessary to get your sister out of the Sunset Lands. I deem your presence necessary. So shut up and let me run in peace."

"Gwen," Lia said, "Gwen, you must see reason. I can give you both more time to—" Her voice cut off as Aris pressed his free hand over her mouth.

He must have put the knife between his teeth because he did not say another word as we ran. More horns sang, this time from several places. I glanced over my shoulder in time to see figures crashing through the brush behind us. My already taxed lungs squeezed in panic. We had escaped once through treachery. If they caught us again, there would be no escape.

"We have company," I told Aris.

We had less than a minute before the Sightscreen failed, and that was only if Delilah had been exact. I had no weapons, no magic, nothing to defend us with. A dark shape, as large as a hound but longer and more lithe, leaped through the break between trees and bushes. It landed on the trail we had just blazed, its nose close to the ground.

It looked like a giant mink, and it was following our scent. Not a second later, Shiverback appeared, following the mink like a master huntsman with his hound. He saw me and his face lit up with malicious glee. The Sightscreen was dead. We were caught.

"Five hundred yards," Aris called, his breath now sawing as hard as my own. "Run, Gwen!"

I turned, pushing my legs for every scrap of strength left in them, and caught Aris up. He held out the knife, which I barely managed to grab, and said, "Protect yourself."

"What about you—and Lia?" I panted.

"Let me—worry about—that."

The enormous animal was gaining, a foot at a time, and would be on our heels in less than ten seconds. I had seen the claws it used to push itself across the ground, curved and as long as my fingers. Those claws would slice across the back of my thighs or my calves as easily as scissors through paper.

We broke into a familiar clearing, one that made my breath stop as hard as if I had just hit a brick wall. Aris dug his feet into the dirt, turned, and swung Lia's legs as if they were a cricket bat. Her feet caught the mink-creature under the chin and sent it tumbling backward through the air with a squeal of surprise.

Shiverback hit me a moment later, his weight crashing into the small of my back and bearing us both to the ground. My already broken ribs screamed in protest, sending electric currents of pain buzzing up to my brain until my eyes watered. On instinct, I planted my right foot, bucked my hips, and rolled the both of us. I slashed at anything I could reach as I tried to pull in a breath.

The knife struck twice, eliciting gasps, and then something hit the side of my head with a flash of light. I careened backward like a felled tree, landing hard enough to knock the air from my lungs with an *oof*.

For a moment the canopy spun over my head, black leaves and branches twisting against a blue-black sky and the first faint dusting of stars. I gasped in enough air to keep myself from fainting and scrambled backward, away from Shiverback and the murder in his eyes.

The mink-creature stood up on its hind legs and shimmered into the dark-eyed woman. She crouched, then attacked Aris. He dropped Lia, caught the woman's flying hands, and casually threw her into a tree trunk. She hit with enough impact to shake the ground.

Shiverback's eyes flicked toward her, registering an instant of pain, and I used that moment to leap to my feet and fly at him. This was different from the sword fight. I had armor of a sort, then, and it wasn't mere strength against strength. I nearly matched him in speed, which had saved me during our duel, but he caught my blows with the same ease Aris had used, batted the knife from my hand, and locked his fingers around my throat.

My toes left the ground.

"If you want to keep your sister alive, General, you had better call off your Raven."

I clawed at his hands, kicking uselessly, and fought for air as blackness swam at the edge of my vision. Lia stood, brushed off her skirt, and locked her eyes on the fae man. It could have been my near-fainting state, but I would swear that her eyes glowed with green fire.

"You should not be frightened of The Raven, sir." She raised one hand and emerald flames bloomed from her palm, licking up her fingers and lighting her face with cruel light. "You should fear me."

She made a twisting gesture and Shiverback screamed. I hit the ground on my side, gasping, watching events unfold in slow motion while I fought to breathe through my burning throat.

The dark-eyed woman had recovered from her blow and approached Aris like a cat stalking a bird. She feinted to one side, then shot in from the other, lashing out with abnormally long nails that tore across his belly.

"They are here!" Shiverback shouted through the pain.

Lia stepped in close, her beautiful face twisted into lines of hate. Fire erupted from both hands and traced up her arms. "Tell me," she said in an icy voice, "do Birch-men burn?"

Aris dodged the woman's next attack, then caught her arm, turned, and kicked her knee. The joint cracked and bent the wrong way. She tumbled to the dirt with a cry of pain.

Lia snapped her fingers.

Shiverback screamed.

The woman rolled to her side, eyes locked on her partner as she clutched her knee. "No!"

Aris hauled me to my feet, but Lia stood over Shiverback, watching him writhe as flames engulfed him, listening to the crackle as his skin popped and burned. The lurid light lit her face from below, turning it into a mask of wrath.

My stomach heaved.

"Come on," Aris said, grabbing her wrist despite the fire and dragging us both away from the clearing. The dark-eyed woman crawled across the ground to where her lover burned, tears streaming down her face in the ghastly light.

When Aris stopped, I knew where we would be. There were no mushrooms growing here. Instead, there was a circle of small, mossy, oval stones of varying heights standing upright like sentinels protecting something of great value.

"Don't step in there," I whispered, dragged back in time to the evening I watched Lia jump into a faerie circle and disappear.

Aris took my face between his hands, forcing me to look at him. His eyes were like coals, intent and burning. "I'm going to open the rift," he said. "I'll be like a bridge to pull you through. It will hurt.

You understand? Wait till I tell you, then take my hand. Gwen, do you understand me?"

I nodded numbly.

After an instant of hesitation, he grabbed my face and kissed me hard. Then he positioned himself outside the stone circle, taking several deep breaths, as if he were going to leap into cold water.

Horns sounded, and this time they were closer.

Lia simply stood watching the green light of her fire glow on the treetops. The dark-eyed woman screamed, a cry of desolation I recognized intimately.

With a grunt, Aris rammed his shoulder forward. The motion looked like a man trying to shoulder open a door. He hit something solid, bore against the invisible barrier, locked his shoulder, and drove with his legs.

Yellow sparks erupted from the place his shoulder met the rift in the magical wall that separated the Sunset Lands from the mortal world. A frisson of power shivered through the air, making my skin rise in goosebumps.

Teeth bared, face locked in a grimace, Aris cried out, "Grah!" as the line of sparks streaked from his shoulder down over his chest, splitting his body into the half pressing into the mortal world, and the half still in faerie.

His clothing smoldered.

"Come on!" he ordered through teeth clenched in pain. He looked like a man trying to hold up a collapsing ceiling with nothing but his legs.

I stumbled forward and took Lia's hands. Another horn sounded, and this time it was only on the other side of the clearing.

"Lia," I said. "Come home with me."

Her face had been eerily blank while watching the flames, and now it crumpled in sorrow. "I can't, Gigi. I can't come with you. Go home and take care of Mama. The Raven will tell you what to do, but I must stay here."

"No," I pleaded, feeling the sky and all its stars come crashing down on me as I forced the words out through the damage in my throat. "I can't live without you anymore. I can't stand it."

She threw her arms around me, and for the first time in a dozen years, every empty space in my heart was filled. Whatever had happened before this, whatever Lia had done and I had suffered, she still loved me. I felt her love like the sun coming up in my soul.

"Gwen!" Aris shouted, his voice wracked with pain.

"I love you, Gigi," Lia said into my hair, squeezing hard enough to hurt, then she pulled away, pushed me, and said, "Go!"

The hound guards broke into the clearing, swords drawn, followed by half a dozen fae warriors sprinting towards us. "Save the general!"

An inhuman cry of pain ripped from Aris's throat.

It was not a decision, not even an instinct or reflex. It was a necessity. I grabbed a double handful of Lia's dress, ignored her surprised cry, and threw myself backward, trusting Aris to catch us.

A strong hand wrapped around my upper arm with bruising strength and pulled. Buzzing heat washed over me in a rush from the back of my head, over my face, shoulders, torso, and finally down to my toes.

My skin felt like it was being peeled back to expose the raw flesh beneath. My conscious mind spun away from my body to somewhere above my head. Visions swam before my eyes, real enough to touch but thin, like wet paper.

A man with dark eyes and mahogany curls, his handsome face wrenched in lines of grief. Two golden heads pressed together in an embrace. New London wreathed in flames that danced to a symphony of screams and mournful cries. A dark silhouette standing with arms raised before a sea of enemies.

I watched from a distance as the three of us tumbled backward through the rift to land, smoking, in a pile in the snow.

Then gravity hit, and my mind catapulted downward and smashed into my body in a rush. Pain flooded every sense like a tidal wave, then eddied back to be replaced by the cold. It was so cold. I rolled toward Lia and wrapped my arms around her, but she lay limp across Aris's torso.

His skin was red in a line, scalded down his face and across his bare chest to the shallow wounds on his stomach. I ran my hands over his face and neck, pressing my fingers against the skin beneath his jaw. My heart thundered in my ears.

Breath of god, Aris, be alive. Please be alive.

He said the passage might kill him. He had warned me, and I'd been so focused on Lia that I hadn't even realized what pain, what danger he'd put himself in.

No heartbeat pressed back against my fingertips.

With a cry, I smashed my lips against his and exhaled, forcing my breath into his lungs. They used this treatment for drowning victims, and I did not know whether it would work on magical injuries, but desperation to do something clawed at my insides with frantic need.

Breathe.

I brushed his blue-black hair off his forehead, sealed our lips together, and forced more air into his lungs. Again and again, until my vision swam with little stars, until tears and sweat made sealing our mouths together impossible.

No, Aris. Breathe!

His lips were turning blue, and my heart was slowly withering in my chest.

Breathe, damn you!

"Gwen," Lia said in a voice like sandpaper. "Gwen, move."

I ignored her.

She pushed my hands out of the way and rested her fingertips on his chest above his heart. Her forehead wrinkled in concentration, her eyes focused. Her arms started shaking, but nothing happened.

"Come on," she breathed, and her lip curled with effort, but no fire appeared. Did she think burning Aris would bring him back?

I prepared for another breath, but a flicker of light, like sparks from a wire, lit up her fingertips for a moment, and hope blazed to life in my gut.

The spark died.

I wiped my mouth and leaned over Aris again...and felt the barest breath warm on my face. Against my trembling fingers, a heartbeat pumped once, twice, three times.

He jolted, gasped in a breath, and color returned to his lips.

We had all made it through. Aris was alive. We were all alive and home. I pressed my cheek against his chest, curled into a ball, and cried.

How long I cried I cannot say, but my hands and feet were numb when Lia stood up. She glanced around the clearing as if she'd never seen it before. Her body shook, either with cold or shock.

"Here," I said, standing to wrap my arms around her. "You're fine, Lia. You made it. We're home."

She pushed my arms off her shoulders and stood shivering. Her hair fell in tangled golden waves down her back and across her face, and her eyes were hard as she flexed her fingers uselessly at her sides.

Despite just saving Aris's life, she must have been disoriented. My head was still fuzzy, and I had not been in the Sunset Lands for more than a week. How was she even standing?

"It's okay," I reassured her. "You're home."

Her eyes narrowed, and pink that had nothing to do with the cold climbed her cheeks. When she spoke, her voice was low and angry. "What have you done? By the moon and stars, Gwen, *what have you done?*"

I stood there, flabbergasted. "What? What do you mean, what have I done? I've brought you home."

"I can't be here! Damn you, I told you to go without me. Haven't you already cost me enough?"

"What...Lia, you're home," I said the word with as much emphasis as my stiff lips allowed, imbuing it with everything home meant. Couldn't she understand? We were safe and together at last. Everything we suffered, all the time apart, those wounds would heal now.

Before she could respond, a wave of energy washed over us, making Aris whimper, and knocking us backward. A hound appeared not a foot from where Aris lay. It wobbled on its feet, disoriented, shaking its huge black head.

"It got through," Lia muttered.

The beast was twice the size of the largest of our hounds, muscled and dark as a midnight sky. It was a hound guard, likely one who had chased us into the clearing. It could have been Harl or Graowh and I wouldn't have been able to tell. I was too tired and weak to be any good in a fight and Aris was still laying on the frozen ground.

I grabbed Lia's wrist and dragged her behind me. "Can you burn it?" I asked.

The sound she made was somewhere between disbelief, anger, and grief. "No."

My eyes flew over the ground for a branch, a heavy rock, anything that might serve as a weapon, but the snow disguised everything.

The hound focused on us, and a rumbling growl shook the air. We circled as it prowled toward us, my bare feet burning with the cold and slipping on the snow. Lia raised a hand and grunted, but no green fire sparked to life. We had nothing to protect ourselves from those teeth. Had we come through all this just to die in the very place we had been separated so many years ago?

The hound's lip curled back in a snarl. It crouched and leaped, the motion so fast that I only had time to turn my back and drag Lia against my chest.

A shot split the air, making my ears ring as the hound hit us. We sprawled on the frigid ground in a heap.

"Gwen!"

A familiar voice, running feet sliding in the snow, a pair of warm hands. Tony lifted me and held me against his chest, one arm around my back as he turned to point his pistol at the limp hound. It didn't move. I allowed myself one moment, just one, to revel in the feel of him. Then my heart fluttered like an injured bird, caught between relief and panic.

Lia did not move from where she'd collapsed.

I gestured to her and Aris with my chin and said through chattering teeth, "We have to get them inside."

Tony, ever the practical man, didn't bother with questions. He bent and lifted Lia to her feet.

I crouched over Aris and pulled his torso off the freezing ground and into my lap. He flinched and said, "God's breath, woman, your fingers are cold."

A weak laugh bubbled up, and I dropped my forehead against his chest, but it was colder than my hands. I pulled his opposite arm to tug him around, then worked my shoulder under his armpit to lever him up.

"You could help me a bit, you bloody oaf."

"I thought," he gasped, "I was a Corinthian."

"You can be both things."

I pivoted us to face Tony and Lia and repeated, "We have to get them inside."

Tony's brown eyes, usually so warm, were wide with embarrassment. "Them?" he asked, eyeing my dress before averting his eyes. "From the look of things, we had better get *you* inside."

I glanced down at myself, realized that what passed for a dress in the fae court would not have even passed for underwear in England—which had not been helped by a fall into the wet snow—and felt the blessed heat of a blush rise to stave off a bit of the cold.

"We are too far from the house to get you back before you freeze," he said. Then turned to Lia and asked in a gentle voice, "Can you stand on your own?"

She nodded.

Tony slung off his backpack and began rummaging around. Before long, he had a small but tidy fire going. We crowded around it, and Tony forced me into his jacket. The gesture was likely more for his peace of mind than my comfort, but it was so warm that I could not complain.

He fired three more shots into the darkening sky. "The groundskeeper should hear that and be on his way," he said.

But he was wrong. One shot would have been enough for Garfield to release the hounds. Several minutes later, baying echoed through the trees. Of course, I may not have any toes by the time they arrived, but when I looked across the fire to see Lia standing there, arms wrapped around herself with Aris close behind, I could not regret it.

She was here. I was not alone. We did it. Every battle, every scar, the years of searching and study and pain and sacrifice were worth it.

We saved the girl.

"Tony," I said, unable to keep tears from streaming down my face, "this is my sister, Ophelia."

28

Loose Ends

TONY

Gwen's sister hadn't been able to walk for long. Despite warm blankets and help from the groundskeeper, her legs seemed ready to give out and her head drooped, so Tony ducked in to pick her up. She gasped at first, then gave him a vaguely dirty look, but after a few moments, she tucked her head and rested it on his shoulder. He thought she might have fallen asleep.

The dark-haired man, who Gwen had not introduced, strode next to her with one arm protectively around her. He was tall and lean, but well-muscled, with sharp, aristocratic features. The wound on his stomach was gruesome looking, but not deep.

Gwen trudged next to him, having already refused to be carried despite her shoeless state, but her face was alight with a quiet joy unlike anything he had ever seen. He couldn't look at her for long. Even with his jacket, the dress was far too revealing. But that didn't matter, and the dark-haired man didn't matter, and even the sleeping woman in his arms didn't matter because Gwen was home.

She was alive and she was home.

The hounds broke through the trees barking and gamboling in the moonlit snow, and the humans followed like a group of weary travelers, trudging toward the glowing windows and smoky chimneys of Wainwright.

When he'd left the manor earlier in the day, he'd only intended to take notes of the site Gwen used for the spell. Instead, he'd ended up wandering the woods, wondering if she was there somewhere, on the other side of the invisible wall. Common sense told him to go back to the warmth of the fire, but he had not been able to shake the feeling she was close.

Then a sound, something like the buzzing of electricity but sharper, spread through the forest like a gust of wind. Instinct drove him toward the sound, a crackling awareness he could not ignore. When he saw her through the trees, a smear of blue gown in the moonlight, his heart had stopped. When the beast leaped at her, everything slowed until the world went still and he fired his weapon on instinct.

The creature still lay in the snow. There was nothing to be done about it yet.

But there was something to be done about Evelyn's daughters. He could not bear to think of her response when both women walked through her door.

"Garfield," Tony said.

"Yessir?"

"Perhaps you should run ahead and warn Her Grace."

The old man's lined face shifted like someone raising the string on a set of blinds. "Oh, of course, sir! Right away."

His legs might have been spindly beneath his corduroy trousers, but Garfield crossed the wide lawn like the lifelong hunter he was and disappeared into the back door of the castle. At least Evelyn would have a bit of warning to prepare herself.

They were nearly to the door when it flew open and the Duchess of Wainwright came flying out of it, her thin wrapper trailing behind her like a broken sail in the wind.

"My girl!" she cried, throwing herself into Gwen's arms.

Gwen was taller than her mother by a head, but the difference didn't stop her from sinking down to rest her head on her mother's shoulder.

"Your Grace," Tony said, trying to sound reasonable and practical, "we need to get the ladies inside. They've been exposed for far too long."

But the women didn't listen, holding one another and crying. It was the dark-haired man who got them both moving by the simple expedient of lifting them both into his arms and dragging them toward the house.

Sam and Sally stood in the open doorway, their faces taut with a mixture of shock, surprise, and hope.

"Clear the door," Tony said gently and turned to carry Ophelia St. James into the house.

Everyone followed in a rush, piling into the foyer where his mother stood as a solid presence.

"Bring her here, Anthony," she ordered, leading him into the sitting room where tubs of hot water had been set up by the fire.

He sat Ophelia carefully on the chair, then lifted her bare feet and slid them into the steaming foot bath. She sucked in a pained breath, her whole body tightening at the pain as Mrs. Hardwicke threw a blanket over her shoulders. After a moment, she sighed and relaxed. After another, she started shivering, which was a good sign.

The dark-haired man chose a seat for himself and plopped his too-big feet into a basin, which meant it was up to Tony to pry Evelyn off her daughter. But when he turned, she was already disengaged, holding Gwen at arm's length and shaking her.

"Don't you ever do that to me again!" she ordered before pulling her back into an embrace.

"Mama," Gwen said, laughing. "Mama, wait." She turned her mother by the shoulders until she was facing the fireplace where Ophelia sat, shivering.

"Who is—" Evelyn began, but her entire body seized up and her face locked into a mask of shocked, desperate disbelief. So slowly he saw every muscle in her face shift, another emotion took hold: hope.

Her knees loosened, and she wobbled forward one shaky step at a time, as if in a trance, until she stood next to the chair. Ophelia's hair had fallen in a golden curtain, hiding her face from the rest of the room. The duchess sank to her knees and, with trembling fingers, brushed the hair back.

Ophelia raised her head, blinking. Mother and daughter locked eyes. Evelyn cupped her daughter's face in both hands. They were limned by firelight, a glowing nimbus in the center of a dark room, and the moment stretched until not a breath broke the silence.

Evelyn said, "My Lia?" in a voice that broke Tony's heart.

Ophelia's lips trembled and a single tear ran down her cheek, catching the firelight like a precious jewel.

"Hello, Mama."

Evelyn St. James Wainwright, the strongest human he had ever met, broke into a hundred little pieces. Her daughter managed to hold them all together with the power of a simple hug.

Gwen stood with her arms around the children, watching her family with tears in her eyes.

The new, and not so new, arrivals, were given hot toddies, warm baths, and bundled in wool blankets till nothing but the tops of their heads could be seen above the fabric. Gwen introduced the stranger as Aris with no last name, and the duchess could not be pried away from her daughters with a crowbar.

Ophelia rarely spoke, and never to her sister, but Gwen seemed content to let it be so, at least for now. Sam and Sally were included in the cuddling. Both of them cried unashamedly.

Tony watched and facilitated but both he, the stranger, and his mother remained spectators.

Once they were certain no one was in danger of frostbite, the servants hauled more blankets down the stairs for a sort of impromptu sleepover.

Tony waited till all was quiet, hugged and kissed his mother, and crept unnoticed to his room.

In the morning, he found them all eating with plates in their laps near a fire that had burned all night long. When he reached the bottom of the stairs, Evelyn glanced up, noticed him, dropped her plate, and threw herself into his arms. He stood for a moment in shock.

A *duchess* was hugging him, and not just hugging but trying to crush him.

"Thank you," she said in a voice throbbing with emotion. "I did not expect you to work so fast." He slipped his arms around her and held her while she laughed and cried at the same time. She was an extraordinary woman.

"Go get a plate and join us," she ordered once the hugging was complete.

He piled food onto a plate without really noticing what he took, and wandered back into the sitting room, full of some emotion he could not name. Gwen and her mother spoke animatedly, but Aris was silent, only watching the women with dark eyes. Every now and then his expression would soften into something tender, but he'd blink and the emotion would disappear.

Ophelia rarely spoke and ate almost nothing. She stared into the fire, which lit her face and hair with golden light. She was a younger, more beautiful version of her mother, if that was possible. But the sadness in her face caught at his heart. What must she have endured to come home to a loving family and still be so alone?

For that matter, how could Gwen be home and he still feel so...bereft? Instead of sitting on the floor in the tangled pile of blankets, he stood near the fire and absently chewed food he didn't taste, wondering what was wrong with him.

"Tony?"

He spun from the window to see Gwen standing at the door to his room. Instead of several layers of blankets, she wore a comfortable-looking wool skirt and blouse. Her dark hair was down, braided over her shoulder as if she were Sally's age. It was difficult not to see her as far younger and more vulnerable than he was used to.

"Good morning," he said.

She smiled. "I wanted to thank you for finding us. We might have been frozen and chewed to death if you hadn't been there."

"Yes, well, your mother did hire me to bring you home, so I suppose I was just doing my duty."

He had intended it as a lighthearted joke, but it came out much too serious and wiped the smile from Gwen's face. Dammit.

"She told me she wanted you to start some kind of private investigation firm for supernatural and magical activity. I must say, I think you are well suited for it. And—I am sorry you lost your position with Scotland Yard. I realize that was at least partially my fault."

"Not at all. It was my fault. Mine, and Lord Rutledge's."

"I cannot say I'm surprised. He appears to have had his hands in more corrupt pies than anyone knew. But a firm of your own," she said, raising her hands, "that seems like the perfect fit. You can track him without the pressure of a corrupt system."

He agreed, but he didn't want to talk about himself, so he said, "How is your sister?"

She swallowed and folded her arms over her chest. "She's angry with me. At least, I assume she is. She won't speak to me. But perhaps that is only the shock of returning after so many years." She looked down at her feet. "She's sleeping. Hopefully, it helps. Otherwise, I shall simply pester her until she has no willpower left to fight back."

"That I can believe."

She gave him a cheeky grin, but it wasn't genuine.

"What are Sunset Lands like?"

"Inexplicable," she said, shaking her head and joining him at the window. "Extraordinary, beautiful, dangerous. Perhaps dangerous, most of all."

She shivered, her eyes far away. Something significant had happened there, something had stolen her brazen self assurance. Dare he ask what it was?

"They are planning to invade, Tony," she said before he worked up the courage.

"Invade?"

"Yes. I do not know how they intend to pass the wall. The rift we used was small and Aris almost died holding it open. But they are preparing to attack us."

"Why?"

"I wish I knew. The Sunset Lands appear to be nearly perfect. It is never too hot or cold, the landscape mirrors this one but on a grander, more beautiful scale. The people defy description."

"What could they possibly want, here?"

"Handsome human slaves?" she suggested, waggling her eyebrows at him.

He snorted, she grinned, and for a moment she was the Gwen he remembered, and the familiar spark of warmth kindled to life between them. But then she said, "I do not know what they want with us, and Lia will not speak to me yet, so I cannot ask her. But they are faster than us, stronger, and their magic is...how can we fight it?"

"With iron?"

She peered at him through dark lashes. "You've been studying."

"If I am going to run an investigative agency specializing in magical mysteries, I had better know something of it."

"Interested in hiring a consultant?"

"Certainly not," he said, then winked at her.

They stood side by side for a while, watching the fresh snow fall. Being with her felt almost like it used to, but something was different and he could not put his finger on what.

"I think things will get worse, Tony," she said in a low voice. "I think all of this is tied together, and I have a few of the threads but...I cannot weave them into a cohesive picture, yet. Rutledge is part of it, though, I am certain of it. If I can question him, perhaps I can find out how."

Should he tell her about his agreement with the Cutthroat King?

A dark figure walked across the lawn with long, lazy strides, headed toward the trees. Seen through the warped glass of the ancient windows, the figure blurred and twisted as it moved, for a moment looking as if it had wings.

Gwen turned, kissed his cheek, said, "We'll talk more, later," then left the room.

Tony began pacing.

Keeping his mind focused on anything in particular seemed impossible, so Tony wandered the manor aimlessly. Laughter echoed from the parlor, but he felt no inclination to see what was happening on the bottom floor. If it was lighthearted, he would only drag it down.

The library doors were ajar, so he pushed in, expecting to find Sally curled in her usual chair. Instead, another blonde head was bathed in the cool light of the huge windows. Ophelia sat in the window seat with a blanket wrapped around her shoulders, hair cascading down her back as she watched the snow fall.

He hesitated in the doorway, but the sight of her was quiet and peaceful, so he entered the room and chose a seat by the fire. An open bottle of whisky sat on the table, but there was no glass to pour it into.

"I have not thanked you for protecting my sister."

Ophelia's voice was light and clear, like stars on a winter night or bells chiming before Yule. He hadn't heard her speak, yet, so he shouldn't have been surprised, but he was. For some reason, he'd expected the same deeper tones he was used to hearing from her sister.

"There is no need," he assured her.

"Because you love her."

He swallowed, caught off guard. "Yes. But I don't think that matters, either."

"Love always matters," she said.

"You love her, too."

Her head fell back against the window frame, and he noticed the empty glass in her hand. "Of course I do. But I'm so angry I cannot feel it, much." She turned to look at him over the edge of the blanket, then raised her glass and said, "Bring me—I'm sorry. Would you mind bringing me the bottle?"

He didn't mind. He poured a finger into her glass, but she made a *keep-going* motion with her other hand, so he poured two. She raised the glass and knocked back half of it, then grimaced and shook her head. "Everything here tastes like ash."

Tony decided to follow her lead and took a healthy swig. It burned a comforting line down his throat and sat like a little fire in his chest. "Gwen said you were sleeping."

"I needed a bit of peace."

"Forgive me," he said, "I'll leave you to it."

"No. Stay. That is, if you don't mind."

He sat in the armchair next to the window and leaned back. The bottle looked a bit too full, so he took another swig.

"How do you know my sister?"

Tony took a deep breath and sighed. "I suspected her of kidnapping orphans."

Ophelia snorted into her cup and took a sip. "I assume she disabused you of that notion."

"With aplomb."

"She is so different from when we were girls. More open than I remember. Then, I'm not much like I was at sixteen, either."

"Who is?"

Her voice was wistful as she stared out the window. "Life changes us all, I suppose."

"You sound disillusioned."

"I am."

That made two of them. They sat a while in silence before he asked, "How could you tell?"

"What? That you loved my sister?" She turned hazel eyes on him, eyes the color of sunlight through leaves that seemed to burn right to his core and stop his heart. She was as extraordinarily beautiful as her mother, but life on the other side of the wall had made her something more than human. His heart was exposed to her, and for some reason, he did not mind.

Her voice was soft and knowing when she said, "By the way you look at her."

"I ought to do something about that."

Why did he feel so comfortable telling this stranger things he found impossible to talk about with the woman he knew much more intimately? Was it her strange fae nature, or the kindness in her eyes? Perhaps it was because she loved Gwen, too.

"Why hide it?" she asked.

He looked down at the bottle. "We don't seem to work out. And when I speak to her now, I can tell something has changed, something that makes me think pursuing what we started to build would be useless."

And he had thoughtlessly hurt her through his own fear, rubbing raw an old wound that left deep scars.

Ophelia released a heavy sigh, hinting at a burden he couldn't understand. "It is never useless to love. But I cannot say you are wrong. The Sunset Lands change people. Perhaps...come here and look."

He found himself following her commands. She had the same gravitas as her mother, able to speak a couple of words and bend people to her will. He peered out the window.

Gwen stood in the snow with a shawl around her shoulders, all that dark brown hair loose and blowing in the wind. Aris stood across from her in black. They were shouting at one another, from the angry looks on their faces and the wild gesticulations. Gwen shouted something that made the tall man lean back in shock.

Tony sympathized. He had never met another woman, another person, so capable of taking others off-guard.

Aris leaned down and replied, pointing a finger in her face. She grabbed it and twisted his arm away, but Aris fisted his other hand in her shawl, dragged her across the space between them, and kissed her.

Tony's hand tightened on the bottle.

Gwen pushed away just far enough to slap the man. He imagined hearing the crack as her palm connected. She was a strong person.

It must have hurt. Tony found himself smiling. At least, until she threw her arms around his neck and kissed him.

He knew the intoxication of Gwen's presence, let alone her kiss. Aris wrapped his arms around her and pulled her against his body. It was the kind of passionate embrace that could melt snow. The whisky tried to climb back up his throat.

Tony swallowed and returned to his chair.

"I did not show you that to hurt you," Ophelia said, her voice colored with sorrow. "But making decisions without knowledge is dangerous. And unfair. You should not be dragged along against your will if you do not wish to partake in the fight."

The only time Gwen had ever kissed him that way, he'd turned her down. She would be right to ignore him. And he had no reason to expect she would welcome it if he fought for her hand.

"Is that what they did?" Tony asked, feeling a flash of insight alongside his aching heart. He had no right to feel betrayed. It was he, after all, who caused the rift between them. "They brought you back against your will?"

"They did not know what they were doing, or what the consequences would be. They couldn't have. But dammit, I told her to go without me."

"And now you're here."

Her fingers, long and elegant, trembled against the glass. She swallowed and tightened her grip, holding the whisky against her chest like a shield.

"Now I am here," she agreed. "And I am deeply, terribly afraid it will destroy us all."

THE END

Continue Reading for the first chapter of Outcast, Book 4 of the Gwen St. James Affair

To read Nicole's books as they are written and access other exclusive and early content, go to https://reamstories.com/nicolemckeon

29

Playing Hero

THE GWEN ST. JAMES AFFAIR BOOK 3, OUTCAST, CHAPTER 1

A ris sat on the chimney and watched the light fade from the rooftops and spires of New London, waiting for his prey to creep through the darkening streets. The last rays of the setting sun turned the forest of chimney smoke and industrial steam into golden pillars that held up the sky.

When the sun winked out beneath the skyline he spotted her, weaving through the labyrinthine streets like a ferret in a warren. Aris flexed his claws, then launched himself into the air, tucked his wings in tight, and dropped below the rooftops like a falling stone.

It was time to go hunting.

His wings snapped open and his body twisted, banking around the side of a brick building as the updraft lifted him above the bottom row of windows. She shot across the side street in front of him, the brass rim of her goggles reflecting the electric lamplight just coming to life on the main thoroughfare.

With a few pumps of his wings, Aris rose high enough to follow as she took a sharp right turn to parallel Main Street, keeping to the shadows to hide the wheeled boots that powered her down the alley. Candles and lamps flickered to life in the windows below him as the twilight glow of the clouds faded into night.

She slowed, cutting the power to her wheels, which retracted far enough to let her heels hit the ground with a soft *thud*. That meant she wasn't going much farther, so he could catch her if he cut her off at the next intersection. Flexing his claws in anticipation, Aris sailed into the next alley, dropped to about six feet from the dirty cobbles, and shimmered into his human glamour.

His feet hit the stone silently just before the intersection of the alley and cross-street, next to the dented door of a boarding house. With a quick snap, he straightened the lapel of his black jacket, grinned, and turned the corner.

She nearly ran into him, squeaked in surprise, and leveled a pistol at his chest before he could blink. With the huge goggles obscuring half of her face and her hair wild from the speed of her wheeled boots, she looked absolutely adorable.

What this situation called for was an expression of shocked dismay that was one or two degrees too ridiculous to be serious. He raised both hands and said in a low voice, "Why, Lady St. James! Threats of violence against someone who is only here to help? I'm shocked at you. Shocked. What would your mother say?"

Growling, she dropped the pistol, pushed her goggles onto her forehead, and glared at him. "She would say that I am well within my rights to shoot you, you interfering corvid. The prospect gets more tempting the longer you stand before me."

He made a *tsking* noise. "Manners, my lady, manners."

"Why must you sneak up on me at every opportunity?"

The woman had no idea how appealing she was when she was a disheveled, irritated mess. He closed the distance between them with one smooth step, bringing his chest nearly into contact with hers, and stared down at her, knowing she'd rather die than back down an inch. It made teasing her so unfairly easy.

With one finger, he touched the space between her brows where the wrinkle from her scowl was deepest. "For this expression, right here. It is unbearably adorable."

His proximity made her react as it always did: her pupils dilated and her breath caught, heart speeding audibly. But she got the better of that reaction, letting her instinctive passion morph into anger.

Gwenevere St. James had a temper she rarely showed the people who loved her, but Aris was particularly good at kindling it. He ought to be, having known her for so long. Pretending to be a pet raven for years had given him unique insights into her life, and an honest understanding of her character that not even a partner could match...which meant he knew every button to push.

And if triggering her temper kept her from deteriorating into the maudlin mess she had been for the past several months, he was more than happy to be on the receiving end of her ire.

Moving faster than any mere human, she grabbed his finger, executed a move he was unfamiliar with, and turned his wrist into something she had called a *joint lock*.

"Gwen," he said, reasonably. "That hurts."

"Do all faeries lie as prettily as you do?" She asked, letting go of him to stuff her goggles into the leather satchel she wore across her torso. "Or have you cultivated that skill on your own?"

"Faeries cannot lie, you know that."

"I wonder. Perhaps you have lived too long among humans."

"There is no question of that. You have thoroughly corrupted me."

With a few deft motions, Gwen tucked her brown curls into something resembling an acceptable hairstyle and made herself presentable. Or as presentable as she could be after motoring around the New London streets on a piece of wheeled artifice. He reached up to pluck a stray leaf from the top of her head.

She waved his hands off and bent to secure the wheels of the foot rig to the clamps on her calves. It was an ingenious bit of artifice that stored the kinetic energy of her every motion in the runes engraved along the sides, and used the stored power to turn the wheels. Leaning forward released more power, and leaning backward slowed the wheels, which required a surprising amount of skill and often resulted in the rider landing on their arse.

Watching Gwen master the tricky device had been one of the more enjoyable experiences of his life.

The contraption was built to fit over her boots and hid nicely beneath the hem of her enchanted coat, so, aside from the lack of hat and gloves she was, at least, moderately presentable. Not that it would make much of a difference to the person they were about to ambush.

"Corrupt or not," Gwen said, glaring at him from the corner of her eye, "you will behave yourself. If you intimidate her into hiding, I will not forgive you."

Aris held up both hands to show his innocent intentions, plucked a pigeon feather from her hair when she wasn't looking, and followed Gwen to the middle of the next street. They stopped in front of a door that was rather nice for the neighborhood and knocked three times.

When the door opened, a small elf woman peeked out. A pair of wide eyes peered at them from a round-cheeked face, and her dimpled chin waggled uncertainly as she tried to decide whether to ask them what they wanted or slam the door in their faces.

"You must be Miss Heatherbloom," Gwen said. Her voice was gentle and disarming, which had an immediate effect on the smaller woman.

"I am. What can I do for you?"

"My name is Lady St. James and this is my friend, Mr. Crow. Our mutual friend, Mr. Bywater, suggested we might visit you. He said you are the finest taxidermist in the city, and that the birds you provide always look the most lifelike on ladies' hats."

Mss Heatherbloom's tan cheeks turned a dusky rose color with pleasure, and she tucked a stray lock of hair behind one pointed ear. "It's very kind of him to say so. He is the most talented milliner in the city, so it is a honor to work with him. But it is getting a bit late and, well," she searched the street behind them with worried eyes, "given the state of things, I'm sure you'll understand that accepting visitors—"

"Of course we understand. These are frightening times. But if we might leave you with this?" Gwen held out a pamphlet for S&P Investigations Inc.

Miss Heatherbloom took it carefully, glanced at the cover, and said, "I'm afraid I don't need any help solving magical mysteries, thank you."

Gwen was not put off so easily. This was where these conversations always got tricky. Aris prepared himself for a quick demonstration.

"Given your circumstances, I understand that you may not want to trust anyone. But please know that we are here to help, should you find you need it. Refugees from the Sunset Lands are always welcome."

Miss Heatherbloom's mouth popped open, her fingers tightened on the pamphlet until it crumpled, and she went as still as a hare hiding from foxes. Poor thing.

With a shaking voice, she said, "I'm sure I have no idea what you are—"

Aris interrupted her by shifting into his raven form. It took no more than an act of will, and his human glamour disappeared. He skipped his fae form entirely and landed on Gwen's shoulder in his raven form to give the woman a friendly croak. She blinked, all the color drained from her face, and Gwen leaped forward to catch her before she fainted.

"Was that really necessary?" She demanded as she lowered the limp woman into a sitting position on the floor of her foyer. He leaped off Gwen's shoulder and shifted back to his human glamour to help. Miss Heatherbloom was a solid little thing, heavier than she looked, which meant she was also likely larger in her true form. While she was unconscious, her glamour began to slip, revealing traces of the faerie beneath. Maintaining a glamour took an act of will, and while only those with years of experience could create a glamour that lasted through even a few hours of sleep, fainting was a different story.

"She's relatively young," Aris said as he began fanning her. "Wake her quickly, or her glamour will fade and she'll be even more terrified than she already is."

Gwen pulled smelling salts from her satchel and swiped them beneath the woman's nose. She snorted, her body spasmed, and her eyes popped open. With a squeak, her glamour solidified and she tried to scoot away.

Gwen let the woman go and held up her hands. "I am so sorry we frightened you. It was not my intention. I simply wanted you to know that we understand, and you have a safe place, should you need it."

Miss Heatherbloom scrambled to her feet, regained her bearing, cleared her throat, and said, "Your visit was most appreciated but I have quite a lot of work to do so, if you don't mind, I'll have to ask you to leave." She bravely hustled them out the door before slamming it in their faces.

They stood there for a moment, facing yet another closed door.

Aris said, "Mr. Crow? Really?"

"You are the one who insists on coming along for these little visits. If you'd like a better pseudonym, you are free to make one up for yourself."

"Perhaps I shall. We couldn't do much worse. Though, she still had the pamphlet in her hand. " The last fae refugee they visited had thrown the crumpled paper in his face.

Gwen sighed. "I doubt she will be able to read it after crushing it so."

"She knows she is not alone, now. That is the important part."

That, and they would be able to warn her when King Obyrron eventually invaded. Whenever that might be. It had been more than six months since he and Gwen escaped the Sunset Lands after stealing Gwen's sister, Ophelia, back from the fae King. Which meant likely only two weeks had passed in faerie time, as mortals reckoned it. That wasn't long enough to adjust invasion plans for the loss of their general. At least, they could hope so. But Ophelia, the general in question, still would not speak to her sister, so they could not be certain.

Whether they would be able to call on the hidden fae to fight when the King invaded was another story.

"Perhaps she would have given us a warmer welcome if you had not gone avian on the poor woman."

"We haven't had much luck either way. Best to make things clear quickly. At least then you have the rest of the night to run about being a hero."

"If you do not like it," Gwen said as she hopped down the stairs, "you can fly home and play chess with Samuel."

"He beats me too often, these days. I do have my pride, you know. Besides, who will be here to rescue you, if I leave?"

She sniffed. "I do not need rescuing."

"If you keep fighting monsters you will."

"No one else is protecting these people," she snarled, suddenly angry. "Scotland Yard does not have either the knowledge or the manpower to make a difference, and they refuse to consult me despite the obviously supernatural nature of the murders and disappearances. Tony's agency is the only one that can recognize the truth of the situation, but he is still so understaffed that he cannot do much good. The witches refuse to tell me what they are doing to help, and this is the only—" she bit off the last words, took a deep breath, and shook her head.

"And it is the only thing that makes you feel alive," he finished.

Gwen made a sound that meant, *I hate that you know that about me,* then bent to unstrap her wheels and lock them in place. Once the goggles were settled back over her eyes, she said, "If you want to be of help, float about and signal me if you happen to see any ne'er do-wells. If you'd rather irritate me with that clever tongue of yours, you can fly home."

"I could think of a few other things to do with my tongue, if you'd like," he said before he could stop himself. A vision of Gwen as he had seen her in faerie, stretched out beneath him with her dark hair spread on the moss around their naked bodies, flashed across his memory, making him hard in a rush. Luckily his glamour could easily hide that, but he doubted she'd missed it.

Gwenevere St. James didn't miss much.

She leaned toward him, bathing him in her scent, and said, in a low voice, "What I would really like you to do with your tongue, is bite it off."

Then she flicked the wheels to their down position and rolled into the darkness at unsafe speeds. Aris swore and leaped, shimmering to his raven form at the height of his jump, and pumped his wings until he was high enough to spot her. He could not smile as a raven, but his amusement bubbled up into a series of caws that made Gwen shake her head.

He would take her angry, frustrated, cutting, sarcastic, so long as she was passionate and alive. But Ophelia had not forgiven Gwen for dragging her back to the mortal world. Adjusting to the change hadn't been easy for Lia, and the happy reunion Gwen dreamed about for a dozen years had turned into a source of constant pain. For weeks she had put on a brave face, smiling and laughing for Sam and Sally, but then she would do almost anything to protect her wards.

In the quiet hours of the evening, however, when she was alone, she sat unblinking before the fire, lifeless as one of the mannequins in Percy's shop. Every now and then he found her curled on the floor, unresponsive.

When he'd been trapped in his raven form as Aristotle, he wanted nothing more than to be able to carry her to her bed on the nights she worked herself to sleep in the study. Now that she knew what he truly was, he could finally carry her safely to her room... but that did not stop the gut-deep sensation of falling he felt every time her saw her suffer. It was the same sensation he felt when the air went flat beneath his wings and he dropped without warning.

Watching the woman who had always seemed more alive than anyone else fade like the pages of the old books she read was something worse than heartbreaking.

Then Tony Hardwicke, the former Inspector for Scotland Yard, had started his agency. He called upon her to consult on a case, and a little life returned. But those cases had been few and far between in the first couple of months. She hadn't come fully back to life until—movement caught his eye, just a simple shift in the shadows between a bakery and rundown public house, but to the eyes of a fae raven, it was enough.

Aris shifted his wings, gliding above the shape that slunk across the alley, and croaked three times. Gwen slowed, oriented on him, and raised a hand. He shifted his wings twice, and she pulled the pistol with silver bullets from her pocket. She was two streets over to the south, but the werewolf raised it's head and scented the air, picking up the smell of her fear. The creature shivered, as if the scent was a physical pleasure.

Then it began stalking her.

Aris stayed above it, giving Gwen a marker to follow, keeping his eyes on both predator and prey. She disengaged the wheels, produced a silver knife in her free hand, and crept toward the cross street on silent feet. If she was careful, she could cut the wolf off and shoot it before it attacked.

Of course, he would have to carry the body out of town under a glamor, which was both tiring and irritating. But better than leaving, what would appear to be, a dead mortal on the street.

If the creatures remained in their wolf shape after death, his role would be much easier. But it had been so long since monsters were common in large cities that the old method of identifying magical creatures, like tying wolfsbane around the wrist or ankle of the dead werewolf, would mean nothing to the citizens or constables.

Instead of ridding the city of a dangerous monster, they would be considered murderers.

The wolf stopped, raised its head with ears erect, and turned its muzzle east. Aris did not hear as well when in raven form, but he saw clearly. A dwarven man plodded down the main street in his heavy smelter's boots, likely returning from his shift at the ironworks. Light reflected from the steel toes of his boots, and the rhythmic thud of his steps echoed off the buildings. He had no idea what danger waited nearby.

The beast growled, a low warning rumble meant to protect his hunt from other predators, but it made the dwarven man freeze. It wasn't the growl of a stray dog anyone might hear on any given night; it was the vicious hunger of something unnatural, something that enjoyed the scent and taste of fear almost as much as the kill itself.

Gwen needed to hurry.

Aris cawed and dropped his head in warning, but it was too late.

The dwarven man spun in a slow circle, searching the shadows for danger as he pulled a heavy mallet off his shoulders. At least he was armed. Gwen's fear wasn't strong enough to keep the wolf on the hunt, not when the scent and sound of more terrified prey echoed through the air.

Aris had a split-second to decide whether to stay aloft so he could monitor everything, or drop to the ground to put himself between the beast and its victim. The wolf sprang into a run, Gwen rounded the corner with her pistol raised, and Aris dropped from the sky, shimmering as he fell.

He hit the ground as she fired the first shot and spun to see the werewolf's tail disappear around the corner, her shot sending chunks of brick flying from the building across from them.

Gwen swore, kicked her wheels down, and leaped forward.

"Two streets to the south!" Aris yelled as he sprinted after her.

Gwen's wheeled boots were fast, but the werewolf had a head start. By the time they reached the street, the beast was already circling the dwarven man, snarling and frothing in a display meant to heighten the fear to a fever pitch. The bulky man held his mallet at the ready, prepared to swing, his arm muscles bulging. And while his hands did not shake, the werewolf's response made it clear that fear and adrenaline were heavy in the air.

"Get me a clean shot," Gwen said, leveling her pistol.

The wolf was relatively small for its kind but still nearly reached Aris' waist at the shoulder, making the burly dwarf look child-like by comparison. It was smart enough to stay on the opposite side of the dwarf, pacing back and forth so that Gwen would not have a clear shot. But the smell of fear must have been driving it mad because it quivered with anticipation and great gobbets of slobber dropped to the ground with audible splats.

He needed to move before the wolf sprang, or the dwarf would likely be dead even if Gwen managed to squeeze off a shot. So Aris edged closer, not even pausing when the werewolf turned toward him and snapped.

"Brace yourself," he warned the man, then coiled and leaped in a smooth motion.

He hit the dwarf, wrapped his arms around the barrel-chested fellow, and turned as he fell, taking the impact on his back and shoulders. The weight of the dwarf drove the air from his lungs as they hit the street.

Gwen opened fire, but the wolf had already leaped, and rock chips skipped off the cobbles where the beast had been. It landed and sprang forward at an angle, aiming at the dwarf's exposed back. Aris raised his legs, planted his feet on the monster's massive chest, and pushed. The creature sailed over his head, the gun barked again, and the werewolf yelped in pain before it hit the ground.

Long claws scrabbled against the cobbles as the beast righted itself, filling the air with scraping and deep-throated growls tinged with a sharp edge of pain. It didn't wait for Gwen to fire another shot, it simply attacked.

Fear squeezed an iron fist around his heart as the beast tore toward her, but Gwen did not flinch. She sighted down the barrel and pulled the trigger once, twice more, aiming as cooly as a veteran soldier. But the monster did not stop.

Gwen tried to leap aside but the beast hit her in mid-air. The two of them spun sideways, going down in a tangle of limbs and fur, claws and teeth.

30

Chapter 21. 5

WITHOUT THE STEAM

C ompared to the madness of the dance and the blood-boiling magic of the wild hunt, the silence of the castle halls was soothing. I may have appreciated the peace if turmoil was not boiling in my guts and twisting my mind into tangled Euclidian knots. We stopped outside the bare wall of our cell, and Harl pressed one paw hand against the bark. Wood fibers slid backward and into themselves until the door appeared.

Manannán walked us into the cell and unclasped the collar from Aris's neck. Aris nodded in respect, and though he didn't rub the red marks away, he clearly wanted to. I did not blame him.

"I believe this belongs to you now, lady," Manannán said, and carefully placed the chain on my palm. "Thank you for accompanying me. I hope you found the experience enlightening."

Enlightening? Was that the word to describe my current state of near collapse?

He winked, then floated out of the cell like a retreating storm cloud. The door grew back. Aris and I stood in silence as I gripped the chain so tightly the links bit into my palms. For days after arriving in the Sunset Lands, the abyss of grief had claimed me. What reached for me now was something else, something darker and more dangerous.

If I did not tip into despair, anger was my only outlet, and I'd fought far too long to let despair win. I turned to Aris and pinned him to the spot with my eyes. When I spoke, the words came rasping up my throat, dry and raw.

"You will accept any other punishment than being stuck here with me?"

"Gwen—"

"Don't try to tell me you did not mean it. You must speak the truth, must you not?"

"Our chances of escape are better if—"

"Must. You. Not?"

Aris's jaw muscle clenched, and he flexed his fingers as if they were claws. "The truth about what? About whom? Do you have any idea how the truth can be twisted? Did I not warn you not to believe anything you saw or heard?"

I was brittle, and my voice cut the words into glittering shards I threw at him like daggers. "Don't pretend you said it to protect anyone but yourself."

"I don't have to pretend, you stubborn fool. Of all the things you could blame me for, and the list is long, this is the only one I will not accept."

"I blame you for lying to me!" I screamed. "For keeping all of this from me for...god's breath! You have known my sister was alive, known where she was for years, and said nothing! You've let me drink myself into stupors when you could have told me she was...that she was..."

She was, what? Not the girl I remembered? A powerful, angry woman who wanted nothing to do with me? An enemy? With a few simple words, he could have saved me from this pain. And he'd chosen not to.

"How could you?"

Aris winced, his lashes flinching as if I had slapped him. He dropped his eyes, swallowed, and clasped his hands behind his back.

"How can you refuse me an answer now, when I already know the truth?" I asked, bewildered.

His gaze lifted, and the pain in his eyes stopped the breath in my throat. Aris looked like a man falling and watching as the ground rose to meet him. His jaw worked as if wanted to speak but could not.

Perhaps...he truly *could not.*

I stumbled backward a few steps as the combined knowledge of half a lifetime of searching and study smashed into what I had just experienced like a wrecking ball. Everything shattered, and my brain scrambled to pick up the pieces and put them together into something resembling the truth.

Hesitant, not daring to believe it, I asked, "Aris, are you under a geis?" Hope flashed in his eyes but he didn't answer, so I changed my question. "If a faerie were under a geis, could they speak of it?"

"No."

"Not even to confirm or deny it?"

"Not even then."

"If I were to ask a faeric questions adjacent to their geis, could they answer them?"

"That depends upon the question."

"Does the geis extend to every form of communication or only speech?"

He didn't answer, which was answer enough. Perhaps I should approach the question even more obliquely.

"You used to work for my sister?"

"Yes."

"In her capacity as general, or for another reason?"

A moment of silence. "I was her chief spy...and assassin."

I paused. Assassin? My mind whirled, and some emotion I did not care to inspect slammed against what was left of my insides until I was tender and bruised. If I examined that too long, I'd find myself back in the pit of grief that yawned hungrily beneath my feet.

Better to focus on things I could use to get us out of here, and to cling to them like a lifeline until the worst of this passed.

Aris was under a geis, a magical injunction that could not be broken on pain of death, which meant I would learn nothing helpful from that angle. When I had asked him earlier why he helped me, he'd said, *because you are a good person.* That had to have been the truth because faeries could not lie, but as he said earlier, that did not mean it had been the *whole* truth.

And he was plenty talkative until I asked him why he had not told me about my sister, so the geis extended to her. But he had spoken of her earlier, so it didn't extend to her purely as subject matter. Or, rather, he had shared possibilities related to her. Which meant the geis was more specific.

If my reasoning was sound, someone made Aris swear a magical oath that he would tell me nothing of my sister or why he had come, or been sent, to me. But he'd been a spy: Lia's spy. An assassin for my human sister, who had become a general of the fae King. She wielded magic unlike anything I had ever seen. My sister, who once held me when I cried and told stories with me in the dark beneath our blanket forts.

She had spies and assassins and used magic to hurt and control people. Thoughts and emotions spiraled like debris hurled by a cyclone, and while I tried to catch them as they flew by, they slipped through my fingers and left me empty-handed.

If I could not focus on something other than the pain, it would kill me. I knew it. Yet the storm would not be held at bay by anything so simple as trying to save my own life.

Because, it turned out, there wasn't much to save. Not my sister. Not my best friend. Not even my ancestry.

"Everything has been a lie," I breathed.

All the air whooshed from my lungs, squeezed out by the building whirlwind inside me. Ophelia—my Lia—was a lie I created to deal with the disappearance of my sister, and the real woman was nothing like I imagined her to be.

Aristotle was not my friend, but a fae spy sent to me for reasons I could not even pressure him to reveal.

Percy was not a talented elvin hat maker, but a selkie who escaped the Sunset Lands.

And, if I were to follow the threads of several circumstances I brushed off, from the vampire to the Cutthroat King, and add them to Lia's magic and position in the court—not to mention the title they used in relation to me—everything would reveal another truth I did not want to confront.

My mind shied away from it, pushed it far back into a dark room, and closed the door as the storm picked up and flung all of my carefully rebuilt fortifications to the far corners of my soul, leaving me bare.

To rescue myself from paralyzing grief, I'd hung onto the hope of escape, of bringing Lia home. But my fingers were bare and bloody. I was losing my grip.

"Gwen," Aris said. He sounded almost as tortured as I felt.

I held up one hand to keep him away and choked out, "Don't."

My legs wobbled. He lunged forward to catch me, and I attacked him. There was nothing else to do. I had to act, and violence felt better than whatever slimy blackness was wrapping around me. But there was no cohesion, no technique in my attack, just flying fists, sobs, and tears that burned down my cheeks to my neck.

"Gwen, stop," he said, fighting to grab my wrists and pin them together at the small of my back. The motion pressed me hard against his chest, so I jerked my knee up between his legs. He turned his hips, and the blow fell ineffectually on his thigh. He sank down, dragging me with him, and I hit the moss floor on my knees, straddling his thighs with my arms pinned behind my back. Strands of hair stuck in the tear streaks on my cheeks.

"You are right," Aris said, his chest heaving from the exertion of trying to capture my arms without hurting me. "I have seen you drink yourself into a stupor. I have watched you study late into the night, and sip laudanum to chase away the memories, knowing I could do nothing to help. Stars, the helplessness was the worst. I could not comfort you or even pick you up and carry you to your bed."

He brushed the hair off my face with his free hand, dark eyes tracing the tracks of my tears as he wiped them away with the pad of his thumb. "So many times I thought death might be a worthy price to pay to take away your pain. But, and I must be honest with you...I could never bring myself to do it because you might send me away if I did and...torturing Mrs. Chapman was simply too much fun. I could not give her up."

An unwilling laugh that was also a sob broke through my trembling lips. How could he tease me now, when a storm of conflicting, uncontrollable emotion raged inside me? When that storm broke, it would either destroy me or turn me into a person I did not recognize.

I had nowhere to run and I could not sit here and wait it out, or I would go mad. My body, my very soul, shuddered with the force of it.

"Shh," Aris said and brushed a cool palm over my forehead. "It will be alright, Gwen. We will find a way out of this somehow." His touch was tender, consoling, and not enough. Not *nearly* enough.

Maybe I did not have to weather the storm alone. "Aris?"

"Hmm?"

I swallowed and blurted before I could stop myself, "Will you kiss me?"

He jerked away as if I had slapped him, releasing my arms and dislodging me from his thighs. "Don't ask me that."

"Why? What is wrong with me? Is this something else you cannot do? Are all your flirtations and sideways glances just another lie you don't tell?"

"No," he rasped, scooting away.

I watched him go, feeling the loss of his presence like a physical blow, leaving me alone against the storm. Alone, again. Unsure whether I spoke to him or myself, I asked, "Are you such a coward?"

"Yes! Yes, damn you, I am a coward." He surged to his feet and glared down at me, eyes burning. I felt in memory his body jerk as the lash fell, saw Aris hit the standing stone as Cassandra hurled him through the air, and remembered the comfort of his small body as I cried myself to sleep. I was being unfair to him and I could not bring myself to feel sorry for it. I was past feeling anything besides the turmoil. But Aris did not seem to notice.

He was too angry.

"For years I wished I could speak to you, or touch you. I accepted the crumbs of your kindness as if they were ambrosia because I knew you could never see me as anything other than a *pet*." His mouth twisted around the word as if it tasted sour. "And now that I stand before you in my own skin, I find that I do not have Tony's strength. He is a better man than I will ever be. If anyone ever deserved your affection, it is him.

"But I cannot turn you away, not even for your own good or my pride. If you tell me you need to cut me to ribbons with the broken pieces of your heart, I will let you do it. I cannot watch you destroy yourself. I am not strong enough for that. So do not ask it of me. Not unless..."

Somehow, between the beginning of his speech and the end, he closed the distance between us and pulled me to my feet. We stood facing one another, chests touching with every breath, the air between us alive with heat. My body shook to the rhythm of my heart, telling me to attack, or run, or scream, the adrenaline demanding that I do something—anything—to release what was building before it destroyed us both.

Aris cupped my face with both hands, his thumbs brushing my jaw as his fingers tightened on the back of my neck. "Is that what you need, Gwen? Someone to hurt? Or—" His eyes dropped to my lips, and he took a shuddering breath. "Someone to punish you?"

Warmth flooded my body, a shocking and distracting counterpoint to the storm of emotions battering my insides. Had there been an herb available, a potion, a spell, a knife, anything other than moss and wood, I would have used it gladly to free myself. But I had none of those things.

I had only Aris. If he offered an escape, I would take it.

"Yes," I heard myself say. "Can you...can you take me away from myself? I can't stand to be alone inside my body anymore."

His hands slid from my face to my neck, then down until he gripped my upper arms, as if he could trap me or keep me still while his eyes searched my face for something. "Once more," he said, his voice raw. "You must ask me once more."

His hands shook.

I could not form words, so I threw myself at him, wrapped my arms around his neck, and kissed him blindly.

There was nothing tender or loving in our embrace. Aris was a bottle, and I drank as deeply from him as he would allow, getting drunk on ecstasy and pouring myself out until there was no Gwen, no Lia, no trials or failures or innocent family members left behind to wonder and mourn.

In his arms, I found the same freedom of forgetfulness offered by alcohol or laudanum, followed by the sweet oblivion of release. When we collapsed, sweaty and exhausted, sleep dragged me down into the blessed darkness and I rested without dreaming.

31

Also By

OTHER TITLES BY THIS AUTHOR INCLUDE

SERIES: The Gwen St. James Affair

Vanished

Eccentric social outcast Lady Gwenevere St. James knows many secret things: magic, alchemy, artifice, and even the truth about the long-forgotten faeries. But she does not know why common criminals are using rare and dangerous magic to kidnap orphans from the streets of New London.

After rescuing one young girl, Gwen vows to save the rest, no matter the cost. But the handsome Inspector of Scotland Yard is also investigating the case, and he thinks Gwen knows far too much about the kidnappings to be innocent.

To save the children, Gwen must dodge the Inspector, bully a coven of witches, and outsmart her marriage-minded Mama, all while managing a wily young pickpocket and a headstrong raven. But an unexpected secret hides at the center of the mystery, one that will force her to confront the most painful event from her past, and possibly sacrifice her future.

Moonstruck

Gwenevere St. James may be a lady, but she's never been interested in playing by the rules. Instead of ingratiating herself into high society, she spent a decade searching the world and studying the occult for a way to find her lost twin sister.

So when a coven of witches offers her a missing person's case in return for a book of spells guaranteed to locate her twin at last, Gwen cannot refuse, even if it means doing something she swore she would never do: attend a country party for the wealthy elite.

But the case is far more complicated and dangerous than she expected. Villagers whisper of ghostly riders in the night, and an unknown monster hunts the nearby forest, putting everyone in danger.

As people go missing and innocent bystanders die, Gwen must make a choice: how many lives will she risk for the thing she wants most?

SERIES: The Eververse Chronicles

The Founding Trilogy

The Laws of Founding

Legends and fairytales aren't all they're cracked up to be; especially when they're trying to kill you.

Since losing her father, Allie Chapter has stumbled through life, using friends, books, and alcohol to numb the pain. When she wakes up in the wrong world and gets kidnapped by supernatural forces, everything changes. Allie learns she is a Walker, blessed–or cursed–with the power to travel between different versions of Earth.

Allie must rely on Ronan, her devastatingly handsome mentor, to guide her through magical worlds she's only dreamed of, and teach her the Laws that govern all Walkers–Laws she must not break at any cost.

But a failed assassination attempt turns her dream into a nightmare. The Eververse is full of danger, and whoever wants her dead may also be behind her father's accident. As she searches for answers, Allie must decide what makes breaking the Laws worthwhile: love, or revenge?

But when she learns she is a Walker, one of the rare few with the ability to travel between different versions of Earth, an entirely new problem arises: can she master her powers fast enough to figure out why someone wants her dead?

The Founding Lie

The monsters we face aren't always the ones we expect.

As the newest member of the interdimensional police force, it's Allie Chapter's responsibility to find out who is stealing magical weapons and bring them to justice before war breaks out.

She's certain the thief is Goll MacMorna, the man who still haunts her nightmares, and she intends to prove it...no matter the cost.

She will either free herself from her nightmares or discover the real monster is the one in the mirror.

The Founding War

"Necessity knows no cruelty. She only makes demands, and we answer as seems best to us."

Allie Chapter went from aimless college student to interdimensional cop in less than a year. Now she's an outlaw, hunted by both sides of an oncoming war that threatens to destroy the Eververse. As her newly discovered magic grows in strength, Allie realizes she might be the only one who can stop the war and save countless innocent lives from obliteration. But her allies have betrayed her, and powers too large to comprehend are manipulating the battlefield, hoping to use her gifts for their own purposes. With no one left to trust, Allie must rely on her wits and her conscience to make the ultimate decision: sacrifice her future–and maybe her life–for the greater good, or save the people she loves and let the Eververse fall.

Acknowledgments

As always, I have to thank my Beta readers: Alix, Abbie, Amy, and Melissa. Your insights, thoughts, and suggestions not only help make these novels better, they give me the confidence I need to push them into the world. I will forever be grateful for the chance to work with you all.

To my lovely editor, Abbie Lynn Smith: you have been a supporter and fan of these books from the beginning and they would be an absolute mess without your keen eye and insights. THANK YOU!

And the incredible subscribers of the Reader's Lounge, my personal community: Katherine, Krista, Button, and a lovely human who chooses not to be named but knows who they are...thank you, thank you, thank you! Your support gives me the leeway I need to get these books finished and produced. Knowing I get to see your feedback, or even that you are just silently cheering me on, helps more than you'll ever know.

Finally, I will always be grateful for the chance to have worked with the incredibly talented Elena Nedeleva, the illustrator for the iconic covers. You brought these books to visual life and created covers that make people want to buy them. I'm so lucky you said yes!